In the Blood

Book Two of The Maker's Song

Adrian Phoenix

POCKET BOOKS

NEW YORK   LONDON   TORONTO   SYDNEY

Pocket Books
A Division of Simon & Schuster, Inc.
1230 Avenue of the Americas
New York, NY 10020

This book is a work of fiction. Names, characters, places, and incidents either are products of the author's imagination or are used fictitiously. Any resemblance to actual events or locales or persons, living or dead, is entirely coincidental.

First Pocket Books paperback edition September 2009

POCKET and colophon are registered trademarks of Simon & Schuster, Inc.

For information about special discounts for bulk purchases, please contact Simon & Schuster Special Sales at 1-866-506-1949 or business@simonandschuster.com.

The Simon & Schuster Speakers Bureau can bring authors to your live event. For more information or to book an event, contact the Simon & Schuster Speakers Bureau at 1-866-248-3049 or visit our website at www.simonspeakers.com.

Cover design by Lisa Litwack, illustration by Craig White

Manufactured in the United States of America

10 9 8 7 6 5 4 3 2 1

ISBN 978-1-4391-5725-1
ISBN 978-1-4165-9406-2 (ebook)

ACKNOWLEDGMENTS

Special thanks to: Sean and Rose Prescott, Karen Abrahamson, and Dean Smith for being my first readers; to my editor, Jen Heddle, and my agent, Matt Bialer, for their passion and for encouraging me to remain true to my vision. It's still one helluva kick-ass ride!

Thanks to: Mippy Carlson, Judi Szabo, Sheila Dale, Louise Robson, and all the members of Club Hell and my street team for your support, enthusiasm, and for giving me even more reason to keep my fingers on the keyboard. *Merci beaucoup*, y'all!

Thanks also to: The members of OWN and Jeri Smith-Ready for friendship and cheerleading; to my sons, Matt Jensen and Sebastian Phoenix, and their partners, Sherri Lyons and Jen Phoenix, and my book-loving little Kylah Phoenix, for all their encouragement and love.

Thanks also to: Abulia Paroxysm (Sebastian Phoenix) for creating music that is original and heart-felt and true. And, last, but never least, Trent Reznor, whose music always provides an emotional soundscape and is a source of inspiration, and whose live NIN shows are not only kick-ass, but relevant and groundbreaking. No one does it better. Period.

And, again, thanks to you, the reader, for picking up this book and plunging back into Dante, Heather, and Lucien's world. If this is your first time, *bienvenue*. Enjoy. Please visit me at www.adrianphoenix.com or at www.myspace.com/adriannikolasphoenix.

PROLOGUE

WALKING IN TWO WORLDS

Outside Las Vegas, NV
March 15

JON BRONLEE CRACKED OPEN the door and peeked out into the motel parking lot. Car bumpers and hubcaps gleamed in the bright Nevada sunshine, flashed dazzling light into his slitted eyes. Perched atop a weathered-wood telephone pole, a crow caw-cawed.

Nothing moved. At least, nothing Jon could see.

He wished he'd never slipped that damned security disk into his pocket. Wished he'd never smuggled it and the padded mailer he'd discovered on Moore's desk out of the center. Wished to hell he'd never looked at either.

As if on cue, and for the thousand-millionth time, his mind chanted: *Gonna sell it and make a helluva lot of moolah. Enough to retire decades early, enough for me and Nora to live easy, enough to send Kristi to gun-free private schools.*

Greed was one helluva con artist, convincing him

to pooh-pooh the consequences—*you'll be rich and long gone before anyone even notices*—until everything had gone to shit.

Yeah, a big old explosion of shit—a regular shitplosion—and then greed suddenly had nothing to say.

The nightmarish images captured by the med unit's security camera flared behind his eyes again for the thousand-millionth time. The woman's scream looped through his mind on endless repeat, a scream that had abruptly ended in a wet gurgle.

And a splash.

Jon desperately wished he could go back in time, back to D.C., back to that night, and rewind events. But since he couldn't . . .

With a fresh mailer tucked under his arm, he stepped outside and sweat instantly sprang up on his forehead. He caught a whiff of Old Spice as his deodorant kicked into overdrive. The rumble of a diesel being downshifted on the highway behind the motel rolled through the taut, heated air like a steel barrel across blacktop.

He hurried to the motel office, pushed the door open, and walked inside. The AC-cycled air cooled his face. He stopped at the counter and a balding man reeking of BO and nicotine bellied up against the other side.

"Help you?"

Jon placed the mailer on the counter. "You have mail service here?"

"Yup."

"Great." Jon poked the mailer with a finger.

With a sigh, the man scooped up the mailer, strolled to a box marked MAIL at the end of the counter closest to the door, and dumped it inside.

With muttered thanks, Jon left the office and sprinted back to his room. He chained and locked the door, then collapsed on the bed and stared at the water-stained ceiling. He needed to plan his next move, but his mind refused to move forward. Instead, it kept padding back to the center, snuffling at the past like a nose-to-the-ground dog.

Jon had scooped up his share of corpses during his ten years on the interagency cleanup crew, and the cleanup at the Bush Center for Psychological Research had been routine. Bodies outside in the snow, a pair of security guards—one slashed throat and one broken neck. Two more bodies inside; one dead agent, one dead serial killer. Hard to say what killed the agent, but bullets had done in the bad guy.

Routine had ended at med-unit one.

Had ended in an exam room inexplicably filled with twisting, thorned blue vines.

Had ended in a puddle of liquid gleaming on the tiled floor.

Stomach acid burned the back of Jon's throat and he swallowed hard. He tried to shut out the scream drilling through his mind. Managed only to muffle it. He wondered what it'd be like to gaze into that pale, beautiful face as you disintegrated.

Moore had screamed. Loud and long and liquid.

A dark thought slithered through Jon's restless mind: Maybe he'd been *meant* to find the disk. Maybe it'd been *fate*, and not just greed. His hand, guided.

During cleanup, his crew had discovered that lightning or something had zapped the center's main transformer. The surge had fried almost everything; the computers, the security cameras, you name it. Every-thing *except* the med-unit cameras; apparently they'd been wired to a different system.

And then curiosity or greed or fucking fate had crooked its finger. . . .

In the days following the cleanup, his team had started dying, one by one. Heart attack, unforeseen, what a shame! Husband caught her with another man and shot her, then himself. Can you believe it? In debt, committed suicide, man, *unbelievable*!

Yes. Yes, it was. Unbelievable.

Jon had gone on the run. Across the country. Dash-ing from one dingy motel to the next, terrified to look in the rearview mirror or even out a café window as he scarfed down a meal. Afraid of *who* he might see.

He'd considered giving the disk to the media, but realized they'd think him a wack job with too much free time and the newest version of Final Cut Pro to play with. He'd even considered sending it back to the center, but suspected that it would be too little, too late. Then, last night, it had dawned on him who needed to see the disk.

Dr. Robert Wells.

Even after Wells had retired from the center and the FBI and moved to Oregon, Jon had kept in touch. His little girl, his honey-haired Kristi, was alive and healthy because of the genetic work Wells had performed while the baby had still been inside Nora's womb, defective and doomed. As far as Jon was concerned, he owed the doc a debt beyond measure. He hoped that the disk and its contents would help Wells prepare for what was com-ing, equip him to survive it.

After all, Bad Seed had been Wells's creation. If anyone knew how to contain Dante Prejean or S or whatever the fuck his name might be, it would be the doc.

Jon closed his burning eyes and prayed his absence had saved Nora and Kristi.

Knuckles rapped against his door.

Jon's eyes flew open, his heart pounding hard and fast. Shadows hid the water stain on the ceiling. The light had faded from the room. He'd fallen asleep. Knuckles rapped again and a voice, low and confidential, spoke his name. "Bronlee? It's Cortini. Open the door. We need to talk."

Jon's heart hurtled into his throat. He bolted upright on the bed and jabbed his fingers through his hair, trying to think. Cortini. He pictured her: shoulder-length coffee-dark hair, hazel eyes, elfin face, slender. Good-looking. Rumored to be vampire. Or a vampire's beloved.

He'd learned about the existence of vampires when he'd joined the cleanup crew. Amazing how quickly he'd adjusted to that reality once the fact had been twisted into his face like a grapefruit half.

But, vampire or not, that wasn't the problem. The problem was that Caterina Cortini tied up loose ends. And he was a *major* loose end. How did the saying go? *If you see God, you're already in heaven; if you see the devil, you're already in hell; if you see Cortini, you're already dead.*

The doorknob rattled again. "Bronlee, we really need to talk."

"Just a minute," he croaked. "Gotta find my pants."

Jon stood and padded to the bathroom, eased the door shut. Stood on the toilet and forced open the window. Grabbing the slick, tiled sill, he hauled himself up and through the window.

Even though twilight glimmered on the horizon, the heat of the sun-baked parking lot slapped him in the face. He gasped, sucking in the smells of hot concrete, sand, and diesel exhaust. He dropped onto the pavement.

"Looks like you found your pants."

Jon whirled around. Cortini stood on the blacktop, one hip cocked, her gloved hands loose at her sides. His heart renewed its assault on his ribcage. His vision grayed and his knees buckled. A hand locked around his biceps. Kept him up on his feet.

"Breathe," she said. "Slow, deep breaths."

Not having much choice, Jon did as Cortini suggested. Gradually his vision cleared and his galloping heart slowed to a canter. He straightened, but Cortini didn't release him. Her fingers felt as hard as steel around his arm. He spotted a holster bulge beneath her light suit jacket.

"Do you know why I'm here?" she asked.

Jon considered lying. Considered feigning innocence. But, looking into Cortini's eyes, he realized there was no point. "Does it matter why I took it?"

"No. Not really."

Jon nodded. Swallowed hard.

Cortini slipped a hand inside her jacket. "But I think it *does* matter that the rest of your team is dead *because you took it.*"

Cortini's words hit him like a hard right to the jaw. He closed his eyes. Nodded again. "I'm sorry for that."

"Be sure to tell them that when you see them again."

Something in her voice opened Jon's eyes; something weary and sad and exasperated. Her fingers slid away from his arm. She pulled out a silencer-lengthened pistol from inside her jacket.

"Let's go inside and chat," she said.

Figuring he had nothing left to lose, Jon bolted, his Keds slapping the blacktop as he ran across the parking lot. He stumbled as he hit the hard-packed dirt, sand, and scrub beside the highway. Blood pounded in his ears. His breath rasped in his throat.

The diesel-powered sound of a semi hauling ass down the highway thundered through the deepening night. Headlights lit up the road like twin suns, growing brighter with each step Jon took. No hands grabbed him to pull him back. Cortini didn't shout his name. He dashed onto the highway and in front of those huge, glowing lights.

Squealing brakes and stuttering tires weren't loud enough to blot out the wet sound of the scream still looping through his memory, Johanna Moore's last breath.

Would he face the same fate?

The smell of burning rubber clogged his nostrils. His vision filled with light. Jon staggered to a stop, turned to face the rig, and closed his eyes.

CATERINA WATCHED AS THE rig, black smoke rolling off its locked-up tires, smashed into Bronlee. He splattered against the front grille like a low-flying june bug. Then his body bounced under the truck, the tires smearing what was left of him across the highway as the semi shuddered to a stop. The stink of burning rubber and scorched blood drifted into the air.

Caterina tucked the Glock back into its holster, then turned and walked back through the weeds and sagebrush to the front of the motel. Doors stood open. People clustered at the motel's edge, staring at the highway and the semi jackknifed across the road. A grim-faced man spoke into his cell phone.

Using an electronic pick, Caterina unlocked the door to Bronlee's room. She unhooked the door chain with a slender, steel pick, and slipped inside. She shouldered the door closed and glanced around the room. Open suitcase on the dresser, rumpled bedspread, a laptop on the table beside the curtained window.

The room smelled stale. Like Lysol and old tobacco. Like lost hope.

The rig's headlights illuminate Bronlee as he swivels to face it.

Caterina blinked the image away. Who the hell opts for a messy roadkill suicide instead of a well-placed bullet into the skull?

She crossed to the laptop and folded it shut. Then she went to the suitcase and rummaged through the wrinkled tees and jeans and boxers. Blank postcards. A few photos. She picked one up. A pudgy little girl of about ten or eleven, her grin framed by brown curls, sat on a swing. The fingers of her right hand flashed a peace-sign vee.

Sorry about your daddy, sweetie.

Slipping the photo back in with the others, Caterina continued searching the suitcase. No sign of the security disk. But a mailer bearing a BUSH CENTER FOR PSY-

CHOLOGICAL RESEARCH return address caught her eye. She pulled the envelope free, then closed and latched the suitcase.

The MAIL TO name, neatly written in black felt-tip pen, was DANTE PREJEAN. Caterina recognized the flowing penmanship—a dying art in the twenty-first century—as belonging to Dr. Johanna Moore. The Bureau's missing ADIC of Special Ops and leading behavioral scientist.

Caterina frowned. Wasn't Prejean part of Bad Seed? One of the study subjects?

She didn't know a lot about the project because she didn't need to; her job didn't require it. All the same, she knew it involved the development and study of sociopaths, a decades-long study that had ended abruptly a couple of weeks ago with a big, messy bang and clusters of bodies in two cities—New Orleans and D.C.

So what would the missing Dr. Johanna Moore be mailing one of her study subjects? Peering into the torn-open mailer, Caterina caught the silver gleam of a CD.

Interesting.

Caterina tossed the room for anything else Bronlee might've stolen, but found nothing. Returning to the dresser, she picked up the suitcase. She tucked the laptop under her arm and walked out of the stale, empty room.

She crossed the parking lot in quick strides, while sirens banshee-wailed through the heated desert night. Blue, white, and red lights whirled and strobed across the crowd gathered at the highway's edge.

Caterina dumped the suitcase inside her rented Charger's trunk. Sliding behind the wheel, she placed the laptop and the envelope in the passenger seat. She drove out of the motel parking lot and headed east toward the interstate.

The rig's headlights illuminate Bronlee as he swivels to face it.

Something besides Caterina had scared him out onto the highway and in front of the semi—something unknown, and that disturbed her.

Bronlee hadn't tried to bluff his way out, hadn't tried to bargain, not even for the safety of the grinning little girl in the swing. And even though that meant he'd already dumped or sold the security disk, it didn't explain his final action.

As Caterina steered the Charger from the dark highway onto the I-15 on-ramp and hit the gas, *why* kept circling through her brain. *Why* wasn't a part of her job. Wasn't supposed to be a part of her vocabulary. And that had never been a problem.

Until now.

She could've sworn she'd seen *relief* on Bronlee's face as he'd faced the rig.

Caterina's hands tightened on the steering wheel. She tried to focus on the road and the white lines blurring past alongside. *Why* droned and buzzed in her mind like a fly trapped between windows. She switched on the radio and country-tinged music twanged from the speakers.

The droning and buzzing faded as she concentrated on the song lyrics. *I hear the train's lonely whistle blow / and I pour another drink / I lift a glass to you, Joe / because of you my heart's on the brink . . .*

Miles rolled past underneath the Charger's tires and song after song rolled through Caterina's mind. Spotting a blue REST AREA sign, she swung the Charger onto the exit ramp, pulled around to the far side of the restrooms, and parked.

She listened to the car's engine click and *tink* as it cooled. She rolled down the window and hot, dry air smelling of baked sand and diesel exhaust wafted into the car.

Her mother's words played through her mind: *You walk in two worlds, Caterina. Dangerous worlds. Never forget that. As a child, you learned a truth most mortals never uncover—they are not alone. So you must listen to your instincts,* cara mia. *Always.*

Caterina unfastened her seat belt and retrieved the mailer from the passenger seat. She dumped the CD from the envelope, then swung open the laptop. She pushed the on button. And slipped the CD into the hard drive.

A list of files popped up on the screen, each marked with a letter of the alphabet. Caterina tapped a finger against her lower lip as she studied the headers. Dr. Moore had addressed the mailer to Dante Prejean. How had Special Agent Bennington referred to Prejean during his debriefing in D.C.?

Dr. Moore warned us—that'd be me and Agent Garth— that E and S were on their way home, led by Thomas Ronin. But Ronin never showed. Only E and S and a third individual—an unsub.

E had been Elroy Jordan.

Caterina clicked the file marked S and began reading.

1

CITY OF THE DEAD

New Orleans, St. Louis No. 3
March 15

"SO WHERE'S THIS WEIRD-ASS bit of hoodoo supposed to be?" Von asked.

"Beside a tomb," Dante said as they scaled the cemetery's locked, wrought-iron fence, both vaulting with ease over the black bars and onto the path below.

"Yeah, but which tomb?"

"Baronne, I think," Dante said, pushing his hood back. He chose the paved central path and followed it past gleaming white crypts. He drew in a deep breath of cherry-blossom-scented air. But beneath the sweet scent, he caught a whiff of decay, moldering bones, and old, old grief.

"These N'awlins cemeteries are creepy as hell," Von commented. "I can't imagine what they'd look like in daylight."

"Didn't you ever check 'em out when you were still mortal?"

"Hell, no," Von snorted. "Like I said, creepy. Especially for a delicate flower like *moi*." He paused, touching a finger to his ear. "Wait . . . breaking news. Correction, seems I *ain't* a delicate flower." He shrugged. "Who knew? Mama musta lied."

Dante laughed. "Yeah, you're gonna be fun on the tour bus."

"Man, I'm fun *anywhere*. And we should be heading to the airport soon."

"Yeah, yeah, I know."

Dante read the names on the tombs as he passed: DUFOUR, GALLIER, ROUQUETTE, and listened for the quiet pulse that had drawn him to St. Louis No. 3. When he caught the letters BA, he stopped, his heart kicking against his ribs.

He hears the sound of his own voice, raw and demanding, the words echoing in the cathedral's vaulted silence. "What was her name? Genevieve . . . what?"

Dante's hands clenched into fists as he struggled with the memory. He closed his eyes. His breathing quickened and fire flickered to life within his veins. Smoldered within his heart. He opened his eyes. Pale moonlight shafted through the thick, twisted oaks, dripped from the Spanish moss.

"Baptiste," he whispered.

<*You okay, little brother?*> Von sent.

Dante nodded. He looked at the tomb and finished reading the name chiseled into the white stone: BASTILLE. He released his breath. His hands unknotted and an emotion he couldn't name curled through him, damping the flames into embers.

Did his mother even have a grave?

A hand squeezed his shoulder and he looked up into Von's moonlit, green eyes. The nomad had shoved his El Diablo shades on top of his head.

"You sure, man? No pain? Cuz I thought I felt—"

Dante cupped Von's whisker-rough face between his hands. He brushed his lips against Von's, tasted him, whiskey and road dust, then smoothed his thumbs along the edges of the mustache framing the nomad's mouth.

"I'm good, *mon ami*," Dante replied. Dropping his hands, he twisted free of the nomad's grip. "And I don't need a fucking nanny."

Von extended a middle finger. Arched an eyebrow. "How about that? You need that?" Extended the finger on his other hand. "How about some more?"

"I'll take it all," Dante said, *"gêné toi pas."*

Dropping his El Diablos back over his eyes, Von shook his head and sighed. "Boy's hopeless as hell."

"Merci."

As they resumed walking the moonlit path, a hush swirled through the city of the dead, isolating it from the world beyond the wrought-iron fence like a deep black moat. The air was so still the muffled clink of the chains on Dante's leather jacket and the creak of Von's leather chaps echoed in the silence.

But beneath the hush, Dante caught the faint rhythm that had—for the last couple of weeks—filled his mind just as Sleep swept over him. Primal. Like a tribal drum beating within the earth's heart.

Like the wordless song that poured, at times, from Lucien and into him, its complicated melody meshing with the refrain of his answering song. Similar, yeah, but not the same. This rhythm reminded him of the unfamiliar song that had rung through his mind that night in Club Hell.

The night Jay had been murdered, dying as Dante had struggled to reach him.

I knew you'd come.

The same night he'd found Lucien broken and impaled on the checkered floor of St. Louis Cathedral, his wings torn, his song nothing but cooling embers. And had learned that Lucien, his closest friend, his *ami intime*, was something else altogether.

You look so much like her.

Pain prickled at Dante's temples. *Send it below. Focus on now. Focus on here.*

The song wisped into his mind again like smoke. A muted, desperate rhythm. Beckoning him. He *moved*, racing past whitewashed and time-weathered statues guarding tombs, standing sentinel to loss. Trees and marble monuments blurred into one flickering shadow as he picked up speed.

The song's deep-earth drumming pulsed in time with the blood flowing through his veins, increasing in intensity until he felt it resonate within his own chest. Then the sound vanished.

Dante slowed to a stop. He stood next to a tomb marked BARONNE. And crouched beside it, holding a bouquet dead and dried, its wings curved forward, mouth wide-open, was a stone angel.

The one rumored on the streets to have appeared in the cemetery overnight.

Magic, some said. *Gris-gris*, others believed. A sign. So mortals whispered, yeah.

And nightkind said nothing, their silence uneasy.

A gust of cool air smelling of leather, frost, and old motor oil fluttered his hair as Von stopped beside him. "Well, there ya go," the nomad said. "Weird-ass hoodoo shit."

"Ain't just hoodoo shit, *llygad*," Dante murmured, his gaze on the stone angel. He felt Von step back a few paces as he took up his duties as Eye.

Observing. Safeguarding. Composing.

Candles in glass holders burned before the stone angel. The smell of vanilla and wax curled into the air. Plastic Mardi Gras beads hung from the wing tips and around the corded throat. Good luck *x*s chalked in blue, yellow, and pink decorated the path in front of the statue, and curled scraps of paper nestled against the taloned feet.

"One of the Fallen, looks like," Dante said. Something *else* Lucien hadn't bothered to mention. "And someone's turned him to fucking stone."

Dante knelt, picked up one of the pieces of paper and read it. *Loa of the stone, grant me protection from evil. Keep me safe in the night.* He returned the prayer to its place beside the stone foot.

He studied the squatting shape. Moonlight glimmered and sparkled like ice along faint patterns etched into the wings. But not feathered wings, no. Like Lucien's, these wings would be black and as smooth as warm velvet to the touch, the undersides streaked with purple. Waist-length hair framed the screaming face. The figure was nude, except for some kind of thick collar-bracelet twisted around the throat and a bracelet around one bicep. And most definitely male.

Von sent an image of the collar-bracelet. *<Torc. Celtic. Ancient.>*

<Merci, llygad.>

Moonlight illuminated a dark stain on the statue's forehead. It looked swiped on, a blood symbol of some kind, maybe a hoodoo *vévé*. Dante leaned forward, leather jacket creaking, and touched the stain. Residual power crackled against his fingertips like static electricity. A tiny blue flame arced in the space between his hand and the statue.

Fallen magic.

Catching a whiff of Lucien's pomegranates-and-dark-earth scent from the blood symbol, Dante pulled his hand back and regarded the angel, wondering what Lucien had done and why. To turn one of his own kind into stone . . .

Then he remembered Lucien's words from *that* night: *Shield yourself. Shut it out. Promise me you won't follow.*

Dante would bet anything he was looking at the reason why for that promise. Touching a finger to the collar—*torc*—around the angel's throat, he closed his eyes and listened. Song whispered in through his fingertips. His breath caught in his throat as his own song, chaotic and dark, answered. The stone beneath his fingers tremored like a rung bell.

Pain suddenly bit into his mind. White light strobed behind his closed eyes. Migraine storm warning. Dante opened his eyes and started to rise, then hesitated, one knee still down on the pavement. The fading song plucked at him like desperate fingers.

Promise me . . .

He wrapped his left hand around the angel's dead

bouquet. The sun-dried stems and shriveled petals crackled beneath his fingers. Flaked away like cindered wood. Like unspoken truth.

You look so much like her.

You knew all this time? And you never said a word?

Anger swept through Dante and music pulsed white-hot at his core. He poured energy into the wasted bouquet's remains. Song, dark and driven and wild, raged through his mind, from his heart, and spiraled around the skeletal stems. Blue fire kindled in his palms and shimmered against the stone.

The cupped stone fingers now held green stems topped by tightly closed buds. But pain shafted through Dante's mind again and his rhythm shifted, blasted harsh and dissonant notes, and his song spilled away into the night.

His hand slid from the angel and he staggered up to his feet. Pain twisted through his mind, snagged his thoughts like barbed wire. He clenched his jaw. Tried to will the pain away.

Send it below.

The cemetery spun; the moonlit tombs wheeled white beneath the cypress. Blood trickled from his nose. Spattered the pavement at his feet.

Behind, he heard Von calling his name.

Within, voices whispered. *Dante-angel?*

Above, he heard a rush of wings.

Dante closed his eyes and touched fingers to his temples. Sweat slicked his skin. A familiar, cool touch pressed against his mind, seeking admittance. Lucien. He tightened his shields, refusing.

Fingers squeezed his shoulder. "How the hell do you

do that?" Von's voice, low and tight, sounded uneasy.

Dante opened his eyes. A black-flowered and thorned bouquet swayed within the angel's stone grip as though caught in a gentle breeze. Or as if it moved on its own, dancing to the song cupped within the heart of each dark blossom.

"Fuck." He'd done it wrong. Pain throbbed behind his eyes. "Not what I intended."

"Intended or not," Von said, "that gift ain't night-kind, least not that I've ever heard. Must come from your dad's side of the family."

"Yeah, my thought too."

Von gently turned Dante around. "How's your head?" he asked.

Dante shrugged and wiped his nose with the back of his hand. Blood smeared his skin. "I'm okay."

Sliding his shades up, the nomad cocked an eyebrow and regarded him dubiously. "Uh-huh," he said, then dropped the shades back over his eyes.

Dante glanced at the stone angel and the midnight twist of flowers in its hand. "Why?" He nodded at the offerings tucked at the angel's feet. "Why do mortals pray this way? What do they hope to gain?"

Von stroked his mustache, considering. "Hard to say," he replied. "A lot of different reasons. Some might be prayers for a friend or relative who's in trouble, maybe for protection or success, or to be healed from something."

Dante's gaze returned to the candles. He stepped forward and fingered a loop of smooth beads dangling from one wing tip. "Did you do stuff like this? When you were mortal? Pray, I mean."

"No, not like this," the nomad replied. "And I never prayed to anyone, ya know? I just kinda said things that I really hoped would happen, like wishing a friend safe on a long journey or saying good-bye to one that'd died."

"Who hears the wishes and good-byes?"

"I forget you don't know this stuff." Von shook his head. "Who hears the wishes and good-byes? The speaker does," he said, voice quiet, reflective. "And you hope that what you say from the heart has power. Power to protect, power to reach the ears of the dead. A spoken thing or a wished-hard thing takes a shape within the heart, man. Takes shape. Becomes real."

"Becomes real," Dante repeated. "And the good-byes?"

"Good-byes can heal the hurt. Or at least start the healing."

This doesn't need to be good-bye.

Heather's words whispered through Dante's memory. An image of her filled his mind: Rain-beaded red hair, black trenchcoat, cornflower-blue eyes, she'd looked *into* him with her steady gaze. She was a fed, yeah, but a woman of heart and steel too. He remembered telling her: *Run from me.*

She had and now she was safe.

From him, maybe. But was she safe from the Bureau? She'd uncovered a nasty secret in D.C. Now she was caught between the truth and a hard fucking place. She was on her own in Seattle, without backup.

But not for long.

The West Coast leg of the tour ended with two gigs in Seattle followed by two weeks of downtime before the tour picked up again. Trey had already ferreted Heather's address, had teased it free from the Seattle DMV's online records with a deft touch.

Easier than rolling a tourist on Bourbon Street, Tee-Tee.

Dante let go of the Mardi Gras necklace, the beads clicking against the stone wing, and turned to face Von. "You got paper? A pen?"

Von frowned. "Fuck, I dunno." He patted his jacket pockets, leather creaking with his movement. "I hope you ain't planning on me taking dictation." He pulled a Bic pen from an inside pocket.

Dante took the pen, holding it between the fingers of his left hand as the nomad fished a wadded-up receipt out of his front jeans pocket and handed it to him.

Kneeling on the pavement in front of the stone angel, Dante smoothed the crumpled piece of paper against his leather-clad thigh. His pulse raced as he scrawled his prayer on the receipt, wondering if it had the power to protect, the power to reach the ears of the dead.

Dante folded the piece of paper, then raised it to his lips and kissed it. Blood from his nose dotted the prayer with dark color. He laid it at the angel's taloned feet among all the other paper prayers and chalk wishes.

Dante stood, glanced at Von. Wondered at the expression on his face, shadowed and a little sad. A smile touched the nomad's mustache-framed lips as he took his pen back and tucked it away again.

"You ready, little brother?" he asked, voice low.

"What time does the plane leave?"

"In about two hours."

Dante nodded. "Let's go."

A sudden gust of vanilla- and wax-scented air blew Dante's hair into his eyes. The candles flickered wildly and a few dimmed to blue, then died. Von's gaze shifted up and his brow furrowed. Dante's muscles knotted. Pain pulsed at his temples. He saw his own tension mirrored in the nomad's face.

Hoped we'd slip away without a scene. But maybe I need to play this out.

"Child, wait." Lucien's deep voice resonated from the sky above.

Pushing his hair back with both hands, Dante drew in a deep breath, swiveled around, and watched as Lucien descended from the star-flecked night, black wings stroking gracefully through the air.

Dressed only in expensive black slacks, Lucien De Noir touched bare feet to the flagstones bordering the Baronne tomb. His wings flared once more before folding behind him, their tips arching above his head. He straightened to his full six-eight height, his black hair spilling over his tight-muscled shoulders to his waist. His handsome face was composed, watchful. Gold light glimmered in the depths of his eyes.

"Wait, huh?" Dante shifted his weight to one hip and crossed his arms over his chest. "Give me one fucking reason why."

"You can't go on tour."

"That's a *command*, not a *reason*. And fuck you."

"You're not well. Your control slips more every day. You're dangerous."

Fire blazed to life, fused with the pain in Dante's head, the ache within his heart. "Fuck you twice," he said, voice low and strained.

Lucien's face remained impassive, but tendrils of his black hair lifted as though breeze-caught. "You know I speak the truth."

"Wow." Dante's gaze locked with Lucien's. "Is that like a first for you?"

A muscle jumped in Lucien's jaw. Shifting his attention to Von, he said, "I need to speak alone with my son."

<You want me to stay? Play referee?> Von sent.

<No, I'm cool. Don't worry. I'll meet you at the bike.>

<Your nose is still bleeding, little brother.>

"Merde," Dante muttered, wiping his nose against the sleeve of his jacket.

Von studied him for another moment before nodding. "Okay. See you in a few." He walked down the path past moon-washed crypts to the cemetery gates. "Play nice, you two," he called over his shoulder.

"I didn't lie to you," Lucien said, voice tight.

"D'accord, you didn't lie. But you kept the fucking truth from me and that's the same as lying. Happy now?"

"How can I be when your search for the truth is tearing you apart?"

"My problem, not yours. Stay outta my business."

"Impossible. You *are* my business!"

"Fuck you! I ain't your business, never was!" Pain fractured Dante's vision, throbbed at his temples. Blood trickled hot from his nose. "We were *friends,* remember?"

Lucien looked away. His fingers reached for the pendant that no longer hung at the base of his throat—the rune for friendship, for partnership, that Dante had given him—then closed into a fist. Dante wasn't sure when Lucien had lost the pendant or how, but its loss seemed somehow karmic to him.

"I made a mistake, one I regret," Lucien said, returning his gaze to Dante's. Amber fire flared in his eyes. "But I refuse to keep apologizing."

"I never *asked* for a fucking apology." Rubbing his temples, Dante closed his eyes. Nothing looked right. Blurry. Distorted. "And I ain't asking for one now either. Quit *pushing*! Leave me the fuck alone so I can find what I'm looking for. I need the truth or the past will always control me."

"The truth is never what you hope it will be, Dante. And the cost is always higher than you imagine. Much higher," Lucien said, his deep voice as low as a sigh. "I thought I could keep you safe in silence. I thought I could hide you, help you heal from all the damage done to you."

Dante opened his eyes and lowered his hands. *Safe in silence?*

"I thought I could contain your song or at least muffle it so it couldn't be heard." Lucien closed the distance between them with one long stride. His dark-earth scent curled around Dante. "But I was wrong."

Dante straightened, suddenly uneasy—something he'd never felt with Lucien before. "Hide me? From who? Are you talking about Bad Seed?"

"I didn't know Bad Seed even existed. No, I hid you from others. *Powerful* others who would use you without mercy."

"Others . . . like him?" Dante nodded at the stone angel hunched on the path.

Lucien's gaze flicked to the statue, resting for a moment on the flowers swaying in its hand, then back to Dante. "Yes, like Loki. I trapped him to protect you."

"Yeah?" Dante questioned softly. "From what?"

"The Fallen."

Lucien's golden gaze pierced Dante to the core, iced his heart. "What the hell are you talking about? Why would I need protection from them?"

"You aren't merely True Blood and Fallen, child. You're much more."

"And that is . . . ?"

"Creawdwr." A reverent note sounded in Lucien's voice. Pride gleamed in his eyes. "You're a Maker. The only one in existence."

A chill rippled down the length of Dante's spine. He looked at the bouquet bobbing in Loki's hand. "Is that why I can do shit like this?"

"Yes. You can create anything and everything. Your song carries the chaos rhythm of life. And you can unmake, as well."

Dante's memory flipped back. The center. *Johanna Moore screams as his song pulls her apart, divides her into elements . . .*

Dante returned his gaze to Lucien, his hands curling into fists. "And how long have you known this? That I was a . . . Maker?"

"From the first moment I met you," Lucien admitted quietly. "Your song, your *anhrefncathl* drew me. Just like it drew Loki. Just like it will eventually draw the rest of the Elohim. Unless I teach you—"

"Forget it. No," Dante said, throat tight, heart pounding out a furious rhythm. "Instead of pretending to be my friend, you shoulda told me the fucking *truth*! Shoulda offered to teach me *then*. Now's a little late."

Pain prickled behind Dante's eyes and suddenly it was as if he was looking through a shattered window as Lucien's image fractured and multiplied. Alarm flickered across Lucien's now diamond-faceted face. "Child . . . ?"

Something abruptly shifted inside Dante, something long broken, carving into his mind with white light and molten pain. The world spun, the stars streaking the night with gossamer ribbons of light, and he felt himself falling, tumbling down, down, down as memory sheared up, sharp and slick and edged with whispers.

You wanna take her punishment, p'tit? D'accord, *take it if you so hellfire eager.*

He's quiet now. Take him down.

Little fucking psycho.

Pain wrenched Dante apart and his vision winked out in an explosion of incandescent light—

Wings rustled.

Dante tasted blood, pomegranate-tart and heady. Felt heated flesh against his cheek. He opened his eyes and looked up into Lucien's shadowed face. He tried to remember where he was and why he was cradled in Lucien's lap, held tight within his arms. Lucien's wings curved forward and purple-tinged darkness folded around them, creating a warm shelter smelling of dark earth and green leaves, of wing musk.

"I was falling . . ." Dante said, then stopped, uncertain. Or had that been a dream?

"Shhh, *mon fils*. You're safe. Rest." Gold motes danced in Lucien's dark eyes.

"You need morphine, little brother?" Von asked, voice pitched low.

Ice frosted the base of Dante's spine. There were only two reasons Von would spike him full of dope. Migraine or . . .

Another fucking seizure.

"No, *mon ami*." The lingering taste of Lucien's blood on Dante's tongue, his lips, told him why red-hot pain wasn't needling his joints and muscles, why he wasn't sapped of strength. "Did you give me blood? Or did I jump you?"

A smile quirked up the corners of Lucien's mouth. "I gave."

"*Merci*," Dante murmured. He felt Lucien gently tapping against their closed bond, urging him to reopen the link. Shaking his head, he pushed free of Lucien's embrace. As he rolled to his knees, kneeling within the circle of Lucien's wings, the *where* and *why* suddenly poured into his mind like water from a broken levee.

The cemetery.

I tried to keep you safe in silence.

The bead-draped stone angel.

Yes, like Loki.

Creawdwr.

Dante's hands clenched into fists on his leather-clad thighs as his rage re-ignited. He met and held Lucien's gleaming gaze.

To Von he sent, <*How long was I down? Did we miss our flight?*>

<*Only a few minutes. We're good to go—if you still wanna.*>

<*I wanna.*>

Lucien's wings swept back and folded behind him. He uncrossed his legs, rising to his feet in one smooth motion. "You are ill, Dante, and hurt. You need time to heal."

Dante stood. "Don't tell me what I need."

A muscle ticked in Lucien's jaw. "Let the past go. Cancel the tour and let me teach you what you need to keep safe."

"No." Dante turned and headed down the path, his fingernails biting into his palms.

"The Fallen *will* find you, one night," Lucien said quietly. "And, if I'm not with you to prevent it, they will bind you."

Dante paused on the path. Deep inside, wasps droned. "*If* they find me, they ain't binding me," he said, his voice low and taut. "They're gonna hafta kill me."

"Not if, Dante. When."

"*Peut-être que oui, peut-être que non.* Same ending."

"Not if I can help it."

"You ain't got a say," Dante said, his throat almost too tight for speech. "And we're done here." He *moved*, racing down the path, the night streaking past in a blue-white ribbon, the smells of moss and weathered marble deep in his lungs.

A few moments later, astride Von's Harley, his hands on the nomad's hips, the wind cold against his face, Dante wondered if Lucien followed. Wondered if any of the Fallen followed. Wondered if Lucien had finally given him the truth.

I hid you from others. Powerful others who would use you without mercy.

The Fallen will *find you. And bind you.*

No, they wouldn't. Not ever. Not unless they knew how to bind a corpse.

One way or another, he would be free—his life, his own.

Dante glanced up. The sky was empty but for stars and moon and pale streamers of clouds. Nothing winged above. Not that he could see. And the Harley's deep-throated rumble swallowed any sound he might hear.

Like a rush of wings.

2

A DARK AND
DELICATE SONG

New Orleans, St. Louis No. 3
March 15

LUCIEN DE NOIR STOOD motionless on the
moonlight-bathed path, Dante's furious words—
They're gonna hafta kill me—battering his calm like brass-
knuckled fists. He drew in a deep breath and forced his
muscles to relax. Unclenched his hands.

Perhaps knocking his stubborn son to the ground
and sitting on him until reason overcame rage—as Von
had suggested a few nights earlier—would *be* necessary.

*Shouldn't have to sit on him for longer than a week or
two, Von says, straight-faced. Maybe three. He's your son,
after all.*

I am patient, Lucien reminds him, not stubborn.

Von laughs.

Lucien bent and searched through the scraps of
paper at Loki's stone feet for the blood-kissed prayer
Dante had placed among them. Finding it, he plucked

it from the pile and straightened. The fading essence of *creawdwr* blood magic tingled against his fingers. Unfolding the liquor store receipt, he read the words scrawled in Dante's lefty slant:

Watch over her, ma mère. S'il te plaît, *keep her safe. Even from me.*

Lucien reread the prayer until the words blurred. He closed his fingers around the receipt, the paper crinkling against his palm. He had no doubt who *she* was—Special Agent Heather Wallace.

Wounded, his child, yes. Damaged, yes. But Dante's heart was whole and in love, it seemed, with a mortal. Perhaps Heather Wallace could bind Dante and help keep his sanity from unraveling.

Insanity. The fate of an unbound *creawdwr*.

Until Dante relented and forgave him, Lucien would be unable to teach his son how to control his gifts. Would be unable to help him keep his balance as *creawdwr* power raged through his mind and heart. Would be unable to lend him the strength to fight madness.

He wasn't the only one Dante hadn't forgiven. Dante also refused to forgive himself. Still sought penance for acts he'd committed as a child struggling to survive, acts he couldn't even remember. Penance unowed, as far as Lucien was concerned.

Lucien studied Dante's handiwork, the bouquet his child had created. The soft-petaled flowers in Loki's hand danced as though breeze-stirred. Thorned tendrils snaked around the stone figure's arms, neck, and wings. The scent of smoky incense, of myrrh, wafted up from each flower's glossy black heart, a night perfume.

A song, delicate and dark, chimed up from the bouquet.

Dante's power strummed across Lucien's heart and radiated into the star-pricked sky—a beacon for any Elohim within range. A cold finger traced the length of Lucien's spine. He straightened and listened to the night. Listened for *wybrcathl*. Listened for the rustle of wings. He heard only the faint pulse of Loki's stone-caught heart.

Lucien looked at Loki's crouched and screaming form. Time was running out. Soon, whoever had sent Loki would wonder at his absence.

Ever since Yahweh's death, well over two thousand years ago, the Elohim had waited for the rise of another *creawdwr*. But only Lucien knew the wait had ended nearly twenty-four years ago, when a Maker had been born, a *creawdwr* like no other—vampire and Fallen.

Only Lucien knew—so far.

And he intended to keep it that way for as long as possible.

Lucien carefully plucked free Loki's bouquet, unwinding its black roots from around the pale stone. A riot of chiming notes rose into the air, a sharp and wild crystalline song. Inky tendrils slithered free of Loki's arm and curled around Lucien's arm, his throat. The song quieted.

A beautiful song. One he would drown in the Mississippi.

Tucking Dante's prayer into the pocket of his black slacks, Lucien fanned open his wings. Air gusted, extinguishing the few remaining candles still flickering and scattering the prayer-etched bits of paper across the cemetery path.

As his wings flared and swept upward, lifting him into the sky, he suddenly heard another heartbeat. Strong and measured. A rhythm he knew. Hovering just above the cemetery's main path, Lucien scanned the shadows.

She stepped out of the darkness pooled beneath the cypress. Flowing midnight hair, creamy skin, and gleaming eyes. A red gown clung to her curves and, at her back, her black wings were folded.

Rubies glittered in the slender torc curving around her throat and in the gold bracelets around her slender wrists. A cold smile played across her lips—lips the color of moonlit ruby wine and just as intoxicating.

"No song of greeting, my *cydymaith*?" Lilith asked.

Without a word, Lucien spun and soared up into the sky. Dante's black blossoms chimed and sang as the wind stroked their petals. He didn't need to look to know Lilith followed; he heard the powerful whoosh as she took to the air. He'd always out-winged her in the past. He hoped that was still true. He flew swiftly for the wide, night-blackened curve of the Mississippi, the night cool against his face.

The lights of the city burned bright beneath him, glimmered with headlight glow, except for one dark, empty section stretching to the east—what used to be the Ninth Ward, now a razed shadow reeking of decay. *Vévés* and *gris-gris* and blessed candles warded its haunted borders, protecting the rest of an unknowing New Orleans from the bitter and angry spirits trapped within—forever drowning, forever waiting for help that never came. And never would.

Moisture beaded on Lucien's face as he veered toward the south and the river. Moonlight rippled across the Mississippi's surface and ship lights glowed red and yellow upon the slow-moving waters.

Lucien caught a glimpse of black and red in his peripheral vision: Lilith had caught up and flew beside him, her wings stroking smoothly through the sky.

So much for out-winging her, he thought wryly.

Ethereal notes rang into the air, clear and lilting. And, for one heart-stopping moment, the centuries dropped away and he was once again flying beneath the deep blue skies of Gehenna, his brilliant and beautiful *cydymaith* winging beside him, trilling her complicated song.

The sky-rumbling roar of an airplane overhead shattered the illusion and the centuries returned. But Lilith singing, that was no illusion; her desperate *wybrcathl* filled the air and Lucien's heart.

What she sang turned his blood to ice.

Gehenna was fading, a land too long without a *creawdwr*'s powerful and sustaining touch. The border between worlds bled and soon the Elohim would return to the mortal world to rule it for all time.

Then the wars for power would begin in earnest.

3

BLEEDTHROUGH

Above New Orleans
March 15

WINGS FANNING THE AIR, Lucien slowed and descended to the weed- and mud-pebbled banks of the Mississippi, Dante's black flowers singing in his hand, Lilith's words echoing in his mind.

Gehenna is fading.

Folding his wings behind him, Lucien knelt on one knee and plunged the blossoms into the dark water, the reek of moss and mud and fish thick in his nostrils. A gust of air swept his hair across his face, and he caught a peripheral flash of red.

"What are you doing?" Lilith cried and grabbed at his arm.

Fending her off with a shoulder flex, Lucien tightened his grip on the flowers and shoved them deeper into the Mississippi. The black tendrils knotted around his hand and arm and throat, twisting tight and digging into his flesh as the bouquet struggled for life. Little bubbles flecked the water's surface. Lucien thought he detected a faint gurgling underwater song. His chest tightened. He had no other choice. To keep Dante safe, he would do whatever was necessary.

"Stop!" Lilith leaped into the water, then bent, her hands searching beneath the surface for his and the things he drowned. Her fingers skittered across the back of his hand. Her talons stabbed.

The bouquet's inky tendrils slithered free of Lucien's throat and arm, limp and lifeless. He released the flowers and pulled his hand from the river. Blood welled up in the punctures, even as the wounds healed.

Lilith swished her hands around in the muddy water for a moment longer, then she straightened, a single black flower, drenched and silent, hanging from her hand. She sloshed from the river, her gown wet from the thighs down and clinging to her shapely legs. She fluttered her wings, shaking water from their tips.

Rising to his feet, Lucien fixed his gaze on her. Like all Elohim high-bloods, she was tall, but at six two, she was still a head below his six eight. He remembered the feel of her silky hair as it slid between his fingers, the softness of her wings—even after thousands of years.

An image of Genevieve draped only in a white bath towel, her wet hair streaming past her shoulders, laughing, dark eyes gleaming, flashed behind Lucien's eyes, and grief closed a fist around his heart.

Lucien was grateful that Dante was gone and on his way to Los Angeles. He was far enough to keep him safe temporarily—but not out of Elohim reach, not yet. Shields tight around his mind and heart, he watched Lilith's approach.

Stroking one taloned finger along the drowned
flower's stem, sadness glimmered within Lilith's golden
eyes. She lifted her head, the fire in her eyes searing
away any trace of the sorrow he'd witnessed just a moment before.

"How *could* you, Samael?" she demanded. "A
creawdwr's beautiful gift and you killed it like an unwanted kitten." She flung the flower at him. It fell into
the weeds.

"I haven't used that name since I left Gehenna," he
said. "Call me Lucien."

"Do you plan on slaying this *creawdwr* too?"

"Perhaps I already have."

"Perhaps."

Lilith crossed the short distance between them,
her breasts shimmying beneath the thin silk with each
step. She stood in front of him, chin lifted, a knowing
smile curving her lips. Her scent reawakened the past,
unearthed memories of heated, soft flesh and urgent
moans. He tensed, breathing in her warm cedar and
amber fragrance, his pulse winging through his veins.

"Perhaps," she repeated. "But I don't think so. Not
yet, anyway. If you *had* killed him, you wouldn't have
been in such a hurry to murder his flowers."

Lucien smiled. "Are you certain of that?"

Tilting her head, she studied him. The river breeze
lifted tendrils of her black hair and blew them across
her face, slashing her lovely face with midnight-black
shadows. "Yes, my *cydymaith*. I'm certain you haven't
killed him . . . yet."

"I'm no longer your *cydymaith*," Lucien said quietly.
"I gave that up as well when I left Gehenna."

"I didn't," she returned with a haughty lift of her chin.

Lucien laughed. "After all this time? Lilith, please."

The fire in her golden eyes intensified, bright and hot, as if she wished she could burn him to nothing but ash with one glance.

"Do you know where this Maker is?" she asked. "I know he's young, male, and powerful from his *anhrefn-cathl*. And unstable."

Dread gripped Lucien with cold talons. Even Lilith realized that Dante was unbound, a *creawdwr* edging toward inevitable madness. Forcing a smile to his lips, he said, "His song brought me, as well. I have no more idea of where he is than you do."

"Really?" Lilith murmured. She slid a warm hand up his bare chest to his lips. "Then who turned Loki to stone and chained him to the earth?"

Without thinking, Lucien kissed her fingertips. It surprised him to realize how easily he reverted to habits he believed long dead. Surprised and disturbed him. Grasping her hand, he lowered it from his face. "It's less than he deserves, I'm sure. Loki has any number of enemies," he said. "Did you send him?"

"No. He's been spending his time with the Morningstar and that wretch, Gabriel."

"Ah."

"How long have you known of the existence of this *creawdwr*?" Lilith asked.

Lucien shook his head. "What does it matter? I won't let you have him."

"So you *do* know him," Lilith breathed. "I knew it."

"Would you like to join Loki, my sweet?"

But Lilith didn't back away as Lucien thought she might. Instead her hands knotted into fists and her wings fluttered in agitation. "You are selfish," she said. "Selfish and full of pride. You'd let Gehenna vanish and leave the Elohim homeless and bereft and for what? Because you think only you know what's best for a Maker!"

"I know I'll never allow another to be chained to Elohim will!"

"Yahweh was never chained! How can you say that?"

"He was used, manipulated, and lied to! You didn't hear him, you weren't with him, you didn't see—" Throat suddenly too tight for speech, Lucien closed his mouth, and turned away.

Let them have me.

"Do you think you were the only one who loved him?" Lilith asked softly. "Astoreth was his *calon-cyfaill*, too. And she died with him. I've never understood how you survived the bond-breaking." Her fingers closed around his shoulder, her touch warm and strong. And damp-sticky. Blood? "You've given me no choice," she whispered.

Lucien jerked free of her hand, and whirled. Pale ethereal light streamed from Lilith's palms. As the binding words slipped from her lips, he dove into the river.

The Mississippi's cold water sluiced away the blood on Lucien's shoulder. He berated himself for being so careless. If he'd been just a split second slower, Lilith would've finished her blood spell and bound him just as he'd bound Loki.

Then she could've returned him captive to Gehenna

to face justice for the murder of Yahweh. Or maybe bargained with him, his freedom in exchange for the *creawdwr*?

Lucien swam underwater for as long as he could. Then, chest aching, he surfaced and gasped in a deep lungful of sweet, cold air. Wiping water from his eyes, he looked for Lilith on the shore and in the sky. He saw nothing—no flash of red, no glowing golden eyes, no movement. She wasn't gone. He knew better than that; she never gave up, not easily. It had been one of the things about her that he'd once loved.

Until she'd severed that love by convincing a tormented *creawdwr* to curl himself into a golden ark to be carried across the desert by mortals who worshipped him; a people yearning for a land of their own, a home. Yahweh had guided them, a sacred and crazed divining rod.

With Yahweh gone, and Lucien and Astoreth searching for their *calon-cyfaill*, Lilith had perched upon Gehenna's black-starred marble throne in Lucien's absence. And gone to war with Gabriel and his golden wings—undoing in one heated moment the peace Lucien had so carefully crafted over centuries.

Wings flaring and flapping against the river's surface, spraying droplets of water in the air, Lucien winged up from the Mississippi and into the night sky.

Gehenna is fading.

Had Lilith spoken the truth? Very possible. The wait for another *creawdwr* to be born among the Elohim high-bloods had never been this long—over two thousand years. Did Gehenna feed on a Maker much like nightkind fed on mortals? And without the one, the other would die?

Only one way to find out.

Lucien spiraled up into the sky. The air was thin and cold and burned within his lungs. It iced his lashes, froze his wet hair, and frosted his wings white, but melted against his heated skin. Miles blurred past beneath him, and the star-field glow of city lights disappeared as he winged over the dark and restless ocean, the smell of brine thick in his nostrils.

His heart beat hard against his ribs as he drew closer to the gate between Gehenna and the mortal world, a border he hadn't crossed in literal ages.

Hadn't dared cross. But he had to know if Lilith told the truth.

A trilling *wybrcathl* drew his attention. Lilith was warning him *away* from Gehenna. Interesting, considering that bringing him in to face the Tribunal could only strengthen her rule.

Perhaps she hoped to keep news of a *creawdwr*'s existence secret until she had him in hand and under her wings.

Refusing to answer her, Lucien flew on, dark doubt brewing deep within him. Loki had said that the Morningstar had allied himself with Gabriel and the two were mounting a campaign against Lilith in another attempt to wrest the black-starred throne out from under her.

If she bound the *creawdwr* and became his *caloncyfaill*, the Morningstar might as well fly down into Sheol, make himself cozy in the embers and pour ashes over his dazzling white hair, because no one would lift wing at his command again—not as long as Lilith ruled with a Maker at her side.

And Gabriel? The amber-haired high-blood would

remind everyone that he'd once been the Voice of Yahweh in the mortal world. And would humbly offer his service to the new *creawdwr*.

A twisted Voice, Gabriel. And heartless. Bitter anger prickled around Lucien's heart. He'd always regretted leaving the pompous, puffed-up *aingeal* alive.

And who, Lucien wondered, would be chosen as the other half of the balance and the triad's third, the second *calon-cyfaill*? A better question would be: Who would Lilith *allow* to be chosen?

For *his* son.

Lucien winged on through the night, his strokes strong and sure. He caught a glimmer of color, undulating waves of purple and pale blue and gold, streaking the sky; an aurora borealis where none belonged.

Lilith's *wybrcathl* ended.

Lucien slowed and hovered, his wings flapping, and stared. Where once a golden gate had spun, visible only to Elohim eyes, there was now only a wound in the fabric of reality, and all the colors and energy-life force of Gehenna bled into the mortal skies.

Lilith had spoken the truth. Gehenna *was* fading.

She hovered beside him, her tresses frozen into long glimmering icicles, the shifting colors reflected across her face. "Why wouldn't you listen to me?" she muttered.

"Who rules Gehenna?" Lucien asked, fearing he knew the answer.

"Gabriel."

So, Loki had lied. Not surprising in itself, but what chilled Lucien's blood was why. Loki had suggested they bind the *creawdwr*–Dante–together, suggested that Lucien could once again rule Gehenna. He now suspected that Loki had hoped to overthrow Gabriel by manipulating Lucien's ambitions, ambitions that had died with Yahweh. But Loki being Loki simply had not known how to speak the truth.

Had Lucien turned an *ally* to stone?

Beyond the new aurora borealis, a song trilled into the night, a trill answered ten, twenty, thirty times. Black wings and gold wings blurred through the dancing curves of light as Elohim swarmed from the tear between worlds.

"I hope you've kept your talons sharp, my foolish, stubborn *cydymaith*."

Sudden calm buoyed Lucien. He'd been waiting for this moment for so long that now it had arrived, he felt relieved. He quickly closed his link to Dante and sealed it against any pushes from his child. He considered severing it, but feared what it might do to them both.

"I've always kept my talons sharp," he said, then met the first *aingeal* head-on, talons slashing. Lilith fought at his side, as though she belonged there, as though all the centuries apart had never happened, her wings lashing the sky and her talons flinging dark blood into the night.

As though she believed escape were possible.

4

IN THE DARK

S HANNON WALLACE DIED BENEATH the sheltering branches of an oak tree, her blood soaking into the pine-needled ground like rain on a hot summer day. She died in the dark without a struggle. She died drunk. And she died looking into the face of her killer.

Of that, Heather Wallace felt sure.

Twigs and dead leaves crunched beneath her Skechers as she stepped through the underbrush. She stopped beside a lichen-laced oak and stood at the spot where her mother's body had been discovered two decades earlier.

Memories whirled like pinwheels in Heather's mind, the revolving images blurring from one into another.

Whirl: *Mom laughing. A smile lights her face and the air shimmers around her like a summer dawn. Rose incense burns in the little brass holder.*

Whirl: *Mom silent and focused as she cleans the house,*

scrubbing every surface with cleanser and stiff-bristled brushes. For hours and hours. For days.

Whirl: *The raw sound of Mom's rage. The crash and crack of thrown dishes, stoneware shrapnel. The heavy stink of cigarettes and booze.*

Whirl: *Mom sits at the kitchen table, elbows propped on the littered surface, her head in her hands. Her hair, uncombed and lank, spills over her knuckles. A cigarette burns in an ashtray full of stubbed-out butts. Empty brown prescription bottles roll on the table beside an empty bottle of vodka.*

Whirl: *Mom laughing . . .*

Heather blinked the images away and drew in a deep breath of sun-warmed air to clear the lingering memory-smell of smoke and roses from her mind.

Shannon had been thirty when she died, mother of three, wife to FBI forensics expert James William Wallace. Heather had already outlived her by a year.

Shannon had been a woman no one had ever championed, not even her husband. The case had gone cold. Forgotten. No justice rendered. Heather wasn't blameless either—even after she'd learned the truth about her mother's death, it'd taken six years for her to act. And watching as Dante had spoken for the mother he'd never known.

"Avenge your mother," Lucien whispers as Dante's eyes open.

Heather hoped finally to speak for her mother.

And maybe, just maybe, the truth would heal Annie.

But before Heather could help her sister or champion their murdered mother, she needed to keep herself alive. And to do that, she wanted the Bureau to see an agent so focused on her job that she voluntarily worked a cold case while on medical leave just to keep occupied, an agent who behaved as though nothing had changed in the last three weeks.

Even though *everything* had irrevocably changed—including herself.

Dante . . .

She touched the spot on her chest where the bullet had pierced her, felt the steady beat of her heart beneath her fingers. Remembered the desperate sound of Dante's voice, his words husky and Cajun-spiced: *I won't lose you.*

Heather closed her eyes and gently pushed the memory aside. *Not now.*

After a moment, she opened her eyes and peered into the gloom beneath the trees, inhaling the thick smells of pine, damp soil, and moss. The trees and shrubs muffled the rush of traffic on I-5. Crouching, she studied the ground, trying to imagine what Shannon had seen and felt that last night of her life. Tried to work it like any other case.

Even twenty years ago, leads in the case had dried up fast. Shannon had left the Driftwood Bar and Lounge in northeast Portland alone around 11:30 p.m. on October first. Employees and patrons were interviewed, barfly statements sifted and compared.

Shannon Wallace frequented local watering holes and often made hookups. Wasn't thought to be too choosy, according to her drinking buddies.

The Portland PD detectives working the case at the time had believed Shannon Wallace to be a victim of a serial killer working the I-5 corridor, the Claw-Hammer

Killer. The CHK preyed on prostitutes and barflies, women who generally wouldn't be missed. Not immediately, anyway. The FBI task force hunting for the CHK had also believed Shannon a possible victim of their perp.

If that *was* true, then Shannon had already been championed.

Special Agent Craig Stearns, then of the Portland field office, killed the CHK—a Hillsboro carpenter named Christopher Todd Higgins—during a violent struggle while serving a search warrant shortly after Shannon's murder.

Stearns.

Heather fixed her gaze on the green and gold leaves above her. Tried to resist the memory flip back to New Orleans. Failed.

Stearns lifts his Glock and calls Dante's name.

Dante, hands braced against either side of the house's open threshold, turns. Fire sparks from the Glock's muzzle. His head snaps to the side as the bullet catches him in the temple. He stumbles, then falls. He sprawls across the threshold, half-in and half-out of the house.

Stearns strides toward Dante's body, gun in hand. Heather bails out of the car before Collins brings it to a full stop. She runs, .38 clenched in both hands. "Drop it!" she yells. "Don't make me do this!"

Stearns spares her a glance, then turns back to Dante. Aims.

She fires.

"Shit," Heather whispered, dropping her gaze to the ground. Only three weeks had passed and the memory still cut deep. She blinked until her eyes quit burning.

According to Inferno's MySpace page, the band was on the road, so Dante was safe—for the moment. And Stearns, her mentor, the man who'd been more of a father to her than James Wallace, was dead, buried with honors in Seattle's Lakeview Cemetery.

She drew in a deep breath. *One thing at a time, Wallace. Just one thing at a time.*

A heavy thunk penetrated the green-lit silence. Car door.

"Wallace? You okay?"

Sounded like Lyons had tired of waiting. Maybe he needed to stretch his legs. Maybe he was bored. She was pretty sure, however, he'd been asked to keep an eye on her, so maybe he was *curious* in a need-to-take-notes kind of way. She hadn't wanted a guide to the kill site in the first place, and for someone of Lyons's rank to volunteer for the job was more than a little unusual.

"Yes, sir, fine."

Heather stood. Brushing dirt and leaves from her jeans, she turned and, ducking under low, slender branches, walked from the grove just in time to see Portland SAC Alex Lyons slide something into the pocket of his hoodie. Cell phone? she wondered. BlackBerry? She walked across the grass to her car. Early afternoon sunshine sparked diamond dazzles from her sleek sapphire-blue Trans Am.

Lyons slouched against the passenger door, smoking. The breeze ruffled his curly blond hair. He looked at Heather, squinting in the sunshine. Lines crinkled around his green eyes, lending him rugged good looks and a Marlboro Man masculinity. Tall and lean-bodied, he wore weathered jeans, a gray Plan B hoodie, and black Rippers. She pegged him in his early thirties, but suspected at heart he remained forever twenty and golden.

"Get what you were looking for?" he asked, straightening. He dropped the cigarette to the pavement. Ground it out with a twist of his Rippers.

"Yes, sir. I appreciate you coming out with me on your day off."

Lyons shrugged. "Not a problem. Glad to help."

"Well, it wasn't necessary," she said. "And thanks for rounding up the Portland PD's file on Higgins to compare with the Bureau's file on the Claw-Hammer Killer."

"Again, glad to help. Especially someone like you."

"What do you mean—like me, sir?" Heather pulled open the Trans Am's passenger door and scooted across the black leather interior to the driver's seat. She grabbed her seat belt and strapped it shut.

Lyons slid into the passenger seat and closed the door. He fastened his seat belt. "I mean, aside from being a fellow agent, someone with a personal stake in the case."

The smell of his cologne curled into the air, a cologne Heather remembered her brother wearing—Drakkar Noir—but in this case, its mingled lemon, sandalwood, and amber scent was edged with cigarette smoke.

"And all those *sirs* are way too formal for a day off," he added with a smile. "How about you call me Alex and I'll call you Heather."

"Wow, good thing that happens to be my name."

"Beautiful, smart, and a sense of humor," Alex chuckled. "A killer combination."

"You just caught me on a good day. . . . Alex."

"So what're your thoughts on the case after reviewing it?"

"Higgins was probably good for my mother's murder," Heather said. "But I'd like to know for sure."

"I understand that completely."

Heather keyed on the ignition. The Trans Am's engine rumbled to life. She hit the gas and shifted the car through the gears to fifth, merging smoothly with the I-5 traffic.

"Can I ask you a question?" Lyons said.

"Sure."

"How did it feel to take Elroy Jordan down? I mean, even after that fuckup of an ME had declared him dead in Pensacola, you still found him."

Heather kept her gaze on the road, guiding the Trans Am into the fast lane to pass a semi hauling Budweiser, but her fingers tightened around the steering wheel. "Just dumb luck," she said.

"Just dumb luck?" Lyons laughed. "Hey, no need for false modesty. Claim your glory. I sure as hell would. You tracked that bastard down and put him where he belonged—in the ground."

The Bureau had named her Jordan's killer and a hero even though they'd known the truth, a truth never spoken aloud by anyone, a truth both she and the powers that be had wanted buried, but for very different reasons.

She to keep breathing and to protect Dante.

They to cover their collective asses.

And the ME in Pensacola that Lyons had so casually mentioned? The one who'd been ordered to falsify the autopsy report? A suicide. Slashed her wrists in the tub. Ended up on one of her own autopsy tables.

A very *convenient* suicide.

It'd chilled Heather to the marrow to realize how far the collective ass-covering would go, but it hadn't surprised her, not after New Orleans. But worst of all was her own silence, a silence that—no matter how necessary—made her feel like an accomplice.

"Yeah, well, I wish Jordan could've faced the relatives of his victims in a court, instead," she finally replied. "It felt like he got off too easy."

"They often do."

"They do," she agreed. "But I still hope to change that with every arrest I make."

"Amen, sister." Lyons paused, then said, "I heard you took a bullet too. How are you feeling? You look good for a woman who nearly died three weeks ago."

"I'll answer your question," Heather said, keeping her voice light, relaxed, "if you answer one for me."

"Shoot."

"I saw you putting something in your pocket when I walked out of the woods. Are you recording this conversation?"

"Something in my pocket? I'm not sure. . . ." Lyons suddenly laughed. "My sister. I called my sister to see if she needed me to pick anything up for her on the way home."

Heather looked at him. Amusement glimmered in his eyes and his level gaze met hers. Her gut instinct said: *He's telling the truth.* Some of the tension drained from her muscles and she eased her grip on the steering wheel.

"So is this FBI-trained suspicion or just natural paranoia?"

Heather chuckled. "FBI trained," she admitted. "But I don't know how to turn it off anymore."

"Another amen, sister. So, my question . . . ?"

"My injury wasn't as bad as you might've heard—" A cell phone's abrupt *beedle-beedle* interrupted her.

"Is that you or me?" Lyons asked, reaching into his hoodie pocket.

"Shit, it's me," Heather muttered, fumbling one-handed behind the seat for her purse. She'd programmed a businesslike ring for the Bureau on her cell; a Leigh Stanz neo-grunge song—"Don't Need Light"— announced her non-work-related calls.

Given that she wasn't on active duty yet, a call from work couldn't be good news.

"Keep your eyes on the road and your hands on the wheel," Lyons said, twisting around in his seat. "I'll get it."

"Thanks," Heather said, doing as he'd advised. A second later, Lyons pressed her phone against her ear.

"Go," he whispered.

"Wallace," she said into the phone.

The conversation was short and most definitely not sweet. When it ended, she reached up and took the cell phone from Lyons, folded it shut, and dropped it into her jacket pocket.

"Trouble?" Lyons asked.

An update on your medical status has been requested. Be here at eighteen hundred hours. Be prepared for the possibility of additional debriefing.

Additional debriefing, sir?

Just a possibility. Eighteen hundred hours, Wallace.

"No," she lied, flashing Lyons a quick smile. "A mix-up, most likely."

"I hear that. The Red-Tape Bureaucracy Boys singing their latest, 'It Needs to Be Filled Out in Triplicate.' "

Despite the hard knot in her belly, Heather laughed. "Exactly."

She had five hours to drive back to Seattle and, although that should be enough time even after dropping Lyons off at the Portland field office parking lot, she'd have to cancel her surprise visit to see Annie at the treatment center. She'd also be cutting it too close to swing by her house once she hit Seattle to change from jeans into office appropriate slacks and blouse.

Maybe that wouldn't matter. *Be prepared for the possibility of additional debriefing.*

The knot in her belly kinked tighter. Maybe they'd found out about her and Dante. If so, that'd give them enough reason to fire her, the hero they'd created. And a chance to transform her into another tragic figure like the ME in Pensacola, a suicide in her tub. Or maybe the victim of an auto accident or a burglary gone wrong.

Heather inhaled deeply, drawing in a breath of Drakkar Noir. *Get a grip, Wallace.* If the powers that be wanted her dead, they wouldn't wait to fire her first. She'd already be on an autopsy table.

Maybe her father was behind this sudden medical status update. Maybe he'd caught wind of her cold case investigation. "Can I ask a favor?" she said.

"Shoot."

"My father is James Wallace—"

"James William Wallace? The fearless leader of our West Coast lab?"

"The same."

Lyons whistled.

"If he should contact you about what I'm doing—about this case, I'd appreciate it if you'd keep him in the dark."

Heather looked at Lyons and something lit in his ocean-green eyes, a connection, an understanding. He nodded. "Can do. I'll keep your old man in the dark."

"Thanks," she breathed, relieved he didn't ask why. "I appreciate it."

"Not a problem."

For the last twenty years, James William Wallace had kept Heather in the dark. About how her mother had died, about how she'd lived; about Annie's illness. She'd had to dig for every little bit of truth, sift it from lies and willful denial. She intended to return the favor. In spades.

5

THE HAND THAT FEEDS

HEATHER KNEW HER LIFE depended on how she answered the question just posed to her by ADIC Monica Rutgers. If she said yes, she'd be little more than a marionette for the Bureau to stage and pose—albeit a well-paid, *breathing* marionette. If she said no, they'd find a way to strip the truth from her mind, and then, in one way or another, she'd die.

"I'm honestly stunned," Heather said, managing to curve her lips into a smile. "And honored. But a decision this important deserves careful consideration."

"Of course," Rutgers replied from the large-screen monitor nestled into the west wall. Graying curls framed a stoic face weathered by decades of subterfuge. "How about Monday? That gives you four days to mull it over."

"Monday would be fine, ma'am," Heather said.

She sat in one of two plush chairs positioned in front of what used to be Stearns's oak desk and his office.

His energy still seemed to permeate the room, steady as granite. And, at times, she thought she caught glimpses of him from the corners of her eyes--behind the desk, standing at the rain-ribboned window looking down into the street. Imagined she smelled coffee and Tums.

"We believe you've more than proven your merit and mettle," Alberto Rodriguez said from behind Stearns's desk.

"Thank you, sir," Heather said. She glanced at the interim SAC and flashed him what she hoped was a winning smile. "Still, it's a big decision . . ."

"You'll make a fine SAC." The shitty sound system rendered Rutgers's voice as thin and flat as her face. "I believe this is a move Craig Stearns would've approved."

Heather doubted that, considering the truth Stearns had learned in New Orleans.

You've been marked for termination. Me too.

How high up does this go?

I think it's best to behave as though it goes to the top.

"I appreciate your confidence, ma'am," Heather murmured, throat tight.

Rutgers folded her hands on the polished surface of her desk, an ill-fitting smile glued to her lips. She studied Heather from the D.C. side of the webcam. Heather forced herself to relax into the chair.

"The latest report from your doctor states that you're fit for duty," Rodriguez said.

Heather swiveled her chair slightly so she could see both him and the monitor.

He tapped a finger against a folder in front of him on the desk, his angular, clean-shaven face thoughtful.

"Though, frankly, he's amazed by your recovery. It's nothing short of a miracle."

"I was lucky, that's all," Heather said. "If the bullet had been a centimeter to the left . . ." She shrugged. "I wouldn't be here. No miracle, just luck and prompt medical attention."

"We still have a few questions—" He looked up when the door opened, then snicked shut again. He nodded his head in acknowledgment.

Just as Heather glanced over her shoulder to see who'd joined the meeting, she caught a whiff of Brut aftershave.

I knew it.

He looked older than she remembered—thinner, hair streaked gray and white, more lines etched into his face.

"I apologize for being late, ma'am," SA James William Wallace said, nodding at the monitor. He stood just inside the door, his rain-spattered tan trenchcoat draped over his left arm. "The traffic was bad."

"No apology necessary," Rutgers said. "You came up from Portland on very short notice."

"If I may ask, ma'am—why was my father asked to attend?" Heather straightened in her chair. "We've never worked together. He couldn't possibly assess—"

"He's here as an advocate for you," Rutgers said, leaning forward against her desk. "We don't want any misunderstandings. And you need to know what's at risk."

A chill iced Heather's spine. "At risk, ma'am?"

James Wallace folded his trench over the back of the remaining chair and sat down beside Heather. With a wink and a smile, he swiveled his chair around to face the com-con monitor and Rutgers.

"She's ready to get back into the saddle," her father said.

"My father does *not* speak for me. Just so we're clear," Heather said.

"Relax," James Wallace murmured. "I'm on your side."

Heather refused to look at him. "Ma'am, you mentioned a risk?"

"That's correct. A few other things for you to consider while you contemplate your decision."

Rodriguez flipped open the file, thumbed through the pages. "Special Agent Bennington mentioned during his debrief in D.C. that he believed Dr. Moore had intended to use you as 'psycho bait,' but he wasn't sure if you were meant to lure Jordan or Prejean." He looked up at Heather. "Any thoughts as to why in either case?"

Heather forced her hands to remain open and relaxed in her lap. She frowned, then shook her head. "I really think Bennington would know more about Dr. Moore's motives than I would."

"And you maintain that when Dr. Moore shot you," Rutgers said, "she was aiming at Jordan? Are you certain she hadn't intended to kill you along with Jordan?"

On the monitor, a man—most likely an assistant—stepped into camera view, a finger to the Bluetooth curving against his ear. He paused to speak into Rutgers's ear, then walked out of viewing range again. The ADIC's expression became grim.

"I'm not certain of anything, ma'am. Between the drugs and the bullet in my chest at the time, very little is clear," Heather said, keeping her voice level. "Again, as to Dr. Moore's intentions, Bennington would know more than I do."

"It could've been friendly fire, just like Heather said in her statement," James Wallace put in. Fabric whispered as he crossed his legs. "Like it was with Craig Stearns when a bullet from Heather's gun ended up in his shoulder during a firefight."

Heather finally looked at her father. Even though her pulse pounded hard and fierce through her veins, ice frosted her from the inside out. "That's all in my original statement," she said, jaw tight. Her father met her gaze, his own composed. "And it has nothing to do with what happened at the center."

"Just pointing out how easy it is and how often it happens," he said.

"Regrettably, yes," Rutgers said. "But I keep coming back to one question. . . ."

Heather shifted her gaze back to the monitor. The knot in her belly tightened. "Yes, ma'am?"

"If Moore *had* intended to shoot you, why? Was she hoping to trigger Prejean?"

Heather's pulse spiked. "I don't understand," she said, her mouth suddenly dry. "Trigger Prejean?"

"Bad Seed," Rodriguez said. "Does that ring any bells, Wallace?"

Heather looked at him. His deep-set eyes zeroed in on her. She shook her head. "Bad Seed? No, should it? Again, if this is something Moore had been working on, maybe you should be asking Bennington and not me."

"Unfortunately, we no longer have that option," the ADIC murmured. "Special Agent Bennington is dead."

Heather held herself very still. She stared at Rutgers's pixelated image. "Dead?"

Face grim, Rutgers nodded. "Heart attack nearly two weeks ago."

Heather judged that Bennington had been in his early thirties and fit. A coronary would be unusual, but not impossible. All the same, she had the chilling feeling that Bennington had been helped into a convenient death, just like Anzalone, the ME in Pensacola.

"I'm sorry to hear that," she managed to say, the knot of dread in her belly pulling tighter. "I can't answer your questions, ma'am. You're asking me things I don't know."

Rutgers studied her for a long moment, then nodded. "Fair enough. While you're mulling over our offer, please keep in mind that refusal or a resignation could result in certain information being leaked to the press."

"Ma'am?" From the corner of her eye, Heather caught a glimpse of movement and another whiff of Brut as her father straightened in his chair.

"Mental illness has claimed two members of your family so far, your mother and sister, I believe." The ADIC's voice was level, conversational.

"That's false, ma'am," James Wallace interrupted. "My wife was an alcoholic—"

"Bipolar," Heather said. "Mom was bipolar. Annie, too."

Rutgers's gaze bricked over, hard and cold, and she shifted it to James Wallace. "I won't brook any more interruptions from either of you." She returned her attention to Heather.

"I'm listening, ma'am," Heather said.

"It'll be made clear that you are the third member of the family to become ill," Rutgers said. "We'll express our regret at seeing one of our finest tragically brought low by ill health. We'll also let it be known that we wouldn't hold you responsible for any delusional comments you might make. And we'll promise to provide all the medical and psychological help needed for you to regain your health."

James Wallace's chair creaked as he leaned forward, elbow to knee, hand to chin. "So you'd shred Heather's credibility and sabotage my career as well."

"Your daughter would be doing that," Rutgers said. "Not us. It's up to her."

Heather locked gazes with the ADIC. "Will that be all, ma'am?"

"Gentlemen?" Rutgers murmured. "Anything else?" Her face was impassive, but Heather detected tension in her body language, in the tight set of her shoulders.

"No, ma'am," Rodriguez replied.

James Wallace shook his head.

"Then we're finished. Until Monday, Wallace. Consider carefully." Rutgers tapped a button on her desk. The monitor went dark.

Rising to her feet, Heather glanced at Rodriguez. "Sir," she murmured. Without even a glance at her father, she strode from the office.

HEATHER CROSSED THE PARKING garage in quick strides. Fury burned a hole in her gut. It'd stopped raining outside, but the air was cool and humid and smelled of rubber, old oil, and car exhaust. She unlocked the

Trans Am with her smart key and reached for the door handle.

"Heather!" Her name boomeranged against the concrete.

She whirled around to face her father, her purse bumping against her hip. "What the hell do you want?"

"I believe the traditional greeting is *hello*," James Wallace said, voice neutral. He stood a yard away, his hands shoved into the pockets of his tan trench. His glasses reflected light from the buzzing overheads. "I came here to vouch for you. We're still blood, whether you like it or not. And my word carries weight."

"I've never wanted or needed your *weight*."

"I know," James Wallace said. A smile touched his lips. "I've always liked that about you."

"Don't you know they just used you?"

"I do . . . now." He sighed. "I was trying to protect you."

"You never have before. Why start now?"

James Wallace slipped off his glasses and rubbed the bridge of his nose. "Are you sure of that?" He suddenly looked weary and worn, in need of a shave; a worried father. He slid his glasses back on without once looking at her with uncovered eyes. "I want us to be a family again, Heather. All of us."

"Really? I don't remember you visiting me in the hospital or even calling," she said, voice low. Tension pulled the muscles in her shoulders taut.

"I couldn't bear the thought of seeing you injured and in pain. Not you, Pumpkin. I hope the media left you alone."

Genuine concern? Interrogation technique? It bothered Heather that she didn't know. "Why do you care if the media left me alone or not?"

He pulled his hands from the trench's pockets and folded his arms over his chest. "Experience. I remember how insane it was when your mother died."

"Murdered."

"I did my best to protect you kids. I wish you could understand that."

"I understand you didn't get Annie the help she needed." She felt her nails bite into her palms. She realized she was slipping into a loop with her father—she accusing, he defending—the same argument over and over.

"How will it help your sister if you dig up the past? Look to the future and let the dead remain dead."

Heather stared at him. How had he found out so fast? Planted bugs? Spies? From Lyons? Or had he been informed by a clerk just in passing? How didn't matter, really. He knew.

"No," Heather said.

"Just no? That's it?"

"That's it."

"Think of your sister, your brother," Dad said. "They don't need to know all the details of your mother's murder."

"I *am* thinking of them," Heather said. "And if you'd been honest with us from the start, we could've helped Annie much sooner. I think the truth will be good for all of us. I've got to go."

Shrugging her purse strap up higher on her shoulder, Heather turned and opened the car door. Her father's hand wrapped tight around her wrist. She stopped, glanced up at him. His gaze, hazel-eyed and clear, met hers.

"Let go," she said.

"I want you to know, for what it's worth, I'm glad you're alive. Glad that Prejean saved your life. If Stearns had killed him . . ." A muscle jumped in James Wallace's jaw.

"Stearns risked his life for me. When he shot Dante—" Heather fell silent, heart pounding. He'd slipped that comment in so casually, so smooth. Hooked her like she was fresh out of the Academy.

Glad that Prejean saved your life.

How could he possibly know?

She'd told only one person what Dante had done; a whispered phone conversation with the only person who wouldn't judge her or think her nuts. A tumbler of brandy in her hand, her throat aching with each word, she'd shared Dante with her sister.

I didn't walk away. I just stepped back for a bit. To figure things out.

Then call him, Heather. Let him know you're worried about him, that you care.

Heather jerked free of her father's hold. She slid into the driver's seat and shut the door. She breathed in the faint odor of vanilla from the Starry Night air freshener hanging from the rearview mirror. She felt as tight and hard as a fist. Struggled to breathe around the twisted knot of anger in her chest.

James William Wallace stepped back, a rueful smile tilting his lips.

Bureau man. Father. Husband. And a coldhearted, lying bastard.

Had her phone or Annie's been tapped?

She keyed on the engine, slammed the Trans Am into gear, and peeled out of the parking garage.

She needed to warn Dante.

THE DOOR CLICKED SHUT behind Caterina and two sets of eyes watched as she crossed the room to stand in front of the ADIC. Rutgers's assistant, SA Brian Sheridan, stood behind Rutgers's chair like one of the royal guards Caterina's mother had described from her time centuries before in the Italian court, his gaze distant and his face serene despite the sweat drying on his forehead.

"I wasn't aware you were in D.C., Cortini," Rutgers said with a frown. She tapped a finger against a neat stack of folders on her desk.

"That was the idea," Caterina said, seating herself in one of the chairs positioned before the desk. Leather creaked. She glanced at Sheridan. "Our conversation needs to be private."

Sheridan's gaze was no longer distant, but fixed on her, hazel-eyed and sharp. Midthirties, and judging by the fit of his well-tailored suit, in excellent shape. No doughnuts and lattes for this royal guard.

"Go ahead," Rutgers told him.

Gaze still on Caterina, Sheridan said, "Yes, ma'am." He walked across the office in quick strides. The door shut quietly behind him.

Caterina set up her audio jammer on the ADIC's desk. The slim, dark metal device was designed to look like an iPod, but she had no doubt that Rutgers knew exactly what it was and why it was being used. Caterina switched it on. It chirped and burbled and squealed as it desensitized all audio recording equipment in the room.

"I've been sent to deliver a message," Caterina said, holding the ADIC's gaze. "A decision has been reached."

Rutgers stiffened. "A decision? Regarding . . . ?"

"The Bad Seed fiasco and the Bureau's mismanagement of the aftermath," Caterina clarified, although she knew perfectly well that Rutgers understood her.

"But we're still looking into the matter," Rutgers protested, leaning forward in her chair. She rested a hand on the stack of folders as if protecting them. "We've destroyed all evidence."

Caterina shook her head. "Not all. The footage from the center's med-unit security cameras is still missing. And some of the evidence is two-legged, walking, and definitely not destroyed."

Rutgers closed her mouth. Her hands slid from the folders to her lap. She regarded Caterina for a long moment. "Dr. Moore and Dr. Wells are the people responsible for Bad Seed. If anyone is to blame for this mess, it's them."

"Moore's still missing and Wells retired from the project five years ago. So responsibility falls to you."

"Am I to understand you believe *me* at fault in this? This wasn't just a Bureau-directed project. Your handlers played a part as well."

"What I believe is of no concern. What *is* of concern are my instructions."

"I see. And what are your instructions?"

"I'm to take care of all loose ends."

Rutgers drew in a sharp breath. "All?"

"All, but one."

"Dante Prejean," Rutgers said, her voice flat. "And what about Wallace? We've offered her the SAC position in Seattle. You can't mean to—"

"She's no longer your concern," Caterina cut in. "End your surveillance of Wallace. Call your people off Prejean. And, if Moore should turn up, please let me know immediately." Caterina had a feeling Moore was dead, scattered ash. But, until she'd confirmed that suspicion, she'd operate as though the missing scientist were alive.

Rising to her feet, Caterina added, "If anyone rabbits, I'll assume they were warned. And I'll assume the warning came from you." She held the ADIC's brown-eyed gaze until the woman finally glanced away, jaw tight. "I hope I've made myself clear."

"Completely."

Caterina scooped up the audio jammer from the desk, but didn't switch it off. She held it in her hand. "This decision is final. There's no appeal."

Rutgers looked at her then, and her eyes were as dark and bitter as scorched coffee. "There never is."

Caterina switched off the jammer and slid it into her pocket. With a quick nod of her head, she spun on her heel and crossed the now silent room to the door.

"I feel like I'm working in the dark here," Rutgers said.

Caterina opened the door. "You shouldn't. Adapting to darkness isn't difficult in our profession." She stepped into the hall, closing the door behind her. "That's the problem."

6

FOOTPRINTS BENEATH HER WINDOW

Seattle, WA
March 22

CHOOSING A WINDOW AT the back of the unlit house, Dante removed the screen and rested it against the white bricks. He forced the window open with a hard, quick, upward jerk. The lock snapped with a wood-muted crack. He paused, his fingers on the window frame, listening. He heard nothing. No barking dogs. No fast-drumming heartbeats. Just silence.

Pushing aside the cream-colored curtains that belled out of the open window, Dante swung a leg over the windowsill and climbed into the darkened room. He straightened. Lowered his hood and shook his hair back from his face.

He breathed in Heather's scent of sage and rain-wet lilac, a fresh after-the-storm smell. Her energy, her presence, warm and strong and sun-spiked with authority, illuminated the room.

He slid his shades up to the top of his head, his latex shirt creaking with his movement. He stepped farther into the room. Plush sofa and recliner, along with the easy chair, coffee table—magazines and books strewn across its polished surface. A blue, star-flecked fleece throw draped the recliner.

Dante walked through the house, drinking in the details of Heather's everyday life. He trailed his fingers along the back of the sofa, the recliner—soft cushions, slick vinyl.

Kitchen: A couple of plates in the sink, a green DONE light glowing on the dishwasher, rose and purple accents, twilight colors. The mingled odors of rosemary, olive oil, and lemon lingered in the air.

Dining room: A runner of green leaves and purple grapes draped the small table. A musty and old-blood odor wafted up from a couple of dinged-up cardboard boxes on the table. Printed in black marker on the sides of the boxes were the words WALLACE, SHANNON, CASE NO. 5123441. Photos were spread like tarot cards across the table's dark wood surface, crime scene photos.

Dante grasped the back of the chair in front of the table, the rings on his fingers and thumbs clicking against the wood, and leaned forward.

In the dirt beneath winter-stark branches, a woman lay half-curled, her gaze on the sky above. Dante's heart skipped a beat. She looked so much like Heather—red hair, heart-shaped face, lovely even in death.

A sister? She'd mentioned that her sister had fronted WMD before the band had split up, a sister who suffered from migraines too.

A sudden thought pulsed through him. His hands squeezed around the chair's hardwood rung. Not her sister. Her *mother*. Murdered and discarded. Like his own.

Pain prickled behind his eyes, snaked through his mind. Voices whispered.

You look so much like her.

Dante-angel?

Shhh, princess. Hush, p'tite. *Sleep.*

Closing his eyes, Dante touched fingers to his temple. Tried not to listen to the whispers. Sweat beaded his forehead. *Focus on Heather. Focus on now.* The voices faded until all he heard was the steady thump of his heart.

Dante opened his eyes. He studied the photos, the report pages scattered on the table. Was she reviewing her mother's case or reopening it? Heather looked for truth in everything she did. No matter how much it hurt. And no matter who it pissed off.

It'd nearly killed her in D.C. He'd bet anything she wasn't any safer here.

He remembered how she'd looked the last time he'd seen her at the hospital, her face pale, eyes shadowed, sorrow pooled in their blue depths. She'd looked vulnerable, fragile. So alone.

He wasn't sure he could trust himself to walk away again. Didn't know if he could actually tell her goodbye. Didn't know if he wanted to heal. Didn't know if he *deserved* to heal. But he wasn't walking until he was sure she was safe.

Shoving himself away from the chair and the crime scene photo collage, Dante walked down the hallway to the bedroom. Heather's scent surrounded him, warm and intimate, and he breathed it in.

An inquisitive mew caught Dante's attention. An orange cat curled at the foot of the bed opened its golden eyes and regarded him calmly.

"Hey," Dante said, holding his hand in front of the cat's nose. The cat sniffed his fingers, then rubbed the side of its face against the edge of his hand. He stroked the small, furred head with two fingers. The cat yawned, tongue curling lazily. "I hope you ain't supposed to be the guard kitty, *minou*, cuz you're sleeping on the job, you."

Dante trailed his fingers across the neatly made bedspread, and a dark restlessness uncoiled within him as he remembered Heather in his lap, her arms wrapped around him, holding him tight as they rocked together. Remembered the feel of her skin—warm and soft and firm, the honeyed taste of her lips, her blood. Remembered the white silence that had cupped around them like hands sheltering flame from the wind.

It's quiet when I'm with you. The noise stops.

I'll help you stop it forever.

But pain still blazed within. White light flickered and strobed.

No. Focus. Stay here. Stay now. Keep her safe.

Forcing himself away from the bed, Dante walked across the carpeted floor to the dresser against the wall. Several framed photos stood grouped together, one of Heather with a girl sporting a purple Mohawk and pharaonic black eyeliner and a guy with reddish-blond hair in jeans and tee. The girl and guy both looked enough like Heather to be her sister and brother. In another photo, Heather cuddled an orange cat, her cheek pressed into the cat's fur, her blue-eyed gaze happy, content.

The same cat now bumping up against Dante's leg, back arched for pats. Smiling, he bent and petted the orange head. "I see you're part of the family and not security," Dante murmured. "Good thing for me, huh?" As the cat swiveled, purring, Dante noticed only three legs. "Looks like a good thing for you too."

Dante straightened, kissed the tips of his fingers, and then touched them against the photo of Heather and her kitty. He'd wrapped a finger around the iron pull-ring of the first dresser drawer when he heard a faint step-step out in the living room—or maybe just outside it—followed by silence.

Dante tilted his head, held his breath, and listened.

A heart's steady rhythm, a *mortal* heart's steady rhythm. A faint scratch against wood. A key? No, sounded wrong. The window.

Dante spun and strode out of the room. As he sprinted down the hallway to the living room, pain prickled, restless and sharp, against his temples and behind his left eye. He stopped when he saw a gym bag tossed into the room through the open window. It landed on the carpet with a heavy *tunk*.

The battered bag with frayed straps reeked of old smoke, pot, and cigarettes. A hand holding a crowbar grasped the windowsill. Dante *moved*. He seized the crowbar-wielding hand and, with one hard jerk, hauled the asshole in through the window. A loud rip tore through the silence as the asshole's hoodie or jeans snagged on the broken lock.

He *smelled* her, this B&E chick, before he saw her, vanilla and cloves and lavender soap, but underneath that a chemical tang smudged her scent. Pain spiked his temples at the smell, scratched like thorns across his thoughts.

Grabbing both of B&E Chick's shoulders, Dante whirled and slammed her to the floor. Her head bounced against the carpet. Her breath *whoof*ed out and Dante caught a whiff of booze—tequila. He straddled her, snugging a knee against either side of her ribs. Held her tight.

Something whistled through the air, moving fast. Without looking, Dante swung his left arm up and out. Cold steel smacked into his palm. The crowbar. He jerked it away from little Ms. Break-and-Enter. Tossed it. The crowbar thunked onto the carpet. Dante looked into her kohl-smudged, dilated eyes.

And realized with a cold shock that he recognized her.

Whipping her head forward, she smashed her forehead into Dante's face. Bone crunched and pain followed hard and fast like a one-two brass-knuckled punch. Blood trickled from his now broken nose. "Fuck!"

"Get *off*!" B&E Chick screamed, squirming and kicking.

Not just B&E Chick, but Annie Wallace. Former front woman for the defunct WMD. He'd recognized her scowling face from the photos on Heather's dresser.

Dante grabbed a double fistful of Annie's black hoodie and jumped to his feet, yanking her up with him. She swung a fist but missed him by a mile. He slammed her against the wall and braced an arm against her chest. When he saw her throat muscles tense, he beat her to the punch and head-butted her first. Their heads met with a loud clonk.

Her head thumped back into the wall, denting the plaster. She looked up at him, blinking, more startled than hurt. Her eyes were sky-blue, not Heather's shade of deepest twilight. She was about the same height as Heather, five four or so to his five nine.

Her hair, streaked electric blue, purple, and black, framed her face and swept razor-cut ends against her shoulders. Metal rings and studs gleamed at her eyebrows, ears, and bee-stung lower lip.

He touched his nose. Pushed. Winced. The bone cracked as it slid into place. He sniffed back blood. "You gonna calm the fuck down? Or we gonna do this all night?"

"Fucker," she spat, her kohl-lined eyes locking onto his face. She stopped struggling. She sucked in air, eyes widening, the pupils dilating even more.

Dante sighed and looked away, muscles taut. He knew his looks hooked into people, mortal *and* nightkind, and reeled them in by the crotch. Hot and bothered. Wanting him, wanting what they *saw,* anyway. Sometimes that was okay. Sometimes it was fun. But only sometimes.

"Hey."

Dante swiveled his head back around. And she kissed him. Warm lips tasting of tequila and clove cigarettes. He pulled back, felt a smile tilting his lips. "First the head-butt greeting, followed up with a sloppy kiss. Is this how y'all do it in Seattle?"

"Who the hell *are* you? How come you broke into my sister's house?"

"*Toi t'a pas de la place pour parler.* I ain't the only one," Dante said, nodding at the crowbar on the carpet. "How come *you're* breaking in?"

She glanced at the crowbar. "Nuh-uh. *You* broke in first."

"I'm a friend. Just wanted to see if Heather was all right."

"Most people knock on the door first to see if someone's home," she said, lifting her chin. "Then wait for them to answer it."

Dante glanced at the crowbar on the floor. "Yeah? And you know this how?"

"Heard it from, like, normal people," she said. She pushed against his arm. "You can let go now. I promise not to make you bleed anymore."

Dante snorted. "You didn't *make* me bleed. The broken nose did that." He stepped back, releasing her.

Annie rubbed her forehead. "Hard skull, man. Your nose looks okay to me, you big baby. By the way, I'm Annie." She extended her hand.

"I figured. Heather's talked about you." Dante grasped her hand and shook it. "I'm Dante." Her grip was firm like Heather's, but hard, like she was still challenging him, trying to make him wince.

Annie released Dante's hand. "And how do you know my sister?" Her gaze skimmed his length from head to toe. "Steel-ringed bondage collar, latex and leather—trust me, you're not the kind of guy she usually brings home."

"We met in New Orleans."

"Holy fuck! Are *you* the guy Heather was telling me about?" Annie poked a finger into his chest. "The guy who fucking saved her life? The guy who is . . . fuck, what the hell did she say you were?"

"Something nice, I hope. But I'm okay with something naughty."

"She said you weren't human," Annie laughed, her voice low and booze-and-smokes scratchy. "Crazy, I know! I forget what she called you. . . ."

"Nightkind."

"That's it! Nightkind. Vampire. Are you?"

"Yup," Dante replied, trailing a hand through his hair. "When did you talk to Heather? Have you seen her? She okay?"

Annie shrugged. "I guess she's okay." She felt along the wall for a light switch. "So, just 'yup'? No denials? No 'get real, there's no such'—"

Dante heard a click as her fingers found the switch. Light flooded the room, spiking pain in through his eyes. He reached for the sunglasses parked on his head, then realized he'd lost them during Annie's head-butt hello. Squinting, he lifted a hand to shade his eyes.

"Fucking hell," Annie whispered. "You're even better looking in the light. That's rare, you know, a lot of times guys you pick up in clubs will be *soooo* pretty in the dark, especially Goth boys, but once you see them the next morning in raw daylight—yikes."

"Been there," Dante murmured. "I feel your pain."

"How in hell did Heather land a hottie like you? Even with blood on your face, you're yummy."

Elroy's words whispered through Dante's mind, words spoken in the back of a blood-spattered van, words that latched tight as handcuffs around the pain in his head: *Your nose is bleeding. That's kinda sexy.*

Dante rubbed his right wrist as the Perv's whisper faded, a ghost sheeted in cold steel, sharp shivs, and bitter lust. But the pain didn't fade. "That's a stupid question," he said, refocusing on Annie. "Your sister's gorgeous, inside and out."

Annie stuck her index finger in her mouth and pretended to gag.

Dante laughed. "I think I like you, *p'tite*."

Spotting his sunglasses on the carpet next to the coffee table, he walked over, scooped them up, and dropped them on over his eyes. His headache eased a little. "Do you have any idea where Heather might be?" he asked, swiveling back around.

"Nope." Annie closed the distance between them until she stood just a handspan away, her weight shifted to one hip. "But I bet I know a few tricks she doesn't," she said, voice low. "She'd be so pissed if I jumped your bones."

"I ain't here to piss her off. And if that's why you're here, I gotta feeling we're gonna be butting heads again."

"Really? Promise? It was *soooo* fun the first time." Her gaze slid over him and the chemical tang underneath her lavender-and-cloves scent thickened, curling into Dante's nostrils like smoke.

Dizziness suddenly whirled through Dante, spinning the room around him. *Something in her scent . . . drugs?* White light flickered at the edges of his vision. Sensations rippled through him, pulled and tugged like a tide of ghostly hands; then the rip current yanked him down. Sucked him under.

A needle pierces the skin at his throat. Cold burns through his veins like dry ice.

Images sheared up into Dante's mind, fractured and confusing: A room with blood-spattered, snow-white walls. A hype with a bead of clear liquid on the needle. A man's voice. *What's the little psycho yelling?*

Pain sucker punched him. He stumbled. A hand locked around his bicep. Black flecks flickered through his vision. Faded slowly. Dante looked into Annie's blue gaze—saw curiosity. Hunger burned through his veins. He needed to feed. He'd waited too long. And his control was slipping.

"You okay?"

"Oui." He pulled free of her hold. Stepped back from her heat, from the tantalizing patter of her pulse.

"Can I see your fangs? You got fangs, right? I wanna see."

Dante walked into the kitchen, stopping at the sink. He twisted the knob to cold. Bending, Dante cupped cold water in his hands and splashed it on his face. Scrubbed away the blood. But not the whispers.

I've mapped your mind.

What's he screamin'?

He's making a very loud, very clear demand.

"Kill me," Dante whispered. Pain spiked his temples and he grabbed the sink's edge. The room spun. He shut his eyes. He tried to hold onto the shadow memory, tried to repeat the words he'd just said, but when he opened his mouth, he no longer knew what to say.

It was gone. Whatever it'd been.

"Fuck." Dante opened his eyes, released his grip from the sink, and straightened. Pain throbbed behind his left eye. Tearing a paper towel from the roll on the counter, he wiped his face. Turned off the water.

In the sudden silence, he heard a sharp gasp from the living room. He hurried out of the kitchen and saw

Annie standing at the dining room table, her attention locked on the photos fanned across its dark wood.

"Is that my mom?" Annie said, voice barely more than a rough-edged whisper.

"Dunno. But I think, maybe, yeah."

"She got herself whacked because she was a drunk and a whore," she said, her tone bored, but strain edged her voice. Manic energy whipped around her like electricity from a downed power line. "If-she-weren't-already-dead-I'd-fucking-kill-her-myself-she-picked-booze-I-hate-her-I-hate-her-I-hate-everyone—"

Annie's hurt and rage punched against Dante like a child's angry fists, pounding and kicking and screaming. Then, with a speed almost nightkind fast, she whirled and ran across the room to the crowbar. Dipped and grabbed. Spun again.

Her eyes gleamed like she was hyped up. Her musky scent saturated the air. Dante had seen this kind of hurt before. Had felt it. Had carried it clenched in his fists and within his heart.

Annie swung the crowbar up into the air, fingers white-knuckled around the steel. A wordless howl escaped her throat and scraped razor-edged along Dante's spine. She shot forward like a launched missile, the crowbar whistling as it arced through the air.

7

NO CONNECTION

HEATHER STEERED THE TRANS Am into a Fred Meyer parking lot, eased the car into a slot, slipped the gearshift into neutral, and yanked up the emergency brake. The engine's rumble eased into a steady purr.

She flipped her cell open. She drew in a deep breath, and then tapped in Dante's home number. She'd memorized the numbers for his home and the club, and had wished more than once he carried a cell phone. She hadn't programmed the numbers into her cell, worried that someone might steal the phone and its data. Someone in a suit and shades, with a Bureau haircut.

The phone trilled and trilled. The metallic crash of shopping carts reverberated through her skull. Unease prickled through her with each unanswered trill. Finally, she heard a click.

"Oui?" Female voice, Cajun. Simone.

Heather pictured the earthy and beautiful blonde

vampire, spiraled locks tumbling past her waist. Pictured her dark eyes and quick smile.

"Simone, it's Heather," she said. "Heather Wallace. I need to speak to Dante. I know he's on tour, but does he—or anyone traveling with him—have a cell phone?"

"No, *M'selle* Wallace."

No longer *Heather*, but *M'selle Wallace*, Heather noted.

"Not even for emergencies?"

"He doesn't always want to be found."

"I need to speak to him. It's important."

"*Je m'en fichu.* Can't help you." Simone's words were cold and flat, all warmth gone from her voice.

Heather's muscles knotted. She looked through the windshield and into the light-washed night. "His migraines, have they been worse? Better?"

"Much worse. And he won't let Lucien near him. As if you care."

"Of course I care," Heather said, keeping her voice steady. "I'm worried about him too. I hope to find some way to help him."

"Like I told you before: You can't help him. Only we can." Simone's voice was cold enough to frost the windows.

"I may be mortal, but I can still help him, whether you think so or not."

"We'll see," Simone said, then ended the call.

Heather flipped the cell closed, then tossed it into the passenger seat. She rubbed her temples with her fingers. Her head ached. She couldn't rely on Simone passing along her message. She'd have to be more direct. Inferno was playing Seattle tonight and tomorrow night at Vespers. She'd even bought tickets online for both shows.

Just in case the sight of Dante didn't hurt.

Heather released the emergency brake and toed the gas pedal. The car's throaty rumble vibrated up through the seat. She slipped the Trans Am into gear and drove from the parking lot, heading for Capitol Hill and Vespers.

She switched on the radio. "Tonight! At Vespers! Inferno!" Rough-edged industrial music poured from the speakers, followed by Dante's almost whispered vocals, his voice simmering and full of rage.

Funny that she was thinking about him and then the next thing she heard on the radio was his band. Funny. A shame she didn't believe in coincidence.

Just three long weeks ago, she'd learned that the world was much darker and more varied than she'd ever imagined. She still didn't completely understand what it all meant or even where she and Dante belonged in this new world, what their roles were. But between the Bureau and Bad Seed, she was scared that she'd never have the chance to find out.

HEATHER TURNED FROM BROADWAY into a cramped parking lot. She parked underneath a sign reading PARKING FOR VESPERS CUSTOMERS ONLY! ALL OTHER VEHICLES WILL BE TORCHED TO KEEP THE HOMELESS WARM. THANK YOU FOR YOUR GENEROSITY.

Heather slid out of the Trans Am and locked it. Slinging her purse onto her shoulder, she walked toward the club's entrance. A sign taped on the empty box of-fice window read DOORS OPEN AT 9. SHOW BE-GINS AT 10.

A small crowd of people stood in several clusters near Vespers's cathedral-styled front doors, defiantly smoking and chatting. Along the arched border sur-rounding the doors lurked handpainted gargoyles and leering demons. Twists of ivy painted in scarlet and black curled up the doors to the arch.

A cool touch to the dark, brooding façade. A venue Annie had yearned to play. Heather glanced up as she headed for the entrance. The marquee read INFERNO and, in smaller letters, DOGSPIT. She hadn't heard any-thing by Dogspit and wondered if they were a local band.

The crowd, with a fairly even mix of male and fe-male from what Heather could see, was a Goth/punk smorgasbord featuring everything from cyber-Goth to old-school punk: metal-strapped latex, stylized strait-jackets, fishnets and red-and-white striped thigh-high stockings, Cleopatra-kohled eyes, black leather and squeaky vinyl, and chain-draped black jeans; some wore stylized Mohawks or had shaved skulls. Piercings glim-mered beneath the streetlights. Tattoos snaked like ivy along hard flesh. Tribal. Stylized. And the air reeked of cloves, patchouli, and sandalwood.

She wondered if any nightkind waited in line with the mortal crowd, but she didn't see any of the haughty grace and cool beauty that she associated with night-kind. Dante was different in even that—his beauty, heated and riveting, his grace natural and unassuming.

Several in the crowd gave Heather the once-over, then looked away when they decided, with her black bomber jacket and boot-cut jeans and unfreaked hair, she probably wasn't associated with the band.

You'd think this Halloween-and-fetish-gear-wearing group would know better than to judge a book by its cover, Heather mused as she walked past. At the door, she pulled on the handles. Locked. Curling her fingers around the huge, black, iron knocker, she thumped it against the door several times.

After a moment, she heard a click, then the door cracked open. A woman with purple-lined eyes and gel-spiked black hair looked her over. "Read the signs. Doors don't open till nine."

"I need to talk to Dante Pre—Baptiste of Inferno. It's important."

The woman rolled her eyes. "Yeah, uh-huh. Life and death, right? Wait for the meet-and-greet after the show." Shaking her head, she started to shut the door.

Sliding her foot against the door, Heather reached into her purse and fished out her badge. Flipped it open. "Please," she added. "If I could just come in . . ."

The door queen's face emptied of all expression. She poked her head out to see if anyone had noticed Heather's badge, then motioned Heather inside. Shut and locked the door behind her.

Door Queen studied Heather's badge for a long moment. "Wow. FBI." She glanced at Heather, worry jittering in her eyes. "And you said Dante of Inferno, right? Is he in trouble? Are we gonna have to cancel the show?"

"No, no trouble," Heather assured her, sliding her badge back into her purse. "But I *do* need to talk to him. Please tell him Heather Wallace is here."

A smile of relief suddenly curved Door Queen's

purple-slicked lips. "Okay. Wait here," she said. She hurried down an ill-lit hallway, her wide-legged black canvas jeans whisking with each step.

Heather glanced at a poster of Inferno tacked on the wall just inside the door. A flaming anarchy symbol against a black background and beneath the symbol: BURN. She combed her fingers through her hair, her stomach suddenly filling with butterflies. She wondered if he'd even come. And if he did, what he'd say.

What *she'd* say.

She caught a whiff of old leather and frost-edged air—crisp and clear. A scent she recognized.

"Okay, little girl. What can I do for you?" A low and easy drawl. Amused.

Heather swiveled around and met Von's green-eyed gaze. A mustache framed the wicked grin parting his lips, revealing his slender fangs. His deep-brown hair was tied back. Six one and broad-shouldered, dressed in leather chaps over faded jeans, a black tee and scuffed-up scooter boots, his good looks played well against his earthy and tough exterior. He extended a callused hand.

"Good to see you, Von," she said, grasping the nomad's hand.

"Same here, doll." Von squeezed her hand once, then released it. "But you sure about that? Your vibe says otherwise." Faint light from the dim overheads glimmered along the silver-etched crescent moon tattoo beneath his right eye.

Heather shook her head, feeling a genuine smile tug at her lips. "Sorry, Von. I forgot how sharp nightkind emo-radar is."

Von laughed. "*Emo*-radar? Hell, woman, what kinda word is that?"

Heather's smile faded as she glanced past the nomad, hoping to see Dante striding along the dark hallway. "Where is he?" she finally asked.

Von's brows knitted together. "Ain't he with you?"

"What?" Heather stared at the nomad.

"He left a couple of hours ago," Von said. "Said he was gonna stop by your place. Said he wanted to talk with you."

Relief cascaded through Heather. "I haven't been home," she said. And she felt a little embarrassed for thinking Dante would avoid her in a high-school-drama kind of way. "Do you think he's still there?"

"I'll find out, doll."

Von's eyes unfocused for a moment and Heather watched as he connected with Dante in a way she envied. She'd experienced Dante's mind touch back at the center—a link blood-forged and temporary and intimate.

Von's green eyes locked onto her again. "He's still there and he ain't alone."

"Not alone?" Dread hooked into her. "Who's with him?"

"Your sister," Von replied.

8

IN THE SHADOWS

Portland, OR
March 22

HIS DAUGHTER WAS PROTECTING a vampire.

James Wallace poured hot water into a mug and over the tea bag nestled inside. As the tea steeped, the faint odor of blueberries steamed into the air. He carried the mug into his office and set it on the small cup warmer plugged into the wall. He sank into his chair, the leather creaking beneath his weight. He rubbed his hands back and forth over his head, his bristle-cut hair soft beneath his fingers.

Heather's reaction to his comment about Prejean saving her life told him everything he needed to know. She'd lied during her debriefing and in her official statement. Was *still* lying. She was protecting Dante Prejean, protecting a goddamned bloodsucking *vampire*.

He didn't know which was worse, that or her investigation into Shannon's death.

On his drive home, several questions had circled

endlessly through his mind: How could he protect his reputation and his stubborn daughter? What had been so important that Rutgers's assistant had felt compelled to interrupt the conference, even briefly? What the hell had Dante Prejean done to Heather?

First thing he'd done when he'd walked in through the front door was get in touch with one of his contacts in D.C.

Keep this to yourself, Jim, but Caterina Cortini was here, paid Rutgers a visit, then left. Rutgers left shortly afterward too—looking pissed as hell.

That news had shaken James. Cortini answered only to the Shadow Branch—the arm of the federal government that'd been formed some time ago by a former vice president; a consortium rumored to be composed of CIA, DOD, FBI, and Homeland Security members, a branch that answered to no one and didn't exist officially.

Cortini was rumored to be one of the Shadow Branch's top wetwork experts, or problem solvers—for the more politically correct, one who permanently tied up loose ends.

Given the subject of his meeting with Rutgers and Rodriguez, James couldn't help but think that the subject of Cortini's meeting was the same: the possible exposure of Bad Seed and containment.

Containment would include Heather.

Scooping up his cell phone from the desk, James pulled up Heather's number and hit SEND. When her voice mail clicked on, he figured she'd IDed his call and was refusing to answer.

James quietly closed the cell. He'd try again later. He picked up his mug and took a sip of tea. He considered calling Annie. She should be at Heather's by now, provided she'd followed his instructions. With Annie, he never knew. She swung hot, then cold. Just like her mother.

Ask her to stop, Annie. Your mother never gave a damn about you kids.

Neither did you. You were always gone. Heather was always there for us.

I was trying to keep a roof over our heads. Food in your tummies.

What if she won't quit?

Then we'll never be a family again. Do whatever you need to—I'll back you up.

The fucking doctor wants to change my meds. He wants me to stay longer.

I'll take care of all that, sweetie. You don't need meds. You're my good girl.

Annie's face had lit for a moment, hope burning distrust from her expression like sunshine through mist, and he'd felt cold and ill, felt like he'd stood in the shadows far too long.

James studied the framed photo on his desk of him and Heather—both in white lab coats, grinning and holding microscopes. Heather was thirteen, skinny and just filling out, her long, red hair in a thick braid to her waist, her smile wide and happy, uninhibited.

Another photo showed him and Heather in grease-stained jeans and tees, posing in front of the classic Mustang they'd rebuilt together. Tendrils of dark red hair fluttered in front of Heather's smudged face as she squinted in the sunshine, her smile, at fifteen, a little more reserved.

Indebted to her father's quick thinking, a grateful daughter just might put aside an investigation into a cold case best left undisturbed.

Of course, if Prejean had transformed Heather into someone other than the girl in the photos on his desk, someone no longer 100 percent human, then the merciful thing, and the thing Heather herself would want, would be to remain silent and allow nature in the form of Caterina Cortini to take its course.

But before that happened, he needed to find out the truth. And there was one person who would know—if anyone did—what Prejean might've done to Heather while saving her life.

Placing the mug back on the warmer, James swiveled in his seat and turned on the computer. While the Dell ran through its startup, he composed in his mind the message he would send.

Has my daughter's humanity been compromised?

9

INSIDE THE
MONSTER'S HEART

Damascus, OR
March 22

D R. ROBERT WELLS FILLED a final syringe with a
fatal dose of atropine, then tucked it out of sight
on the lintel above the bedroom door. He'd hidden
other syringes throughout the house in drawers, cup-
boards, under furniture, even under his wife's pillow.

All fatal doses, yes—for mortals. If the assassins were
vampire, the atropine dose would either knock them
to the floor for an unplanned snooze or, depending
on age, slow them down enough to afford him a slim
chance at escape.

Wells suspected it was just a matter of rapidly passing
time before the Bureau—*no, let's be accurate, the Shadow
Branch* puppeteering *the Bureau heads*—sent someone to
kill him. All because of Bronlee's theft.

Unless he acted first.

"How long, do you think?" Gloria asked, her voice dry and paper thin.

"They could already be on the way. Or it could be weeks." Stepping away from the door, Wells returned to his wife's hospital-style bed and adjusted the flow rate on her morphine drip. "It *is* the government, after all," he added with a wry smile.

Gloria's eyes shuttered closed and the lines pain had chiseled beside her mouth eased. A sigh escaped her lips, a soft sound, almost wistful. "No time to waste," she whispered. "Send Alexander to Seattle."

"Those plans are underway, honey. Don't worry."

The room smelled of ammonia and bleach, but all the disinfectants in the world couldn't hide the lingering stink of decay.

Of failure.

Wells went to the window and cracked it open. Cool air fragrant and sweet with pine and early tulips breezed into the room. He sat on the bed beside his wife and wrapped his hands around hers, tried to rub warmth back into her fingers.

She was only fifty-seven years old, but cancer and chemo had stolen all youth from her, erased all traces of the woman he'd carried, laughing and tipsy on champagne, across the threshold of their first house thirty-five years ago.

Gloria's head turned to one side and her lips parted. Her breathing deepened, slowed, as the morphine stole her away like Hades carrying Persephone into the underworld.

His throat tightened. Gloria was now the cancer's bride and he couldn't rescue her, no matter how much he tried, no matter how much he yearned, no matter how much he sacrificed. The battle had been lost. He lifted her hand to his lips and kissed her cold fingers.

If he continued to prolong her suffering, then his love for her had warped into something small and selfish. If he truly loved her, he'd release her.

Truth was rarely kind. And rarely what you hoped for.

All he needed to do was increase her morphine until she went with grace to the great below. Simple and easily done.

Wells remained hunched on the bed, Gloria's fingers against his lips. He would wait until she was awake again so he could speak to her, tell her good night one last time.

His iPhone beeped. Kissing Gloria's fingers once more, he laid her hand across her blanketed waist. He pulled the iPhone from the pocket of his sweater and clicked open a red-flagged message in his e-mail inbox.

What he read trip-hammered his pulse and re-ignited hope.

James Wallace of the FBI's Portland forensics division, a man Wells knew only by reputation, had a problem.

My daughter claims that Dante Prejean saved her life. But he didn't feed her his blood, didn't turn her. He breathed blue fire and music into her. I don't claim to understand that. I don't even claim to know if such a thing is possible. But, if it is, what are the long-term effects? Has her humanity been compromised?

Wells texted: *Good question. I'll look into it. Study her medical records. Maybe it was a hallucination caused by pain and blood loss.*

Thank you.

Have you mentioned this to anyone else? Anyone at all?

No, of course not. I only contacted you because you've studied Prejean.

Good. Keep quiet about this and I'll get back to you. . . .

Wells slipped the iPhone back into his pocket feeling champagne giddy.

First the security cam footage. Now this.

Right after the incident at the center, Wells had been contacted and interrogated about Johanna, Bad Seed, and S. He'd also been asked, almost offhandedly, if Johanna had been working on a project that included vampire genetic material. He'd replied that he hadn't been involved with Johanna's work since he'd retired.

At the time, he had wondered what had prompted that question, but now, after viewing the pilfered footage Bronlee had mailed to him and seeing the puddle of liquid on the floor that had once been a living being, Wells suspected he knew.

The cleanup team and their handlers believed they'd found a spilled experiment. It had never occurred to them that they'd found the woman they sought. Or, rather, all that remained of her.

Johanna wasn't missing, no. She'd never left the center.

S had made sure of that.

Poor Johanna had had no idea—right up until the end—of what S truly was. Of what their little night-bred beauty had become. Or what he was capable of.

Truth be told, neither had Wells. Until the disk from Bronlee had arrived in the mail.

S had kept a secret from them both.

But Wells had kept one as well. From Johanna. From the Bureau. From S.

A secret he planned to unveil very soon.

Leaning over, Wells kissed his wife's pale cheek, then straightened and stood. He padded out of the room, leaving Gloria in Morpheus's narcotic embrace.

If S could unmake one woman and heal another, Wells felt confident the boy could cure Gloria. All he needed to do was bend a god—a young and damaged god, one he'd delivered himself—to his will.

And all it would take would be one whispered word.

But before Wells used S to heal Gloria, the threat against his own life needed to be neutralized. Perhaps it was time to begin shifting power from the Shadow Branch puppeteers and into his own hands. His and Alexander's—a new order, a new reign.

In the living room, moonlight filtered through the skylights in the high-peaked ceiling, filling the room with pale light. He looked out the window and into the woods.

Alexander, dressed in jeans and a gray hoodie, walked across the pine-tree shadowed yard toward the main house, a leather satchel slung over his shoulder, a shotgun in one hand. Moonlight gilded his hair silver, and an inner light seemed to radiate from him as if he truly were the embodiment of the Macedonian conqueror-god he was named for.

In that moment, his son was unutterably beautiful, Apollo's true heir.

Wells heard the front door open, then heard it click shut again. Reaching into the front pocket of his trousers, he clicked on the psi-block emitter that would shield his thoughts from his son's telepathic mind.

"I brought extra shells for the shotgun," Alexander said as he sauntered into the living room. "Did you pick up a Taser?"

Wells nodded. "It's in the kitchen. I've made other preparations, as well."

"I've double-checked the security system. All green."

Ah, so have I. And, my ambitious son, I changed the codes, Wells thought, but said instead, "Good."

"I'll finish securing the cottage tonight," Alexander said. "I'll make sure Athena's safe and occupied before I head out for Seattle tomorrow."

"I think we're as ready as we're going to be."

Alexander perched on the edge of the leather easy chair beside the sofa and shrugged the satchel off his shoulder. He cracked open the shotgun barrel. "If it weren't for Mother, you could go underground until things were settled." He looked up at Wells through thick blond lashes. "A lethal dose spiked into her IV. You'd be doing her a favor."

"A few minutes ago, I would've agreed with you."

Alexander reached into the satchel and withdrew a handful of shells. "What's changed?"

"I've just learned that S can heal."

"*Any* vampire can heal if they offer up enough blood." Alexander slotted shells into the shotgun, then snapped the barrel shut. "Of course, that usually means the person healed turns into a bloodsucker." He lifted his gaze to Wells's. "So how's this different?"

"S healed a mortally wounded agent *without* using

his blood. Since my source happens to be the agent's father, I have no reason to doubt his veracity."

Alexander frowned, his brows angling down. "Mortally wounded . . . do you mean Heather Wallace? The agent in the med-unit footage?"

"The very same. And where *is* the disk, by the way?"

"Thena's watching it again. She enjoys it."

Wells couldn't blame Athena for that; the footage *was* fascinating. Revelatory. A dark thought curled through his mind. And *inspiring*? "Make sure she keeps it safe."

"Of course," Alexander murmured.

"I plan to get ahold of Wallace's medical records," Wells said, crossing the room to the dark mahogany bar at its other end. "Ideally, I'd really like to get hold of *her*, run a few tests. See what S has done." He selected the bottle of Courvoisier, lifted it for his son to see. Alexander shook his head, so Wells poured one snifter of cognac.

"Maybe that's possible," Alexander said carefully. "I'd bet good money she'll be at Prejean's gigs in Seattle, especially if he saved her life. I could alter our plan to include her—"

"No, Wallace would be a distraction. You'll need to remain focused. S will kill you if you make a mistake. He's fast and unpredictable. Dangerous."

"Singing to the choir, Father," Alexander sighed. "We watched the footage too."

Wells took a swallow of the amber liquor. The Courvoisier burned down his throat, tasting of oak and vanilla. "Give S the encoded MP3 player or, better, leave it for him; keep at a safe distance. Once he's finished with his task, sedate him and bring him home."

Alexander propped the shotgun against the easy chair and rose to his feet. "Bring him home to heal Athena," he said, his gaze steady.

"And Mother," Wells said. "Listen to me carefully and keep this thought forefront: Only *I* have a map to the labyrinth within S's head, a labyrinth *I* created."

"Do I hear an amen?" Alexander said, a cynical smile twisting across his lips. "I understand, Father. But I need *you* to understand *this*—Athena first."

"Athena first, agreed," Wells said, lying with a sincerity learned from decades of work within the Bureau. A pang of regret bit deep into him. Athena was Alexander's twin. He feared his son might never be the same without her, and that was the reason he hadn't already ended her life.

But as Athena descended deeper into madness, he feared that her insanity would seep into Alexander through their indefinable bond, the womb link of twins. Feared it was seeping into him even now, threading delusion through his veins.

"Agreed then." The cynical smile vanished from Alexander's lips. He crossed the carpet to where Wells stood in front of the mahogany bar and bowed his head.

Wells stepped forward and kissed the top of Alexander's golden head, bestowing paternal blessing with a touch of his lips.

"Bring S home," Wells murmured. "And I'll teach you how to wield him."

"I'll hold you to that."

"As you should."

Wells stepped back and Alexander lifted his head. He looked at Wells for a long moment, the Aegean depths of his eyes unfathomable. "I've always wondered why you hide your thoughts from me when you're the one who made me telepathic."

Wells chuckled. "To build character. To give you grief. To keep you guessing. Take your pick."

The cynical smile returned to Alexander's lips. With a flipped half-salute, he turned and walked from the room.

"Alexander," Wells called. His son's tread stopped. "Keep in mind that the MP3 player is designed to play the message only once. Preview it, and you'll be giving S nothing but static to listen to."

The front door creaked open, then shut again.

Wells drained the snifter in a second long swallow. Sweat popped up along his hairline. Heat flushed his face. He poured a second drink. Sliding his fingers around the snifter's stem and cupping the bowl in his palm, he carried the glass, along with the bottle of cognac, down the hall to his office.

Mortal Wells might be, but the fires of creation burned within his mind. Genetics was his hammer. Human flesh his metal. His son was the proof of that—his daughter his only shame.

"Do what needs to be done, Bobby." Gloria rubs her hands over her still-flat belly. "Maybe that's why I'm carrying twins. Maybe that's why we have one of each gender." A small, knowing smile curves her lips. "And maybe that's why I chose you."

With those words, Wells had finally seen beyond the self-sacrificing madonna to the calculating mother-goddess. Through her, the path to divinity unfurled beneath his feet. Father to a new age. Creator of gods.

But Athena . . . He still didn't know what had gone wrong, how he'd made a mistake. The twins had been designed with the utmost care, their genetics altered and enhanced as they curled together within Gloria's womb, all flaws deleted.

Or so he'd believed. Until Athena's mind had quietly, slowly, and irrevocably unwound. Paranoid schizophrenia. A flaw unforeseen.

Settling into his comfortable and well-broken-in leather chair, Wells set the cognac bottle down on his desk and picked up a copy of the disk his daughter was watching at this very moment.

Thena is watching it again. She enjoys it.

Athena wasn't alone in that; Wells had watched it many times as well. But he didn't *enjoy* it; that wasn't the word he'd use. No. A better, a more accurate word would be *scared*. It scared and exhilarated him. But he didn't enjoy it. He slipped the disk into the drive.

Taking another sip of the cognac, Wells clicked PLAY. A corridor appeared on the monitor, the dim lighting tinted night-vision green. A figure moved into view—waist-length black hair snaking into the air like night-blackened seaweed caught in a current. His wings, black and smooth, arched up behind him, half-folded, as he knelt on the floor and reached for one of two figures crumpled together on the tile.

A voice curled from the computer's speakers, low and deep, with a trace of a European accent. But, just like the first time he'd heard them, the words trailed a finger of ice down his spine.

"Avenge your mother. And yourself."

And S rises from the speaker's arms, rises up from the

floor, bathed in dim red emergency light, his body tight and coiled, blood smeared across his breathtaking face. Rises up like a god from the ashes, a burning, beautiful, terrifying god.

Wells hit PAUSE and poured himself another drink. Until he'd viewed the disk, he'd considered the late Elroy Jordan—sociopath, sexual sadist, and serial killer—to have been Bad Seed's greatest success. No longer.

The beautiful boy who'd risen from the floor on the monitor had eclipsed Jordan.

Smiling, Wells poured another drink.

10

WHISPERS

Damascus, OR
March 22

"IS THE DISEASED OLD cow still breathing?" Athena asked. She sat cross-legged on the sofa, her gaze on the laptop cradled in her lap. The lab smock she wore over her jeans was smeared and spattered with blood and other fluids.

"Mother's still breathing, yes," Alex replied, kicking the door shut behind him. He set his sister's tray of night meds on the cluttered coffee table.

"Good. I don't want her dying before I can kill her."

"That's the spirit."

The room smelled of hot circuits and cinnamon potpourri, but underneath Alex caught a whiff of something that stank of rotten eggs and singed hair drifting from Athena's study lab. "How did your experiment go?"

"Unsuccessful," Athena murmured. "I need more material."

"Okay, I'll take care of it." Alex sat on the sofa beside her. "What else have you done today?"

"Studied." Her eyes scanned the images on the monitor, sliding right, then left.

"Ah." Meaning she was studying Dante, watching the med-unit footage yet again. He sighed. "We need to talk."

"About . . . ?" Athena looked up. Lamplight glimmered in her eyes like sunshine on calm water and, for a moment, her eyes seemed translucent, palest ocean-green.

"What happens next."

"I'm listening," she said, returning her gaze to the laptop's monitor.

Alex wrapped his fingers around the monitor's edge and folded it shut. "Enough. It's time for you to stop studying." He pulled the laptop from her reluctant grip and placed it on the coffee table.

"But I need to understand him," she protested. "When I *look*, I can't see anything beyond him and I don't know what that means."

"You're tired, that's all," Alex said. "You need rest." The dark smudges beneath her eyes testified to that and to all the restless, sleepless nights she paced away. But her visions were always right, sleep or no sleep, meds or no meds.

Visions Father knew nothing about.

"I've got to figure out how to undo Dante's programming."

"You can worry about that after I bring Dante home. C'mon, fresh air. Meds. Move your butt." Alex grasped Athena's hand and pulled her to her feet. He led her through the kitchen and out the back door, easing the screen door shut behind them.

He released her hand as she settled into the swinging bench on the porch, then he sat beside her, wood creaking comfortably beneath him. Without looking, he grasped Athena's hand again. Her fingers, warm and hard, curled around his.

Alex drew in a deep breath of moist, pine-scented air. "So much better."

"If you say so."

A quick glance revealed the smile shadowing his twin's lips. He smiled too.

"The SB is probably planning on killing Father," Alex said, his gaze on the night sky. He watched the stars light up one by one like votives in a church. "Hell, the Bureau might've even rubber-stamped it after the fiasco with Moore."

"Do they know Father's the one who tipped Ronin off to Bad Seed?"

"I doubt it. That'd require some *real* intelligence work."

"What if they kill Father before he teaches you how to use Dante?"

"We'll have to hope that doesn't happen," Alex said. "I've armed Father and the security's tight, but . . ." He shrugged. "A pro could get past all of that. I've tried and tried to get Father to go underground."

"Maybe they'll send a bumbling amateur or a poor shot instead of a pro. It's not like it's the mafia. It's the government."

Alex laughed. He leaned in and pressed his forehead against his sister's. Heard her quiet, never-ceasing thoughts: *Does Father dream now? Of power and gods? Of all he can never be? And shall never have?*

Athena's mind refused silence, refused to rest.

Alex straightened, relaxing into the bench as it swung back and forth, back and forth. The wood creaked, drowning out the sound of Athena's thoughts/whispers. He didn't have to look to know her lips struggled to keep up with the ideas streaming through her mind.

"I don't think Dante knows about Father's role in his conditioning," Athena said. "I don't think he knows about Father, period."

"That's good. Then he won't be expecting us."

"What happens next?"

"I go to Seattle," Alex said. "Trigger Dante, dope him when he's finished doing what he's supposed to do, then bring him home."

"How are you going to get close enough to him to dope him?" Athena looked at him, her blonde curls tumbling across her face, curls she brushed back automatically.

"Shoot him from a distance. In the back, preferably." Alex considered all that he'd read about Dante, replayed in his mind the footage that his twin obsessively watched: *Dante cups Moore's face. His hands tremble. Glow with blue light. His hair snakes up into the air and energy crackles.*

Dangerous.

"Amen, brother," Athena whispered. "But soon he'll be a part of us. We'll give him Father to play with—after we restore his memories."

"Can we do that? Restore his memories?"

"I don't know, but there must be a way . . ."

"Unless the damage is too great," Alex finished.

"Green waters of remembrance," Athena said, her voice a low monotone, her oracle voice. "He'll need the green waters."

Alex's skin prickled as his twin's gaze turned inward, seeking the sacred. "Green waters? For Dante? What do you mean?"

"Green and green and green."

"What else do you see?"

"The old cow's time is almost here," she murmured.

"Do you *see* it? Mother's death?"

Athena laughed. "Yes, a vision of a near-future event. I see a pillow over her face and my hands over the pillow."

"An overdose would be simpler, less suspicious."

"Ah, but less fun, Xander, and I have so little."

Alex squeezed his twin's hand and listened to her circling thoughts: *A pillow over her face, my knee and heart and hands over the pillow. Welcome to hell, Cow. Let me be your guide.*

Call me Hades.

Madness or divinity? Was there even a difference?

Father had tinkered with his and Athena's genes while they were still in the womb. He'd wanted gods. But believed himself disappointed.

He was wrong. He had his gods. Just not the ones he'd planned for. Dante hadn't been the only one to keep secrets. Father had designed his and Athena's telepathy, but he knew nothing about their other gifts.

"Yes and yes and yes," Athena whispered. "Secrets. Godhead. With Dante we'll have the perfect trinity—Conqueror, Counselor, and Creator. We'll begin a new age. After we punish the wicked first, of course."

"But of course," Alex agreed. "Isn't that the first rule in the *Godhead and Divinity for Dummies* handbook?"

"Prick."

"Thank you for noticing."

Athena squeezed his hand. As always, her touch somehow completed him, closed a circuit. He shared the silence with her as they rocked back and forth in the swing.

But it wasn't truly silent for her. No.

If only Father had devoted his medical and research skills toward helping Athena instead of funneling it into the swirling drain that was his dying wife. If only he hadn't viewed Athena as a flawed project instead of a daughter.

A daughter who'd needed him. Once. But not anymore.

The wind-in-the-pines sound of Athena's whispers ended the silence. Alex squeezed her hand, then released it. "Time for your meds," he said, standing.

Still whispering, Athena rose to her feet. Her gaze was turned inward, truly lost in thought. Alex opened the screen door, guided his twin into the house, and walked her into the living room. Whispering, she sank onto the sofa, automatically crossing her legs under her.

Kneeling beside the coffee table, Alex picked up the little paper cup holding Athena's meds—antipsychotics, antianxiety, tranquilizers—and placed it carefully in her hand. "Put in your mouth and swallow."

Athena raised the cup to her lips, tossed back the pills. Alex slapped a bottle of water in her hand and she drank obediently. He picked up the syringe containing her sleep dose.

Alex glanced at his twin. Listened to her oracle whispers and wondered: Could he keep Athena under control until Dante arrived? Could he keep her balanced and calm for a few more days? She was slipping deeper into madness and it terrified him to think she might plunge so deep into the abyss, he'd never find her again, never recover her.

Rolling up the sleeve on Athena's left arm, Alex swiped the injection site with an alcohol swab. His nose wrinkled at the sharp odor.

"Coldandcoldandcold," Athena whispered.

"Sorry. I should've warned you."

A few more days, he could do that, keep her calm. He *had* to—for both of them. He'd pick up more material for her experiments.

"I need you to stay here while I'm gone," he said. "Don't go into the main house, and avoid Father. I figure the SB operative will target only him, but collateral damage is usually allowed if necessary."

"Yesandyesandyes."

"If you could be well again," Alex said, his voice low and rough. "If you could return to your career and everything you've had to leave behind, would you?"

"Xander."

Alex looked up and into Athena's eyes. Her gaze seemed more lucid than it had in years. "There's nothing wrong with me," she said gently. "I see more clearly than I ever have. I don't need to be healed."

Something twisted tight in Alex's chest. He nodded. He inserted the needle into his sister's cleaned skin, and thumbed the plunger.

"I'll never leave you. I promise," Athena whispered.

Alex leaned forward and brushed his lips against his twin's forehead. She'd said the words he'd longed to hear from her, but instead of the joy he'd imagined—the circuit closed once again, the womb bond that she'd unraveled five years ago to protect him finally restored—he felt only a stark desperation.

Her promise was empty and beyond her power to fulfill.

The bond would never be restored. The circuit would never be connected, closed, an infinite loop. Not until Dante repaired her misfiring synapses and stilled the lightning storm within her hyperactive brain.

Athena tilted her head as though listening—and Alex knew she was—to all the ideas and thoughts pinging through her never quiet mind; she unhooked her thoughts from his.

"Is there anything else you need me to get for you when I go out?"

A smile dimpled Athena's cheeks. "My Xander," she said; then she giggled, a sound Alex hadn't heard from her in years, girlish and light, happy; it spun like a Ferris wheel through his heart.

"What's so funny?" he asked, a grin pulling at the edges of his mouth.

"Could you pick up a copy of *Godhead and Divinity for Dummies*?"

Alex laughed. "C'mon, let's get you in your PJs and into bed."

He scooped her up from the sofa and into his arms. A pang of sorrow shafted him as she looped her arms around his neck. She was so light, his goddess of wisdom, buoyant with far-sight, untethered to the earth.

He imagined her floating away from him, rising higher and higher into the midnight sky until she disappeared from view.

As Alex carried his sister to the bathroom, the wind-rushing-through-the-pines whisper of Athena's voice filled the hallway, and the corridors of his heart.

11

FRAGILE

Annie zeroed in on the rumpled boxes marked WALLACE, SHANNON. She'd knock the fucking things clear out of the dining room, out of the universe, a fucking home run. She swung the crowbar with every ounce of her strength, weighted the piece of steel in her hand with every dirty, festering bit of her hate.

She caught a blur of movement at the edge of her vision, then the crowbar struck hard, smacking into flesh instead of cardboard. The force of the impact shuddered up her arms and into her shoulders. She stumbled forward, slamming her hips against the table's edge as the crowbar was wrenched from her hands. Her gaze fell across the photos arced across the polished wood.

She looked into her mother's sightless eyes. Saw her curled up and dead on the ground like some fucking Raid-gassed cockroach.

Your mother's been killed in a car accident. She's not coming home.

With a guttural scream, Annie threw herself onto the table, sweeping everything off–photos, papers, table runner. Grabbing one of the boxes marked WALLACE, SHANNON, she hurled it with all she had. It exploded against the wall. Glass shattered. Steel-hard fingers wrapped around her upper arm and spun her around.

Black hair. Sunglasses. White skin and hot hands. One hand held the crowbar, the other held her. "Who you pissed at, *p'tite?*" Dante asked, tossing the crowbar across the room and out the open window.

Hawking up a big loogie, Annie spat on him. Spittle gleamed on his pale face. Lifting his arm, he wiped his face clean against his latex-clad shoulder. A smile quirked up one corner of his mouth. "Good shot."

"I swear to fucking God, I'll fucking *kill* you, if you don't let go!"

"Guess you're gonna hafta kill me then, cuz I ain't letting go."

Annie hooked a fist at Dante's gorgeous face, swinging right-left-right, but she missed him. She rammed a knee at his crotch, but missed again. "Goddammit," she snarled. "Quit moving!"

Not able to wrestle/kick/punch her way free of Dante's grip, she decided to change tactics and went limp, collapsing to the floor. His fingers slid away as she fell.

Annie rolled over on the carpet, her fingers closing around a jagged piece of glass, and she rose to her knees. She sliced the glass shard across her scar-ridged wrist. Blood welled up dark and thick. Catching a peripheral blur of movement, she slashed out. She felt the splinter

bite into flesh and smelled coppery blood. Heard Dante
suck in a breath.

Suddenly he was kneeling in front of her, his pale
face tight, his unshaded dark gaze determined. She
ducked and weaved, tried to climb to her feet, but he
shadowed every move. She stabbed at him, over and
over, the glass splinter whistling through empty air as
he seemed to vanish.

Then his fingers locked around her wrists. He
yanked her in close, held her tight against him. The
shard of glass finally slipped from her blood-slick fingers and he wrapped his arms around her.

Annie felt her muscles bunch, snap taut, and then
give. Her knees folded and even as she collapsed into
Dante's embrace, she felt lighter than air, buoyed by the
feel-good magic of tequila and oxy, but she could never
rise high enough.

Leather and latex creaked as he sat on the floor, cradling her in his lap.

"I fucking hate her," she whispered, curling against
him, against his heat.

"I got that," he murmured.

"I'm glad she's dead," Annie managed to say through
a throat gone tight. Her heart felt like a red-hot knot in
her chest, burning her up from the inside out, a fire she
couldn't douse, a knot she couldn't untangle.

Dante pushed her hair back from her face. "Wanna
tell me why?"

"No. I hate you too."

"*T'es sûr de sa?*" His scent swirled around her, like
autumn, like Halloween—burning leaves and frosted
earth and ripe apples.

"What's that mean?"

"It means: You sure about that?"

"Oh. Yeah, I'm sure I hate you. Kinda."

"Okay," he said. Then he started singing, his voice soft and husky and sexy. *"Laissez-faire, laissez-faire, ma jolie, bons temps rouler, allons danser, toute la nuit . . ."*

Annie wasn't sure if he was singing in French or Spanish or fucking Cajun, but the melody was as soothing as a hand stroking her hair.

As she closed her eyes, she thought she glimpsed black wings arching high behind Dante, the undersides glimmering with a hint of deep blue. Held within this dark angel's arms, she listened to his song, and his voice fell like a cool waterfall against her rage, tugged like nimble fingers at the tangled knot of her heart.

Annie opened her eyes and touched bloodied fingers to Dante's pale face. Blood trickled from one nostril, so one of her punches must've landed, after all. His skin felt fevered. She traced his lips. He shivered and closed his eyes, but kept singing.

"Si toi t'es presse et occupe, mon ami, courir ici, courir la-bas . . ."

"Kiss me."

Dante's eyes opened, dark and wary, but Annie saw hunger in their depths. His song ended as he lowered his head and kissed her, a quick amaretto-and-blood flavored smooch on the lips.

"No." She reached up and captured his face between her hands. "A *real* kiss."

"I don't think so," Dante said with a wicked smile. "You've been naughty."

Annie stared at the slender fang tips his smile revealed. Her heart kicked hard against her ribs. *Night-kind*. Could be implants. *Had* to be implants.

"If you're a vampire, do you kill when you feed?"

Dante's smile faded. "Sometimes, yeah."

Annie paused, mulling over his answer and deciding he was trying to scare her—the fucker. "No big deal, but do you *hafta* kill?"

"Not always, no."

"Can you make me into a vampire?"

"Yeah, but I won't, so don't fucking ask."

Before Annie could ask another question, he pulled free of her hands and lifted his head. "Heather's here," he breathed, easing them both to their feet. His gorgeous, bloodstained face lit up like an autumn bonfire and Annie knew she no longer existed.

Outside, Dante heard the low rumble of a car's engine, a sports car or muscle car, throaty and powerful. But he also heard Annie's heart hammering against her ribs, triple-timed by drugs and adrenaline. He glanced at her. She pressed against him, her eyes dilated and wide.

"Kiss me," she said urgently. "Kiss me hard."

Dante shook his head, listening as the car's rumble grew louder, vibrating in up through his boot soles and into his spine. Through the front window, he caught a glimpse of the car, low-slung and sleek, turning into the driveway, gravel crunching under the tires. With a low purr, the engine died. Silence filled the house.

"Kiss me," Annie repeated, voice low. "Or I'll tell my sister you broke in and attacked me." Her fingers wrapped around his belt and tugged.

Dante heard a door open and then heard shoes on gravel. The car door thunked shut. He tilted his head and regarded Annie through his lashes. "Yeah?"

"Yeah. I'll tell all kinds of stories." Dark hope edged her words.

"She already knows I'm here. And she knows you're here, too." He remembered Von's brief message: *Your FBI sweetie's here—looking for you.* He pictured her walking up to the house, imagined her red hair loose and curling past her shoulders and framing her lovely face. Pictured her slim curves. Was she in jeans? Slacks? A dress?

Dante closed his eyes and counted her footsteps.

She was safe. She was breathing. He intended to make sure she stayed that way.

Run from me. Run as far as you can.

She'd tried. But he'd followed. And he couldn't explain why. She knotted him up in ways he'd never felt before.

"Bullshit. Kiss me, Dante."

Annie's busy little fingers tried to unbuckle his belt, but he plucked them loose and gently shoved her hand away.

"I'll tell her *you* cut me," she whispered.

Dante's pulse thundered. He opened his eyes. Heather would walk into the house in a moment. He heard the jingle of keys.

Dante cupped Annie's face between his hands. A satisfied smile ghosted across her lips as she offered up her face for a kiss. She rested her hands on his hips and closed her eyes.

Hearing the scrape of a key sliding into the lock,

Dante lowered his head, brushed his lips against Annie's ear, and whispered, "Fuck you. Tell her whatever you want."

Annie's eyes flew open and Dante released her. The door opened and streetlight shafted in around the slim figure standing at the threshold. The smell of lilac and rain drifted into the room, the sweetness undercut by frustration and uncertainty.

The streetlight dazzled Dante's eyes and he lifted a hand to shade them. He was right about her hair; it tumbled loose past her shoulders. And she was wearing a black jacket and curve-hugging jeans. Her gaze locked onto his and her breath caught in her throat. A split second later a smile curved her lips, lit her twilight-blue eyes.

"Dante . . ." she said, stepping into the room. Then she stopped.

Her gaze skipped from the papers, broken glass, and photos on the carpet to him. To the open window behind him. To her disheveled and bloodied sister standing in front of him, her hands still on his hips. Her brows drew down. "What the hell's going on?"

With a wink, Annie shoved away from Dante, whirled, then crumpled to the floor.

"*De mal en pire,*" Dante muttered. *From bad to worse.*

12

THE ART OF
SELF-DESTRUCTION

Seattle, WA
March 22

ANNIE CRUMPLED TO THE floor and, for a moment, the image of their mother half-curled on the leaf-littered ground flashed behind Heather's eyes. Dante muttered something, an exasperated expression on his face, then dropped to his knees and pressed his fingers against Annie's temples.

Heather rushed across the front room, skirting around the crime scene photos, papers, and folders littering the carpet. She knelt beside her sister and brushed her multicolored hair back from her face.

"Is she okay?" Heather asked. She reached into her jacket pocket for her cell phone and flipped it open. Dante's warm scent, burning leaves and deep, dark earth, curled around her. She was close enough to him to feel his heat.

"Don't call. She's okay. High, maybe drunk, maybe faking, but okay."

"Faking?" Heather shut the cell and slipped it back into her pocket.

Dante shrugged. "Maybe." He slid his hands from Annie's temples and rested them on his leather-clad thighs. "She's mad at me."

"She's not alone in that," Heather said, leaning over her sister.

"Yeah?"

"Yeah. But we'll talk about that later."

"Fair enough."

She smelled booze on Annie's breath. *Dammit, Annie.* Blood stained Annie's right hand, her wrist. She turned her sister's wrist over and tensed at the still-bleeding gash sliced into the flesh.

"She did that before I could stop her," Dante said. "I'm sorry."

"Not your fault," Heather said.

Night-cooled air poured in through the open window at Heather's back. *Must be how he got in. Jimmied the window.* Or had Annie broken in first? Anger simmered. She'd been worrying about him, trying to reach him by calling Simone, and going to Vespers, and he was busy breaking into her house and . . . what . . . wrestling with her sister?

"What happened anyway?" Heather asked, looking into his dark eyes.

"She's hurting inside," Dante said. "And she didn't want to hurt alone."

Heather's anger faded as she took in the dried

blood smeared beneath Dante's nose. "Were you—did she—" she paused and looked at her sister, searched her smooth, expressionless face, then returned her gaze to him. "Was a memory triggered?"

Dante shook his head. "Not that I recall." His lips tilted into a smile.

"Not funny." Heather studied his bloodied hands— defensive wounds—and then she saw the jagged slash at belly level in his latex shirt. Sucking in a sharp breath, she gingerly touched the cut in his shirt and plucked it open. "Shit! Did she hurt you?" The pale skin beneath the sliced latex was bloodied and sticky.

Dante's warm fingers wrapped around hers and pulled her hand away. "I'm okay, *chérie*. Don't worry. Nightkind, remember?"

"I remember." Relief flooded through her and she squeezed his hand before releasing it. "But you can still be hurt."

Dante shrugged. *"Oui."*

He scooped Annie into his arms and then stood, his movements fluid and graceful even with a woman cradled against his chest. Annie's head slumped against his shoulder, her face veiled by black, purple, and blue strands of hair. "Where do you want her?"

"This way," Heather said, rising to her feet and leading him into the hallway, to the guest room. She stepped aside at the threshold as Dante walked through and eased Annie down onto the comforter-draped bed. It sloshed beneath her weight.

"A water bed? Seriously?" Dante said, straightening.

Heather felt a smile quirk up one corner of her mouth. "I happen to like this bed, Mr.-I-Have-a-Futon, so shut up," she said, stepping into the darkened room. She clicked on a little bedside lamp. A small yellow circle of light appeared on the ceiling.

She sat on the bed beside her sister, the bed wobbling beneath her weight for a few seconds. She stroked Annie's hair from her face. Was this the start of a manic episode or the downward spiral of depression?

Heather looked up, intending to ask Dante to give her a few moments alone with Annie, but he was already gone. For a moment, she worried he'd just leave, but he hadn't broken into her house just to saunter off without saying whatever it was he'd come to say. A band of tension buckled across her shoulders.

Von's words sounded through her memory: *He's been worried about you.*

But she'd had a feeling, standing there in the dimly lit corridor at Vespers, that Von had left a whole lot unsaid.

But despite what Von'd said or hadn't said, the concern crinkling his eyes, his tense posture had made one thing clear—*he* was worried about Dante.

Heather carefully turned over Annie's cut wrist, examining the wound; even though it still bled a little it wouldn't require stitches. She checked Annie for other injuries, discovered cuts to the insides of her fingers and a faint, bluish bruise on her forehead.

Heather stood and then watched her sister as the bed sloshed gently for a few moments. A strand of blue hair clung to one cheek. The skin beneath her eyes was smudged with kohl and bruised by lack of sleep. A faint smear of dried blood streaked her lips.

Annie must've seen the crime scene photos, given their current arrangement on the living room floor. *I never would've left them out if I'd known she was coming.*

Turning, Heather went to the bathroom for a wash-cloth, antiseptic, and Band-Aids. In the hall, she caught a glimpse of Dante gathering the scattered papers from the floor. "You don't need to do that," she called. "I'll get it later."

He snorted and continued with what he was doing. Heather shook her head. Still pigheaded. She thought of him carrying her sister and easing her onto the bed with care and tenderness, even after she'd tried to share her hurt with him. Still Dante. But now she needed to add B&E expert to his list of finer qualities.

Returning to the guest room with her supplies and a warm, damp washcloth, Heather sat back down onto the bed and waited for the sloshing to stop.

"Hey."

Heather looked into Annie's kohl-rimmed eyes and noted her dilated pupils. She also noted that for a woman who'd passed out and awakened somewhere else, she didn't seem very confused. A muscle tightened in her jaw. *Maybe faking.* She had a feeling Dante'd been right about that. And it wouldn't be the first time Annie had pulled a fake.

"Hey back. How are you feeling?" She gingerly cleaned the blood from the gash in Annie's wrist.

"Your boyfriend's a goddamned vampire! With fangs and . . . and . . ." Annie's breath hitched. She bit her lip and looked away.

Working up tears? "I'm sorry if he freaked you out," Heather said, daubing antiseptic on the cut. The sharp, medicinal smell masked the odor of booze drifting from Annie. "I told you he was nightkind."

"And you expected me to just *believe* that? *Vampires?* Jesus Christ!"

"Do you believe it now?" Heather bandaged the wound.

"Yeah," Annie whispered. "He cut me and I think he was gonna drink me dry."

Heather looked at her sister. "He didn't cut you, Annie. And he was trying to help you, not hurt you."

"How the hell do you know? You weren't even fucking there! Why are you taking his side?"

Here we go, Heather thought. "I'm not taking anyone's side."

"Yes, you fucking are!"

The sudden roar of the vacuum from the living room startled Heather. What the hell was Dante doing? Given the acuteness of his hearing, maybe he was trying to keep from listening, and Annie wasn't exactly being quiet.

"Stop it," Heather said, managing to keep her voice even. "You've been drinking and drugging and you broke into my house. When did the treatment center release you?"

Annie clamped her mouth shut and looked away.

"They didn't, did they? You bailed out and quit taking your meds."

"Why should I take them? All they do is turn me into a fucking zombie. But that makes things easier for you, huh?"

Annie's words stung and Heather stiffened. "I want you to be well, not a zombie. I want you to have your life back. I want to see you onstage again."

"Yeah, right. Your boyfriend kissed me, by the way. Twice."

Annie watched her, a smug smile on her lips and a knowing light in her eyes. Was she telling the truth, finally? And using it like a knife? Annie's hands had been on Dante's hips; his hands had been at his sides. But the blood smear on her lips—transferred there from Dante? His nose *had* been bleeding.

Did it matter whether Dante had actually kissed her?

The sudden tangle of feelings—jealousy, yearning, sorrow—twisting in her chest surprised Heather. Yes, it did. It mattered a lot.

"Score one for you," Heather muttered and looked away. "But he's not my boyfriend." Sighing, she closed her eyes. But he *was* her friend. And more, maybe.

"*Not* your boyfriend? Yeah, right. I saw his face when he said your name. I saw how he looked as he watched you come in through the door." Annie's voice was a cynical near-whisper. "Nothing else mattered. Nothing else existed. Just you."

"Annie . . . no."

Annie sat up on the sloshing bed and hugged her knees to her chest. "Those pictures and stuff of Mom, why do you have them?"

Heather studied her sister, her body hunched, closed in tight as a fist. She almost seemed to vibrate with energy, wired. *Manic, then.* "I'm trying to find her killer. I'm doing what Dad should've done."

"When you find the guy who whacked Mom, let me know, so I can thank him."

Handing Annie the washcloth, Heather stood. "Finish up, then get some sleep."

"Dad did the right thing in forgetting the bitch."

Heather stared at her sister, the blood pounding in her temples. Annie's therapist's advice uncoiled through her mind like a lifeline: *Don't buy into her drama, don't let her push your buttons, just show her you care.* "If you need anything," she said, her voice strained even to her own ears, "I'll be in the front room."

Annie flopped back down on the bed, rolling over onto her side as the bed sloshed and waved. Curled up her knees. "Whatever. Fuck you."

Drawing in a deep breath, Heather walked out of the bedroom and into the front room. His face washed clean of blood, Dante sat cross-legged on the floor in the dining room reading her mother's file; the crime scene photos gathered neatly in front of him; the glass vacuumed up; the broken poster frame gone; and the poster, a copy of Leighton's *Flaming June,* lying on the dining room table.

Heather felt some of the tension drain from her with this unexpected act of domesticity from Dante. Given the disorderly state of his bedroom at home in New Orleans, she never would've guessed him capable of it.

He tucked a strand of hair behind his ear as he read, his dark brows slanting down in concentration. Her thoughts whirled back to the file footage of Chloe teaching him to read, and her throat tightened.

"I'm sorry about all that," she said, sitting down on the floor beside him. "Annie's bipolar—"

Dante lifted his gaze, touched a finger to his lips, then nodded toward the hallway.

His meaning was clear: *She's listening.*

Heather nodded. She didn't want to close the door out of fear of what her sister might do behind it. Nor did she want to move to a room beyond Annie's hearing, for the same reason. Heather trailed a hand through her hair, suddenly exhausted.

"You caring for her alone?" Dante asked, his voice barely above a whisper.

"Mostly," she murmured. "My brother lives in New York and my dad—well, forget him. Annie generally lives on her own, but when she's like this . . . she needs me."

"*Chérie,* I'm sorry."

Dante's words, his voice, low and warm and sincere, brushed against her heart. But the cool breeze blowing in through the open window, smelling of rain and wet, green leaves, reminded her of how he'd gotten into her house.

Rising to her feet, Heather crossed to the window in quick strides and slid it shut. She fingered the broken latch, and then glanced at Dante from over her shoulder. He watched her, his beautiful face suddenly wary. *He reads the tension in my movements, hears it in my voice. You bet he's wary; that's how he survived his childhood and the streets.*

"Why'd you come in through the window?"

"Door was locked."

"So was the window."

He shrugged. "I figured the window'd attract less attention."

"What the *hell* were you thinking, anyway?" she asked, swiveling around to face him. She grasped the windowsill behind her. "You could've called. Or knocked on the door. Or just waited for me to get home!"

"I wanted to make sure you were all right."

"And *that* makes it okay? Breaking in because you're

worried about me?" She held his gaze. Fire burned through her veins. "Who broke in first? Christ! I can't believe I even have to *ask* that question!"

"Me."

"You had no right! None. Neither did Annie."

Dante nodded, and light glinted from the hoops in his ears. "I hear you."

"What the hell does that mean?"

"It means I–" Dante tapped his index finger against his chest. "Hear–" He touched both ears. "You." He pointed at Heather.

She stared at him, chest tight, anger burning in her veins. "Don't be an asshole. You could've waited for me to get home."

"Yeah? Really?" Dante placed the folder beside him on the carpet. "I wasn't so sure about that."

"I said I needed some time. I *never* said good-bye. Or didn't you *hear* me?"

Fire ignited in Dante's eyes. "*Oui,* I heard you."

"So . . . did you prowl through the house? Go through shit? Did you kiss Annie?"

"Yeah," Dante said, stretching the word out, voice low and mystified. "I kissed her. What's that got to do with anything?" Then it clicked, and his gaze darkened. He buried his face in his hands and shook his head. "Fuck," he muttered, and then lowered his hands. He rose to his feet.

"She said you kissed her twice."

"You fucking kidding me? This is about me kissing your sister?"

"No, this is about you breaking in," Heather replied, crossing the room to stand in front of him. "But since you mention it, why *did* you kiss her?"

"It shouldn't matter," he said, voice low and wire-taut. "It was just a kiss."

"She's my *sister*, Dante! It matters!"

A muscle in Dante's jaw flexed, but he said nothing, his smoldering gaze locking onto hers. Dante kissed for many reasons, and in many ways, she reminded herself. Out of friendship, in greeting, in parting, with desire. Maybe he really *didn't* get it given the lack of boundaries during his upbringing.

"You know what? You're right, it shouldn't matter," Heather said. "It's none of my business who you kiss or why."

His dark eyes searched hers, his expression suddenly unguarded. *"T'es sûr?"*

She knew a little French, enough to help sometimes with his Cajun. But if she was right, what he just asked confused the hell out of her.

"Did you ask if I'm sure? About it being none of my business?"

Dante trailed a hand through his hair, and he looked almost as confused and unsure as she felt. "Yeah," he finally said with a tilted smile. "I think I did."

Heather couldn't help but return his smile. "I don't want to fight with you, Dante," she said, voice soft. "I'm glad to see you, I really am."

"Me too."

"But we need to talk," Heather said. "Seriously talk."

Something close to relief flashed across Dante's face. "I've been wanting to talk to you too, *chérie*. You still working for the FBI?"

"For the moment, yes." She nodded at the dining

room table. "Pull up a chair, I've got some stuff to show you."

Dante shrugged off his hoodie and hung it over the back of a chair. He wore a black latex shirt with silver-buckled straps across the chest and black leather pants. His silver belt buckle and the rings on his fingers, thumbs, and on his collar were the only other bits of sharp color amid all the snug-fitting black. He swung the chair around and then straddled it.

Heather felt his watchful gaze on her as she walked the room and closed all the curtains. Going to the front door, she twisted shut both dead bolts. The locks slammed into place with solid thunks. She didn't know if anyone was actually keeping surveillance on her. She hadn't spotted any unfamiliar cars or work vans, but that didn't mean they weren't out there.

Maybe Dante climbing in through a back window was a good thing, after all.

Heather returned to the table and sat down. She picked up a pile of papers and thumbed through them, looking for the data she'd printed out last night. As she did, she tried to organize her thoughts, shape her suspicions.

"I'm sorry about your mother, by the way," Dante said. "I didn't know."

Heather met his dark gaze and smiled. "How could you? But thanks anyway."

"How old were you when she died?"

"Almost twelve. My birthday was a couple of weeks later."

"Aw, *chérie*, that sucks," he said, and she could tell he meant it.

Heather glanced over her shoulder toward the hall. Lowering her voice, she said, "My mom's murder is a cold case, officially, anyway. At the time, her death was attributed to a serial killer known as—"

"The Claw-Hammer Killer, Christopher Higgins," Dante supplied.

"That's right." Heather looked at him for a long moment, impressed. He hadn't had much time to go over the file while she tended to Annie, so he must've scanned it quickly and well.

"The FBI won't let you go, will they?" Dante said.

Heather shook her head. "I was hoping they'd let me walk if I kept quiet and pretended not to know anything about Bad Seed or what happened at the center after I was shot."

"But . . . ?" Dante folded his arms along the chair's back.

"They called me into a meeting today and offered me my boss's position as SAC." Heather shook her head. "The offer not only went completely against protocol, I was warned about what would happen if I refused."

"Tell me." Dante's voice was low, razor-edged.

She did, recounting the meeting with Rutgers and Rodriguez, and highlighting the bits that had made it such a *special* occasion—her father's unwanted appearance, the intense interest in her medical recovery, the not-so-veiled threats. She also told Dante about the visit to her mother's murder site accompanied by an honor guard in the tall and lean form of the Portland field office's SAC.

"They gave me until Monday to make my decision."

"And if you tell them no, you'll suddenly go wacko and end up confined in a looney bin or in a morgue after taking a dive from a very tall building. Mother-*fuckers.*"

"Yeah, basically." Heather leaned back in her chair. "Such a way with words, you sweet-talker you."

A tilted half-smile tugged at Dante's lips, but he held her gaze, his own dark and simmering. "So what's your new boss's name again?"

Heather's smile vanished. She straightened. "No, you're *not* killing anyone. Don't even kid about it."

"Ain't kidding."

"That wouldn't stop it! He has a boss who has a boss who has a boss and so it goes. Killing him wouldn't solve this."

Dante suddenly stood. He paced, jaw tight, hands clenched into white-knuckled fists. A chill touched Heather's spine. *His anger is closer to the surface. What happens when he can't control it anymore?*

After a moment, Dante stopped and drew in a long, shuddering breath. His hands opened and smoothed against his thighs. Leather squeaked. He turned around to face her. His gaze was calmer, the fire banked, but his body language was just the opposite, tensed and tight, almost vibrating with checked emotion.

"You okay?" Heather asked. "Dante, do you need anything?"

He looked at her, his dark eyes drinking her in, his gaze so heated and intense that Heather felt her pulse pick up speed. "I mean . . . do you need a . . . drink?" *Say it*, she told herself. *Say it out loud.* "Blood," she amended.

"Yeah, but it'll wait," he said, trailing both hands through his hair, his skin white against his blue-black tresses. "Okay, killing your boss ain't the answer. So, whatcha wanna do? I'll help you any way I can."

"That's the thing," Heather said. "I'm worried about you too."

"Yeah? *Pourquoi?* I'm okay."

Eerie announced himself with a soft mew and rubbed up against Heather's leg. Just as she bent to pet him, he hopped away for the kitchen, mewing as he went, moving as fast on three legs as he had on four.

"Hey, *minou*," Dante said. "*Now* you raise the alarm?"

Heather stood and followed Eerie into the kitchen. His dish was empty. "Mommy's bad," she said, pouring more kibble into his bowl. "Sorry about that." Eerie chirped in agreement—*yes, Mommy's bad*—or in acceptance of her apology or both. She stroked his head for a moment while he crunched salmon-flavored nuggets.

"You want some coffee?" she called. "I can make some."

"Sure." From right beside her.

"Shit!" Heather whirled, heart pounding, fists lifting automatically.

Dante stepped back, hands held up defensively. She hadn't heard him get up or walk into the kitchen. She'd forgotten how fast and silent he was, even more so than regular nightkind, and that was saying something, from what she'd seen.

"Whoa, hey! Sorry," he said, laughing. "I didn't mean to startle you."

"Christ! Maybe I should bell you like a cat!" She

shoved past him to t...
from the coffeemak...
coffee was brewing, ...
she returned to the ...

Bending over its ...
ping through the p...
your father, told you ...

"Nothing," Dan...
been exactly friendl...

Heather glanced ...
deep. "He should've been honest with you."

Dante trailed a hand through his hair and his pale face suddenly looked weary. He nodded at the papers she was busy searching. "Why you worried about me? Bad Seed died with Johanna Moore, right? It's over."

Heather shook her head. "No, it's not over, not completely. There was another person involved in the project—the man who conceived it and who recruited Moore." The paper she was looking for finally appeared. She pulled it free and set the stack aside on the table. She looked at Dante.

"Go on," Dante said. His gaze was steady, his beautiful face wary. "What's his name?" His fingers white-knuckled around the back of his chair.

"Dr. Robert Wells." Heather stepped beside him and showed him the paper. He looked at it, his gaze fixed on the photo at the top. "He delivered you and ordered the death of your mother."

The sharp crack of splintering wood ricocheted through the room as the chair back snapped beneath Dante's fingers.

13

IN AN HONORLESS WORLD

In the Skies
March 22

CATERINA GLANCED OUT THE plane's small window. Thousands of tiny lights burned and flickered in the darkness below, a reverse sky with the stars beneath and cold infinity above. Pulling up the edge of her sleeve, she looked at her watch. Twelve twelve a.m. EDT, which made it nine twelve p.m. in Portland, Oregon. She'd travel back in time as she flew across the country, away from the dawn and toward the night.

Relaxing into her seat, Caterina closed her eyes for a moment. She'd told Rutgers the truth about the missing security cam footage and it irked her no end that she hadn't yet recovered it. But she had an idea of where it might be.

After Brolee's death, she'd traveled to Gaithersburg to express her condolences to his widow, Nora. This was an action she took whenever possible to remind herself that it'd been a life she'd ended, not simply an assignment accomplished.

While sitting with the grieving woman—*I'll never know why he up and left us. Kristi was the world to him*—Caterina had learned that Bronlee and his widow practically worshipped Dr. Robert Wells.

The plane bumped up and down violently for a few seconds and Caterina's eyes flew open. Her heart slammed into her throat. Turbulence. She hated flying, hated entrusting her life to a stranger. She picked up her plastic cup from the fold-down tray and drained the rest of her vodka. The Absolut Vanilla burned smooth and warm as it went down. She felt her muscles unkink.

Apparently, Wells had performed delicate and controversial genetic work on Jon Bronlee's only child while she'd still been in Nora's womb. Fragile X syndrome. Without Wells's work, Kristi Bronlee would've faced life mentally disabled, possibly autistic as well, and that would've been only the start of the problems. Providing special care for Kristi, medical and schooling, would've kept the Bronlees in deep debt.

Dr. Robert Wells had changed that future by altering their daughter. Because of his work—free of charge, no less—Kristi Bronlee had been born healthy, free of handicaps, and with a future of limitless possibilities.

It'd be interesting to find out if Wells had received a package from Bronlee.

Caterina handed her plastic cup to the flight attendant and shook her head when he asked if she'd like another. As he moved down the aisle, Caterina listened to his cheerful voice as he tended to other passengers. She closed her eyes again.

Half-dozing, her thoughts curled back to her mother and her soft bedtime songs—ages-old lullabies sung in Italian, her voice warm as flannel. *Fi la nana, e mi bel fiol / Fi la nana, e mi bel fiol / Fa si la nana / Fa si la nana / Dormi ben, e mi bel fiol / Dormi ben, e mi bel fiol . . .*

Caterina pictured Renata Alessa Cortini—slim and small and graceful, dark eyes and pale skin, her dark, rich brown hair a Roman cap of ringlets and curls that swept against her white shoulders.

Renata had told Caterina about True Bloods, admitting that even in all her centuries, she'd never met one, although she'd heard jaw-dropping tales from elders who had. True Blood encounters were becoming ever more rare, and that had deeply disturbed Renata.

She'd feared the Bloodline was breaking down, its purity diluted, tainted.

After viewing the CD in Bronlee's laptop, Caterina had been able to temper her mother's fears: *The Bloodline still holds. I've seen it.*

A True Blood had been born. His mother slaughtered. His father unnamed.

How could Johanna Moore—as a vampire, as a woman, as a living being—have done that to her own *fille de sang* and the child of that daughter's womb?

Fire flared to life within Caterina with the memory, rushed through her veins, wild and hot. She drew in a deep breath and counted to one thousand. The fire smoldered, banked and under control.

She still needed to find Dr. Moore or at least learn what had happened to her at the center. She suspected the missing med-unit security camera footage that had cost Jon Bronlee and so many others their lives held the answer.

In Caterina's work, the completion of the assigned task was everything. No questions. No hesitation. Honor demanded no less. She'd become what she was with her eyes wide open. Was she a sociopath? She didn't think so. She only killed when it was required and not for personal gain, power, or sexual kicks. She was samurai in an honorless world.

Caterina had always believed that the work done at the center, including the projects initiated by Moore and Wells, had been for the collective good, mortal *and* vampire. She'd known their work had involved studies of the mind, but had never given thought to how those studies had been conducted, had never considered the cost.

Her job hadn't required her to know.

But her heart had wondered, a wondering she'd muffled with duty.

Now she knew. Now a True Blood child named Dante Baptiste had put a breathtaking face on Moore's studies.

Create sociopaths to study. And—unspoken and un-written—control.

Dante had been placed in the worst foster homes available, shuffled around constantly; everything and everyone he had ever cared about or loved had been systematically stripped from him.

Dante had been mind-fucked in many ways, another experiment in psychopathology, his memory fragmented and buried.

A True Blood prince.

A couple of images of Dante from the photos she'd

seen on the CD played through her memory: Dante as a dark-haired teenager, androgynous and gorgeous; sexy, tilted half-smile on his lips, flipping off the photographer. She liked the boy's defiance, his dark and direct gaze.

The other image was recent: Dante as an adult, a stunning beauty with a been-there-done-that-just-might-do-it-again-so-fuck-you gaze, wearing a leather jacket and torn jeans, a battered guitar case in hand, his pale face confident.

The plane jolted and dropped suddenly and Caterina's stomach dropped with it. As the plane's passage smoothed, the captain's urbane voice soothed the passengers with apologies for the rough flight. Caterina kept her eyes closed and her grip tight on the armrests.

Caterina's thoughts slipped back to her most recent conversation with her mother, remembered the breathless catch in her voice:

"True Blood. You are certain?"

"Sì, Mama. *But he's been damaged. I don't know how extensive—"*

"It doesn't matter, cara mia. *He is only a child."* Cold fury iced Renata's next words: *"That mortals would hide a child born of the Blood, hide him and misuse him—"*

"Mama, *I've been ordered to kill the mortal woman he rescued and all others involved in the project, including the man who designed it."*

"Kill that one slowly, very slowly. And the True Blood? What of him?"

"We are to let him be for the moment, let him remain free."

"Buono. Find him and earn his trust, then bring him to us."

"Sì, Mama. *But that's why I want your advice. If I dis-*

cover he's damaged beyond repair, if he truly is a monster, how do I kill a True Blood?"

"If the damage is too great, then bring him to us so we may end his life with love and respect." The fury was gone from Renata's voice, replaced with sorrow. "He belongs to us. Alive or dead. Not in the hands of mortals, not even yours, my little love, child of my heart."

Another violent jolt shook the plane, but Caterina kept her eyes closed this time, although her fingers latched onto the armrests. More turbulence. Several rows back, a baby wailed.

She suddenly yearned for a cigarette and imagined sucking the smoke down into her lungs. Even though she hadn't smoked in six years, sometimes the intense desire for a cigarette would sneak up on her and kick her in the ass, leave her tensed and jonesing like a nicotine junkie fresh on the patch. And she wanted one now. Bad.

Caterina pondered her mother's parting words yet again, turning them over and around, contemplating their meaning from every direction: *You walk the tightrope between worlds with more grace and balance than I've ever seen, my sweet Cat. But one day you* will *fall. Which world will you tumble into—mortal or vampire? You shall have to choose even as you slip from the rope.*

And if she refused to choose? Just stepped off, head back, eyes closed, allowing fate or destiny to guide her fall? Could she keep her honor in the heart of turbulence?

She knew how to kill her own kind and knew how to kill vampires. And since Renata wouldn't instruct her on how to kill a True Blood, she'd have to find out some other way. Just in case.

Let's be clear. Let's be honest. What would it take to kill a True Blood child?

But if Johanna Moore's project had failed and Dante hadn't been shaped into a monster like Elroy Jordan, he was young enough to be reshaped, guided, tutored.

Young enough to be redeemed.

She would find Dante Baptiste and then, listening to her heart, she'd do whatever honor and mercy required of her: Kill a True Blood monster. Or protect a True Blood prince.

SA BRIAN SHERIDAN SMILED at the waitress as she refilled his cup with coffee. He dumped a packet of Splenda into it, along with a splash of the shit that passed for cream. He stirred idly, watching a plane taxi over to the runway, lights winking in the darkness. The plane rolled down the tarmac, building speed, the engine roar muffled by Dulles International's thick walls.

Cortini's plane had departed right on schedule an hour ago.

Sheridan had heard many things about her, had studied a few photos, but had never seen her in the flesh. He sipped at the coffee, ignoring its burned and bitter taste.

When Cortini had walked into Rutgers's office—five seven, slender, confident stride—Sheridan had been riveted by her graceful motion. Fluid, yet poised. Like a gymnast or martial artist. He'd bet anything her reflexes were fast and stiletto-sharp, that she could shift from shaking your hand to snapping your neck in an instant.

She'd worn a tailored black suit, a white blouse underneath, and silver had flashed at her wrists and ears. Dark, coffee-colored hair had brushed her shoulders and framed her attractive face. Thirty-four, but she looked younger. An unexpected impish smile had curved her glossed lips—just a hint of rose—and lit her hazel eyes.

It'd be easy to be caught off guard by this woman, this wetwork expert, easy to underestimate her with her mischievous smile. And fatal.

The plane he was watching vaulted into the sky, a moving constellation of blinking wing lights. Sheridan watched until the plane vanished from sight. He finally gave up on the coffee in disgust and ordered a Foster's. No harm in one beer while waiting for his red-eye flight to Seattle. It was going to be a long night.

Rutgers had given him very specific instructions while walking together outside the building and away from listening ears, flesh or otherwise.

"If I have to lose a good agent like Wallace and a valuable resource like Wells, then Dante Prejean goes too," Rutgers says, head bowed, her words clipped and tight. "I refuse to let him walk from this mess. He dies. The SB can shove their decisions up their collective asses." She looks up and her eyes are shadowed, her voice bitter and cold. "Adapting to darkness isn't difficult in our profession. Be sure to remind Cortini of that when you kill her."

14

EVEN DEEPER

Seattle, WA
March 22

Dante stared at the paper, his heart drumming out a frenzied rhythm. The photo blurred and pain skewered his temples with each attempt to focus on it.

Avenge your mother and yourself.

But if what Heather said was right—and he had no reason to doubt it—then he'd *failed*. Genevieve Baptiste's killer still breathed and ate and slept. Enjoyed life.

But not for much longer.

"Give me that name again," Dante said, chest tight, muscles coiling. "I can't read it. Say it again. Say it slow."

Heather's brows slanted down, worried. "You don't look so good," she said.

"The name."

"Robert Wells."

"Robert . . ." Dante repeated. He opened his mouth

to say the last name, but it was gone, slipped from his grasp, pain-greased. Deep inside, wasps droned. Pain needled his temples. "Fuck," he muttered. "Say it again."

"Robert Wells. Dante, I don't think—"

An image strobed into Dante's mind: *A man with gray-flecked blond hair and a friendly smile leans over him. Blood spatter decorates his white lab coat. His hand strokes Dante's hair as he sticks a needle into Dante's throat.*

My beautiful boy. You'll survive anything I might do to you, won't you?

And pushes the plunger.

The image broke apart. Vanished. Pain scratched across Dante's awareness, white light flickering at the edges of his vision. "Say it again," he whispered, knuckling his fists against his temples. "Again."

Fingers grasped his chin, forced his head around. He met Heather's concerned blue gaze. Her lips moved, but all he could hear were the voices rising like a hurricane from within.

We need the straitjacket. And the chains. Hurry!

Little fucking psycho.

Say that again, and I'll give you to that little fucking psycho.

Run, Dante-angel, run!

"Dante, come back." Heather's voice cut through the whispers and he locked onto her face. She looked in so deep. Deeper than he thought was safe. Safe for him? Safe for her? He wasn't sure, but he had a feeling it wasn't safe for either of them. Things stirred in the darkness within. Restless. Hungry.

Dante's muscles tensed. Drawing in a deep breath,

he focused on Heather's twilight gaze. Breathed in her lilacs-and-sage-in-the-rain scent. Then her arms wrapped around him and the whispers faded. The droning vanished.

All was quiet but for the mingled beating of their hearts, a dual rhythm of daylight and moonrise. He laced his arms around her and rested his face against her head, breathed in the lilac fragrance of her hair.

"Dante?"

"J'su ici."

"How's your head?"

"Comme çi, comme ça." He lifted his head and saw the pieces of broken wood at his feet, and then looked at the ruined chair. "Fuck. Sorry."

"Don't worry about it. Sit down," Heather urged.

Dante released her, then shook his head. "No, I gotta go."

A strange look crossed Heather's face. "What did I just tell you a moment ago?"

Dante searched his memory, felt something shift and slide from his grasp. Pain snaked through his mind. He sniffed. Tasted blood. "Something about the guy who delivered me, killed my mother, but I can't remember his name," he muttered. He wiped at his nose, smearing blood across the back of his hand.

"Robert Wells," Heather said. "Dr. Robert Wells. And your nose is bleeding."

"Robert . . ." Dante said, then searched his memory. He knew the name was there, could almost hear it as an echo, but an empty one. "Fuck!"

"Sit." Heather pushed at his shoulders. "Dante, sit down."

He sat, and ran his fingers through his hair. Something felt wrong inside, almost like something was winding up, some broken, splintered thing trying to spin to life. His heart pounded hard and fast. Heather knelt in front of him and dabbed at his nose with Kleenex. "How come I can remember Johanna Moore's name, but not this asshole's?"

Heather shook her head, her face dead serious, worried. "I don't know, but I've got a feeling Wells programmed a safeguard into you that Moore was unaware of, maybe something to keep him alive in case things went sour between them."

"Okay, then let's bypass that fucking safeguard. Where does he live? How do I find him?"

"Later. Put your head back."

"I'm fine," he said, grabbing for the wad of tissues in her hand. "Give me that."

"You are *not* fine!" Heather threw the bloodstained Kleenex at him. Fire blazed in her eyes, and he smelled the blood flushing her cheeks. "Your mind has been messed with since you were born, Dante. You are *far* from fine! Why are you so goddamned pigheaded?"

"It's the only way I know to be."

A sad smile brushed Heather's lips. "And that's how you survived."

"I ain't the only stubborn one in this relationship."

"I'm tenacious, not pigheaded," Heather murmured. "There's a big difference."

"Keep telling yourself that."

Heather chuckled deep in her throat, a warm, sexy sound. "Do you remember what I told you a bit ago?"

Dante nodded. "A guy whose name I can't keep. A

guy who's responsible for my mom's death." The Perv's words snaked through his mind. *Being a bloodsucker and all, they cut off her head and torched her.*

"That's right. We'll deal with all this tomorrow. I think we've both had enough tonight and you've still got to perform."

"And you've got Annie," Dante said.

"Yeah," she sighed. Exhaustion shadowed her eyes. "I've a couple of leads I want to follow up tonight after I get my sister settled. I'm safe until Monday. And you, you're probably safe on tour. But watch your back in case I'm wrong."

"You too. Keep your gun handy, *chérie.*"

"Yeah, of course."

Dante walked over to the window and shoved it open. "I'll fix this tomorrow, first thing in the evening," he said, tracing a finger over the broken lock.

"Damn straight you're gonna fix it," Heather said, though she couldn't picture him wielding a screwdriver. She joined him at the window, then asked, "Why don't you use the front door?"

Dante shrugged. "Going out the way I came in."

He turned and lowered his head, and Heather found herself tipping her face up for his kiss, her heart pounding hard and fast, but instead of the heated touch of his lips, she felt his fingers brush against her face, a lingering touch. His forehead touched hers and she breathed in his smoke and deep, dark earth scent.

"Je te manque," he whispered. His fingers trembled, then vanished from her face.

Heather looked up into Dante's eyes; hunger glinted in their dark depths. She touched his face and, tensing beneath her fingers, he pulled away. Her breath caught in her throat.

Dante kissed for many reasons—he kissed friends, he kissed strangers, she'd even seen him kiss an enemy. So what did it mean when he *didn't* kiss? When the touch of his lips was denied?

Pushing the curtain aside, Dante ducked down and swung a leg over the windowsill. Straddling the sill, he glanced up at Heather. "I'll put you and Annie on to-morrow night's guest list if you'd like to come to the show."

"I'd like that," Heather said with a smile. "Thanks."

"Bonne nuit, chérie," Dante said, dropping to the ground. "I'll see you tomorrow."

Dante pulled up the hood on his hoodie, his fingers tugging the edges past his face. He stepped backward several paces, his gaze on hers, his lambent eyes gleaming in the darkness. Sliding on his shades, he whirled, and *ran*.

Heather closed the window, leaned her forehead against the glass, and closed her eyes. The pane felt cool against her skin. Her fingers grasped the window-sill. The weeks apart hadn't changed her feelings for Dante. But she still hadn't yet sorted out those feel-ings or her fears. Before she could do anything about those feelings, they both had to survive the fall of Bad Seed.

Closing the curtain, Heather turned and walked over to the sofa where she'd tossed her purse when she'd come in—blindsided by Annie's dramatic swoon and Dante's breathtaking presence. She eased her Colt Super from her purse, then tucked the .38 into the back of her jeans. The cold barrel nestled against the small of her back.

Quiet sobs, forlorn and raw, drew her back to the guestroom and her now weeping sister. Dante's whispered words circled through her mind: *Je te manque.*

I miss you too, she thought.

15

NEW GODS ARISE

On I-205 Between Damascus and Portland
March 22

ALEX LYONS STEERED HIS Dodge Ram along I-205 north, headed for Portland to pick up more material for Athena's experiments. She slept, but he knew it'd be brief, even with the drugs. Her restless mind would soon have her on her feet, chasing her thoughts.

Inferno's music pounded from the truck's speakers, filled the cab with raging, sharp-edged sound. Dante's voice snaked around Alex's awareness, husky and heated.

I'm waiting for you / I've watched / and watched / I know your every secret . . .

I don't think so, Alex thought. *But I know yours.* An insistent off note trilled underneath the music and Alex realized his cell was ringing. Muting the music, he pulled the Ram over into the emergency lane and stopped. He flicked on the hazard lights. He yanked the cell from his hoodie pocket. The ID read *unknown*.

Thumbing the answer button, he said, "Lyons."

"Did your meeting with Heather Wallace produce anything of interest?" His SB contact's voice was smooth and deep and slightly nasal. A New England native, Alex mused, maybe Boston.

"Nothing new," Alex said. "She kept everything close to the vest. She's smart enough to know she's being watched, pumped for info."

"She said nothing about Prejean? Or Bad Seed?"

"No."

"And nothing about Moore or the events at the center, I imagine."

"You imagine right."

His contact sighed. "Ah, well, it probably wouldn't have made much difference even if she had, I suppose."

"What do you mean?" Alex went still, listening carefully for nuance.

"She'll be joining your father in . . . retirement."

"Is that necessary?" Alex asked.

"Yes."

Alex pictured Heather's lovely heart-shaped face, her deep blue eyes. Remembered what she'd asked of him: *Could you keep my father in the dark?* And his promise. "I learned some interesting info about Wallace, indirectly," he said.

"And that would be?"

"It wasn't luck or prompt medical attention that saved her life like she claims. Dante Prejean healed her, but he did it without using his blood."

"Interesting, indeed. I also find it interesting that you didn't give up that fact until *after* I mentioned Wallace's retirement."

A cold sweat beaded Alex's forehead. "Sorry, I just thought of it."

"Is there anything else I should know? Anything else you just thought of?"

Alex paused before replying, pretending to give it thought. "No."

The line went dead, his contact's typical good-bye. Alex slid his cell phone back into his pocket and wiped the sweat from his forehead with the heel of his hand. He hoped he'd bought Heather more time; hoped the SB would be more interested in studying her now than in ending her life. She was smart and sexy and full of secrets, one of which they now shared.

I'll keep your old man in the dark.

Alex switched off the hazard lights and, hitting the gas, merged the Ram back into traffic. A few drops of rain hit the windshield and he clicked on the wipers. Inferno shredded the silence, Dante's whispered lyrics slicing to the bone like a razor-edged shank.

Break me / I'm daring you / see if you can / break me / with your whispers and your lies / fucking break me / with your kiss / I'm daring you / put me on my knees / see if you can . . .

The Ram's headlights silhouetted a figure walking backward in the emergency lane, thumb out. Alex lifted his foot off the gas and guided the truck off the road. Even before he'd stopped, the figure was loping toward the truck.

A moment later the passenger-side door yanked open and a rush of cool, rain-laden air swirled into the cab. A youthful, bearded face poked inside. "How far you going?"

"Portland," Alex said.

"Cool, that works." The hitchhiker tossed his stained and road-weathered backpack onto the floorboards and climbed into the passenger seat. He fastened his seat belt and grinned. "Thanks, man." His damp, collar-length hair curled at the edges.

"Sure," Alex said, returning the hitchhiker's grin. "You're doing me a favor too."

"By keeping you awake?"

"By helping me out with an errand."

The hitchhiker's grin faded. "What kinda errand?"

"Don't worry. You won't have to do anything." Telekinetic energy surged through Alex, rushing up his spine, electric and tingling, as he focused it on his passenger.

Energy snapped against the hitchhiker, pinning him to the seat and knocking the air from his lungs. The hitchhiker gasped. The hair on his head and beard lifted. His eyes widened as he flailed to free himself, but remained right where he was, held by invisible hands.

Alex reached into his hoodie pocket and pulled the syringe free. "You're saving me a lot of time and trouble," he said over the hitchhiker's panicked grunts. "Now I won't have to arrest another unlucky vagrant camping under the Burnside Bridge."

Alex wondered what Athena hoped to accomplish with her experiments. He knew she was trying to emulate what she'd seen Dante do to Johanna Moore, fascinated with the idea of unmaking.

How else will I understand him?

Alex didn't have an answer for that, but the experiments kept her happy and occupied and that was all that mattered.

Sometimes Alex lay awake at night, listening to the Athena-wind rushing through the house, and pictured her spinning out of control. Murdering their parents. Torching the main house. He could even smell the acrid smoke, hear the fire crackling, felt its heat tighten the skin on his face.

Call me Hades.

Then he'd remember the Bad Seed CD he'd watched of beautiful fourteen-year-old Dante murdering his abusive foster parents, then torching their house. And Alex would grow calmer. Perhaps such scenes were rites of passage. Fires to forge and temper blades of flesh.

When the old gods are slain, the new gods arise, drenched in blood.

So it was. So it would ever be.

"Amen, brother," Alex murmured, then jabbed the needle into the hitchhiker's throat and thumbed the plunger.

16

NOTHING MORE
THAN MYTH

Seattle, WA — Vespers
March 22

DANTE STRODE INTO THE greenroom backstage
at Vespers. Von, sprawled in a ratty-looking easy
chair, glanced up from the issue of *Newsweek* he was
reading.

" 'Bout time," he drawled. "You missed sound
check."

"Nope," Dante retorted. "I didn't miss it one bit."
He grabbed the back of the metal folding chair set up
in front of the dressing table and mirror, flipped it
around, and straddled it. He watched in the mirror as
Von draped his magazine over the chair's arm.

"Y'know, that line never gets old," the nomad said.

"Glad to hear it. That's me all over, aiming to
please."

Von snorted.

Dante took off his shades and tossed them onto the

table. He closed his eyes. He still saw Heather at the window looking into the night, still smelled her, lilac and sage and bittersweet hurt, still felt the softness of her cheek beneath his fingers.

Opening his eyes, Dante shoved his hood back, then combed his fingers through his hair. He shivered, cold and knotted up. He rubbed his hands over his face. He just needed to feed, and he would, after the gig. "You and Silver fed yet?" he asked.

"Yeah . . . but is that a cut I see in your shirt?" Von's voice was low with suspicion. "You been scrapping again? Or did tough little Heather greet you with a big ol' knife?"

Dante looked at Von's watchful reflection in the mirror. "Nah. Her sister did."

The humor vanished from Von's face. He sat up. "Seriously? You okay?"

"Yeah, I'm okay." Tugging off his hoodie, Dante draped it over the chair. His personal kit was on the table, beside a tall, deep green bottle of black market European absinthe; he unzipped the kit and felt around inside for his kohl stick. Pulling it out, he uncapped it, leaned forward, and touched up the kohl smudged around his eyes.

"Seattle nightkind are here for the show," Von said. "Well, some of 'em, anyway. The Lady of the leading household asked for some time with you before the show."

"She can wait for the meet-and-greet like everyone else," Dante replied. "Why should she get special attention just cuz she's nightkind?"

"That's you all over, aiming to please," Von said.

"My fucking mission in life," Dante agreed. He paused, the kohl stick pressed against the outside corner of his eye as sudden movement drew his gaze.

Eli hurried past the curtains and into the room. "Dante! I was beginning to worry," he said, his words rapid, spring-loaded. "Which set list do you want for tonight?" He hunkered down beside Dante's chair. His patchouli and ganja scents curled up into Dante's nostrils.

"The first one. Why you so anxious, *mon ami*?"

Eli shook his head, his dreads swaying with the movement. Tension played across his face. "I've been having some programming problems with the keyboards."

"Okay, I'll take a look in a bit," Dante said, "and see what's up."

"*D'accord.*"

Dante dropped the kohl stick onto the table. Worry still darkened Eli's hazel eyes. "What *ain't* you saying? What's got you worked up?"

"Nightkind in the crowd," Eli said.

"That ain't nothing new."

"Looking for easy out-of-town meals."

"Yeah? Where're Jack and Antoine?"

"Watching Dogspit set up. Silver's with 'em, keeping an eye on things."

"I'll say a few words to the nightkind in the audience at the start of the show." Dante touched a finger to the hollow of Eli's throat, his black-painted fingernail underlining the tiny iridescent bat tattoo etched into the skin—visible only to nightkind. "Make sure you don't cover that up. Remind the guys; the mark needs to be seen."

"Will do."

"Anything else?"

Eli shook his head again, smiling. "That takes care of it."

Dante twisted around, bent his head. Eli lifted at the same moment, and Dante cupped a hand against his face, and kissed his offered lips. Murmured, *"Bonne chance, ce soir."*

"Et toi." Eli straightened, and then walked from the room.

"So why ain't Heather here?" Von asked. "The way she was looking for you, you woulda thought you'd burst into flames and she was the only one with a bucket of water."

Dante stood, then turned around. He trailed a hand through his hair. "Her sister's kinda messed up at the moment, not well, y'know? She needs to be with her."

Von nodded his head at the slice in Dante's latex shirt. "No shit."

"The Bureau ain't letting her go either," Dante said, his voice low. "They plan bad fucking shit for her if she refuses to sign over her soul. She's got till Monday."

"She never said a word about that," Von said, looking a little indignant. "She only talked about the trouble you might still be in. Told me a bit about Bad Seed."

"Yeah, well, I'm only concerned about Heather," Dante said. "I'm gonna help her win her freedom, one way or another."

"Naturally, you're counting me in on the action."

"Yeah?" Dante said softly. "Okay, then, *mon ami. Merci.*" Some restless part of Dante drummed a fast-paced tempo within, a rhythm he paced out across the floor. "After I make sure she's safe, I'll walk away."

"Dante, man, walk away? What are you saying?"

The tone in Von's voice, troubled and tight, drew Dante's gaze and stopped his feet. Von parked his shades on top of his head, and an emotion Dante couldn't name flickered in the nomad's green eyes.

"What I have to do."

"Have you talked things out with Heather?"

Dante shook his head. "Why? What's to talk out?" He resumed pacing, his boots silent on the floorboards as he walked back and forth, measuring with his stride the rhythm pulsing in his veins. Underneath the rhythm, voices whispered, droned like angry wasps crawling beneath his skin.

She trusted you. I'd say she got what she deserved.

Tainted. Everything you touch, boy, dies.

I knew you'd come for me.

Little fucking psycho.

Whirling, Dante kicked the metal chair he'd been sitting in, knocking it across the room—a blurred, gray streak. It hit the wall with a loud clang, then clattered to the floor. The noise pierced his head, scraped down his spine like flint, sparking pain in his mind.

Hands suddenly latched onto his biceps, spun him around, and held him tight. Von's frost and leather and gun-oil scent enveloped him. Dante heard the steady beat of the nomad's heart, and looked up into Von's face. Light gleamed in his eyes, sparkled along the edges of his crescent moon tattoo.

"You honestly don't know, do you?" Von said.

"Know what?"

A smile lifted one corner of Von's mustached mouth, but it wasn't amused or laughing, just kind of sad, which perplexed Dante. *What the fuck?* He tensed beneath the nomad's hands. "C'mon, let go."

"You're in love, little brother."

Dante stared at him. "Yeah? I know what love feels like, but *this*, this, man . . . *fuck* me. Steals my breath. Knots me up. Torches me."

Von shook his head. "No, this is what *denying* love feels like, man. Why you denying your heart?"

Dante flexed free of the nomad's tight-fingered hold and stepped away. Images flickered behind his eyes, like pictures seen in a burning-white lightning flash.

Flash: *Gina's tear-streaked face turned toward the door, her eyes empty.*

Flash: *Jay, straitjacketed, blood pouring from his throat and puddling around him, staining his blond hair red.*

Flash: *Heather, falling, a wet circle of blood spreading on her sweater, her twilight-blue gaze locked on his face.*

Flash: *A child's hand, fingers curled in toward the palm . . .*
Dante-angel?
Here, princess.
Chloe.

Pain spiked through Dante's head. He tried to capture the images that'd just lightning-stroked through his mind, but he couldn't hold onto the last one, couldn't even recall the name that'd flared like a candle in his mind and was just as quickly snuffed.

Blood trickled from his nose and he wiped at it with the back of his hand. Sniffed, and tasted blood. Pain jabbed like an ice pick behind his left eye. "Penance," he whispered.

"Fuck. Sit down, and put your head back," Von said. "You're bleeding."

Dante shook his head. *"Tracassé toi pas.* I'm okay." As he walked to the table, he saw Eli, Antoine, and Jack clustered near the curtains, their faces solemn. Silver stood just behind them, his arms crossed over his chest, his purple, gel-spiked hair glistening under the lights, his expression pensive. Dante paused, wiped at his nose again. "I'm okay," he repeated. Their expressions didn't change.

"Like hell you are," Von muttered, grabbing him by the arm, whipping him across the floor, and practically flinging him into the easy chair. "Head back, you stubborn sonuvabitch."

"It's nothing," Dante protested, but he tipped his head back. Pain prickled at his temples and behind his eyes. He pinched the bridge of his nose. "Damn thing got broken earlier this evening."

"Heather's sister?"

"Yeah. She's got one mean head-butt."

Von snorted. "Sounds like she needs to teach Heather that particular move."

Dante pictured that and smiled. "Fuck you."

Von chuckled. "Thank you. My work here is done."

The ice pick lodged behind Dante's eye burned red-hot. White squiggles of light bordered his vision. Sweat trickled down his temples. A sudden breeze smelling of cinnamon and hair gel fluttered across him, blowing several strands of his hair across his face. Silver. Von murmured a thanks.

"Here," Von said, and wrapped Dante's fingers around a cold compress.

"You need us?" Silver asked. "Or can we get back to what we were doing?"

"Show's over, yeah," Dante said, replacing his pinching fingers with the compress. "But thanks." He sat up, and suddenly thought of Lucien, of how he could cool the fire raging in his skull with one touch.

"You heard anything from Lucien?" Dante asked.

Von shook his head. "Not a peep." He looked at Dante for a long moment before asking quietly, "You ever gonna forgive him?"

"I honestly don't know."

"He fucked up hard-core, but he cares about you. Hell, he's your dad."

"Yeah, that's the problem, ain't it?"

"You need to talk this out with him, little brother."

"Drop it."

"I'll leave it for you to pick up," Von drawled. "I think I'll go scan the audience for dudes in trenchcoats and shades. Just in case."

Dante lowered the compress. Blood stained its blue fabric. He watched as the nomad walked across the room, leather creaking and tiny chains jingling, then slipped behind the curtains.

Rising to his feet, Dante returned to the table and opened the half-full bottle of absinthe. He wrapped his fingers around the bottle's neck and lifted it to his lips. The liqueur smelled of anise, hyssop, and wormwood, and promised answers. So far, though, it'd only shaken loose a few memory glimmers that'd quickly slipped out of his grasp. Fucking *naturellement*. Just like at Heather's place.

He delivered you and ordered the death of your mother.

Dante wanted to remember that motherfucker's name and face. Wanted to tattoo both into his mind. He took a long swallow of the absinthe. Tasting like black licorice, sweet and strong and bitter just underneath, it burned through him. Lit up his mind. Uncoiled his muscles.

Dante lowered the bottle back to the table, but kept his fingers locked around it. As the absinthe trickled into his veins, the pain in his head faded. But another pain strengthened, hard-knuckled and relentless.

Why you denying your heart?

He met his reflection's dark-eyed and dilated gaze. "Can't trust it."

DOGSPIT LAUNCHED INTO THEIR set with a kick-ass drum solo while their front woman screamed, *"Fuuuuuck you Seattle!"* The crowd roared, a hungry beast, and the sound of it vibrated the floor beneath Von's boots.

The crowd moshed beyond the curtains, booted feet jackhammering the floor as Dogspit created an aural firestorm. But Von wasn't watching the band or the crowd. He stood at the curtain's edge, a fold of worn velvet between his fingers, watching Dante.

Dante lifted the absinthe bottle to his lips again, tipped his head back, and drank. Boy was hurting. Hurting bad.

Ever since D.C., Dante had been tossing back a lot of the green-tinted psychoactive. Von suspected it wasn't to ease migraine pain or even just to catch a buzz. He had a feeling Dante hoped to pry open the locks on his past with a wormwood-scented crowbar. And given what Lucien had told him, that wouldn't be good.

Lucien's voice rumbled through Von's memory: *I fear for him. He refuses to rest or to grieve. Refuses to release his rage.*

So why'd you hide the truth from him? Truth he needed?

He needs time to heal before facing his past. Or before facing who and what he is. I need you to guide him, llygad. *And guard him, especially from himself.*

I chose Dante over the Road. Of course I'll fucking guide him. Watch out for him. But Dante's a big boy and I trust him to make his own decisions.

You shouldn't—not until he heals. Not until he's bound.

Bound? What the hell you talking about?

Guard him from the Fallen, llygad. *Guard Dante from them, most of all.*

Why?

Dante is a Maker.

Von stares at Lucien, unable to corral his thoughts into any semblance of order.

Von had figured Makers were nothing more than myth, a nightkind fairy tale of Fallen power. But here he was, watching as the myth downed a bottle of absinthe.

Dante lowered the bottle to his side, turning as if he meant to head backstage, maybe to work on the keyboards, but he stumbled instead, like he'd taken a punch to the temple. He nearly lost his grip on the absinthe bottle. He held himself still, eyes closed, pain shadowing his face.

Von heard the breath catch in Dante's throat. Smelled his hunger, sharp and alkaline. "You haven't fed, have you?" he said quietly, walking up behind Dante.

Dante shook his head. "After the show."

"You fucking kidding me? You ain't gonna make it through the show."

"Yeah, I will." Dante set the bottle on the table.

"No, you won't. You may be the most mule-headed sonuvabitch I've ever met, but you're too young and in too much pain."

Opening his eyes, Dante whirled around to face him, his hands knotting into fists. "What the fuck do you expect me to do? There ain't time!"

Von pulled off his leather jacket and tossed it onto the chair. Unbuckling his double-shoulder holsters, he shrugged them off and placed them, along with his guns, on top of his jacket. He touched fingers to one bare, muscle-corded wrist. "I expect you to take enough to get you through the show. Think you can do that?"

Dante trailed a hand through his hair, then nodded. "Yeah," he said, voice husky.

"Okay, then." Von sat down on the floor in front of the ratty-looking easy chair, resting his back against it and stretching his legs out in front of him. He slid his shades to the top of his head, glanced at Dante, and patted his thigh.

Dante straddled him and sat. Leather and latex creaked as Dante leaned in and kissed him, his mouth opening as Von's lips parted. His tongue flicked against Von's, tasting of licorice and alcohol. Von breathed in Dante's heady scent, pulse racing.

"Merci beaucoup, mon ami," Dante murmured, when the kiss ended. He held Von's gaze, gold flames flickering in the depths of his dark, unshielded eyes.

"My honor," Von whispered. He lifted a hand and

stroked Dante's hair. Slid a silky black tendril between his fingers.

Dante wrapped his fingers around Von's wrist and raised it to his lips. He closed his eyes. Von felt the warmth of Dante's lips, then a quick sting as his fangs pierced the skin. In restrained sips, Dante drank him in.

A sigh escaped Von's lips. His fingers tightened in Dante's hair, looped, and pulled. Dante shivered and moaned softly. Pleasure flowed between them like warm honey, pulsing from lips to flesh, from mind to mind, heartbeat to heartbeat. But Dante ended it just a few minutes later by lifting his head and pushing Von's arm away. As Dante rose to his knees, Von released his hair.

"That wasn't enough, little brother. Sit back down."

Bending, Dante kissed him deeply, sharing the grape-sweet taste of his blood, sharing fevered heat. "It's gonna hafta be enough," he whispered against Von's lips. "I can't stay. Something's . . . waking up . . . inside."

"Dante . . ."

Slipping free of Von's hands, Dante jumped to his feet, turned, and walked away. Energy crackled along his fingers. Blue fire haloed his hands. He clenched his glowing hands into fists.

Maker. And *uncontrolled*.

Sweat beaded Von's forehead, but inside he was cold. The question Dante had asked him at Louis Armstrong International while waiting for their flight to Seattle reverberated through his mind: *If I'm the only Maker in existence like Lucien says, then who can teach me what I need to know?*

Lucien held the answer to that question.

And Lucien had gone silent a week ago, a silence that left Von uneasy. A silence that left Von watching the skies at night, listening for the sound of wings.

Guard him from the Fallen, llygad. *They will use him without mercy.*

Lucien wouldn't have cut off communication, not willingly, not when he was counting on Von to keep him posted on Dante's well-being.

Watching Dante walk away, blue flames licking around his knotted fists, desperation on his pale face, Von realized he needed to find an answer for Dante's question.

Before it was too late.

17

GEHENNA

C LAWS RAKED ACROSS LUCIEN'S torso, scoring his flesh open from collarbone to hip. Pain seared his consciousness like a red-hot branding iron as he swung suspended in the air, the movement twisting the hooks barbed into his shoulders even deeper into his muscles. The rapid flutter of multiple pairs of wings fanned hot, sulfurous, stinking air across his face, and the nameless *chalkydri*'s chittering filled his ears.

Lucien refused to open his eyes as the *chalkydri* demanded. He'd looked long enough upon his tormentor. He knew it hovered beside him in the dark pit, held aloft by its twelve pairs of hummingbird-quick wings, its long, serpentine body coiling in the air, black scales glittering with tiny decorative sapphires.

Gold wings, the *chalkydri* was always quick to point out, its lizardlike head lifted with pride, the feathered crescent atop its skull bristling, taloned paws patting its jeweled hide. *High-blood gold,* it insisted.

"Yahweh always regretted making *chalkydri,*" Lucien lied, voice hoarse. "Your creation was proof of his madness, and he—"

"Murderer!" the *chalkydri* hissed. "*Creawdwr*-slayer!"

Claws slashed across Lucien's chest again. Another searing brand upon his consciousness. Every time his wounds healed the *chalkydri* inflicted fresh ones. As it had been doing ever since he and Lilith had been captured.

"He always intended to unmake you," Lucien finished, through gritted teeth.

Angry chittering filled the air. Furious chittering. The rush of wings intensified. *So,* he mused, *more* chalkydri *have arrived to defend their honor.*

And, in so doing, provide amusement for Gabriel and his court.

Three Elohim guards drag Lucien through the air by his chains, sweeping past the gold-flecked, black marble columns guarding the palace-aerie's wide mouth, flying into the massive cave. Pain bites at the edges of his banded wings, chafes his chain-wrapped ankles and wrists, but his mind is calm and his shields tight. He wonders if Lilith is chained and clipped as well, and hopes she isn't.

She tried to warn me.

Lucien's escorts release him in midair and he plummets to the gleaming marble floor, his banded wings futilely trying to lift him up. He hits hard, landing on his side, chains ringing against the stone. Black specks whirl across his graying vision.

Wybrcathl—fluting, trilling, warbling—from hundreds of

throats echoes throughout the palace's throne room as Elohim high-bloods voice their songs and dissenting opinions, a beautifully orchestrated choir. Lucien suppresses the instinctive urge to warble a response to the kilted and gowned aingeals ringing the sky-blue floor.

Blinking his vision clear, he pushes himself to his knees before the golden-winged Uriel or black-winged Yng can descend and kick him to his feet. Straightening with as much dignity as his chains and wing bands allow, Lucien stands and faces the throne from which he once ruled. The smells of home—jasmine and smoky myrrh and deep, dark earth—fill his nostrils, and he breathes deep.

But what he sees closes a cold fist around his yearning heart, turns it to ice. Gabriel, golden wings folded at his back, stands before the ancient black-starred throne, its carved-marble wing blades surrounding it like the petals of a flower. And sprawled on a smaller, less ornate version of the throne, his long legs stretched out before him, is the Morningstar, his star-white hair cut short and framing his handsome, bored face.

And beside him, in a twilight blue gown, stands Lilith. She meets Lucien's gaze, chin lifted, sudden color touching her cheeks.

Always the chess player, his Lilith. Holding her gaze, Lucien bends forward at the waist, chains clanging; a half-bow. The color in her cheeks deepens and her chin lifts higher.

Gabriel waves a hand and the wybrcathl choir stops. "So, at long last, the murderer of Yahweh faces justice," he says, his melodic voice carrying through the aerie. He walks down the dais's steps with slow deliberation, his face thoughtful, his caramel-colored hair curling in thick waves against his purple-kilted hips. Lamplight glints from the silver bracers on each wrist. "I've often wondered if we'd been denied another creawdwr *because this* aingeal—*this* creawdwr-slayer—*still drew breath.*"

Gabriel stops in front of Lucien. Scorn sculpts his golden gaze, chisels a smile on his lips. "What say you, Samael? Any excuses? Please, amuse us."

"I thought you were amusement enough," Lucien says, his voice clear and deep, his words resonating against the palace's polished marble walls. "Still trying to siphon power and respectability from others because you lack any of your own?"

Gabriel's smile becomes strained. His wings flutter. "Perhaps you don't understand, Samael. I rule Gehenna."

Lucien touches a hand to his chin thoughtfully, chains clinking. "Rule? As-in keeping the throne warm until someone worthy arrives to occupy it?" His gaze skims the watchful faces, marking those he knows, and those he doesn't; then he nods. "Wise, my brothers and sisters. Gabriel should soon have it warm enough for even the coldest ass."

Someone in the semicircled flock gasps, but several others barely stifle laughter. Behind Gabriel, a smile flickers across the Morningstar's lips.

All amusement vanishes from Gabriel's face and he stiffens, the muscles in his shoulders suddenly taut. "I think time in Sheol is in order," he says, voice as tight as his muscles. "Some quiet time to reflect."

"Quiet time to reflect is always good," Lucien murmurs. "But perhaps you could stand in a corner? No need to drop yourself into the pit."

Open laughter resounds through the aerie, and is just as quickly cut off.

Brows knitted in a furious scowl, Gabriel lifts his hand, palm up, and then curls his fingers closed, his simmering gaze *holding Lucien's. His amber talons pierce the skin, and blood, dark and fragrant, wells up.*

"You're going to need more than blood and spells to hold me, seat-warmer," Lucien says.

"Yes," Gabriel agrees. He dips a talon in his own blood and touches it to Lucien's forehead. "I need your true name." A dark smile twists across his lips.

Cold dread prickles in Lucien's belly. He looks at Lilith. She drops her gaze to her pretty sandaled feet.

"I bind you, Sar ha-Olam of the Elohim," Gabriel intones, "to the soil of Gehenna and bind your power within you, unused and unvoiced, until I set you free again." As Gabriel paints a blood-glyph on Lucien's forehead, translucent light streams from his palms and coils around Lucien, binding him with an ethereal rope. "As Gehenna fades, so shall you. Upon my name it is done."

Lucien holds Gabriel's gaze as the aingeal's *spell spirals around him, into him, cold and tingling, encasing his energy, his fire, within gossamer ice, and traps his* wybrcathl *beneath the glacial flow, silencing his song.*

"One day I will free myself of your spell," Lucien whispers. "And on that day, for you, the dawn will end forevermore. Keep this in mind, Gabriel Seat-Warmer; I know your name, as well. Think on that. Think long."

Sudden doubt shadows Gabriel's fair face. He steps back several paces at whatever he sees in Lucien's eyes. "Take him to the pit!" he cries.

How much time had passed since that day? Suspended by chains and caught in a never-ending wheel of pain, exhaustion, and shielding his knowledge of Dante from probing minds, Lucien had lost all track of time. He'd known what he risked in irking Gabriel, but he'd been unable to resist pricking the preening *aingeal*'s pride full of holes.

If his capture and punishment as Yahweh's murderer, and as the soon-to-be murderer of Gehenna itself, kept Gabriel from listening for a *creawdwr*'s song, for Dante's song, then every second of pain was worth it.

I guard our son, Genevieve, with all that I have.

But for how much longer? Sooner or later, Dante would use his gifts again. How could he protect his son while hanging above the pit's red-embered floor?

The alliance between Gabriel and the Morningstar seemed fragile and certain to shatter in time. Was there a way to manipulate that and earn his freedom? Otherwise he might still be dangling here like a jeweled pendant when that schism occurred.

Lucien yearned for the pale sky.

Pale, when once the skies had been cobalt blue, rich and deep.

Claws scraped furrows across his chest, while others tore at his bound wings. Pain flashed white-hot behind Lucien's closed eyes, and he cried out, the sound echoing within the cavern, raw and full of rage.

Wybrcathl trilled into the air, and the chittering *chalkydri* fell silent, the high-pitched *burr* of their whirring wings an agitated sound. One of the Elohim was descending, then, Lucien thought. A hot wind blew through his hair and across his face as the demons winged away into the pit's ever-night.

Ah, perhaps a moment's rest. A moment's sleep.

Fingers touched his face, gentle fingers, a familiar touch. "I never meant this for you," Lilith whispered. Her warm, amber scent cleansed away the *chalkydri*'s dry, musky odor. "You could've ended this torture by telling Gabriel about the *creawdwr*. He still doesn't know one walks in the mortal world."

Lucien opened his eyes. Lilith hovered in front of him, her black wings sweeping through the heated air; a red skirt draped her legs, a silver torc graced her slender throat, and her breasts were bare, her nipples rouged. Behind her, light shafted into the pit from above, illuminating dust motes and sparking bursts of orange flame from the smoldering rocks.

"You haven't told him?" he asked, voice hoarse.

Lilith shook her head. Long tendrils of glossy black hair drifted across her face. "Of course not. If Gabriel found out . . ." Her words trailed away. She looked down into the darkness beneath her feet, her expression troubled.

Lucien suspected he knew what she was thinking. "If Gabriel knew, he *would* chain the Maker to his will. Make him dance like a bear in a circus."

Lilith lifted her gaze. "Yes." Regret shadowed her face. "Gabriel yearns for the days when he was Yahweh's voice in the mortal world and humankind trembled at his approach. Yearns for the days of mortal worship."

"He dreams of power, as always," Lucien said. "So it wouldn't be enough if the *creawdwr* healed Gehenna and the rift between worlds was closed."

"No," Lilith agreed, her low voice sorrowful. "Not as long as Gabriel rules."

"Why tell me this? What do you want from me?"

"The *creawdwr*."

Lucien laughed. Laughed until tears filled his eyes.

Indignation flashed across Lilith's lovely face. "Do you think so little of me?" he asked, once the dark and bitter amusement had drained from him. "A week of torture at the claws of *chalkydri* and I'd just give you the *creawdwr*?"

"Do you think so little of *me*? I wish to keep this Maker *from* Gabriel."

"And keep him for yourself."

"And if I do? I suppose you think you're protecting him, but what happens if you never return to the mortal world?" Lilith's keen eyes watched him closely. "He's unbound. Untrained. Destined for madness, and he'll take the mortal world with him. And Gehenna. Eventually Gabriel *will* hear his *anhrefncathl* and find him. What then, Samael . . . *Lucien*? What then?"

Good question. And it galled him that everything Lilith had said was true. He'd hoped to keep Dante hidden, but had failed. In keeping the truth from his child, he'd not only earned Dante's fury and contempt, but had lost his trust. He refused to accept anything from Lucien, including knowledge.

Unbound. Untrained. Destined for madness.

Could he trust Lilith? An even darker thought circled endlessly through his mind: *Do I have a choice?* If it came down to Gabriel or Lilith, he'd choose Lilith. Gabriel had done everything in his power to encourage Yahweh's delusions. Had twisted Yahweh's words into something ugly among mortals.

He couldn't protect Dante hanging in the pit of Sheol, his wings banded. And, as if to underscore that thought, sudden song whispered into Lucien's heart, wild and clear and soaring, and iced him to the core.

Dante's chaos song. The song just as quickly faded, and pain brushed briefly against Lucien's shields.

Lilith tilted her head, her expression questioning. "Is something wrong?"

Relief flooded Lucien. "You mean aside from me hanging in space, bound?" She hadn't heard the song. Maybe only he had because of his bond with Dante.

A small smile touched Lilith's lips. "Aside from that, yes." She held his gaze. "I understood why you fought so hard for Yahweh; you were his *calon-cyfaill*. But why do you fight so hard for this Maker?"

"What did it take for you to reveal my name to Gabriel?"

Lilith's wings fluttered. "I offered it to gain his trust. I wanted him to believe that the only reason I fought at your side was to betray you. Like you once betrayed me."

"That I did," Lucien agreed softly.

Blinking, she glanced away. "Did you ever regret it?"

"At times, yes."

Lilith looked at him. Emotions danced across her face—resentment, sorrow, bruised pride—but her gold-flecked, violet gaze was steady. "And now?"

"We start anew."

"After thousands of years?"

"Absolutely. What else is there for us to do? We've both changed."

Lucien regarded Lilith for a long moment, remembering the trust they'd once shared, remembering their love and her honeyed kisses. But he also remembered her ambition. Perhaps that ambition could be used. Perhaps the memory of love, as well.

"His name is Dante, a born vampire," Lucien said. "He's twenty-three years old, and he doesn't understand what he is."

Lilith's eyes widened. "He's just a child! How could you leave him alone?" She frowned. "Did you say born vampire? *Fola Fior?* But how can he be a Maker?"

"He's my son," Lucien said quietly.

18

FOREVER SILENCED

Seattle, WA
March 22/23

ANNIE FINALLY SLEPT, CURLED up on her left side, just like she always had since she was little. Bending over her sister, Heather pushed a lock of blue hair away from Annie's face. The memory of an old promise—still as vivid as the night she'd made it—played through her mind.

Annie-Bunny, in her Tinker Bell jammies and clutching a plushie bunny, stands in Heather's doorway. She rubs her eyes with her fist. Tangled strawberry-blonde curls frame her plump toddler face. Mommy and Daddy are screaming at each other again, their voices scraped raw with rage.

"C'mere," Heather whispers, lifting the blankets.

Annie climbs into Heather's bed and snuggles against her. "Scared," she says.

Heather drapes the blankets over them both. "I won't let anything happen to you," she promises Annie, even though she's scared too. But Annie-Bunny's her baby sister, just like

Kevin's her little brother, and she'll always take care of them, no matter what.

Annie-Bunny snuggles closer, her plushie bunny a soft squashed lump between them. Her eyes close.

"Sleep tight," Heather whispered. Despite her promise, she'd been helpless to prevent all the bad things that had happened to her sister over the years.

It seemed like when Mom had died, she'd left a part of herself behind, rooted deep inside Annie, dark and bitter and self-destructive, a part that resisted all attempts to uproot it.

Maybe if Annie'd stay on her meds.

Heather walked from the room, leaving the door partially open behind her. She went into the kitchen and set coffee to brew. As it trickled into the carafe, she leaned against the counter and rubbed her face with both hands. She was exhausted—the visit to her mother's death site, the meeting with Rodriguez and Rutgers, her father, then Dante and Annie—and the day wasn't over, not quite.

And Dante . . . what else had that bastard Wells done to him?

Give me that name again. I can't read it.

Wells still needed to answer for his crimes, past and present. The victims of all those who'd died at the hands of the killers he and Johanna Moore had created and set loose upon society needed a voice, someone to speak on their behalf.

Dante had tried to speak for his mother, Genevieve Baptiste, the only way he knew how—through violence—but who had ever spoken for him?

And Dante's victims? Chloe and the Prejeans?

Heather's thoughts spun back to the tavern murders in New Orleans. Two dead NOPD detectives, three dead tavern patrons, bodies and building torched. She was afraid that Dante, heartbroken and fevered and lost to darkness after Jay's death, had spoken for him with blood and gasoline-fueled flames, his programming triggered.

She dropped her hands from her face. Cold fingers squeezed her heart. Programming that could be triggered again and again. But if she killed Wells . . .

She sucked in a sharp breath. She steered her thoughts away from that dark path.

Murder is murder is murder, no matter how much the person deserves to die.

And the murders at the Flying Crow Tavern?

Dante never tells or forgives a lie. When the time was right, she'd just ask him. Deal with it then.

One thing at a time. Just one thing at a time.

Heather poured coffee into her kitty-face mug; the aroma, rich French roast and fresh, normally tantalized her nostrils. But now, she wasn't sure she could even drink the coffee; her stomach felt like it was full of cold stones.

A little more work. Then sleep.

At the table, she set her mug down, the coffee untasted. She picked up a pile of the papers and reports that Dante had gathered. A photo slid out and fell onto the table. Placing the stack aside, she picked up the photo. The first known victim of Higgins, a young woman with a hard-drinking and easy-loving reputation, and a wistful smile. Heather carefully tucked the photo back in with the reports.

Higgins had forever silenced twenty-four women, including Heather's mother. Each one had been lonely and hurting, seeking warmth in a bottle of booze or a stranger's embrace or on a barstool surrounded by cigarette haze and drunken laughter. Most had been running from bad marriages, from uncaring parents, from themselves. Each woman had so desperately wanted to belong somewhere or to someone.

Just like Annie.

Annie's photo would never end up in a crime scene report, the victim of an anonymous killer. Heather wouldn't allow it. She rubbed the back of her neck and flexed her shoulders until some of the tension eased from her muscles.

Heather fetched her laptop from her bedroom and eased it onto the table. Once the laptop was up and running, she mulled over which search to begin first.

Search A: Who was SAC Alex Lyons and why had he been assigned to guide her on her magical murder tour?

Search B: What had been SAC Alberto Rodriguez's previous assignments? Why had he been chosen to head Seattle temporarily? And why had he been pushing so hard on the medical issue and Bad Seed?

Search C: Where oh where was the retired Dr. Robert Wells?

Heather typed in DR. ROBERT WELLS and initiated search C.

19

JUST BENEATH THE SKIN

Seattle, WA
March 22/23

DANTE WALKED ALONG THE sidewalk, listening to mortal thoughts, feeling drum tight. Neon from the strip clubs on both sides of the street flickered and buzzed–JIGGLES and GIRLS GIRLS GIRLS and LAP DANCES!–too bright, and he slid on his shades. The winking colors muted. He drew in a deep breath of air and smelled car exhaust, fried chicken, and brine from the bay.

Hunger pulsed through him, strong and insistent, but still under control, thanks to Von. He'd fucked up by waiting too long to feed, and he knew better, but his hunger for Heather had been stronger.

Hood up, shades on, he slipped past small clusters of people gathered in front of some of the clubs smoking and laughing, making deals–dope, sex, break-ins. Most didn't pay him any attention, their thoughts focused elsewhere.

Dante *listened*. But all he picked up were horny thoughts, horny and lonely and desperate thoughts, a few worried—*I'll just say I was out with the guys, took in a ball game, had a few beers*—and others challenging—*I'm an adult, I'll fucking do whatever I want*. Some thoughts were all business, flat and bored. *Hey, baby. Wanna date? Wanna blow job?*

A few of the clubs were closing, and cars trickled steadily from parking lots. Dante stepped over one of the yellow-painted parking blocks and walked through the nearly empty lot for HOT XXX BUNS. Several cars remained parked near the employee exit at the side of the building.

Dante followed the noise of two fast-drumming hearts, their rhythms overlapping and twisting into one thundering sound. In the darkness pooled in front of the exit, courtesy of a burned-out bulb, a guy in a windbreaker struggled with a woman, his hand locked around her upper arm.

"Let go of me!" she cried, trying to jerk free. Fury edged her voice, but Dante heard fear underneath. She swung her purse.

"Goddammit!" The guy dodged, then grabbed her bag and wrenched it from her hand. He tossed it into the parking lot. It hit the concrete, spilling its contents across the pavement. "I spent a helluva lot of money on you! You could at least be nice."

"I don't—"

Dante *moved*. He ran across the parking lot, breezing past the woman's purse, and stopped beside the grabby guy before the woman finished speaking.

"—owe you shit!"

The guy, potbellied but thick-muscled, scowled at Dante. "None of your business, asswipe. Get lost."

"Yeah, y'know what? *Fuck* you." Dante shoved the guy with one hand. Potbelly slammed into the building like he'd been fired from a cannon. He slid down to the pavement, expression dazed.

The woman blinked, not exactly sure what had happened, but when she noticed Potbelly was down, she ran over and kicked him in the thigh, then gathered up her purse and its contents. Whirling, she hurried back into the club. The steel door slammed shut behind her.

Potbelly groaned.

Dante leaned over him, twisted his fingers into the windbreaker's collar, and yanked the guy to his feet. He dragged Potbelly around the club's edge to the Dumpster-filled back lot. Hurled him against the building and pinned him there, hand to shoulder, thigh snugged between legs. Potbelly stared at him, mouth open, eyes dilated, and Dante realized his hood had fallen back.

"My God . . ."

Dante breathed in the mortal's adrenaline-and-lust-spiced scent, listened to his jackhammering heart and thought of the blood pumping through his veins. Just beneath the skin. Promising pleasure. Promising relief. Hunger uncoiled.

He shoved Potbelly's head to one side, before he could say another word, and tore into his warm, pulse-pounding throat with his fangs. Burrowed into his flesh.

And fed.

20

LET THE DEAD
REMAIN DEAD

Seattle, WA
March 23

*S*hannon staggers along the highway's edge, thumb out, peering into the darkness. She really has to get home. She only stopped for a few drinks while out on errands. The kids were at soccer practice or guitar lessons or Scouts, and she had a few moments to herself.

A few moments to concentrate on all the amazing ideas and thoughts and plans buzzing in her head like busy little bees that won't let her sleep. Light seems to fill the darkness behind her eyes at night, illuminating her mind, and working in cahoots with the stupid busy little bees.

Just a few moments to drown the fuckers and put out the light.

The next thing she knows, it's dark, and the moon's high in the sky. Her new friends try to talk her into staying and, for a second, she considers it. Then she remembers Jim saying: I'll take the kids from you, Shannon, I swear to God!

You need to pull yourself together. You need to get back into rehab.

So she pulls free of her friends' beseeching hands—C'mon! One more drink!—and escapes into the chilly October night. Car won't start and she can't find her cell phone. Screw it. She abandons the car, and decides to thumb a ride home. Probably will piss Jim off—he'll rattle more crime statistics until she blocks out the sound of his voice by humming to herself.

Sometimes she wishes he'd never joined the fucking FBI. She can't compete with that kind of love, that kind of devotion. He was like a priest, and forensics was his act of communion with the Holy Bureau.

October, and the air is crisp. But she's not cold, she's on fire and alive and flying. Heather's birthday is coming up. She'll be twelve. Twelve going on forty. She sees too much and maybe not enough.

Have I lost her?

Shannon stumbles, her heel catching on the asphalt's ragged edge. She giggles. Good thing she isn't driving. Point in her favor. She licks the tip of a finger and strokes an imaginary line in the air. Sliding off her shoe, she peers at the heel.

Headlights pierce the night. Shannon sticks out her shoe instead of her thumb, cocking her weight onto one hip and smiling. The headlights glow, twin moons filling her vision and dazzling her sight.

The car pulls over, tires crunching on gravel, the muffler streaming a plume of exhaust and the heady smell of gasoline in the air. The engine purrs.

Headlight-blinded, she wobbles as she tries to put her shoe back on. She hops backward before sprawling on her ass. She throws back her head and laughs. Good thing she isn't walking the line for a cop. Another point in her favor. She draws another imaginary line in the air. Slipping off her other shoe, damned heels playing havoc with her balance; well, that and all the booze, Shannon climbs to her feet, stumbling only a little. She's brushing the dirt off her hind end when the driver's door opens.

A man slips out of the purring car, and something gleams in his hand.

"Need help, Shannon?" he asks.

WITH THE SMOOTH IDLE of a well-tuned engine still in her ears, Heather awakened, heart racing. Light filtered into the room between the slats of the closed blinds. Rolling over onto her side, she pulled open the nightstand drawer and fished out a memo pad and pen. She wrote down as many details as she remembered: the car not starting; the lost cell phone; the cold, crisp air; the smell of pine and rain-wet blacktop; the man speaking her mother's name.

Shannon and her killer knew each other.

Heather stopped writing. *Wait.* This was a dream—only a dream. Not a glimpse into the mind of a woman twenty years dead. Just a dream, a recurring one that she'd had for years, not an interview with a victim.

Sighing, Heather tossed her pad and pen onto the nightstand and sat up. She wrapped her arms around her sheet-draped knees. Eerie was on his back at the foot of the bed, his belly up for pats. He watched her through slitted, contented eyes.

"Morning, you," she said.

Just a dream, yes, but one that was refusing to fade. She still heard the creak of the car door opening, Shannon's drunken giggles, still smelled cigarette smoke from the tavern. Just a dream, but one that'd dropped her deeply into her mother's mind, a dream laden with more details than ever before.

Ever since D.C.

Sighing, she glanced at the clock. The red, glowing numbers shocked her completely awake. 11:45 a.m. Shit! Jumping out of bed, Heather plucked her robe up from the chair and slipped it on over her PJs, belted it.

Ever since she'd been shot, she'd been sleeping later and later. She wondered if the shock to her system had altered her biorhythms. She'd never really been a morning person, but had learned to cope over the years, like most people in the human workaday world. Could Dante, while healing her, somehow have *changed* her? She went still inside at the thought.

Mantra: One thing at a time.

Drawing in a deep breath, Heather pushed aside her troubling thoughts, knowing she'd examine them again later and in more depth. She stepped into the hall and smelled fresh-brewed coffee, the welcome scent filling the house.

She paused in the hall, combing her fingers through her hair for several moments before she realized she was gathering energy, preparing for Annie.

But instead of moving forward, she closed her eyes, uncertainty and desperation twin spikes nailing her in place. *Could* she help Annie? She was running out of options, running low on hope. Sure, the truth about their mother might grant insight into Annie, but would it be enough to save her?

Shannon's bleak thought echoed within her: *Have I lost her?*

Heather opened her eyes. *No. I can't. I won't.* Shoving aside her doubts, she walked into the dining room. Annie sat cross-legged on the floor in front of the sofa, flipping through one of Heather's books on vampires— *While We Sleep*. A mug rested on the coffee table.

Annie glanced up. "Hey. Good noon. There's coffee."

Heather smiled and nodded. "Yeah, same to you. And thanks." Going to the kitchen, she pulled a mug from the cupboard and poured coffee into it, sugared and lightened it with half-and-half. Curling up on the sofa, she asked, "How you feeling? No hangover?"

Annie closed the book, and placed it back on the coffee table. She shrugged. "I'm fine." She glanced over her shoulder at Heather, her blue, black, and purple hair swinging against her face. "I'm sorry about last night, about all the stuff I said about Mom. Seeing those pictures . . . I mean, I never imagined . . ."

"I know," Heather said. "Nothing ever prepares you for the reality."

Annie's apology surprised her. Normally when she spun out of control, lashing out at everything and everyone around her, she'd pretend afterward like it'd never happened. Or excused it away as just being drunk.

"How do you handle it? Seeing bodies, I mean? Does it ever freak you out?"

"Sure, it freaks me out from time to time. And to be honest, I don't know how I handle it, I just do." Heather took a sip of coffee, then added, "I have to if I'm going to find out who killed them."

"But Mom's been dead for ages," Annie said, pushing her hair back from her face. "Why are you digging into it now?"

"Because I watched someone else speak for his mother and realized no one, not even Dad, had spoken for our mother."

"Who are you talking about?"

"Dante."

"His mom was murdered too?" Annie asked. She curled a lock of hair behind one ear, revealing the studs circling its rim, her face thoughtful. "No wonder . . ."

"No wonder what?"

"Nothing." Annie shook her head. "He's nothing like the other guys you've dated. Well, I mean, aside from the fact he's a freaking vampire."

"True."

"And he looks awfully young. You robbing the cradle? Or is he like centuries old?" Annie scooted around to face Heather. Sunlight glinted from the rings looped through her eyebrows.

"Thanks, thanks a lot, Little Ms. I'm-Twenty-six. Wait till you're thirty-one. He's twenty-three, so he's been out of the cradle for a while and we're not dating, anyway."

"Oh. Excuse me." Annie rolled her eyes. "Sleeping together, not dating."

"Okaaay, let's turn this conversation to you," Heather said. Eerie hopped up onto the sofa and, purring, graced her lap with his warm presence. She set her mug on the arm of the sofa and petted him, smoothing her palm down his silky, furred back. "So what's the plan? Is this just a visit, or are you seeking sanctuary?"

Annie's shoulders hunched forward, her body stiffened. "Fuck, I haven't even been here a day and you're already trying to get rid of me." Setting her mug back on the coffee table, she rose to her feet.

"Don't start," Heather said. "I'm not trying to get rid of you. You broke into my house and I want to know if you have a plan. What about your apartment in Portland? Are you moving here? What about a job? Your meds? Therapy?"

"Oh, I get it." Annie turned around, her hands clenched into fists. "Let's just lobotomize Annie. Make everything much simpler for you, wouldn't it?"

Heather picked up Eerie and placed him on the cushion beside her. "Quit twisting things around! This isn't about me!"

"Sure. Uh-huh." Pointing her middle, fuck-you finger at the carton on the table, Annie said, "That dead bitch is more important to you than me."

Fury pushed Heather up from the sofa and onto her feet. "Annie, stop," she said, voice low and tight. "Stop, right now."

"You only care about the *dead*! That's all you think about! Talk about!" Annie yelled: "Maybe if I died—"

Heather grabbed Annie's shoulders. "Don't say that!"

"It's true!" She knuckled a fist into Heather's shoulder. "What if *you'd* died, huh? What if you'd fucking died and left me all alone?"

Hot pain knotted Heather's shoulder, but Annie's words hurt worse than her punch; her words knifed Heather's heart and stole her breath. *What if you'd died?*

Heather wrapped her arms around Annie and pulled

her stiff, but unresisting body into hers. Hugged her tight. "It's all right. We'll figure it out. You know I'd never ditch you. It's just that things aren't safe—"

"Let mom stay dead, Heather. Let mom stay dead so we can be a family again."

Heather went still. She felt cold, like winter had awakened within her, gray and icy and stark.

I want us to be a family again. All of us. But don't dig up the past, Heather. Look to the future and let the dead remain dead.

Maybe no one's phone had been tapped.

She'd only told one person what Dante had done. She poured her secrets and confessions into Annie, believing that as keeper of Annie's whispered yearnings and manic desires, her sister wouldn't judge her. Believed their shared secrets strengthened the bond between them—sisters and survivors.

Glad that Prejean saved your life.

How many secrets had Annie bartered away over the years?

Numb, thoughts reeling, Heather held Annie, realizing for the first time just how alone she truly was.

21

IN THE DIRT

Damascus, OR
March 23

ALEX FINISHED BURYING THE remains of Athena's latest experiment, tamping the dirt in place with the back of the shovel. Sweat stung his eyes. He straightened, wiping his sleeve across his forehead and arching his back to work out the kinks. He sucked down pine-scented and river-cooled air to wash the stink of melted flesh out of his nostrils.

Leveling the shovel over his shoulder, he headed back to the cottage and the shower. After toweling his hair dry, he pulled on jeans and a black Inferno tee, one with flames licking up from the sleeve hems and the word BURN to the left of center on the chest. He laced his Rippers, shrugged on his hoodie, then followed the wind-through-the-trees rustle of Athena's whispers.

She sat cross-legged on the sofa in the front room's closed-curtained gloom, light from the laptop monitor flickering across her face, sparking in her eyes. Her lips moved as she whispered.

"I'm leaving for Seattle," Alex said, stopping beside the sofa. Blue light flashed across Athena's rapt face as she watched Dante unmake Johanna Moore yet again. He suspected she had that scene on a repeating loop.

"I'm leaving," he repeated gently, crouching beside the sofa. "Can I trust you to stay here while I'm gone?"

Athena nodded and her hair tumbled into her eyes. She brushed it back with an absentminded sweep of her hand. Blue light danced in her eyes.

"Stay away from Father. Which means you can't snuff Mother either. Promise."

"Promise."

"What do you *see*?" Alex asked.

"A night sky full of black and gold wings," she murmured. "The Fallen descend, setting the sky afire with their song. I see a woman balanced on a tightrope."

"What does this mean?"

"Ask Dante."

Alex grasped his twin's hand and squeezed. "Thena, will you be all right? You could always come with me."

She looked at him then, the glare from the monitor vanishing from her eyes. "I'll be fine, Xander." A small smile brushed her lips. "And you'll do much better in Seattle without me." She squeezed his hand back, warm and quick.

The circuit closed again and, for a too-brief moment, Alex felt connected and whole. Then Athena released his hand. Her gaze returned to the monitor. She touched the keypad and light flashed across her face again. Danced in her eyes. Her lips moved, whispered.

He'd lost her. Again.

Alex rose to his feet, opened the front door and left the cottage. The misty rain had stopped. Pale and ragged streamers trailed from the gray clouds, combing across the tops of the trees. A breeze smelling of pine and moist earth rustled through the trees, a soft sighing whisper.

Call me Hades.

A chill swept over him, goosebumping his skin.

Time was running out. Faster than he wanted to imagine. Faster than he *could* imagine.

Alex sprinted across the yard to the gravel driveway and his Ram. Rain beaded on the truck's ruby-red finish, glistened on the windows. Sliding in behind the wheel, Alex glanced at the floorboards.

The former shotgun satchel now contained everything he needed to restrain Dante. The iPod encoded with his father's instructions to Dante and a small, slim trank gun were in his hoodie pockets. As was something Father didn't know about and sure as hell wouldn't approve, a flash drive containing all of Bad Seed's history and Dante's past.

Just in case everything went south.

"Amen, brother," Alex murmured, starting up the truck.

DOWN IN THE DIRT, pine needles, and bugs, Caterina watched through binoculars as a tall, lean-muscled blond man in jeans and black hoodie climbed into a pickup. He backed the pickup down the driveway to the highway below and drove away.

Looked like Alexander Lyons had the day off, given the way he was dressed and the late afternoon hour. That left his twin in the cottage and his dying mother in the main house with his father.

"Wonder how long the son'll be gone," Beck said.

"Does it matter?" Caterina asked, keeping her attention focused on the expensive house nestled in the pines. "It'll only take me a moment to finish Wells."

"Yeah," Beck sighed. "Little Ms. Bad Ass."

"Keep your commentary to yourself."

"Got it. Little Ms. Bad Ass is working."

Caterina's muscles tensed, and for a moment, she held in her mind a very clear picture of herself garroting Michael Beck with her binoculars strap, imagined twisting it tight, her knee in his broad-shouldered back. And, for some reason, that image cracked her up. It was like a scene from a retro action flick full of cheesy puns and stiff dialog.

Ah'll be back . . .

The day she was reduced to strangling someone with a binoculars strap would be the day she resigned. And took up action flicks? Her resentment of Beck's presence eased. A deep breath in, tension out. A brief, heated conversation with her handlers at the Portland airport had gotten her nowhere.

I don't need a backup. Call him off.

Wells and Wallace are yours, Caterina, and yours alone. Beck is there if something should go wrong. Better to be prepared, than caught unaware.

Nothing will go wrong. Have I ever—

Beck stays.

And that had been that. Even though she usually

worked alone and preferred it that way, her handlers sometimes saddled her with a backup on assignments with multiple targets. Like this one.

Calmer, her pulse slow and steady, Caterina reviewed what she knew of the house's occupants:

Alexander Apollo Lyons: He'd taken his mother's maiden name in an effort, an apparently successful one, to carve a career of his own without any juice from his father's name. FBI agent, Special Agent in Charge of the Portland field office, thirty-five, six two and one-ninety, the younger twin by two minutes. His power climb through the Bureau had come to a screeching halt when his twin had become mentally ill and he'd transferred from D.C. in order to care for her.

Athena Artemis Wells: A noted clinical psychiatrist specializing in abnormal psychology, thirty-five, five ten and one-forty. She'd been overtaken by schizophrenia, or a form of it, at age twenty-five. She'd managed to function for five more years before her madness landed her in a lockdown ward, drugged and restrained.

Below, the house and the guest cottage beside it were quiet. Two more cars were parked in the driveway, a Saturn and a tarp-covered vehicle. The covered car was most likely Athena's.

Caterina's research had revealed that Wells's wife, Gloria, had been diagnosed with uterine cancer five years ago. She'd undergone surgery and radiation treatments. A year ago, Wells's receipts revealed purchases of chemotherapy drugs and morphine and other medical supplies, so it would seem that the cancer had returned.

Scanning the yard, Caterina saw no sign of a dog, or pets of any kind. Perhaps the Wellses weren't a cuddly kind of family. The smell of pine and wet grass filled her nostrils.

Had Bronlee sent the med-unit footage to Wells? Caterina planned to find out as soon as it was dark. Her mission that day was twofold: Clip Wells. Retrieve the missing footage—if it was in Wells's possession.

Several quiet hours later, the cottage door swung open and a figure stepped out. Caterina focused the binoculars on Athena Wells. Dressed in a stained lab coat and brown cords, she walked barefoot into the yard, leaving the door open behind her. She headed toward the main house, then stopped abruptly. She swiveled.

And looked directly into Caterina's binoculars.

Athena touched a finger to her lips. *Shhhh.*

"Christ," Caterina breathed. Her skin prickled. "She knows we're here."

"Impossible," Beck said. "She's a basket case. She doesn't know shit."

Caterina had the distinct feeling that *they* were the ones who didn't know shit.

Athena Wells looked away, then skipped the rest of the way to the main house. Opening the front door, she slipped inside. It closed behind her. A moment later, Caterina's handheld scanner beeped an all-clear on the alarm system.

It was down. Off or disabled.

Caterina watched the house for another half hour, feeling the tightrope stretch taut beneath her feet. "I'm going in."

"Roger that," Beck replied, finally in work mode. He touched the com bud tucked into his ear. "I'll signal you if the son returns."

Caterina packed up her binoculars and other gear, and started down the hillside, gun in hand.

WELLS SAT DOWN BEHIND his desk, resting the shotgun against it. A slide show of family pictures flashed across his computer monitor: Gloria in the surf on the beach at Lincoln City, the twins as towheaded toddlers, Gloria laughing. The deep ache in his chest eased for the first time in months.

Soon Gloria would be laughing again. In a matter of hours, Alex would ensure that S listened to the message on the iPod. Then S, beautiful and deadly, would spin into action and his assigned target, SAC Alberto Rodriguez, would die. Hopefully in great agony. And looking into S's pale, merciless face, Rodriguez would know who had sent him and why.

Once Alex brought S home, Dante Prejean would disappear forever. Wells would direct S to heal Gloria, to steal his beautiful Persephone from Hades's heated grasp once more, and restore to Wells his laughing bride.

A dark excitement uncoiled within Wells. He tapped his keyboard and the slide show disappeared. Scrolling through his files, he clicked on the one marked S and opened it. He relaxed into his chair as images filled the monitor.

Locked inside a rabbit hutch, the toddler, black hair curling at the nape of his pale neck, watches as his few toys are tossed into a debris fire one by one. Following Wells's instructions, the boozed-up foster parents tell the child that it's his fault his toys are being burned.

"You was a bad boy, you. Bad, bad, evil boy. All your fault, you."

A small plastic guitar melts in the flames. A ball joins it. But when the last toy, a ragged, chewed-up turtle plushie, is dangled above the blaze, the toddler tears his way free of the cage. Firelight glints on his tiny fangs as he snatches the turtle from his foster mother's hand.

"Shit and hellfire!" the foster father cries, then recovering from his shock, he grabs the toddler. The toddler's hand and the turtle clutched in the little fingers are shoved into the flames.

Let someone try that now, Wells mused. He scrolled forward through the file seeking other choice bits, other fond memories, then paused. Had he heard the front door open? An alarm beep-beep-beeped in a rapid cycle and Wells's heart slammed into his throat. His pulse drummed so fast his vision grayed. He lowered his head, gasping for air, thinking, *Lovely. All your preparations and you get caught gasping for air like a land-drowning goldfish.*

As he reached a shaking hand for the shotgun, the frantic beeping stopped. Locking his fingers around the gun, Wells grabbed it and strained to listen past his thundering pulse. After a moment, he became aware of a soft sound, like the whisper of the wind through the trees.

He exhaled in relief. Only Athena. He drew a still trembling hand across his sweat-damp brow. The whispers preceded his daughter down the hall, the words she was repeating over and over, becoming clear.

"Threeintoonethreeintoonethreeintoonethreeinto-onethreeintoonethreeinto one . . ."

But then a chilling question occurred to him—how

had Athena silenced the alarm? Not even Alexander knew that he'd changed the codes, not yet.

Still whispering, Athena walked into his office, her dirty, bare feet tracking mud across the pale carpet. She shuffled past his desk, her hands stuffed into the pockets of her spattered and stained lab coat.

"Athena," Wells said, tucking the shotgun under his arm and reaching for the psi blocker in his pants pocket. The whispers stopped. "What are you doing here?" He swiveled around in his chair.

Athena stood in front of his collection of Hellenic spears, shields, and breastplates. She plucked a spear free and spun around on the balls of her feet. Her Aegean eyes gleamed, a sunlit tide. Smiling, she yanked from her pocket the Taser he'd hidden.

The prongs pierced his chest. Electricity jolted through his body. Pain wiped all thought from his mind. His body twitched and convulsed and flopped onto the floor.

Through a haze of thrumming, heated pain, he heard his daughter's voice.

"I'm breaking a promise, Daddy," she said.

22

NOT MEANT FOR ME

Seattle, WA
March 23

SUDDEN SCRATCHING AT THE window in the front room along with an inquisitive chirp from Eerie caught Heather's attention. She looked up from her laptop. "You hunting moths, kitty boy?" Another thought flared in her mind: Nighttime. Dante. *First thing tomorrow evening*.

She pushed back from the table and rose to her feet, reaching for her purse and the .38 tucked inside in case it *wasn't* Dante crawling in through her fricking window again.

The window slid open, pale hands grasping the edge, then Heather saw a black-clad leg edged from ankle to hip with vinyl straps and buckles swing over the windowsill, and into the room, quickly followed by the rest of Dante. A hood hid his face, but not the lambent gleam of his eyes.

"Hey," he said as he straightened, pushing his hood back. A smile tilted his lips.

The sight of him caught at her heart. As always. Heather's muscles unknotted. "I could've shot you, you know. Why the hell don't you use the front door?"

Dante shrugged. Turning, his leather jacket creaking, he slid the window shut. He fingered the broken hasp. "I bought stuff to fix this."

"Do you even know how to use a screwdriver?"

Dante snorted. "How hard can it be? Slide A into B, twist. Could be fun."

"Sounds sexy, but where's the kiss?"

Dante puckered his lips and blew her a kiss. "Good enough?"

Heather glanced over her shoulder. "You missed, Cupid. But Eerie's purring."

Dante laughed. He nodded at the computer. "You find anything out? Like where to find . . . *him*?"

Heather shook her head. "Not yet. All of his Bureau records have levels of security like I've never seen. The last known address was in Maryland and it's five years old. I've tracked him to the West Coast, then he vanishes. I'm still looking, though. But I've made a few other interesting discoveries."

"Yeah?"

Heather hesitated. "You get into this with me, you'll be in the crosshairs, Dante. More than you are now."

"Doesn't matter. You were there for me, Heather. I'm here for you."

Heather held Dante's gaze. "It was my job."

"Nuh-uh. You'd been called back. Case closed. You stayed, alone, and without backup, to help me."

And she'd failed him. More than once. "I didn't do a very good job of it either."

"Yeah, you did," Dante said. He crossed the floor in quick strides and joined her at the table. He cupped her face between his hands, fevered hands, and she looked into his dark eyes, drawn into their unguarded depths. "You risked *everything* for me. You never gave up."

"Neither did you." Heather grasped his right hand and pressed it against her chest over her healed heart. Something chimed within her, triggered by his touch, and resonated from the palm of his hand to her heart and back, ringing between them like struck crystal, pure and clear and true.

Her breath caught in her throat, and for a moment, she thought she saw black wings arching up from Dante's back and sweeping around her.

Wonder lit Dante's eyes. "Listen," he said, lowering his face to hers.

Pulse racing, Heather tilted her face up and he kissed her, his lips as fevered as his hands, his kiss hungry and a little rough. As the kiss deepened, Heather thought she heard a song—wild and dark—its complicated melody weaving in and around the crystalline hand-to-heart refrain dancing between them. The song arced electricity through her heart, her mind, and sparked fire in her blood.

She hears a rush of wings.

All too soon, Dante ended the kiss and took a step back, his hands sliding away from her breast, from her face, and curling into fists. The song vanished. His jaw tightened.

"What's wrong?" Heather asked.

He shook his head, then trailed a hand through his hair. "How's Annie?"

Bewildered by his abrupt physical and conversational shift, Heather shrugged. "She's okay for the moment. She walked up to the market to get a pack of smokes."

"*C'est bon.*" Dante nodded at the table. "So what'd you find?"

"Pull up a chair," Heather said. "I'll show you."

Dante shrugged off his leather jacket, then the hoodie beneath it, and hung both over the back of a chair. He wore a long-sleeved mesh shirt under his black tee. White letters on the chest read BLOW ME. In his usual manner, he swung the chair around, and then straddled it. He folded his arms along the chair's back.

Heather pulled her chair around so she could sit beside him. She awakened the laptop with a quick tap to the keypad. A file appeared on the monitor and she clicked it open. A photo flashed onto the screen.

"SAC Alexander Lyons," Heather said. "Portland office. He's the one who accompanied me to my mom's death site. Spotless record, amazing test scores, exemplary field work. He transferred to Portland from D.C. about five years ago."

"Why?"

"An illness in the family. His mother had cancer, I believe."

"So how come he was asked to keep an eye on you, instead of someone lower in the food chain?"

"Good question," Heather said. "Near as I can find out, Rodriguez in Seattle gave him the assignment . . . oh, excuse me, the *request* to ensure my safety. And that's another interesting thing."

"Interesting how?"

Heather minimized Lyons's file and clicked open another. She scrolled through text for a few moments until she found the section she was looking for and highlighted it. "Read it," she said softly.

" 'William Ricardo Rodriguez, whose reign of terror as the Boxcar Strangler ended ten years ago when he was captured by federal authorities, died in prison while serving out multiple life sentences. He was killed by another inmate during a dispute. Rodriguez's father, FBI agent Alberto Rodriguez, had been instrumental in his capture.' " Dante quit reading and gave a long, low whistle. "Holy fucking hell."

Heather nodded. "Can you imagine? Not only is your son a serial killer, but you bring him in. Yet as amazing and tragic as that is, it's not the *interesting* part."

"Yeah?"

Heather held Dante's gaze for a long silent moment, then she said, "The next part might be hard, maybe impossible, for you to read. I'll–"

Sudden understanding lit Dante's eyes. "No, I'll read it," he said, voice low. "You take over if I . . ." He twirled a hand in the air.

"Okay."

Dante returned his attention to the monitor. " 'Years earlier, SA Rodriguez filed a malpractice lawsuit against Dr. Robert . . .' " Dante's voice trailed off. He closed his eyes and rubbed his forehead. "Hold on. Let me try again."

Heather reached over and squeezed Dante's arm. "You don't have to."

"Yeah, I kinda do." Dante opened his eyes and looked at the monitor again. " 'Filed a malpractice lawsuit against Dr. Robert . . .' " His voice trailed off again and he blinked several times. He glanced at Heather, his pupils dilated. "What was I saying?"

Heather stared at him, her fingers tightening on his arm. Cold panic crackled through her veins. "You were reading, do you remember?"

Sweat glistened at Dante's hairline, at his temples. "An FBI agent . . ."

"Look at *me*, Dante, not the monitor."

"Yeah, *d'accord*." Dante's dark eyes fixed on Heather, focused.

"An FBI agent, Rodriguez," she said. "He filed a malpractice lawsuit against the man you can't remember because that man had treated Rodriguez's son for an antisocial disorder."

"And the son became the Boxcar Strangler," Dante said. He pushed his hair back with both hands. His pale face was thoughtful, but pain glimmered in his eyes. "You wanna bet Rodriguez's son was part of Bad Seed?"

"It's a sure bet," Heather said. "Which would explain why Rodriguez asked an SAC like Lyons to accompany me. Anything or anyone connected to Bad Seed, like me and like you, Rodriguez would want to keep tabs on. And he'd want people he trusted to keep him informed, people with skill. He must trust Lyons."

She shifted in her chair and cupped her palm against Dante's face. "You okay? I shouldn't have let you read–"

"Nuh-uh, don't even go there. My choice."

"I'm going to make some coffee," Heather said, sliding her hand from his face and standing. "I'd offer you something stronger, but with Annie around, I'd rather not."

"Je comprend, catin."

Eerie bunted Dante's chair with his head, mewed. Dante picked him up and placed him in his lap.

"He's really taken to you," Heather said, walking into the kitchen. "I expected animals to be wary of nightkind, predator to predator, but so far, Eerie's proved me wrong on that account."

"Nah, I've never had problems with animals," Dante said. "Some nightkind do, but only the dickheads, y'know? I think it's because we're a part of the natural world."

Interesting thought. Vampires a part of the natural order. Heather spooned coffee into the filter, poured water into the coffee maker, and switched it on. Returning to the table, she sat down again.

Eerie was curled in Dante's lap, purring, eyes closed while Dante scratched under his chin with his left hand. He held a photo in his other hand. Heather took a quick glance—it was a photo of Shannon and James sitting on a floral-patterned sofa just before they married, before she'd been born.

Shannon had been captured in the act of planting a kiss on James's cheek, her hands with their purple-lacquered nails clutching his jeans-clad thigh. Her long red hair, teased into a retro-nineties stripper-chic bouffant, framed her face. A grin parted James's lips, and behind his glasses his eyes were closed. A lock of honey-blond hair had tumbled across his forehead. They both looked so young. Happy.

If Heather asked her father, would he even remember one laughing minute from twenty-plus years ago? Laughing moments slipped away, transient, light as a summer breeze; but tragedy was etched into hearts and souls, indelible, a lightning strike altering lives in a split second . . .

Your mother isn't coming home.

. . . forever.

"You look a lot like her," Dante murmured, voice husky.

"Maybe a little," Heather allowed. "Ever since she died, I've had dreams about her death, nightmares, I guess I mean."

Dante nodded.

"The thing is, ever since D.C., the dreams have become more vivid and detailed, but they don't feel like dreams. It feels like I'm seeing it all through her eyes. And last night, it was like I *was* Shannon Wallace." Heather paused a moment, then said, "Is it because of you?"

Dante carefully placed the photo of her parents on the table, then met her gaze, his own troubled and thoughtful. "Could be, yeah. If it is, it wasn't deliberate."

"I know that," Heather said softly. "I'm not trying to blame you. I'm just trying to understand it. Or maybe nearly dying triggered a latent ability."

Dante nodded. "That's possible too."

It was, but she'd bet a year's salary on Dante being the originator of the change within her. The real question, one that Dante couldn't answer, was: Had he woven any *other* changes into her while saving her life?

"How about you? Have you learned anything about your mom?"

"I had Trey search for info on her," Dante said. "We found nothing. Like she never existed. They not only killed her, they fucking erased all trace of her."

"There's gotta be something," Heather said. "She lived in New Orleans. Someone had to know her. Worked with her. Something." She caressed his arm, her fingers whispering across the mesh, feeling the heated skin and hard muscle beneath. "You might consider asking De Noir." The muscles beneath Heather's fingers tensed.

"No." Dante's gaze smoldered, his jaw tight.

"You look like her, you know," Heather said softly. "A lot. She was a beautiful woman. Black hair, dark eyes, warm smile."

Dante nodded and looked away. "Yeah, Lucien said so too."

Heather wished De Noir hadn't destroyed the Bad Seed CD documenting Dante's birth and his hellish childhood. Wished she had a picture of Genevieve Baptiste she could give Dante, a memory he could look at whenever he wanted, and keep. Wells and Moore *couldn't* have erased Genevieve's existence. Not completely. She and Dante would just have to dig a little deeper, that was all.

The aroma of fresh coffee drifted into the room. Releasing Dante's arm, Heather rose to her feet and went to the kitchen to pour coffee for both of them. When she turned around, Dante was walking into the kitchen and brushing cat fur from his velvet-and-vinyl pants.

"I can pour my own, y'know," he said.

Heather handed him a mug. "Yeah, yours is so tough to remember. Black."

He smiled. *"Merci beaucoup."*

"I want to thank you for last night," Heather said.

Dante looked at her, his pale face puzzled. "For what?"

"For picking up the mess, and for being so good to Annie, even when she was telling lies about you. I owe you an apology for that too."

"No, you don't," Dante said. "You owe me nothing."

"Yes, I do, Dante, I do," Heather said. "I gave you shit over kissing my sister and I had no right—"

"Shhh." Dante pressed his fingers against her lips. "Forget it." Leaning in, he bent and replaced his fingers with his lips, a warm kiss, lingering. She laced her arms around his waist, his earthy and intimate scent teasing her nostrils. Heat kindled in her belly, stoked a fire she realized had never died.

Looking into her eyes, he said, "Annie's home."

Heather heard the front door open, then shut. "Gotta love nightkind hearing," she murmured. Sliding her hands from his waist, she stepped past him and walked into the living room. Annie flounced onto the sofa and switched on the TV with the remote.

"Hey," Heather said. "I was starting to worry about you."

Annie rolled her eyes. "No need. I was good. I didn't drink or buy anything illegal, I—" Her words ended abruptly, her gaze sliding past Heather. Her eyes widened.

Heather felt Dante step up beside her.

"Hey, Annie," he said.

"Holy fuck," Annie breathed. "It wasn't the tequila and oxy. You really *are* that fucking gorgeous."

"Thanks, but I've been told. Ain't nothing I care about. Just so you know."

"You'd care if you *weren't* good-looking," Annie declared, settling back into the sofa, a sardonic gleam in her eyes. "Then every compliment would melt your heart and make you fall in love with the person saying them."

"Annie . . ." Heather sighed.

"Nah, she may be right," Dante said. "But, tell me, Annie, you know this *how*?"

Annie lifted a hand and flipped him off. Dante pointed to the words on his shirt—BLOW ME—and lifted an eyebrow.

"Yeah?" Annie challenged. She pointed at her crotch. "You first."

"Is this a new game?" Heather asked, pretending innocence. "How does it work? You point at body parts until someone misses and pokes an eye out?"

Annie stared at her for a moment, then said, "Y'know that might work as a drinking game."

Dante looked at Heather and amusement gleamed in his eyes. He looked happy and untroubled, relaxed. She liked seeing him that way, and she liked that she was the cause of it. Liked it very much.

She realized that she knew so many dark and painful things about Dante's life, more than he did, but she didn't know any of the simple things about him like his favorite color or his favorite band or what he liked to read or what size shirt he wore. And his birthday was coming up in . . . oh . . . twenty-four days.

Dante walked over to the table and set his cup on its cluttered surface. "I should fix your window before I head over to Vespers," he said, pulling tools and a lock kit from the pockets of his leather jacket. He headed to the window, Eerie hopping after him, then bent over the windowsill, twisting the screwdriver with precision.

Heather smiled. "So you *do* know how to use a screwdriver."

"Great for jimmying locks."

"Don't make me arrest you."

Dante laughed. "No ma'am. We've already been there, done that."

"Yes, we have."

A few minutes later, he'd installed the new lock. Eerie leaped onto the sill and mewed his approval. Grinning, Dante scratched the top of the cat's orange head. "Couldn't've done it without your supervision, *minou*," he said. Glancing at Heather, he added, "He's got a lotta grace for having only three legs."

"He does," Heather said. "The shelter I got him from said he'd been attacked by a dog. He survived somehow and it's never really slowed him down."

"Slow he ain't, eh, *minou*?" Dante said, giving Eerie one last pat.

Dante plucked his hoodie and leather jacket free from the chair and tugged both on, chains jingling. He slid the screwdriver into his pocket. He pulled up his hood, shadowing his beautiful face. Heather understood why he hid his looks, but it made her a little sad that he felt it was necessary. She walked to the window with him.

"So what do you want for your birthday?" she asked.

"*My* birthday?" Dante's voice was *what the hell* puzzled. His expression matched his voice. "What birth-day?"

Heather stared at him. "Didn't you ever have a birthday party growing up?"

"Nope, not that I remember. I just thought it was something not meant for me, y'know, like school and daylight." His voice was even and matter-of-fact—no big deal.

Anger flashed through Heather, a full-on wild-fire, scorching through her veins. Her heart pounded so hard, it seemed like her entire body shook with the force of it. Dante had no idea how old he was or when he was born. No one had told him. The bastards had stolen even that from him.

"Heather? You okay?" Dante's dark brows were knit-ted together.

She drew in a deep breath. Calmed herself. "Yeah, I'm fine," she replied. "Your birthday's on April six-teenth."

"Really? April sixteenth. How old will I be?"

"Twenty-four, Dante," Heather said, chest aching. "You'll be twenty-four."

"Yeah?" A smile tilted his lips, lit his eyes. "Good to know."

"You ever going to use the front door?" she asked as he slid the window open.

"Dunno." Dante climbed out the window. "Maybe. See you at Vespers, *chérie*."

23

TIGHTROPE

Damascus, OR
March 23

CATERINA PICKED THE LOCK, then eased the back door open. Slipping inside, she pressed her back to the wall. She scanned the room, a kitchen—refrigerator, butcher's block, wall oven, and stove. Quiet, except for the hum of the refrigerator. The smells of chili, hot peppers, and cucumber spiced the air.

Caterina crossed the faux-brick tiled floor to the doorway. A hallway stretched in both directions and a glimmer of light spilled from a doorway to the right. To the left, she saw light from the room at the end of the hall.

Caterina paused, tightened her grip on her Glock. The refrigerator clicked off and the sudden silence shocked her senses, like an unexpected zap of static electricity.

She touched the com bud in her ear.

"Here," Beck said.

"Keep sharp," she sub-vocced.

She had no doubt that Athena Wells had somehow

known she and Beck were on the hill, watching. Had no doubt Athena Wells had also shut off the alarm system.

Time to find out why.

Rolling the tension from her shoulders, Caterina stepped into the hall and listened. To the left, she caught a faint whisper, like a breeze rustling through the trees late at night: a female voice. A low groan, deep and male, cut intermittently through the whispers.

Staying against the wall, Caterina followed the whispers to the lit room at the end of the hall. As she drew closer, she heard the steady beep of medical machinery. Gloria Wells's room, then. Now she could just make out the words whispered over and over: *shewalksonatightropeshewalksonatightropeshewalksonatight ropeshewalksonatight—*

The whispers suddenly stopped and fear knocked an icy fist against Caterina's sternum. *Tightrope?* Drawing in a deep breath, she centered herself and pushed her fear aside. She whirled into the room. She went low and to the left, swinging the Glock up as she moved.

Caterina scoped the scene in milliseconds—two beds, only one occupied, one at either side of the room, medical equipment between, a chair, a man sprawled on the floor, a blonde in cords and a blood-spattered lab coat at the foot of one bed, a spear clutched like a walking stick in one hand, a gun or Taser in the other.

Caterina halted, gun aimed at the blonde, and straightened. "Athena Wells?"

She shook pale curls back from her face and said, "Once. I'm Hades now."

Lying in the bed, a thin and wasted older woman watched Caterina, her eyes narcotics-glazed but lucid. IV lines threaded into the back of one bruised hand. "Help me," Gloria Wells whispered. "My daughter's insane."

Understatement, Caterina thought.

She swung her gun around to the man on the floor, aimed. Taser prongs protruded from Dr. Robert Wells's chest and his head lolled to one side. Foam flecked his lips. His eyelids fluttered and Caterina caught a glimpse of rolled-up white. He groaned deep in his throat. A faint odor of piss and singed flesh drifted up from the floor. She wondered how many times Athena Wells had zapped her father.

"She's come to kill you," Athena said to her father. "But I won't let her."

Athena was wrong about that, but Caterina saw no point in telling her so.

Caterina's finger tightened against the trigger. But instead of pulling it, she heard herself say, "How did you know we were here?"

"I knew the *tightrope walker* was here."

Athena's words hung in the air, charged and potent. Caterina's skin prickled. She kept her finger against the trigger. She nodded at Wells. "Why?"

"I'm warming him up for Dante."

"Explain that."

"Xander went to Seattle to get Dante and bring him home. We're going to give Father to him."

Renata's furious words hissed through Caterina's memory—*Kill that one slowly, very slowly*—searing the strangeness of this encounter into her mind.

Wells had tortured and twisted an innocent child, a *True Blood* child, and murdered his mother. If anyone deserved a chance to kill this man, it was Dante

Baptiste. If she could give him that, she might earn his trust. Then she could take him to Rome and her mother. Caterina's pulse quickened.

She shifted her gaze to Athena. "When will your brother be back?"

Athena's sea-green eyes seemed almost translucent in the light. "As soon as he has Dante."

"Please help me," Gloria Wells whispered again, her words clicking from a dry throat. "My husband . . ."

"Is a monster," Caterina said, lowering the Glock to her side. But maybe the monster's wife was a victim also. She moved to the bed and handed Gloria a glass of water from the nightstand. Gratitude glinted in Gloria's eyes. Slipping the straw between her lips, she drank.

If Lyons didn't return with Dante Baptiste, Caterina could still kill Wells and fulfill this part of her assignment. She felt the tightrope quivering beneath her feet.

She tucked the Glock back into her shoulder holster. She stepped behind Wells. Bending, she hooked her arms around his shoulders. She glanced at Athena. "Grab his legs. Let's get him on the bed."

Without a word, Athena leaned her spear against her mother's bed and slid to her feet. She ghosted over to the closet, her dirty, bare feet soundless on the carpet. Pulling the accordion-style door open, she rummaged through its contents. A moment later, she turned around, a girlish smile lighting her face. She held up leather restraints.

"He used to put these on me back in the days when I was still his daughter."

"We'll use them now," Caterina said.

Draping the restraints over her shoulder, Athena

crouched and grabbed her father's ankles. Between the two of them, they managed to wrestle Wells's slack body up off the floor and onto the second bed. A few moments more and he was restrained at wrists and ankles. Caterina wiped sweat from her forehead.

"Do you know if your father received a package from Nevada a week or so ago?"

Athena glanced at her father, a dark smile twisting her lips. "Yes," she said and walked into the hall.

Caterina followed Athena, listening to the sound of her renewed whispers, down the hall to the faint pool of light and the room beyond, a well-appointed office decorated with spears, shields and breastplates—most likely Hellenic, given Wells's interests in all things Greek.

Athena led her to the desk. She bent over the computer and tapped her fingers across a couple of keys and clicked open a file. She stepped back. "There."

Caterina took Athena's place at the desk and glanced at the monitor. Black wings arched behind the back of the man—*man? No, Fallen*—who held Dante in his arms.

"Do you remember Genevieve Baptiste? My son's mother?" the fallen angel said.

Knees weak, Caterina sank into the chair, her heart pounding hard against her ribs, her thoughts whirling.

At long last, she learned what had become of Johanna Moore.

And why Jon Bronlee had stepped in front of a semi.

24

THINGS FALLING APART

Seattle, WA—Vespers
March 23

VESPERS REEKED OF SPILLED beer, clove cigarettes, and patchouli. Heather grabbed Annie's hand and held it tight as she steered her away from the gleaming brass and mahogany bar and into the sweat-soaked crowd jammed up against the rail in front of the stage.

Dogspit had finished their set and Heather was sorry she'd missed them. Annie had taken forever to get ready, changing clothes at least three times and fussing with her hair, but that was her little sister.

The crowd buzzed and chattered as people waited for Inferno to hit the stage. Goth princesses in velvet and black lace and fishnet stood side by side with cyber-Goths in PVC and fetish wear; neo-punks in Mohawks spiked in purple and red shoved against muscular misfits in leather and latex, their black-dyed devil locks hanging over sullen faces; a handful of nomads in road-weathered leathers stood off to the side, the black bird-vee tattooed on their right cheeks marking their clan as Raven.

Male and female, the crowd fought for places along the rail, anchoring themselves in place with double-handed grips and feet braced against the struts.

Heather felt underdressed in her Skechers, black jeans, and purple fishnet shirt pulled over a purple bra. Or overdressed, depending on who you were looking at, she thought as she sidled past a woman crammed into a black leather bustier and leather hot pants, flesh spilling over at both ends.

"Have you been to an Inferno show before?" Annie shouted above the drunken buzz. The pungent smell of pot curled into the air.

"No, first time I've seen them perform." Heather worked an elbow path through the crowd to a spot at the right of the stage, near the nomads, and behind the first phalanx wedged up against the rail. "Dante said he'd heard WMD," she shouted. "Said he thought you guys were among the fucking best."

"Yeah? Cool." A pleased smile curved Annie's lips. With heavy kohl around her eyes, glittering purple shadow on her lids and smeared across her lips, she was a sexy club beauty in her tight, black GRAVEYARD tank, black and purple crinoline skirts, fishnet stockings, and latex-strapped boots.

The crowd stirred as someone—tall, lean, and mustached—strode out onto the stage and waved for the lights to be lowered. The crescent moon tattoo beneath his eye glittered like sun-struck mica under the lights.

"Hey, darlin'!" Von shouted, striding to the edge of

the stage. He crouched. "Whatcha doing in the crowd? Dante has y'all signed up as VIPs."

Heads at the rail craned around to see who he was speaking to. Attention riveted on Heather. People whispered to each other.

"Hey, Von," Heather called to the nomad. "I wanted to see the crowd."

Von lowered his shades and winked at Annie. "This must be your sister. Looks sure as hell run in the Wallace family." He grinned wolfishly.

"Thanks," Heather said, and glanced at her sister. Annie stared intently at the fangs Von's grin revealed.

He jumped down off the stage and into the area between the stage and the rail. He motioned for people to move aside and, reluctantly, they did. "C'mere, doll," he said, motioning to Annie.

Chin lifted, Annie stepped forward and a path to the rail opened up for her as people shuffled to either side. Von slid his hands around her waist and lifted her to the stage as though she weighed nothing.

"Your turn."

Heather walked to the rail and Von slipped an arm around her waist and jumped onto the stage with her at his side. For a moment, she felt like they were flying.

Von led her and Annie across the darkened stage, past the shadowed equipment and speakers, to the curtained wings. Dante walked out, pale face lit, eyes gleaming, light glinting from the steel ring in his bondage collar. And Heather stopped, her heart in her throat, breathless.

Dammit. Gotta quit doing that. It's just Dante.

And that was the whole thing in a nutshell: *It's just Dante.* No one else like him.

"*Catin.*" He looked her up and down, appreciation lighting his eyes. "*Très* fucking sexy." He looked at Annie. "Hey, *p'tite*. You clean up good."

"Gee, thanks," Annie said, rolling her eyes.

Dante wrapped his arms around Heather. His latex-and leather-clad body burned against her. His hands slid up to her face and cupped it, his rings cool against her skin. He lowered his face to hers and kissed her. His lips tasted sweet, like black licorice, and she tasted alcohol. Electricity arced to her belly and between her legs.

"Glad you're here," he said when the kiss ended.

"Me too," Heather murmured.

"Geez," Annie said. "Get a room, why don't you?"

"*Tais toi, p'tite.*"

"Speak English, dork."

"Fuck you."

"That's better. Heard you were a WMD fan."

A smile tilted Dante's lips. Releasing Heather, he stepped back and gave his attention to Annie. "Yup. Y'all ever gonna get together again?"

"Maybe," Annie said. "Depends. You ever gonna let me put that collar to use?"

Dante laughed, but Heather sucked in a breath, stung, and whirled on her sister. "What the hell do you think you're doing?"

"Nothing. Just teasing. Fuck, relax!" Annie crossed her arms over her chest and a familiar, sullen look masked her face.

"He's . . ." Heather paused. What was she about to say? *He's mine? He's taken?* Was that true? Sudden heat warmed her cheeks. When had she made *that* decision?

"You're fucking blushing," Annie said, her tone incredulous.

A smile tilted Dante's lips. "I think I like it when she blushes," he said. Then he stepped forward and touched his forehead to Heather's. His hands settled on her waist, his fingers hot against her mesh-draped skin. Heated tingles rippled through her. "Anytime you want," he whispered. "I'm yours."

"Yeah?" she whispered back.

"Yeah. Leash optional."

Heather laughed, her embarrassment fading. She was grateful Dante hadn't asked her to finish what she'd been about to say. Especially since she still didn't know what she'd intended to say in the first place.

Dante lifted his head, his hands sliding away from her waist. He clasped her hand, his fingers folding through hers. He walked her and Annie backstage to the sparsely furnished greenroom. "C'mon, let me introduce you and Annie to the guys." Sticking his index finger and thumb into the corners of his mouth, he whistled—sharp and loud. All activity in the greenroom stopped. All faces looked in his direction.

"Everyone, this is Heather," Dante said, inclining his head toward her, "and her sister, Annie." He draped an arm around Annie's shoulders.

People nodded, smiled, waved and yelled *"Hey!"*

Dante directed Heather's attention to the easy chair and the person just rising from its sagging depths. "This is *mon cher ami* Eli," he said, his voice warm and low and affectionate. "We've been making music together for . . . how long?"

"Almost five years, Tee-Tee," Eli said. He was a blend

of bloodlines. Café au lait skin, almond-shaped jade-green eyes, tall and rangy, mid-to-late twenties.

"And over there in front of the mirror," Dante said, "is Black Bayou Jack. A helluva drummer. Kicks fucking ass."

Jack grinned. "A pleasure, *m'selles*, for true." His Cajun-musical tone marked him as another Louisiana native. His faux hawk had been transformed into a braided horse mane, the dark blond hair buzzed short at sides and back, the braids dyed deep cherry red. Black-ink stylized tattoos twisted around his neck and muscular arms.

"And over there, twitching to go out and triple-check the fucking equipment, is Antoine, the man who puts the funk and the sex into the bass."

"Hey," Antoine murmured, shifting his weight from foot to foot. Also in his mid-to-late twenties; dark brown skin, toffee-colored eyes. Topped by a sexy, untrimmed and natural 'fro, the last member of Inferno was clearly itching to get away.

Dante jerked his head toward the curtains and, flashing a smile, Antoine disappeared behind their thick velvet folds.

"Gonna go make sure things are set up right," Dante said, squeezing, then releasing Heather's hand. His breath caught. He touched his fingers to his temple.

Panic burned through Heather when she saw his eyes dilate. She reached for his hand, but he backed quickly out of reach. "You're hurting," she said.

He shrugged. "No big. See you soon, *chérie*."

But Heather saw his jaw tighten as he turned away. She looked at Von, but the nomad's attention was already fixed on him, brow furrowed. Dante slipped past the curtains and out of sight.

"Simone said his migraines were getting worse," Heather said.

"Ain't the half of it," Von said, voice low. "He's been having seizures, too."

"Seizures?" Heather suddenly felt cold.

"Keep it quiet for now, doll," Von said.

"He shouldn't be going onstage."

Von snorted. "*You* tell him that."

"I will." Heather turned and started for the curtain. Fingers latched around her arm. She jerked, but the fingers still held. She looked up into Von's serious face.

"Let him be," he said. "Now's not the time. You understand? Not now."

Heather paused, then nodded. "Okay. Not now." Von released her arm. She held his gaze. "But he needs help. He can't heal if he refuses to admit he's hurting. And I don't think he can heal alone."

Von nodded. "That's the fucking truth. What happened between you two, anyway? He's never said."

Heather hesitated, mingled regret and uncertainty pricking her heart. She drew a breath and said, "I saw him *unmake* a woman." Understanding flickered in Von's eyes. "He saved my life and I'll always love him for that alone, but . . . what do you know about True Blood?"

"Just a little," Von admitted. "I've only been night-kind for forty years and I ain't heard much because born vampires are fucking rare. I know they're supposed to be powerful and light-speed fast and brimming with magic. Hell, just take a look at Dante."

"Do the nomad clans know about vampires?"

"Oh, hell yeah," Von said. "But the clans see True Bloods as night elementals; y'know, as Nature's voice, avatars of the night." He shook his head. "But since Dante's also Fallen, he's something else altogether." He hesitated for a moment like he was about to say something more, but he shook his head again instead.

Heather had known that the nomad clans were mostly pagan, holding to ancient nature rites and worship, but she hadn't realized nightkind—vampires—were a part of the nomad belief system.

We're a part of the natural world.

"C'mon, let's get you and your lovely sister set up to enjoy the show."

"I'm looking forward to it." She glanced over her shoulder, and stiffened when she saw who Annie was talking to.

Midnite Purple dyed hair gelled to maximum bed-head effect, his lean frame draped in black jeans, biker boots, a vintage TV ON THE RADIO tee, and looking no older than sixteen, Silver smiled a fanged smile and chatted with Annie.

Annie shifted her weight to the ball of her foot and pivoted one shapely and booted leg back and forth while her fingers plucked at the edges of her short crinoline skirts. Her gaze was bewitched and dazzled, her blue eyes gleaming with desire.

"What's he doing here?" Heather asked. She'd never gotten a good handle on the enigmatic vampire while in New Orleans, had bristled at his knowing smiles.

"Silver's under Dante's tutelage," Von said with a

shrug. "An exchange student kinda thing among night-kind. Anyway, since Dante's responsible for him, he couldn't leave him in New Orleans."

"Ah, I see," Heather murmured. "Well, I don't want him messing with Annie."

A puzzled smile quirked at one corner of Von's mouth. "Funny. She looks old enough to make her own decisions, doll."

Ignoring Von's comment, Heather joined Annie and Silver, wedging her body between them. "This is my sister," Heather said to Silver, holding his gleaming silver gaze. His *amused* silver gaze. "Hands off. Got it?"

"Butt out," Annie said, her voice low and tight. "I'm twenty-fucking-six years old and more than capable of running my own life."

"Really? Since when?"

Silver opened his mouth to say something, then glanced in Von's direction and closed it again. Shrugging, he walked away.

Heather grabbed her sister's hand. Annie yanked free. "Quit treating me like a baby!" she yelled. Fire burned in her eyes. "I'm bipolar, not retarded!"

"I'm *not* treating you like a baby," Heather said, struggling to keep her voice level. "But I'd appreciate it if you'd quit acting like one. Silver's nightkind. I'm just looking out for you."

"Really? Is this another guy you're not dating, but want to keep for yourself?"

"No!"

"Oh. Okay. So only *you* can date nightkind? Is that it, Ms. I Have Everything?"

"Annie, no—"

"Well, y'know what? Fuck you!" Annie whirled and dashed past the curtains.

"Shit!" Calling her sister's name, Heather shoved the heavy curtains aside and ran across the stage after her. But Annie dove into the crowd pressed up against the rail. Arms passed her to the back. Dropped her. Her multicolored head disappeared from view.

Heather jumped down from the stage, ducked under the rail, and pushed her way through the crowd. The house lights dimmed, and the crowd roared. Heather found her way blocked by burly male bodies reeking of sweat and beer. She bounced up on her toes and looked for any sign of Annie, but a swaying field of heads blocked her vision.

The crowd surged forward, jabbing and shoving Heather with elbows and hips, and the roar intensified. Knowing she couldn't get free at this point, not as Inferno hit the stage, Heather turned around and resigned herself to watching the show.

ALEX SHOVED AWAY FROM the bar, plastic cup of Rogue ale in hand, and joined a group of idlers at the back of the crowd. Colored spots lit up the stage as four figures took their places. Fog machines churned pale, incense-scented mist into the crowd. Alex downed a swallow of the frosty ale, then twisted earplugs into his ears.

Hard-edged industrial music, a pissed-off wall of sound, slammed into the crowd, and Alex's heart pounded in time with the heavy bass throb. He fixed his gaze on Dante's lean, shadowed figure standing before a microphone at the front of the stage, his hands wrapped around the stand, his gleaming black guitar hanging at crotch-level.

Dante curled his hands around the microphone as he sang. His voice, low and simmering with rage, meshed with the music pounding through the club and up along Alex's spine.

"On my hands and knees," Dante sang, his voice a seething whisper. "For you. I'll crawl, on hands and knees, across shattered glass, over splintered hearts, nothing is left of us. Nothing remains. But to crawl. On hands and knees."

The music came to a sudden halt. But the crowd didn't stop hurling themselves against each other with bruising and skull-jarring abandon.

"Now that I've got y'all's attention," Dante said, "I've got something I wanna say to the nightkind in the audience."

Several people—male and female—shrieked *"I love you, Dante!"* A few laughed, thinking he was just doing a bond-with-the-audience spiel. Enthusiastic screams pierced the air.

Most had no idea that he truly was what their dark fantasies imagined: vampire.

And more.

"Everyone here came to enjoy a show, have a few drinks, and maybe get laid," Dante continued, his voice clear and strong, his rhythm Cajun-spiced. "If you're here for a different reason, if you want *la passée*, go hang out at a Smashing Pumpkins revival show or some other lame-ass gig and drink your fill. Touch anyone here without their consent and you'll fucking regret it."

A voice rang out from the crowd. "Is that a challenge?" More laughter followed.

A spotlight focused on Dante, lit him up with blue-gelled light. He slowly extended a middle finger. "Whattya think *this* means?" Then he lifted his head.

Alex's heart jackhammered against his ribs, a stunned and frantic tattoo. The sudden collective intake of breath that he felt, more than heard, told him that this preternatural beauty, this Medusa of heart-stopping loveliness, hadn't ensnared him alone. Lifting the plastic cup of ale to his lips, he drained it.

Light glimmered from the row of hoops in each ear, gleamed blue upon Dante's glossy black hair; slender coiled muscles; and that pale, breathtaking face—full lower lip, high cheekbones, kohl-rimmed eyes. He moved across the stage with natural and untamed grace.

"Crawl with me, on your hands and knees, for me," Dante growled, jerking the stand back up, rocking back, and pressing his lips close to the rounded microphone. "I'll kiss away your fears. If you crawl. With me. Fall with me. For me."

Every move of his tight-muscled body, every toss of his head, whispered sex. Promised dark pleasure. Hinted at willing, pale flesh. His leather pants clung to his thighs and blue light sparked from the ring on the collar buckled around his throat.

Dante nestled the curve of his guitar against his thigh as his white hands flashed across the strings and frets, his attention riveted on the searing music pouring out from beneath his fingers. His body moved with the music, booted feet sliding, stomping, bracing.

Alex realized as he watched Dante, unable to slow his pounding heart, unable to tear his gaze away, that Dante was dangerous in ways he'd never anticipated. Never would've believed possible.

Seductive. Irresistible.

"We'll go down together. I won't let you fall alone." Dante's low, smoky voice curled into Alex's heart and set it ablaze. "We're both to blame. Crawl crawl crawl . . ."

Alex forced himself to turn around and fought his way through the heaving, moshing, sweat-rank crowd, making his way outside. He leaned against the wall, sucking down fresh night-chilled air, Inferno's music vibrating into his muscles through the masonry. Alex pounded his fists against the stone until they bled, until the pain cleared his head.

Fury, blade-sharp and cold, cut into him. He straightened and pulled his Winstons and Zippo from his hoodie pocket. He shook a cigarette from the pack, jammed it between his lips, and sparked it up. As he smoked, a new plan mapped itself out, a way to conquer and control Dante after he'd seized him from Father and made the True Blood his own.

Alex would hurt Dante. Over and over. Long and deep and often. If Heather figured into that plan, so be it. And if hurting him in every way possible wasn't pain enough to keep Dante from spinning another sticky web of lust to snare him in—*and Athena? Would she be trapped the same way? Burning hot as a star?*—then he'd tell Dante the truth.

Cram it down his throat. Every last bit of it.

And let him choke.

* * *

THE CROWD JUMPED AND slammed to the music, smashed into each other, sweat and fists flying as those behind tried to dislodge those up front from the rail. The crowd handed along a girl in a latex dress and little else, Heather noted, over the heads of the venue's security guards and to the stage.

Eyeliner-streaked face glowing, she darted for Dante, but he stepped out of reach, still singing. Since her slow speed marked her as mortal, the odds she would ever catch him were nil, Heather reflected, unless he *wanted* to get caught.

Heather wasn't sure how she'd feel if Dante allowed the girl to touch him, kiss him, feel him up. The tightness in her chest at the image that particular thought created told her: *Not well, Wallace. Not well at all.*

One of the venue's thick-muscled security guards, his bulky torso sausaged into a yellow VESPERS T-shirt, climbed onto the stage, scooped Latex Girl up and tossed her back into the crowd. The crowd roared, but whether in approval or anger, Heather couldn't tell.

Dante whirled, so fast his movement was a blur, a streak of motion. The mike rolled across the floor. Then the security guard flew into the air, mouth open, eyes wide. The crowd parted, and he hit the concrete floor. Hard.

The crowd roared again, louder than before, and this time Heather had no doubt they were cheering Dante's violent action. Before Dante had stepped back from the edge of the stage, three other figures hurtled over the rail and the open-mouthed security guards, jumping onto the stage and whirling on Dante—nightkind fast.

The crowd yelled and screamed, unaware of what

Heather had just realized: Dante's challenge had been accepted.

A female in a PVC tank and velvet mini, her hair pulled back into a glossy black and red ponytail, swung on Dante, her fists blurring beneath the blue spots.

Dante was already gone when Ponytail's fists cometed one-two through the air. She nearly overbalanced when her punches didn't connect and spun around, confusion on her pale face. Dante tapped her on the shoulder and she spun again, fists flying. Dante ducked, straightening up right in front of her. He grabbed her by the shoulders, kissed her, then tossed her back into the crowd.

Stuck between a sweat-soaked burly guy in an IN-FERNO T-shirt and his equally burly and sweaty buddy, Heather watched, heart in her throat, hating the fact that, unless she was willing to pound on these two guys, watching was all she *could* do. She scanned the stage for Von.

Ponytail's companions—a male in jeans and an ancient Ramones tee, his hair a waxed and bristling Mohawk, and a devil-locked male in leather and latex— appeared behind Dante in twin streaks of motion. Mohawk's long-nailed fingers arced like knives for Dante's sides, while Devil Lock, fists clenched and lifted, swung around to face Dante.

But Dante was already going low and whirling, one hand holding his guitar steady. Heather caught only a glimpse of black hair and gleaming leather as he lunged, his movement so fast it was over by the time it registered in her mind.

Dante's left fist slammed into Mohawk, followed almost instantly by his right forearm into the guy's face.

Blood spurted from his nose. Seizing the dazed vampire by the shoulders, Dante yanked him in close and kissed him too. Devil Lock pounded a fist into Dante's ribs as Dante tossed Mohawk into the crowd, the other fist blurring toward Dante's temple.

Dante ducked and spun, slashing his fingers across Devil Lock's midsection. Blood sprayed into the air, glistening for a moment beneath the blue lights, a dark, jeweled mist. Devil Lock pressed his arm against his gut, his expression both pained and surprised. Dante reeled him in by the long strand of gel-slick hair hanging over his face, but before Dante could kiss him, Devil Lock jerked free and dove back into the crowd.

The crowd roared. Jumped. Pumped fists into the air.

Heather drew in a deep, relieved breath. She spotted the gleam of lambent eyes in the dark wings—Von, she hoped. She was worried about what would happen if ten or twenty more nightkind rushed the stage.

Dante licked blood from his lips, scooped up the mike, stalked to the edge of the stage, and screamed, *"Fuck you!"* Then he stepped back and resumed singing while the other members of Inferno thrashed their instruments—flying dreads, light-starred piercings, sweat-gleaming skin—pouring energy and heart into the music.

"I'm coming for you!" Dante screamed, neck muscles taut, bending over, the mike stand between his legs. He lifted his head, tossed back his hair, and his gaze locked onto Heather.

For one moment, music, wild and wordless, pulsed between them like it had in her kitchen, and Heather's breath caught in her throat. Dante's song. Beautiful. Lonely. Forsaken. She pressed her hand to her heart, to the healed wound that now vibrated beneath her fingers.

Dante straightened. Sweat trickled down his face. Black tendrils of hair clung to his forehead. "Nothing can stop me. I have nothing left to lose. I'm coming for *you*!" He screamed the last word, a long, drawn-out sound of animal rage.

Heather pushed and elbowed her way through the moshing, sweat-pungent crowd, fighting her way to the stage. Hearing the loss behind the rage in his voice, she struggled to keep her gaze on Dante's white face. She shouldered her way to the row behind the rail riders, knowing she wouldn't get any closer without drawing blood.

Dante knelt on the stage, holding his guitar against his side, his dark gaze on her face. Fingers and hands waved in the air, stretched toward Dante. Voices screamed.

"I dream of you, in the dark," he sang, voice strained. "Taste you. Smell you. Feel you burning inside me. I stand beneath your window and watch you sleep."

Dante touched several of the hands waving in the air, his own trembling. He rose effortlessly to his feet, swung his guitar around, and then stumbled. Heather tried to shove closer, but the tight press of bodies held her back.

Dante fell to his knees. The mike tumbled from his fingers and feedback squeal reverberated through the club. The other members of Inferno stopped playing with a hesitant strum of chords.

A tremor shook Dante's body. He keeled over to the floor, his limbs locked, back arching. Heather fought and pummeled her way to the edge of the crowd. She caught a glimpse of blurred movement—Von running in from the wings. He dropped to his knees beside Dante's convulsing body, unstrapped his guitar, and tossed it aside.

Ducking under the rail, Heather dashed up the short flight of stairs leading to the stage and ran across the wood floor. The spots had been dimmed, and voices buzzed and whispered and shouted out on the floor. The other members of Inferno semicircled around Dante and Von, blocking them from view in an effort at privacy. Eli looked up, then stepped forward as if to block her.

"Now's not good—"

As Heather tensed to duck and dodge, she heard Von's voice. "Let her through." She brushed past Eli as he stepped aside. She stopped beside Von, then knelt. The nomad held Dante's convulsing body, his face grim. Blood trickled from Dante's nose and across his foam-flecked lips, spattered the wood floor.

"What can I do to help?" she asked.

Without taking his gaze from Dante's pale face, Von said, "In the greenroom's a black zippered bag. Get it."

Jumping to her feet, Heather slipped between Jack and Antoine and pushed past the heavy curtains. She scanned the room, spotting the bag tucked into the side of the easy chair. Grabbing it, she raced back across the stage.

Her relief vanished when she saw that Dante was still convulsing. His booted feet pounded holes in the stage floor. His body arched and twisted and jerked with a speed and violence that left Heather's mouth dry.

She dropped to her knees beside Von. "Now what?" she asked.

"Get one of the hypes outta the bag and fill it to the brim with morphine," Von grunted, struggling to hold onto Dante. "In the vials," he clarified.

Heather stared at him, heart pounding. "To the brim?"

"It won't do nothing but ease him into sleep," Von said, voice tight. "But do it *now*. This seizure's gonna fuck him up if it goes any longer. Gonna fuck me up too."

Heather unzipped the bag. Syringes and vials of morphine were neatly tucked into slots. She pulled a syringe free, flicked the cap off the needle tip and stabbed the needle into one of the vials, sucked in as much painkiller as it would hold. She squirted a little out to eliminate air bubbles.

"In the neck," Von said. "I can't let go of him."

With a deep breath to steady her hand, Heather jabbed the needle into the vein in Dante's taut throat and pressed the plunger. Syringe emptied, she withdrew the needle and dropped the syringe on the floor. A few seconds later, Dante's thrashing limbs and twisting body went still and he slumped within Von's embrace.

Heather sighed, and closed her eyes in relief. Her pulse pounded in her temples.

"Fuck," the nomad breathed. "Holy fucking hell."

Heather opened her eyes and looked at Von. Sweat beaded his forehead. His fight-scarred knuckles unclenched as he relaxed his hands. "How often does this happen?" she asked.

Von shook his head. "Too often."

The blood trickling from Dante's nose slowed. His eyes fluttered half-open, the pupils ringed by a slim circle of darkest brown. His gaze focused on Von's face. "What's up, *mon ami*?" he slurred, his voice opium-thick and dreamy.

"Not you, man," Von said, pushing Dante's hair back from his sweaty forehead. "You decided to take five on the floor."

"J'su pas fou de ça," Dante murmured, eyes closing.

"You okay?"

Von chuckled. "Fuck, yeah, I'm fine. It's you I'm worried about."

Dante's eyes opened again. "I didn't hurt no one, did I?"

"No."

"Heather." Dante shoved at Von's arm, trying to get up.

"Here," Heather said. "Dante, I'm right here." Leaning forward on her knees, she cupped his pale face between her hands. He burned, fevered. His gaze shifted to her face and a smile brushed his blood-smeared lips. "Thought I'd lost you," he said.

"You're gonna have to try a little harder if that's your plan," she said.

"It's quiet, *chérie*."

"I'll be right here," she whispered.

Dante's eyes shuttered closed and his breathing dropped into a low, barely perceptible nightkind rhythm as false Sleep claimed him.

Heather slid her hands away from his hot, smooth-cheeked face and knotted them on her thighs. He looked peaceful held in Von's arms, drugged and dreaming, his dark, thick lashes curving up from his pale face. Peaceful. Yes.

An illusion.

She'd heard the dread in his voice, the near panic as he'd asked, *I didn't hurt no one, did I?* She knew why he'd asked that question, even if he didn't, and her chest ached as she remembered the look on his face, the raw anguish in his voice when he'd seen Chloe, his little Winnie-the-Pooh princess, snow-angeled in a pool of her own blood.

"Eli, man, Dante's done." Von cradled Dante against his chest and rose to his feet in a fluid, easy movement. "Tell 'em the show's over."

Shouts of *"Inferno! Inferno!"* built as the crowd shifted restlessly. A few laughed, delighted, as if the front man's seizure had been part of the show and, Heather realized, some of them probably hoped it was. Or thought Dante was faking, though how a person could fake the muscle-and-tendon-torquing convulsions Dante'd just endured was beyond her.

Heather gathered up the syringe and vial and placed them back inside the bag. Zipping it shut, she tucked it under her arm and stood.

Von's gaze skipped from Eli to Jack to Antoine. "Y'all stick with Silver and avoid other nightkind. Dante pissed the fuckers off and they just might cause a ruckus now that he's down."

Eli nodded, gathering his dreads together in both hands, his expression worried. "Silver isn't here," he said quietly.

"He chased after Heather's sister," Jack volunteered.

Heather stiffened, suddenly cold. "He followed Annie? I need to find—"

"Hold on," Von murmured, his gaze turning inward for a moment.

Heather realized he was seeking contact with the missing vampire. She swiveled, searched the crowd for any sign of Annie's blue-purple-black tresses or Silver's gleaming eyes, but too many people filled the small venue. She sighed. Annie was a big girl, like Von had pointed out, but . . . she turned back around and met Von's steady gaze.

"Did you reach Silver?" she asked, tapping a finger against her temple.

"Let me get Dante settled," he said, nodding his head toward the curtain.

Heather followed the nomad backstage as Eli announced that the show was over due to circumstances beyond their control. Shouts winged into the air like angry wasps. Even though the show had been going for over an hour when Dante collapsed, Eli said refunds would be available.

Von eased Dante onto a worn, stained sofa. Strands of black hair slid across Dante's face, partially veiling it. One arm hung off the sofa, his hand brushing the floor. The nomad tucked Dante's arm against his side, then gently patted his cheek. "Sleep tight, little brother," he murmured.

Then he turned and looked at Heather. "Silver's with your sister," he said. "They're okay. But she ain't in no mood to come back."

"Dammit." The sinking feeling in Heather's gut told her that her sister was out drinking with Silver, drinking, doping, fucking—whatever helped her fill the void swallowing her up inside.

I want us to be a family again.

Heather could hit the streets and search the bars, but she knew from bitter experience that it wouldn't do any good. Annie would refuse to leave and would create a huge, screaming scene that'd end with someone jailed or hospitalized. All she could do was go home and wait.

"Look, doll, she's okay," Von said. "Silver knows how to deal with troubled mortals, and he won't hurt her."

"What does he know about troubled mortals?"

"He used to be one."

"She's bipolar," Heather said. "Not just troubled."

"I'll let him know."

Heather nodded, feeling like she had no other choice. The thought of the night ahead, waiting sleeplessly for Annie to come home drunk and hostile, or bruised and bleeding from a drunken brawl, or waiting for the phone to ring, left her tensed. She glanced at Dante. Maybe she should stay with him. Talk to him.

And if Annie needed her in the meantime? Got arrested again? Sighing, Heather knelt beside the sofa and kissed Dante's lips, tasted amaretto underneath the tang of his blood. His face still felt fevered, but at least the nosebleed had stopped.

"Where are you guys staying?" she asked, glancing over her shoulder at Von. "In a hotel or on the bus?"

"Hotel. The Red Door."

A sudden thought occurred to Heather. Maybe she wouldn't have to just sit and wait, unable to focus on anything but the anxiety coiling through her body.

"My house isn't huge, but I've got a sofa, two beds, and a very comfy recliner," she said. "How about you guys come and stay the night with me? In case there's more trouble."

Von stroked the sides of his mustache with thumb and forefinger thoughtfully. "Let me ask the guys," he said. "I'm gonna help 'em pack up and stow the gear first, okay?"

Heather nodded. "Fair enough."

Von reached inside his leather jacket, then slipped out a pistol. He handed it to Heather. She examined it, checked the safety, then checked the sights. It lined up beautifully. A Browning Hi-Power. She'd left both her purse and .38 at home, knowing how easy it would be to lose both jammed in the middle of a club crowd.

"Nice," she said, hefting it in her hand.

"Just in case the Seattle crew cause any problems. Aim for the—"

"Head or heart," she finished.

Von grinned. "You got it, darlin'." Then he walked away.

Heather got up from the floor and perched on the arm of the sofa farthest from the curtains. Her fingers wrapped around the Browning's grip. Her pulse was steady and her breathing relaxed. She couldn't explain it, but she felt like she was right where she needed to be, protecting a friend.

Just a friend? No, Dante was more than that—how much more, she wasn't sure. But whenever she imagined life without him, she felt hollow inside.

If the Bureau *was* keeping a watch on her, their suspicions would be confirmed when Dante and his band arrived at her house. Would they simply rescind the job offer or spin their threats into reality? She voted for possibility B.

Run from me. Run as far as you can.

Too late, she thought. Much too late.

25

NOTHING IS WHAT IT SEEMS

Damascus, OR
March 23

"**A**BOUT TIME," BECK SAID, climbing to his feet as Caterina hiked up the hill. "I was beginning to worry. What took so fucking long?"

"Sorry," Caterina said. "The daughter was still up. I waited."

"I was thinking I should do Wallace and make you wait in the dark and the dirt for a change. See how you like it. But we don't need to worry about her since the orders just changed." Beck bent and gathered up the blanket. "You got off easy, Ms. Bad Ass."

Caterina looked at him. "Changed? How?"

"They want her bagged and brought in, so they've sent Norwich and Shep."

"Brought in? Why?"

Beck straightened, the blanket draped over his arm, and looked at her for a long silent moment. "How the hell would I know?" he finally said. "When did you start asking why?"

"Right now," Caterina said.

"Well, knock it off and let's hit the fucking road," Beck said. "I'm hungry and I'm tired and I have a zillion bug bites." He started down the other side of the hill toward their rented Mazda.

Caterina drew in a deep breath of pine-scented air and lifted the Glock. "Beck."

Beck turned around and his eyes widened. The blanket fluttered to the ground. His fingers locked around the grip of the Colt in his shoulder holster. She aimed. The moment stretched, time suddenly elastic and streamlined. Their eyes met.

Beck yanked the Colt free of its holster. Caterina squeezed the Glock's trigger. The bullet hit Beck between the eyes, and he was dead before his body crumpled to the ground and rolled down the hill.

Lowering the gun, heart triple-timing, Caterina closed her eyes and stepped off the tightrope.

THE VAMPIRE NOMAD STRODE out from behind the curtain and onto the stage, joining the Inferno members already tearing down and packing up their equipment. Sheridan moved, climbing up the side steps and sidling along the curtain's faded edge. He slipped behind it. Then froze.

Dante Prejean was stretched out on a well-worn sofa, unconscious, black hair half-hiding his pale face. Perched on the sofa's arm, a beautiful red-haired woman lifted a gun in a steady two-handed grip and aimed.

"Turn around and walk away," Heather Wallace said quietly.

Sheridan had no doubt that she'd pull the trigger if he didn't comply. His mind raced almost as fast as his pulse. *Wallace is guarding a fucking vampire.*

For one heart-pounding, crystal-clear moment, Sheridan envisioned shooting Wallace, then Prejean, but knew he'd never have time to kill the bastard properly before someone—the nomad, one of the mortal band members, a groupie—wandered backstage.

Forcing a smile, Sheridan lifted a conciliatory hand, showed the digital camera in his other hand. "I'm with *Spin* magazine," he said. "Just hoping for some candids."

Wallace didn't return the smile. Didn't lower the gun. Didn't say squat. Sheridan backed away, hand still lifted, then slipped past the curtain. He didn't breathe easy again until he was outside.

He crossed the parking lot, sidestepping the puddles and ignoring the cold rain trickling down his face. Time to return to his original plan, which had been to follow Prejean to his hotel, then wait for daylight to snuff him; but the seizure had seemed like a perfect opportunity.

Live and fucking learn.

As for the lovely and treacherous Heather Wallace, he'd hoped to warn her, but she was beyond redemption. Cortini could have her.

ALEX STOOD OUTSIDE VESPERS and kept watch on Inferno's bug-spattered tour bus. Shaking another cigarette from his nearly empty pack of Winstons, he stuck it between his lips and lit it, hands cupped around his Zippo. He breathed in the smoke, felt the nicotine rush through his veins.

The show had ended early and, according to the buzzing conversations swelling around him, it became clear that something had happened to Dante. Some whispered *overdose;* others whispered *seizure.* Alex wondered if something dark and deadly and hungry had awakened within the young vampire and knocked him on his ass.

Most of the people who'd been hanging out near the bus hoping for a photo, an autograph, or maybe a quick fuck had dispersed when the nomad vampire in his Nightwolf leathers had strolled outside and squelched their hopes.

No photos. No autographs. No fucks, quick or otherwise. Dante was down for the count, but he'd make it up to his fans later, that was a promise.

Inferno's fans had lingered for a moment longer in the rain-damp parking lot as if they thought the nomad would laugh, say it was just a joke, that Dante was actually waiting to see each and every one of them with the intention of fulfilling their wettest dreams.

When that didn't happen, they finally gave up and wandered away, their makeup-streaked faces disappointed. Quite a few were discussing Dante's "drug overdose" in heated tones as they passed Alex, trailing the pungent nostril-pinching aromas of patchouli and sweat.

Alex sucked in one last drag from his cigarette, then flicked it into the gutter. It looked like the opportunity to talk to Dante was growing slimmer with each passing moment. He'd planned to pose as a fledgling musician

with a Inferno tribute song on his iPod and ask Dante—
Oh, would you, please? It'd mean so much to me!—to listen.
The only possible hitch would've been Heather, but he
could've worked his way around her.

Time to improvise. He'd follow the band to wherever they were staying, bide his time, and hunker down
until twilight. Then he would knock on Dante's door.

Better let Father know about the delay.

Alex leaned against the building, stone gritting beneath his shoulders, and pulled his cell from his hoodie
pocket, his fingers brushing against the iPod's slender
shape. For a moment, he thought he'd punched the
wrong button when Athena answered the phone and on
the first ring, no less.

"The tightrope walker wants to talk to you," she
said.

Alex stood up straight, pulse double-timing. "Who?
Athena, what's going—"

"Your sister's safe." An unfamiliar female voice
curled into his ear. "But I have the muzzle of my gun
against your father's temple." The SB's assassin's tone—
and Alex had no doubt that's who she was—was low and
level, reciting facts. "I can pull the trigger and walk away
or I can holster my gun, for the time being. It depends
on how you answer the next question."

"BOB? SWEETHEART?"

Wells shifted his gaze from the artfully textured
ceiling—*like whirls of cake frosting*—and looked at his wife.
All the little glowing lights that displayed Gloria's vitals
beeped and blipped, a steady and reassuring sound.

"How on earth did *Athena* get the drop on you?" Gloria asked, her voice as parchment thin as her fragile skin.

Wells managed a rueful chuckle. "I planned for the SB, I planned for a coup d'etat from Alexander, but I never planned on our daughter."

Leather creaked as Wells twisted his wrists once more, testing for any hint of slack. And, as with each prior attempt, he found none. How long since Athena and the other woman—*a killer, an assassin, but one who hadn't pulled the trigger . . . yet*—had left the room? An hour, perhaps.

"Bob?"

"I'm listening, honey."

"Alexander probably instructed Athena. This *is* his coup d'etat."

Wells frowned. That made no sense. "No," he said. "Alexander would wait until after he'd learned how to wield S. He'd want to look in my eyes as he twisted the knife. No. Athena acted on her own."

"Alexander the Great had his father assassinated."

A familiar argument. Even now, with Gloria dying in one bed and himself strapped to another, they still disagreed on one point of history. Wells sighed. "He had nothing to do with King Philip's death. It would be complete foolishness for Alexander, *our* Alexander, to kill me before I've passed on my knowledge. It'd be—"

"Insane," Gloria finished flatly. "Didn't I warn you to put the twins down the moment Athena started slipping? Her madness is Alexander's madness. I warned you, sweetheart, I warned you."

"You did. But I still think Alexander had nothing to do with this."

Beeping and blipping. The creak of the straps. His wife's fretful silence.

"Is the syringe still under your pillow?" Wells asked. Neither Athena nor the assassin would be expecting an attack from Gloria.

"Yes."

"Get it. Keep it in your hand." Wells watched as his wife weakly fumbled a hand beneath her pillow. "Careful." She pulled her hand free, the syringe clutched in her palm. She offered her husband a faint smile.

Wells smiled back. "Good. Keep strong."

Gloria tugged the cap from the needle's end and angled the syringe toward the inside of her arm. The syringe slipped from her grasp and her fingers frantically patted the blankets, searching for it.

Wells stared at her, mute and motionless. Cold iced him from the heart out, rimed his soul. "No," he whispered finally. "Not for *you* . . ."

"Your heart is and always will be your undoing," Gloria said, her voice tender.

"Alexander will bring S. The boy can heal! He can remake you—"

"Bobby, please. I'm so tired. Let me go."

Gloria's searching fingers discovered the syringe and closed around it. She looked at Wells, a relieved smile on her lips, lips that had once known his own so well.

S could save Gloria, he *knew* it; felt it bone deep.

A soft sound breezed into the room, snaking around all the beeping and blipping, a sound like the wind in the trees.

"Welcometohellwelcometohellwelcometohell welcometohellwelcometohell . . ."

Wells's heart thundered in his chest. Gloria's eyes widened and she yanked up the syringe, but it flew from her shaking fingers and bounced onto the carpet.

"No," she moaned. She grabbed the bed railing and pulled herself over to the side of the bed. Teeth gritted, sweat already beading her forehead, she reached a trembling hand to the floor.

"Welcometohellwelcometohell." Athena stepped into the room, spear in hand.

Gloria's fingers scrabbled for the syringe, but it was just out of her reach.

"Athena," Wells said, struggling to keep his voice calm, hoping to distract his smiling daughter, "has your brother called? Does he know what you're doing?"

Athena ignored him. She stepped between the beds, bent and picked up the syringe. "Drop something?" Straightening, she fixed her wild, Aegean gaze on Gloria.

"Athena, sweetie, listen to me—"

"Shut up, Daddy."

Gloria hauled herself back up and sank into the pillows, gasping. Athena sauntered to the chair beside the door and propped the spear against it. Wells breathed a little easier with the weapon out of his deranged daughter's grasp.

"Athena, child, Father never helped you, but I will," Gloria said, her voice breathless, but steady. "I've always fought for you. You've always been my favorite."

Yes, Wells thought, that approach might work. Bad parent–good parent.

"Call me Hades," Athena said, turning around to face her mother again. Her smile vanished and her eyes darkened. She dropped the syringe into her lab-coat pocket. Returning to the bed, she yanked one of the pillows out from under Gloria's head. Pressed it over her mother's face.

"Welcome to hell," Athena whispered.

Wells screamed.

26

THE LINE BEGINS TO BLUR

Seattle, WA
March 23/24

V ON CARRIED DANTE INTO Heather's room and
eased him onto the bed. Dante never stirred. "Are
you sure he's okay?" Heather asked, dropping Dante's
travel-worn duffel bag on the floor beside the bed.

"Yeah," Von replied, brushing Dante's hair back
from his face. "Pretty sure."

"Pretty sure? What does that mean?"

The nomad shrugged, leather jacket creaking. "We
just pumped him full of morphine, doll. He's as good
as the need to do that implies."

Heather bit her lip, then nodded. "Gotcha."

Von bent, his fingers working the straps on Dante's
boots.

"I'll do that," Heather said. "You go get the guys
settled. There are blankets and towels in the hall closet.
And there's a sleeping bag on the bottom shelf, too. You
can help yourselves to the food in the kitchen."

A smile flashed across the nomad's lips as he straightened. "You got it, doll." He headed for the door, then paused. Bracing a hand against the threshold, he looked at her from over his shoulder. "For what it's worth, you're good for him," he said.

Heather looked up at him, surprised.

Von's green gaze held hers. "Family," he said. "It all comes down to who has your back when your tires are running down a strange road and who'll stop to help you patch a flat when that road turns nasty. Family." He paused, his hand tapping the threshold once, twice, as though he was considering saying something more, or maybe something else, then he walked away.

Von's words played over and over in Heather's mind as she sat down on the bed and set her fingers to work unstrapping Dante's boots. Tugging off one boot, then the other, she dropped them on the floor. She looked at Dante. *You're good for him.* She hoped that was true. She was having a hard time imagining her life without him. And she still didn't know if that was good or bad.

She pulled his socks from his feet and tucked them into his boots. She thought of the music that'd rippled between them at the show and in her kitchen—wild and dark and restless. Joining them somehow, defining them.

Scooting to the head of the bed, Heather peeled Dante's T-shirt off, followed by the long-sleeved mesh shirt underneath. Flat belly, hard chest, lean muscles, his white skin gleamed under the low lamplight; and his scent, burning leaves and dark earth, dizzied her.

Anytime you want, I'm yours.

I want.

But she drew in a deep breath and slowed her racing pulse. She was a grown woman and she would *not* take advantage of him when he was drugged and sleeping. The thought of all the people who'd walked down into the Prejean basement and *had* taken advantage of him was all the cold water she needed.

Sliding off the bed, Heather gathered up the quilt folded at the foot of the bed and settled it over Dante's sleeping form. Eerie jumped onto the bed with a concerned trill. He hopped over to Dante and sniffed him delicately for a few moments before curling up beside him.

Heather smiled. "Little guardian. You watch over him for me, okay?" Eerie lifted his orange head and blinked at her as if to say, *Duh*.

Switching off the lamp, Heather walked from the room to check on her other guests. Eli was curled up on one end of the sofa, the TV remote in his hand, light from the screen flickering across his face.

The clunk of the refrigerator door being closed drew her gaze to the kitchen. Jack was slathering mayonnaise across multiple slices of bread. Scattered on the counter was a package of cheddar, a bottle of mustard, lettuce, sliced tomatoes, ham and turkey lunch meat—all the makings of a bunch of sandwiches or one monumental Dagwood-award-worthy sandwich. Playing drums was obviously hungry work.

The sound of water spraying against glass told her Antoine was in the shower.

Her stomach rumbled and she realized she was hungry; starved, actually. She was about to join Jack in the kitchen when it dawned on her that she didn't see Von.

Swiveling around, she asked Eli if he'd seen the nomad. He nodded. "Outside," he said. "Checking the perimeter."

Perimeter? "Thanks."

Outside, it was sprinkling again, a fine mist more than actual rain, and cool water quickly beaded on Heather's face and clothes. The driveway held only her Trans Am.

The tour bus, its driver, a couple of roadies, and the band's equipment were already headed home to New Orleans, rolling along the Interstate southeast. Everyone else had tickets for an evening flight home tomorrow.

Heather's Skechers crunched on the gravel as she walked around to the side of the house. A pale hand grabbed the top of the wood fence, and Von vaulted over as easily as if he'd jumped from a trampoline. He landed with feline grace.

"Everything looks clear," he said, ambling over to join her. His eyes gleamed in the dark, reflecting street-light. Rain glittered like diamonds in his dark hair. "I don't think there's gonna be any trouble from Seattle nightkind. Not here, at least. What good's an ass-kicking if the guy you're pissed at ain't conscious enough to ap-preciate it? Ruins the whole thing."

"Ass-kicking appreciation. Could be a freshman course at college," Heather said with a quick grin. "But right now I'm more worried about mortals with an agenda."

Von nodded. "Yeah, I was thinking about that too—that Bad Seed shit you told me about, not to mention that so-called *Spin* photographer. You see any cars that don't belong? Anyone outta place?"

"No," Heather said. "But that doesn't mean they're not watching."

"Better to be too paranoid, doll, than not paranoid enough. I'll be taking the night watch," Von said. "Jack said he'd take over at dawn."

"Does Jack know how to handle a gun?"

"Yup, he's a bayou boy."

"Has he ever played guard before?"

"Nope. Lucien was always there in the past."

Heather shook her head. "Then I'll take dawn duty. Jack's gotta be tired after the show. He can take over later in the morning."

"You've got time to catch a nap. It's only two."

"Annie's not home yet, and I—"

"It's okay, doll. I hear you."

"So . . . how do the clans feel about one of their own being turned?" she asked.

"It's an honor, yeah, a big deal," Von said. "You shoulda seen the bash my clan threw when I was chosen and turned. Everyone was drunk for *nights*."

"So it was something you wanted? Being turned?"

"Yeah, you could say that." He looked at Heather for a long moment, stroking the sides of his mustache with forefinger and thumb, thinking deep.

"Tell me," Heather said. "Whatever it is. I'll keep it safe."

Von stopped stroking his mustache. "I know you will," he said softly. "No matter who or what Dante might be, no matter what he has done or might do, his heart's true. I've never regretted giving up the Road for him."

"Did Dante ask you to?" Heather asked.

"Nah, my choice. I saw him. And I knew."

"Knew what?"

"He *is* the never-ending Road."

"But to where?" Heather said, holding Von's steady gaze.

"Don't matter and don't care. I'll be with him."

"I'm glad you are," Heather murmured, then added, "Nightkind for forty years, huh? So how old are you, anyway?"

"What kinda question is that, woman? How *old*. Seventy-one. I'm still jailbait, nightkind-wise." Von bumped her with his shoulder, a surprisingly catlike gesture. A mischievous grin parted his lips. "You're wet."

"So are you."

"Okay, then. Inside?"

Smiling, Heather bumped him back. "Inside, Mr. I'm Still Jailbait."

Von laughed.

Inside, all was quiet. Eli snoozed on the couch while Jack watched TV, plate of sandwiches in his lap. Antoine relaxed in the recliner, reading one of Heather's books about vampires, a look of amused disbelief on his face.

Heather locked the front door and twisted the dead bolts into place before grabbing a towel from the bathroom and then walking into the bedroom to check on Dante. He'd moved; he was curled on his side, facing the door, Eerie tucked in the crook of his arm. Eerie's eyes slitted open. He mewed, then closed his eyes again. Very content.

She'd never seen him take to anyone like he'd taken to Dante. And that particular endorsement meant a lot to her, since she trusted Eerie's judgment. Heather kicked off her shoes, then pulled off her wet clothes. Toweling herself dry, she slipped into her jammies and slippers.

Pulling her .38 from her purse, she automatically checked both the safety and the magazine, then, gun in hand, she hung the towel up in the bathroom to dry. As she walked back into the living room, she saw Von unbolting and unlocking the door.

"What's up?" she asked.

Von opened the door. Annie walked in, followed by Silver. Both were wet and disheveled—Annie's makeup smudged, her skirts in reverse order—and, in her sister's case anyway, reeking of booze and cigarette smoke.

Relief flooded through Heather and she felt her tension unwind. She opened her mouth, then closed it. No point in saying anything to Annie when she was drunk and, besides, she was just glad she was home, safe.

"Hey," Silver said. "Everything okay?"

"Golden," Von said, relocking the door.

"How's Dante?"

"Still out."

"Oh."

Heather heard something sad and a little lost in Silver's voice, and she wondered at it, remembering some of his pensiveness in New Orleans. She wondered if he was homesick.

"I'm back," Annie announced, lifting her chin. "C'mon," she said, grabbing Silver's hand. She led him into the guest room—her room now—and slammed the door.

Heather looked at Von. He was grinning at her. "What?"

"Little sheep–covered jammies and a gun," he said. "Now how hot is that?"

"Not half as hot as a nightkind nomad dripping water on my carpet," she replied. "Rowr. There's towels in the closet, doofus."

"The closet." Von smacked his forehead. "Never woulda thought of that."

"Since Annie's home, I'm going to bed. Wake me before you Sleep, okay?"

Von nodded. "You got it, darlin'. Sleep tight."

Back in her room, Heather placed her .38 in the nightstand drawer, kicked off her slippers, and left the door open just enough for Eerie to come and go. She slipped beneath the quilt and up beside Dante. She spooned him, tucking herself against his fevered heat, and draped her arm over his waist. As she slid into sleep, his warm scent enveloped her and perfumed her dreams.

27

HER GUN AT HIS FEET

Portland, OR
March 23/24

CATERINA LOCKED THE MOTEL room door behind her, then tossed her overnight bag onto the bed. She was exhausted after the long, dirty night and was looking forward to a hot shower and a few hours of sleep. She reeked of soil and sweat and decay, the smell of the dead clinging to her like a fetid perfume.

She eased her laptop onto the lacquered desk, then opened it. She needed to report her progress. She needed to buy time. Keying open the minibar, she pulled out an ice-cold bottle of SoBe Green Tea, twisted the cap off, and poured a long, cooling draft down her throat.

Plunking down on the desk chair, she clicked on NEW MESSAGE and typed in: *Wells assignment completed to satisfaction. Since Wallace is no longer ours, we'll catch some sleep, then a flight home.*

Caterina hit SEND and folded the laptop. Closing her eyes, she rested the cold bottle of tea against her forehead. Burying Beck and Mrs. Wells had taken more energy than she'd expected, energy she hadn't planned on expending.

Caterina regretted Mrs. Wells's murder. It had never occurred to her that Athena would off her terminally ill mother. Her father, yes, given her hostility toward him. But since Athena was determined to see him in Dante's hands, Caterina had thought it safe to leave her with her parents while she disposed of Beck.

A mistake.

Remembering what Wells had so enthusiastically done to Dante Baptiste from birth, Caterina had believed the man empty of normal human emotions, soulless.

But Wells's spittle-flying fury after Gloria's death had proven her wrong on that score, at least where his wife was concerned.

I'll have S rip you out of that body and pour your mother into it! I should've had you put down like your mother advised! You're nothing but a flawed and bitter mistake. Alexander will be happy to kill you! He's looking forward to it!

Wells's threats had stopped only when Caterina had slapped several layers of duct tape across his mouth.

Small wonder Athena Wells's sanity had unraveled.

Watching Athena, listening to her, Caterina had realized that the woman who'd renamed herself Hades was a precog. An unusual gift for a mortal, but not unheard of. But was Athena's future sight warped by madness, the clarity of her visions whirling with debris from the storm raging within her mind?

Caterina had a feeling the answer to those questions would be both yes and no.

Later Caterina had walked Athena to the guest cottage and put her to bed as Alex Lyons had requested. As per their arrangement—she would care for his sister and guard Wells, for Dante's sake, and Lyons would make sure that Dante arrived safe and sound. And he'd make sure the team coming to collect Heather Wallace failed.

Dante Baptiste had saved Wallace's life, had carried her from the center cradled in his arms. As far as Caterina was concerned, that marked Wallace as Dante's beloved. Reason enough to protect her.

"Time for bed," Caterina says. "I promised your brother."

Athena strips to her bra and panties, then crawls onto the bed like a child, and slides beneath the blankets. She stares at the ceiling, her lips moving as she whispers. Shadows smudge the skin beneath her eyes, hollow her cheeks.

Cold ices Caterina from the inside out as she looks around the room. Pictures of Dante are pinned to each wall—night-vision shots from the security cam footage—his pale face rapt, his eyes closed, rays of light whipping around him, from him.

Caterina bends and smooths the blankets over Athena's chest, tucks them in securely. She seems insubstantial, a ghost, the flickering memory of a woman, and Caterina brushes Athena's hair back from her face. A pretty face, smooth-skinned and oval, pale brows, gently sloping nose over curving lips. But her eyes are incandescent, as though moonlit. And gazing upon things only she can see.

Athena lifts her arm and Caterina injects her with the sleep meds as Lyons had instructed during their conversation. Athena's lids droop. Pale lashes flutter.

"Fi la nana, e mi bel fiol, fi la nana, e mi be fiol," Caterina sings softly, her voice more husky than her mother's, not as sweet.

Athena's whispers falter. End.

Caterina finishes her lullaby, and then walks from the room, easing the door shut behind her. She leaves the cottage, Athena's words spiraling through her mind like a never-ending staircase and chilling her blood—Dante will make us three, holy trinity.

Relaxing into the chair, Caterina lowered the SoBe bottle to her mouth and finished the tea. She'd considered giving Athena a lethal bedtime dose, but honor wouldn't allow it. She was trusting Lyons to fulfill his end of his agreement; she needed to tend to her end.

But that obligation was now satisfied.

Whatever the twins had planned for Dante would never come to pass. They'd never live long enough to do him harm. Caterina would make sure of that.

Eventually, it would be discovered that Beck was dead and that Caterina had gone rogue. One of two things would happen: she'd be named traitor, her life forfeit, and she'd be hunted by the best; or fear of Renata Alessa Cortini and the hellstorm she would unleash upon the SB if anything happened to Caterina would convince her handlers to look the other way.

No matter the outcome, Caterina knew she'd be wise to look over her shoulder and watch her back for years to come. Many, many years. Some of her soon-to-be former handlers had long memories, indeed.

Caterina set the empty SoBe bottle on the desk and rose to her feet. Walking into the bathroom, she turned on the shower and undressed while waiting for the water to heat up, folding her clothes neatly as she removed them.

She stepped into the shower, the hot water easing

the kinks from her muscles and the weariness from her limbs. Steam curled into the air. As she tipped her head back and wet her hair, an image from the footage she'd watched flashed through her mind.

The energy surrounding Dante shafts into Johanna's body from dozens of different points. Explodes from her eyes. From her nostrils. Her screaming mouth. She separates into strands, wet and glistening. Dante's energy unthreads Johanna. Pulls apart every single element of her flesh.

Unmakes her.

Johanna Moore spills to the tiled floor, her scream ending in a gurgle.

Energy continues to emanate from Dânte, snapping like whips into the air and altering everything touched. The counter transforms into a heaving twist of vines thick with thorns; Johanna's gun slithers into the vines.

Dante's beautiful face is ecstatic. He closes his eyes and shivers as energy spikes from his body, flames from his hands.

With a shudder, the energy and light recedes, vanishes. Dante lowers his hands. Opens his eyes. He looks down at the moist strands that used to be Johanna. Kicks them apart with his boots. And walks away.

For a moment, excitement burned away Caterina's exhaustion. She had so much to tell her mother; the Bloodline not only still held, but was evolving, and a whispered myth from the ancient past now walked the earth in a slender, tight-muscled, breathtaking form.

A True Blood prince *and* Fallen Maker.

Did Dante represent a new path for all—Fallen, vampires, and mortals?

After Caterina had slept, she'd return to the Wells house. After Dante Baptiste arrived in Damascus, Caterina would go to him and lay her Glock at his booted feet. She'd humbly ask to serve him as samurai and protector.

And refuse to leave until he agreed.

COLLEEN SHEP STEERED THE rented Lexus ES into a slot in the Doubletree's parking lot and shut off the engine. She leaned back in the seat and sighed.

"I hear that," Norwich said, raking his fingers through his tousled hair. "The flight sucked, the rental desk sucked bigger, and the traffic from the airport sucked huge."

"Wanna bet they screwed up our reservation?"

Norwich laughed. "You're on. If they screwed it up, I'll buy you a nightcap in the bar. If everything's in order, you'll buy."

"Deal." Shep reached under the dash and pulled the trunk release lever. "How do you wanna handle things tomorrow?"

Norwich opened his door, then paused. "Swing by Wallace's house during the day, when her neighbors are at work." He rubbed his face as he considered, and in the silence, Shep heard the whiskers rasping against his palm. "Tell her she was exposed to something top secret and potentially lethal, tell her she's being escorted to the CDC in Atlanta."

Shep nodded. "We can even ask for a list of everyone she's been in contact with to make it sound good."

"I like that," Norwich said, stepping out of the car and unfolding his length. "Should keep her cooperative." A cool breeze smelling of rain blew into the car and ruffled Shep's hair before Norwich closed the door.

Shep glanced in the rearview mirror and swiped at her razor-cut black hair, trying to spike it back into edgy life. The Lexus bounced as Norwich freed their suitcases from the trunk. She heard a couple of dull thuds. Grabbing her purse, she slid out from behind the wheel. With a tap to the smart key, she locked the car.

"Y'know, we could spend part of the day checking out the waterfront first," Shep said as she walked to the rear of the Lexus. "I've never been to—" She halted, staring at the tall man in hoodie and jeans bent over the trunk's opened mouth. He sure as hell wasn't Norwich. Her hand darted for the Colt in her purse.

Not-Norwich straightened and turned, his pulled-up hoodie shadowing his face. He aimed a small black gun—*trank gun,* Shep realized in that split second—held in his gloved hand.

Shep yanked the Colt up and out of the purse. Wrapped her finger around the trigger. But before she could squeeze off a round, something dropped over her, something prickling and charged, like a net woven of electricity. Shep tried to squeeze the Colt's trigger. But nothing happened when she attempted to flex her finger. She couldn't move.

Jaw clenched, Shep willed her muscles to action. Willed her finger to squeeze the goddamned trigger. Sweat trickled down her temple. Nothing. Not-Norwich walked over and plucked the gun from her short-circuited hand.

"I'm a federal agent," Shep rasped. This close, she caught a glimpse of blond curls under the hoodie.

"Yeah, I know," Not-Norwich said. "And I'm honestly sorry about this. It wasn't my idea."

Shep's gaze cut to the trunk, and her heart stuttered against her ribs. Norwich was accordioned inside, eyes half-open, mouth lax. Her mouth dried. "Who—"

"You can thank the tightrope walker."

Something stung Shep's arm. She lifted into the air, floating toward the trunk's Norwich-crammed interior, then dropped inside. Liquid pain boiled through her veins. She tried to scream, but her bubbling lungs refused to take in air. The trunk shut with a solid *thunk*.

And then, Colleen Shep died in the trunk of a rented car, in the darkness, jammed against her partner's lifeless body, just fifty minutes after arriving in Seattle.

ALEX PICKED UP THE purse that had fallen from Shep's shoulder and dug through it for the Lexus's keys. Finding them, he plucked them free, then unlocked the car. He stuffed the suitcases into the backseat. Relocking the car, he trotted to the Dumpster. The ripe smell of rotting vegetables and dirty diapers drifted into the air as he lifted the lid. He tossed the purse and keys inside, then strode across the parking lot.

He'd just used tranks developed for vampires on humans. He felt a little queasy. It was one thing to kill a vagrant or a hitchhiker for Athena's experiments, another thing entirely to kill fellow agents.

Correction: SB agents.

But since protecting Heather Wallace had been part of the assassin's price to ensure Athena's safety, he'd had little choice.

Do you intend to give your father to Dante Baptiste?

Amen, sister. That's my plan, my humble offer to him.

Good. I'll keep your father alive, then.

The assassin with the low, sexy voice had requested that Alex divert the arriving team from their mission, requested he warn Wallace. True, she hadn't mentioned *killing* the team, but death was one helluva diversion.

Beneath the halogen streetlights, Alex's shadow jittered and jerked on the pavement as he trotted across South 188th to his parked truck. He climbed in and peeled off his gloves, tossed them on the floorboard. He tucked the trank gun under the seat for safe-keeping.

The Dodge Ram's engine started with a deep rumble. Alex reflected on the fact that with his father lunatic-trussed to a bed, his instructions were now null and void. Yet his father's voice rippled through his thoughts: *Only I have a map to the labyrinth within S's head—a labyrinth I created.*

Alex reached a hand into his hoodie pocket, touched the iPod's smooth shape. Why not test that claim? Why not see if the message actually triggered Dante? If Alex understood his father, Dante would be triggered long enough to follow the instructions from the iPod. Doping him unconscious would nullify his programming again, kick it back into the cluttered cellar of his subconscious.

Pulling his hand free from his pocket, Alex shifted the truck into first and steered it into wee-hours traffic.

S needs to be used in precise strikes against our enemies, Alexander, then returned to sleep. If S remains triggered, there'll be no stopping him.

Inferno's latest pounded from the speakers. And Dante's voice, smoldering and pissed, whispered, "Break me / I'm daring you / see if you can . . ."

"Amen to that, brother," Alex said. "Amen to that."

28

THE CHAOS SEAT

Gehenna, in the Royal Aerie
March 23/24

L ILITH LIFTED HER VEIL and glanced behind her. The gleaming marble corridor was empty, the lights dimmed to a low orange. Dawn was still several hours away and most within the royal aerie slept, except for a few night-duty servants and guards.

Lilith carefully extended her senses, seeking spiked psionic or mental energy, anything out of the ordinary, but detected nothing.

Dropping her veil back into place, tinting her vision red once again, Lilith drew in another calming breath of myrrh-smoked air and slipped inside the *creawdwr*'s receiving chamber—a room that had been empty for over two thousand years.

Moonlight filtered through the floor-to-ceiling windows in the east wall, pale and sheer, a thin, ghostly reflection of the silver and vibrant light that used to flow in through those windows.

Gehenna dies.

Pushing back her veil, Lilith forced herself to cross the sky-blue marble floor at a normal pace, forced herself to keep her mind ordered and her heart calm. She couldn't afford to be discovered in this chamber, not with what she carried. She stopped at the black marble dais leading up to the silk-draped perch.

His name is Dante, a born vampire.

The air smelled stale and dusty, as empty as the throne above her.

Stepping onto the first riser, Lilith seized a corner of the protective silk sheet and yanked. The gold material rippled to the floor like water over rocks and fell against Lilith's feet. Watery moonlight waved against the black, blue-veined marble chair. A center support arrowed up at the back with hollows at either side for wings. The legs and armrests had been carved into scaled dragon limbs, taloned paws inset with sapphires and iridescent opals.

The Chaos Seat. From here a *creawdwr* wove chaos into ordered life.

Twin pangs of loneliness and regret bit into Lilith. She remembered the face Yahweh had possessed before he'd transformed it into a pillar of blazing light in his madness—handsome, golden-haired and golden-winged, intelligent dark eyes, a smile that had needed to be coaxed to his lips, but a smile well worth the effort.

A smile that his *calon-cyfaill*s, Samael—no, *Lucien*—and Astoreth, had good-naturedly competed with each other to elicit. Later, Yahweh's smiles had flowed freely and at moments that had held no laughter, no joy, no cause for celebration.

She remembered *Lucien's* anguish: *We can't stop it. His sanity's slipping.*

Remembered her answer: *Perhaps he needs to be bound by more than two, my love. Perhaps his power is too strong, too chaotic, for a simple triad balance.*

Lilith pushed away the past. Regret had burned bright within her once, but had long since flickered out. Right or wrong, she'd done as she'd believed necessary for Gehenna and for Yahweh.

Lucien claimed the same, but the memory of that awful night so many centuries ago still poisoned her dreams.

"What have you done?"

Lilith whispers her question, but each word bangs like a hammer against her temples. Her head throbs with pain. Outside, the ground ripples and quakes and it feels as though Gehenna will tear itself apart. She clutches at the doorjamb.

Newly made beings wing into the sky only to unravel and scatter into the wind.

Samael . . . Lucien . . . bleeds from his nose and ears. He clutches Yahweh close against his chest. No light blazes from the creawdwr's *face. Motionless on the marble floor beside her* calon-cyfaills, *honey-haired Astoreth stares empty-eyed at the ceiling. Blood rims her eyes like kohl and her lovely face is bloodied at ears and nose.*

"What have you DONE*?" Lilith screams the last word. Pain drops her to her knees on the cold, hard floor. She grabs at Yahweh's shoulder.*

Lucien smacks her hands away and levels her a look that chills her to the bone and freezes her hands in midair. "You'll

never use him again." He returns his gaze to Yahweh, his ex-
pression tender. "He's free." Lucien drapes his hair over the
creawdwr's *face, a silken black shroud.*

"Murderer!" Lilith wails.

Lilith drew in a deep breath of incense and jasmine and shoved the past away once more. Lucien's
unexpected presence had dusted off her memories and
lifted them into the light. She centered and calmed
herself, then climbed the steps to the Chaos Seat. She
needed to verify her former *cydymaith*'s claims.

His name is Dante, a born vampire. He's twenty-three
years old.

Reaching into the black velvet purse tied to her belt,
Lilith pulled out the prize she'd slipped unnoticed from
a pocket of Lucien's trousers while he hung in the pit.
Blood dotted the wrinkled scrap of paper like a seal.
Creawdwr magic whispered against her fingers. Her
hands trembled ever so slightly.

If this was genuine and not some trick Lucien had
designed to make a fool of her, then the gems on the
Chaos Seat would glow. Only a *creawdwr*'s magic could
awaken the Seat.

Bending, Lilith touched the blood-smeared paper to
the black marble.

The Chaos Seat burst into flame.

Lilith stumbled backward and her sandaled foot
slipped off the step. She fell from the dais, but caught
herself with a quick sweep of her wings and lowered her
feet to the hard floor.

Fire engulfed the black marble throne, cool flames
radiating out around it like a twilight aura—blue, green,
and purple. The sapphires and opals blazed with in-

tense color, and Lilith lifted a hand to shield her eyes from the Seat's cold-sparkling brilliance.

Luminescent color like evening's first blush glimmered throughout the room.

Lilith's heart winged frantically against her ribs. She'd never seen such a display from the Seat before, not even when a *creawdwr* had occupied it. And with only a drop of a child-*creawdwr*'s magic-infused blood. Her mouth dried.

His name is Dante, a born vampire. He's my son.

Fola Fior and Elohim.

Never in the history of the Elohim had there been a mixed-blood *creawdwr*.

Possibilities pranced through Lilith's mind. Her pulse soared.

Lilith swooped to the top of the dais and snatched up the blood-dotted piece of paper. The fire and shimmering color vanished. The room darkened, and she blinked bright spots from her vision.

Swinging around, she dipped her wings, grabbed the silk sheet, and redraped the Seat. Unshielded minds pressed unknowing against hers and she knew it was just a matter of time before one of the servants stumbled across her.

Or worse, Gabriel.

Landing on the marble floor, she folded her wings behind her, and hurried from the room. She reached for her veil, but it was gone. Panic waterfalled down her spine. Spinning around, Lilith raced back into the receiving chamber.

Her veil rested on the dais's bottom step, a streak of blood against all the black stone. She picked it up and slipped it over her head, draping the ends over her shoulders.

"What a pleasant surprise, little dove," a low and honey-sweet voice said.

Even though her heart jumped into her throat, Lilith managed not to jump along with it. She finished arranging her veil, then turned around to face a red-tinted Gabriel. "I hope I didn't disturb you," she said, pleased her voice was level. "I couldn't sleep."

He leaned against the doorjamb, in kilt and sandals, his hair plaited into a single, thick braid, his wings tucked away into his back pouches. A knotted torc encircled his throat. He flashed her a sympathetic smile. "Me either."

"No rest for the wicked," Lilith said, returning his smile.

"True. Very true."

She walked to the door, then paused when he showed no inclination to move.

He touched a finger to her veil. "What brought you to *this* room in search of sleep? Why not a walk in the garden or a night flight?"

Lilith met Gabriel's gaze. "My conversations with Samael have resurrected memories I thought long dead," she said, allowing just a hint of sorrow to soften her voice. "And . . . old feelings."

Gabriel's hand dropped to his side, amusement lighting his eyes. "Conversation? Is that what you call it?" He chuckled. "Hanging in the pit and namebound, all thanks to you, I can't imagine he'd have much to *chat* about."

"Perhaps I enjoy watching him suffer. Perhaps I like hearing him rant and curse."

"Now *that* I believe," Gabriel murmured. "I think you came to this room to stoke your rage, to remember what he stole from us, little dove."

Lilith smoothed the pleats in her gown. "When did you get to know me so well?"

Gabriel straightened and stepped out into the corridor. "You've never fooled me," he said, his gaze locking onto hers. "Not once."

"Truly? So you meant to fly your army into my ambush on the Golden Shore?"

Gabriel waved a hand. "That was a long time ago. I've learned since then."

Lilith smiled. "I would hope so." She walked into the corridor.

A servant, one of the half-mortal and wingless *nephilim,* bowed her blonde head and slipped silently into the *creawdwr*'s chamber, a broom and feathered dust-sweep in her hands.

"There was another reason I was surprised to see you here," Gabriel said. "The Morningstar has invited Samael to his aerie for a predawn breakfast and a bit of conversation."

Lilith stared at Gabriel, a cold knot in her belly. "I lost track of time," she said. "Thank you for reminding me. Good night." She whirled and started down the corridor, but Gabriel's voice stopped her.

"Do you think he's hiding a *creawdwr*?"

"The Morningstar?"

"Don't play games, little dove."

"I don't know," Lilith said, her voice thoughtful. "I don't think so, however."

"Ah, well, when Samael's strength has waned enough

to eliminate his shields, I'll just root through his mind and find out for myself."

"Sounds delightful," Lilith said dryly. "Good night, Gabriel."

"Shall I tell Hekate her mother dropped by?" His voice was honey-sweet again.

Thorns pricked Lilith's heart. "Now who's playing games? No matter how I answer, you'll tell her anyway."

"True, little dove. Pleasant breakfast."

Lilith resumed walking, head high. She was halfway down the corridor before it dawned on her that she'd never tucked the bloodstained paper back into her purse. Her blood turned to ice. She couldn't turn around and go back—she felt Gabriel's presence behind her, knew he scrutinized her movements, her body language. She could only hope the servant would sweep the paper up and throw it away.

She had another concern to add to the lost bit of paper. Why hadn't Star informed her of his forthcoming breakfast interrogation of Lucien?

Had he been hoping to surprise her and catch her off guard, perhaps? After all, she should've still been in their bed. Now, he was most likely wondering where she had gone in the small hours of the night.

Perhaps she'd simply tell him she'd been to see their daughter, but that thought left a bitter taste in her mouth. What if Hekate told him otherwise?

Lilith hurried from the aerie's mouth and launched herself into the night sky.

29

SACRAMENT

Seattle, WA
March 23/24

S HE TASTED AMARETTO AND parted her lips for more.

Fingers brushed against her cheek, trailed along the line of her throat and then down, whispering across the curve of her breast. Sudden heat fluttered through her belly, ignited between her legs. And the scent of burning leaves and early frost filled her nostrils like incense, summoning her from sleep.

Heather awakened and looked into Dante's gleaming eyes. Up on one elbow, he watched her, his fingers still caressing her breast through her pajamas, then he lowered his pale face and kissed her again.

Rolling onto her side, she kissed him back, drinking in the sweet taste of his lips. The intensity of her hunger, her need, surprised her. It burned at her core, white-hot. She skimmed her hand along his back, the feel of his silk-smooth skin and the hard muscles beneath sending hot tingles down her spine.

As the kiss deepened, Dante's hand slid from her breast, down along the curve of her waist, to her hip, and yanked her closer still. His heat baked into her, merged with the fire blazing within her. He shoved her pajama top up, baring her stomach and her breasts. He cupped her breast, and his mouth abandoned her lips to trail hot kisses down her throat to her nipple.

A small moan escaped her as he licked the stiffened peak, then sucked it into the wet heat of his mouth. The flutters in her belly intensified. She heard the sound of her own rapid breathing as she worked a hand between them and unbuckled his belt, unfastened his pants, regretting that she hadn't peeled them off when she'd put him to bed.

Dante brushed her fingers aside and finished unzipping his pants. With a low, impatient growl, he kissed her breast, then lifted his head. A blur of movement, a quick heated breeze, and then she heard the clink of his belt buckle as his pants hit the floor. Another blur of movement—white hands, sure and fast, and her pajamas and panties joined his leather pants.

Heather pressed herself against him again. They were still on their sides, face-to-face and skin to skin. She hooked a finger through the ring in his collar. Tugged and claimed him. *Mine,* she thought.

Dante's mouth closed over hers and she felt a sudden sting as he bit her lower lip, the pain vanishing almost instantly. He sucked blood from the wound, his kiss hungry and rough. His hand tucked between her legs, his fingers stroking and dipping and finding all the right spots.

She moaned softly against his lips, moving to the urgent rhythm of heated flesh and hungry lips and exploring hands, caught up in the music of small gasps and rapid breathing and pounding hearts.

Sliding her hand between them, Heather grasped him, stroking his hard, heated length, his skin velvet-soft beneath her fingers. Dante sucked in a breath, shivered, and the heat fluttering through her belly whirled into a thought-ashing firestorm.

Inching up against the pillows, she eased herself onto him. Dante moaned low in his throat and drove into her, pumping against her, with her. He kissed her, deep and wild, ravenous.

Heather gave in to her hunger, a dark and primal surrender. She grabbed at Dante's shoulder, his back, his hard-muscled ass, digging her fingers in with all her strength as she pounded against him.

His motion matched hers, driving hard and fast, his fevered heat torching a bonfire blaze within her, sweat slicking their skin.

Heather gasped as his mouth slid down to her throat and his fangs pierced the skin. The quick sting vanished beneath his lips, and he sipped, drawing her into him, like she'd drawn him into her.

Without a word, he grasped her hand and interlaced his fingers with hers, their palms pushing together—a balance, a promise.

Pleasure pulsed through Heather and blue sparks lit the darkness behind her eyes. Dante drove deeper and faster, harder, and she came suddenly, the orgasm's intensity stealing her voice. Dante's breath quickened and his lips returned to hers. She tasted her own blood on his lips, his tongue, copper and amaretto. Electric tingles prickled along her spine, fluttered through her belly.

I'm inside of him.

Pleasure pyramided within her again, building and building. Music—vibrant, dark, and yearning—resonated between them, palm to palm, heart to heart. Blue fire lit Heather's mind and she cried out as pleasure poured hot through her veins like melted wax, rippling through her center and out, in wave after molten wave.

A low moan escaped Dante's lips. Heather opened her eyes and watched through her lashes as pleasure illuminated his beautiful face. Blue flames haloed their joined bodies, shimmered in the darkness.

His lips parted and his breathing became rough and ragged. He pounded into her faster, deeper. Cupping her hand against his face, she kissed him as his muscles tensed and he came. She came again with him, moaning against his lips as the orgasm intertwined with the song pulsating through them.

One midnight-dark note held—burning and bittersweet, yet edged with hope—gradually fading as Dante's movement slowed. Heather wrapped herself around him, her thigh over his hip, her fingers in his hair. Dante held her tight, his breathing slowing, his heartbeat steady and strong against her cheek. His body fit against hers as though he'd been made for her alone, the second half of a locket clicking into place.

She never wanted this moment to end.

Just her and Dante, curled together. Bodies glistening with sweat, fingers entwined. Breathing as one.

No government conspiracies or buried memories; no deep, dark secrets; no loss.

Nothing beyond this moment, a moment that couldn't last.

Heather realized neither one of them had said a word. But that was okay. Everything she had to say to Dante at the moment, she'd said with her body and her lips. She hoped it was the same for him.

Dante stroked her shoulder, his touch soothing. He planted tender little kisses on her forehead and eyes and lips as she drifted back to sleep, satiated and relaxed, thinking, *We'll go slower next time. Play more. And I swear to God I'm going to learn how to get his goddamned pants off.*

DANTE WATCHED HEATHER SLEEP, her head resting on his shoulder, her body warm and snug against him, one leg over his. He brushed her hair back from her face, trailed his fingers through its soft, tousled length. She smelled of lilac and musk, smelled warm and sticky and of him. She breathed easily, her lips slightly parted, her lashes shadowing the skin beneath her eyes.

Inside, it was quiet, the whispers hushed, as though Heather's embrace was a sacrament of silence, white and tranquil. He kissed her lips. Memorized her night-shadowed face, the feel of her against him, soft skin and taut muscles. Memorized the rhythm of her heart.

The noise has stopped, chérie.

Gray, predawn light spilled around the edges of the curtain, and he felt Sleep uncurling within him, mingling with the last of the morphine in his system.

He tried to remember what had happened at Vespers, but smacked into a wall. A hard, blank wall. *D'accord.* One step at a time. Onstage at Vespers. Singing. Performing. Scrapping with Seattle nightkind. Heather pushing through the crowd. Then nothing. Dante sighed.

The next thing he knew, he was waking up beside Heather, not knowing where he was or how much time had passed. It wasn't anything new, the not knowing or the loss of time. Yet he felt uneasy, and he wasn't sure why.

Something Heather had told him earlier? *Rodriguez filed a malpractice lawsuit against . . .*

Pain, like a red-hot skewer, lanced through his skull. Dante sucked in a breath and shut his eyes. Orange light cobwebbed the darkness behind his eyes. The pain faded. Sleep snaked through his veins, slowing his heart rate and damping down his heat. He forced his eyes open. Try again. *A malpractice lawsuit against Dr. Robert . . .*

Another red-hot skewer twisted through his mind. This one didn't fade. *Yeah, well, fuck it.* Dante grabbed for the thought again. Pain corkscrewed in behind his left eye, intense and sharp and unrelenting. His vision grayed.

Dante eased out from under Heather and sat up, rested his aching head against his upraised knees. He tasted blood and wiped at his nose. He waited for the pain to either subside or kick him ass-first into Sleep.

Something soft bumped his calf and mewed a quiet question. Dante's fingers found and stroked Eerie's head, the warm fur soft as silk. He drew in a shuddering breath as the pain gradually released him. Eerie arched up into his hand, twisted around and arched again.

Sniffing back blood, Dante raised his head and looked at Eerie. He smoothed his hand down the length of the cat's spine. A song curlicued into his mind, a symphony composed of sweeping genetic strings and twisting DNA rhythm. Electricity crackled along Dante's fingers and its reflected blue light danced in Eerie's eyes. Purring, the cat leaned against Dante's leg.

Dante closed his eyes and plucked at the strings, rearranged the rhythm, adding measures, new beats. Composed. Strummed new chords. Imagined Eerie whole. Imagined Eerie walking and running.

Just as Dante lifted his hands, pain slashed a dissonant cross-rhythm across the melody he wove and the song split apart and unraveled, as did the white silence within, fraying beneath the sudden angry droning of wasps.

Let's see how long you can stay under.

I think he's dead. I think you killed him.

Tais toi, *you fool. Put him in the trunk.*

Pain jack-knifed Dante's thoughts, stole his breath. He opened his eyes. White light strobed at the edges of his vision. Then Sleep rushed over him in a black tide and shoved him beneath its lightless surface, but one image followed him into the dark—the image of Eerie jumping off the bed and slipping through the cracked-open door, blue sparks trailing from his fur.

30

SALT IN THE WOUNDS

Gehenna, the Morningstar's Aerie
March 23/24

LILITH PULLED THE VEIL from her head, wadding it into a ball in her hand, as she marched into her aerie's spacious living chamber. The Morningstar stood at the window in a purple kilt and white platinum torc and bracers, his gaze on the dying night beyond the glass. He tilted his head in her direction, but didn't look at her.

"Ah, there you are, my love," he said. "I was beginning to wonder."

"When were you going to tell me about your plans for this morning?"

"At the last moment." He turned around to face her. "But you weren't here."

"I couldn't sleep."

"Truly?" Star murmured. "You certainly looked asleep when I saw you last." A smile brushed his lips. "Faking, my love?"

"When necessary."

He chuckled. His blue eyes gleamed in the darkness pooled beside the window. "That's my Lilith."

"I am not *your* Lilith," she said, throwing her veil at him. It floated like a crimson leaf to the pale, polished floor. She stared at the veil in frustration.

"Funny," Star said. "I could've sworn that for the last five centuries or so, you've been exactly that."

A *nephilim* servant in a rose-colored kilt entered the room and lit the incense brazier. As he tucked a lock of hair the color of sun-ripened wheat behind one ear, Lilith was able to put a name to him—Vel, another of the Morningstar's half-blood and never-ending brood. The myrrh's smoky scent mingled with the fragrance of the white-blossomed jasmine climbing the room's north wall.

After a glance at his father for any other instructions, Vel padded from the room.

"You must've spoken to Gabriel," Star said, ambling away from the window. "Since he's the only one I told about this meeting."

"I went to see the Chaos Seat," Lilith said, deciding to tell the same story she'd told Gabriel. She had no doubt he and Star would compare notes. "I wanted to remind myself of everything we've lost because of Lucien."

Star arched one white eyebrow. "Lucien?"

"Samael," she clarified. Before she could say another word or draw in another breath, a faint song curled through her mind, dark and beautiful and haunting. The song faded like a half-heard whisper, like the last dregs of sleep, then disappeared. Lilith's pulse raced.

Anhrefncathl.

One look into the Morningstar's wide blue eyes told her he'd heard it too, but the furrow between his brows told her he wasn't certain. "Did you hear that?"

"Hear what?"

"Chaos song. Faint, but . . ." He searched her eyes. "I didn't imagine it."

"I heard nothing," Lilith said, keeping her voice even. "Are you sure?"

She crossed to the window and looked outside to see if anyone else had heard and was now winging with joy into the predawn sky. The graying skies were empty. She breathed a little easier. Perhaps no one else had heard because they still slept.

"Yes, I'm sure. I'd wager my wings that our so-called Lucien knows exactly where this Maker is."

Lilith swiveled to face Star. "Why do you think Lucien knows?"

"He was living in the mortal world, my love. The *creawdwr*'s song would've plucked at his essence like fingers upon harp strings. Drawn him. And Samael or Lucien or whatever he wishes to call himself would've answered."

"If you *did* hear a *creawdwr*, then we need to claim him or her before Gabriel does," Lilith said. "And, if Lucien has hidden this Maker like you believe, you'll need my help to discover where."

Star regarded her for a long moment through his silver lashes, his handsome face thoughtful. "You betrayed his name. Why would he want anything to do with you?"

"He owes me," Lilith said, her hands gripping the tiled windowsill behind her. "He's even admitted as much. If I arranged for his escape, he might trust me enough—"

"To lead you to the *creawdwr*," Star mused. "Perhaps . . ."

<*We might win back the throne,*> he sent, eyes alight. <*We might win back our daughter.*>

"Of course," Star murmured. "But first the throne."

"Whatever you desire, beloved," Lilith said. She marveled at how her voice managed to sound so tender when her heart felt so cold.

THE CLINK OF CHAINS drew Lilith's gaze up from her cup of wine and its pomegranate-red depths. Escorted by a fluttering-winged *chalkydri*, Lucien walked into the room, wrists manacled, wings banded.

Lilith's former *cydymaith* stood proud, his black hair spilling to his waist, shoulders back and head high, a cool smile on his lips as if he'd just strolled in from a dawn flight, hoping for refreshment.

But his pale face and bloodless lips revealed the lie. His vitality ebbed with Gehenna's, his fate now bloodbound to the land.

A pang of regret nicked Lilith's calm. She took a sip of wine, tasted the tang of limes beneath the pomegranates and grapes. *For Hekate,* she told herself. *For Gehenna.*

"Welcome, brother," the Morningstar said. He reclined on a velvet and gold-brocaded couch beside Lilith's. "It seems you found something that fit."

"I did," Lucien said. "Although it wasn't necessary."

"Or even desired?" Star said with a smile.

The clothing Star had provided Lucien in place of his tattered trousers fit him with breathtaking perfection, in Lilith's opinion—the silver-belted black kilt flowed from his hips to just above his knees, and silver-edged sandals protected his feet.

The past slipped past her guard and winged into her mind: *He catches her in the air and gathers her against him—chest to chest—heated skin and the rush of wings, counter-tempo. He tears her gown from her body.*

Lilith pulled her gaze from Lucien and shoved the memory away. Everything between them had died with Yahweh.

"Leave," Star said, flipping a hand at the *chalkydri.*

In a buzzing *burr* of wings, the *chalkydri* obeyed.

"Please, brother, seat yourself. Eat." The Morningstar gestured at the low table laden with fruit—oranges, limes, pomegranates—breads and chilled pitchers of wine, and encircled by couches.

Lucien sat with grace despite the manacles and banded wings, but he didn't relax. He kept his back straight, his muscles taut and ready. Lilith noticed he held a length of the manacles's chain between his hands.

As if he planned to strangle his way to freedom.

He's my son.

Maybe that was exactly what he'd do if given half a chance. Her amusement at the thought vanished. Drawing in a breath of jasmine-and-myrrh scented air, she centered herself, and pushed the image of the burning Chaos Seat out of her mind.

"Is this little get-together your idea," Lucien said, "or are you merely doing Gabriel's bidding, like a good little lapdog?"

"Gabriel knows, naturally," Star said, ignoring the dig, his voice smooth as sun-warmed silk. "But he'll only know what I wish him to know."

"The Seat-Warmer, as you named him, is busy planning the quickest way to conquer the mortal world," Lilith said.

"Once Gehenna no longer exists," Lucien murmured. "And me with it." He leaned forward on the couch, chains clinking, and grabbed an orange and a hunk of bread.

"That doesn't need to happen," Star said. Pale peach dawn light shimmered on his star-bright tresses. "Not if there's a *creawdwr* to heal the land, and you."

"There is no *creawdwr*," Lucien said.

"Really?" Star asked. "I sent Loki to the mortal world to search for one."

Lilith kept her face and mind still. She'd mentioned nothing about discovering Loki trapped in stone, forced to play crypt-guard in New Orleans.

Lucien peeled the orange and said nothing.

Star sighed. "Perhaps you saw him?"

"I saw him," Lucien said. "He annoyed me, so I chained him to the earth." He ate an orange slice, his face thoughtful. "I imagine he'll remain that way until I return to free him."

Star arched one white eyebrow. "That would explain his silence. As I said, I sent him because I believe there's a *creawdwr* hidden in the mortal world."

"Why would you believe that?" Lucien asked.

"A few times as I dreamed," Star said, voice low, "I caught the fading edge of an *anhrefncathl*. A wild and beautiful song."

"Perhaps it belonged only to your dreams," Lucien said. "If a *creawdwr* walked the mortal world, I would've known."

"Yes, you would've," the Morningstar said. "And you would've been close—whether to guard or kill, I don't know—but I have a feeling that's how Loki found you and that's why you bound him."

"If you say so." Lucien finished the orange, then bit into the bread.

"Samael . . ."

"He prefers Lucien," Lilith murmured, sipping at her wine.

"*Lucien*, then, as my beloved *cydymaith* advises."

Lucien looked at them, amusement glimmering in his black eyes. "Congratulations," he said. "Did this blessed union happen to coincide with Gabriel's claiming of the throne?"

Heat rouged Lilith's cheeks. "My unions ceased to be your business the moment you fled Gehenna, our *creawdwr*'s blood still wet upon your hands."

Lucien's amusement disappeared and gold light awakened in his eyes. "We all do what we must. Each one of us. Then once we've done what was necessary, we begin anew." He held her gaze, scorching through all her shields and barricades as if they'd never existed.

<*We must forgive each other.*>

Cold anger swept through Lilith. How was it possible for him to do this to her after all the centuries that had passed? To make her feel as if he'd never betrayed her, never winged away from her side? As if *she* had wronged *him*?

Lilith closed her mind to him, snapped her shields

up tight. She lifted her cup and drained it. A rose-gowned servant seized a moisture-beaded pitcher and hurried over to refill her cup. The *nephilim* poured carefully, then returned to her place in the shadows.

"Yes, we begin anew. I like that," Star said, voice earnest. He sat up and leaned toward Lucien. "I pledge to protect this Maker, to keep him from Gabriel, and safe. I will restore Gehenna and place the *creawdwr* on the Chaos Seat where he belongs. We'll bind him and love him—"

"You've made a mistake," Lucien said. "There is no *creawdwr*."

"But there is! I heard his song just before dawn." The Morningstar's face blazed incandescent, caught up in emotions too intense for Lilith to even attempt to untangle or name.

"Then you've drank too much wine," Lucien said, his voice cold and distant. He stood, the length of chain in his hands again.

The image of Lucien cradling Yahweh's body flashed through Lilith's mind. Would Lucien kill his own son in a deranged effort to protect him from his rightful place on the Chaos Seat?

"If you were to bring this young *creawdwr* home," Star said, "I'm confident past crimes would be forgiven. You would be free, brother, to remain here or return to the mortal world."

"This conversation bores me," Lucien said. "Take me back to the pit."

The Morningstar trailed a hand through his short hair, glanced at Lilith, then nodded. "As you wish. Once you're hanging in the heat and darkness again with the *chalkydri* flaying your flesh, I hope you'll remember our conversation."

"Oh, every word," Lucien said. "I enjoy a good laugh."

<*Your turn, my love,*> Star sent to Lilith, a wry smile on his lips.

<*I'll plant the seeds of trust, beloved. Make an exit and leave me with him.*>

As though summoned, the rose-gowned *nephilim* servant stepped from her place in the shadows and approached the Morningstar. The girl was new, Lilith mused, but she looked familiar. Given her wheat-colored tresses, she was most likely yet another of Star's half-blood offspring.

The girl whispered into Star's ear, then stepped back. He rose fluidly to his feet, his purple kilt swirling around his legs. "Another matter has come up," he said. "So I'll leave it to you, my love, to arrange for our guest's return to Sheol."

Lilith nodded. "Of course, beloved."

Star strode from the room, his servant-daughter following in his wake. Absent of the Morningstar's radiance, the chamber seemed to dim despite the rising sun, seemed to quiet and relax as if releasing a long-held breath.

Lucien looked at Lilith. A sardonic smile tilted his lips. "So it's your turn now, is it?"

<*The Morningstar needs to think so, yes,*> she sent. <*Please follow my lead.*> She eased up from her couch and walked around the red oak table to where Lucien stood, his face still. "I know you want Gabriel off the throne as much as we do."

Lucien nodded. "Yes, I do, but I'm not hiding a Maker. I don't know how to make it any plainer."

"The fact that you turned Loki to stone indicates otherwise," Lilith said. "And if Gabriel hears of what you've done to Loki, he'll be convinced you're hiding something."

"All it indicates is that Loki irritates me."

Lilith chuckled. "He irritates me too." *<I heard your son's song this morning too. Tell him to be silent.>*

Weariness shadowed Lucien's eyes. *<He's closed our link. If I force it open, it'll not only injure him, it'll reveal the bond between us.>*

<A bond others could follow.> Lilith pulled the weight of her hair over her shoulder and plaited it as she pondered. *<Why has your son closed the link?>*

<He believes I lied to him.>

<Did you?>

"Perhaps," Lucien whispered. He stumbled forward a step, sweat gleaming at his hairline. Lilith grabbed his shoulders and steadied him. "Sorry. Seems I'm fading." A smile ghosted across his lips. His skin burned beneath her fingers. His dark earth-and-green-leaves scent filled her nostrils, coiled around the past.

Releasing him, Lilith turned to the table and poured a cup of wine. She pressed it into his trembling hand. "Drink," she urged.

<Gabriel plans to ransack your mind once you're too weak to shield against him,> she sent. *<The coward.>*

A muscle jumped in Lucien's jaw. He drained the wine in one long swallow. He touched the dewed cup to his forehead and closed his eyes. "You might as well send me back," he said. "I've nothing more to say."

<*Is there any hope of escape?*> he sent. <*If not, I need you to guard Dante from Gabriel and the Morningstar.*> Lowering the cup, Lucien opened his eyes and the desperation Lilith saw in his gold-flecked eyes splintered her heart.

She thought of Hekate, thought of how it had felt to have her silver-haired daughter wrenched from her grasp, remembered the fear on her child's face when Gabriel, triumphant after battle, had seized her.

She will be a hostage in my court, to ensure your cooperation.

You don't have to do this, Gabriel. I swear upon my name, I won't trouble you.

Ah, Lilith, but I do. The moment I turn my back, you'll be plotting to steal the throne yet again.

Not this time. Not now. Leave me my daughter. Please.

Shhh, my love. Hekate will be perfectly safe. Gabriel assured me of that.

You knew? *You* bargained *our daughter away?* Our daughter, Star?

Lilith recalled Lucien's words to her millennia ago: *You'll never use him again.* Everything that had happened to her since that day had its roots in Yahweh's murder by her *cydymaith.*

Lilith plucked the cup from Lucien's fingers and set it on the table. With a flick of her mind, she summoned a pair of *chalkydri.* She met her former *cydymaith*'s gaze. "I'll do what I can to help you," she lied. <*If nothing else, I will guard your son.*>

From you.

Lucien lifted a hand, chains clinking, and brushed his fingers across her cheek. "We all do what we must,

Lili," he murmured. He lifted his head. "Each one of us."

"Yes," she said. "We do."

And when I find your son, I'll be able to free my daughter.

THE MORNINGSTAR STRODE FROM the mouth of his aerie and onto the landing gallery. Pale apricot and rose dawn light shimmered over the stone. He paused at the balustrade, then turned around to face Eris.

"All right," he said, folding his arms over his chest. "What did you find?"

Eris pulled a piece of paper from her gown's pocket. "As you instructed, I followed Lilith—"

"She is Lady and mistress to you," the Morningstar snapped.

Eris stiffened, then bowed her head. "Yes, my Lord Father. I followed your Lady to the royal aerie where she visited the Chaos Seat and spoke with Lord Gabriel."

"Ah." The Morningstar held out his hand. "Give it to me, child."

Eris handed him the paper, then backed away.

Power tingled against his hand. The Morningstar stared at the crumpled bit of paper, his heart fluttering against his ribs. He touched a finger to the dark spot of blood at the paper's center and felt a *creawdwr*'s distinctive energy.

He was right—had been all along. Samael or Lucien or whatever he wished to be called was lying.

The Morningstar smoothed the paper—a receipt—and read it.

Vieux Carre Wine & Spirits
422 Chartres St.
New Orleans

He flipped it over and read the words scrawled across the back: *Watch over her,* ma mère. S'il te plaît, *keep her safe. Even from me.*

The Morningstar's white wings unfurled and swept through the warming air. He swirled up into the dawn sky, his heart buoyant.

A Maker was in New Orleans. And judging by these words, possibly in love and unable to trust himself. *Keep her safe. Even from me.* A child in need of guidance. A child in need of bonding. A child he needed to find before he himself was caught in the web Lilith and Gabriel were spinning.

31

THE MARK HAS BEEN MADE

Seattle, WA
March 24

HEATHER PAUSED ON HER way to the front room window to make sure that the moon-and-stars throw still completely covered Von. He Slept in the recliner, the throw draping him from his head to his stocking-clad toes. His scuffed-up scooter boots stood neatly on the floor beside the chair, his shirt and leather jacket folded over the fireplace screen.

Eli sat cross-legged on the couch, Eerie nestled in his lap, eating oatmeal and cantaloupe, and watching a game show on TV. The ding-ding-ding of a winner's bell sounded through the living room. Since it was only a little past ten a.m., everyone else was still asleep.

And as badly as Heather wanted to crack open the bedroom door and check on her sister, she refused to give in to the urge. Like Von had pointed out, Annie was a big girl and he'd promised that Silver wouldn't hurt her.

Heather twitched the curtain aside and studied the quiet, rain-wet street. The rain had stopped, for the moment. Most of her neighbors, people she didn't know well, were at work, their driveways empty. She didn't recognize a couple of the cars parked along the street—an SUV, a rust-pocked old Chrysler—both with Washington plates.

A blade of sunlight sliced through thinning clouds and cut ruby dazzles from a pickup parked a block down. Heather squinted, thought she could make out Oregon tree-in-the-center plates. An image popped into her mind of the Portland field office's parking lot and the vehicle she'd watched SAC Alex Lyons climb into, a sparkling red Dodge Ram. Her pulse picked up speed.

Couldn't be on official surveillance, she thought, dropping the curtain back into place. Not in such an easily spotted vehicle. She wondered how long he'd been watching the house and for who. Rodriguez?

She planned to find out.

Turning, Heather crouched beside the sofa and shook Jack's shoulder. The drummer opened one eye and grunted. "Your shift," she said. "I've gotta check something outside."

Jack forced himself away from his pillow and sat up on the sofa, yawning. He stretched, then smoothed a hand along his mane of cherry-red braids.

"You awake?" Heather asked, rising to her feet.

"Sadly, yeah."

"Do you need a gun or did—"

Jack pulled one of Von's Brownings out from under the pillow. "Don't worry," he said. "I'm strapped, me."

A snort sounded from Eli's end of the sofa. "Nutria beware."

Without looking at him, Jack flipped Eli off. "Damn straight."

"I'm going out the back door," Heather said. "And coming back that way. Don't let anyone in but me."

Jack nodded, and his braids swept across his muscled shoulders. "If anyone tries to get in here, I'll make 'em dance like a turkey in hot ashes, for true."

"Now *there's* a disturbing image," Heather said with a smile.

"You need help?" Eli asked, setting aside his breakfast. The smell of fresh cantaloupe drifted through the air.

Heather shook her head. "No, I should be fine. Just being cautious."

With an inquisitive trill, Eerie jumped from Eli's lap to the carpet and padded over to Heather, rubbing against her legs, his back arched for pats. She reached down to pet him, then froze.

Padded. Not hopped. Eerie had four legs, not three.

"Holy Christ," she whispered and knelt. Eerie mewed happily as her trembling fingers stroked his head.

"I thought you knew," Eli said.

"Knew?" she repeated. She touched Eerie's new leg, felt its solidity and strength.

"Yeah, I mean, he was that way when he came out of your room this morning," Eli said. "I figured Dante . . . I mean . . . how else?"

How else, indeed, Heather thought, her mind spinning. She'd known Dante could *unmake*. She'd been too troubled by Johanna Moore's destruction to even consider that Dante might be able to *make,* as well. Yes, he'd most likely made changes within her when he'd saved her life, but she'd never carried that realization all the way through, never stopped to consider its implications.

Could Dante create? Not just fix or heal, but *create?*

Eerie bunted his head against her fingers and she petted him. He sat and extended his new leg, grooming it as if to say, *See? It was there all along.*

Heather stood and walked to the bedroom. She eased the door open and looked into the darkened room. Dante's pale face was turned away from the door, his black hair trailing across the pillow, one white arm across his blanketed waist.

He is *the never-ending Road.*

Heather touched her hand to Dante's chest, waited for the reassuring thump of his heart against her palm. When it came, she removed her hand, bent, and kissed the tiny bat tattooed into the pale flesh above his heart.

With a mew, Eerie jumped up onto the bed and settled himself beside Dante, yellow eyes gleaming.

"Watch over him, little guardian," she whispered.

For answer, Eerie licked a paw and swiped it over his head, the very epitome of nonchalance. *Cats.* Heather backed out of the room, leaving the door cracked open for Eerie's passage.

Jack, Browning Hi-Power snugged into the back of his jeans, walked Heather to the back door so he could lock it behind her.

"I'll be back in a few minutes," she said, stepping out into the gray day. The air smelled of impending rain and wet pavement. "Look, there's probably nothing to be worried about, but I'd rather be safe than sorry."

"We'll keep the Sleepers safe, for true," Jack said, meeting her gaze. "If someone's hunting Dante, he ain't gonna get through us."

Heather smiled. "Thanks, Jack."

"*Ça fait pas rien.*" He closed the door. The dead bolt clunked into place.

She swiveled around and headed across the lawn for the padlocked gate in her backyard's northwest corner. Once through it, she'd follow a short alley between the houses and to the street, but *behind* Lyons's Dodge Ram.

Slipping her hand under the back of her blue turtleneck sweater, Heather touched the grip of the .38 tucked into her jeans at the small of her back.

SHERIDAN YAWNED.

The SUV's interior smelled of coffee and greasy hamburgers. His stomach rumbled, but he didn't feel hungry. The buzz from the pick-me-ups he'd swallowed during the night when he'd begun his surveillance was fading, leaving him twitchy and tired. Sighing, he rubbed his eyes with thumb and forefinger.

Dawn had come and gone and he was still waiting and watching; Prejean was still Sleeping and breathing, and Cortini was nowhere in sight. Nothing was going the way he'd hoped.

With another yawn, Sheridan returned his gaze to the handheld mini-mon. The small camera rigged to the rooftop bike rack provided a steady feed of the street outside of Wallace's white-brick house. He rested fully

reclined on one of the car's rear seats and he doubted
Cortini or anyone else cruising past would be able to
make him. To all intents and purposes, the SUV looked
like nothing more than a parked neighborhood vehicle.

But that couldn't be said about the truck parked
across the street and down half a block or so. It had
shown up a couple of hours before sunrise had smeared
the sullen horizon with bruised color, a red pickup with
a black cover or tarp protecting the bed. The rumbling
diesel engine had shut off, but no one had emerged from
the cab. The flare of a lighter and a cigarette's glowing
end proved someone was in there.

Someone watching, just like he was.

More than a little curious, Sheridan had run the
plates. The Dodge Ram was registered to Alexander A.
Lyons of Damascus, Oregon.

Portland SAC Alexander Lyons. The agent who'd
accompanied Wallace on her little field trip to her
mother's murder site.

Sheridan's curiosity levels had blasted through the
roof. So he'd put in a call to Rutgers and, ironically, that
was the reason Prejean was still breathing.

*SAC Lyons is here keeping an eye on Wallace. Any of-
ficial reason why?*

*None that I'm aware of. Rodriguez wanted to interrogate
Wallace more thoroughly about Bad Seed. I wonder if he's initiated action of his own?*

Instructions?

*Don't proceed until Lyons is out of the picture. And keep
me apprised. If he's working for the SB and not Rodriguez . . .*

*Roger that. Prejean and his band are holed up at Wallace's
place.*

This seems to indicate that Wallace lied to us.

Definitely. She was guarding Prejean earlier.

A shame. Prejean corrupted her somehow. Goddamned vampires.

Ma'am, is collateral damage acceptable? If I can't get Prejean alone?

Absolutely not. We're not the SB. Only Prejean and Cortini are acceptable.

Yes, ma'am. Roger that.

Yawning, Sheridan dry-swallowed a couple more pick-me-ups. Prejean wouldn't be going anywhere until twilight. Maybe he could risk a run over to a nearby restaurant for real food and a restroom. The urinal he'd picked up at Walgreens was doing the trick, but it'd be nice to wash up.

And if Cortini cruised by while he was gone? Circling her prey before moving in?

Movement drew Sheridan's gaze back to the minimon. Someone strode purposefully along the opposite side of the street—a red-haired, slender figure in sweater and jeans, one hand at the small of her back.

Sheridan's sleepiness vanished.

Heather Wallace sidled up alongside the red pickup and tapped on the driver's window with the barrel of her gun.

CATERINA KNOCKED ON THE guest cottage's front door, then opened it and walked inside. Gray daylight seeped around the edges of the closed drapes and into the room. Athena's laptop rested on the coffee table, folded shut. The air smelled faintly of fresh-turned soil and vegetable decay, like a just-mulched garden. Caterina frowned. She didn't see any potted plants, no window-box flowers.

She glanced at her watch. It was nearly ten thirty. She hadn't given Athena the shot until the wee hours, so she should still be out cold. Thick silence layered the shut-in air, weighted the atmosphere.

No whispers. No constant murmur.

Caterina's inner alarms prickled. The silence felt *wrong* somehow. She reached into her jacket and drew her Glock from its shoulder holster. She listened. Refrigerator hum, dripping faucet in the kitchen.

She padded across the room and into the hall; a nightlight at the hall's end twinkled like an evening star. Dark clumps dotted the carpet at irregular intervals. Crouching, she touched one of the clumps—mud. She stood and chambered a round.

Back to the wall, Caterina ghosted down the hall to Athena's room. The door was still open, just like she'd left it earlier. A quick peek inside revealed a form curled under the smudged and smeared blankets. Mud clumps led to the bed like a trail of bread crumbs.

Glock in a two-handed grip, Caterina stepped into the room. The smell hit her immediately, a mingled stench of mud, shit, and death. She crossed to the bed and yanked down the mud-smeared blankets.

Gloria Wells's corpse, muddied and crawling with insects, rested on the sheets. Caterina stared, stunned, absorbing the fact that the body was dressed in a fresh nightgown and a blue ribbon adorned the mud-stiffened hair.

"Welcome to the Underworld."

Caterina felt a sharp sting against the back of her neck and whirled, Glock lifted.

Athena held a syringe between her dirty fingers, her hair and underwear-clad body streaked with drying mud. "I am Hades, Lord of the Underworld," she said. "The dead do my bidding and soon, so will you."

Caterina squeezed the trigger. The gun crack sounded like a cannon blast. Cold spread through her, icing her blood and spinning a white-out blizzard across her mind. She tried to fire another round, but heard only a dull *tunk*.

Looking down, she saw her gun on the floor. The room tilted and she reeled against the bed. A fetid odor wafted into her nostrils as her hand grabbed hold of the corpse's arm for balance. Things writhed under the already-moldering skin beneath Caterina's fingers.

Jerking her hand from Gloria Wells's cold arm, Caterina stumbled, then fell to the floor. The ceiling spun and spun, faster and faster.

"I think I'll call you Little Red Riding Hood," Athena/Hades whispered. "And I'm going to let Dante eat you all up."

Caterina spun into the abyss, the Lord of the Underworld's girlish whispers guiding her into the darkness.

LYONS'S HEAD JERKED AWAY from the rain-beaded window he'd been snoozing against and his hand dove inside his hoodie.

"I wouldn't," Heather warned. "Hand out. Slow."

Lyons turned his head and looked at her, then focused on the gun she aimed at him through the glass. He eased his hand from inside his hoodie. "Hell, Heather," he said, his words clear, but faint. "You scared the crap outta me."

Lyons seemed a little too alert for a man abruptly awakened, especially for one who'd been sleeping in what she assumed wasn't his normal napping spot. Heather's thoughts shifted to Annie, and Dante's words rolled through her mind: *Maybe faking . . .*

Heather motioned with her .38. "Roll down your window and keep your hands where I can see them."

Lyons did as she asked. Warm air smelling of cigarettes, sweat, and Drakkar Noir wafted out of the truck. He wrapped his fingers around the steering wheel. "This isn't what it looks like," he said, offering her a sheepish smile. "If you'd let me—"

"Keep your hands on the steering wheel." Heather leaned in through the window and reached inside his gray hoodie. Her fingertips brushed against his body-heat-warmed leather shoulder holster.

"I'm usually a third-date kinda guy," Lyons murmured. "But, for you . . ."

"Lucky me," Heather said, unsnapping the holster guard and slipping his gun, a Smith & Wesson M&P .40, from its holster. She straightened and met Lyons's sea-green gaze. His smile faded at whatever he saw in her eyes.

"Who ordered surveillance? Rodriguez?" she asked, tucking the S&W into the back of her jeans.

"No one ordered surveillance."

"That's a good thing, because you suck at it." Heather lowered her .38 to her side. "Your truck is probably visible from space."

"Ouch." Lyons winced. "To be honest, I was keeping watch—well, I was, until I dozed off. Christ."

Warning tingles prickled along Heather's spine. Her fingers tightened on the grip of her gun. "Care to explain that? Watching for what?"

"Apparently, your father can't keep secrets. He spilled the beans about Prejean healing you," Lyons said. "A team's coming to bring you in."

Heather stiffened, her gaze locked onto Lyons's. "You know this how?"

A dark SUV turned onto the street, and Lyons stiffened, studying its progress with narrowed eyes, his hands white-knuckled on the steering wheel. When the SUV cruised past behind Heather, he said, "Could we talk about this inside?"

Heather glanced up the now empty street. Was Lyons telling the truth? She had a feeling he was parceling it out, but even so, it might be information she needed and soon. Returning her gaze to Lyons, she saw genuine weariness on his beard-stubbled face. Portland to Seattle took four hours, less if you floored it and burned up I-5.

"Wouldn't a phone call've been easier?" she asked.

Lyons shook his head. "This is stuff you need to hear face-to-face."

"Okay," she said. "We'll talk inside."

PALMS PRESSED AGAINST THE living room wall, legs spread, Alex kept his gaze on the cream-colored carpet beneath his feet. He felt the drummer with the mane of red braids—Jack—standing beside him, and was pretty damned sure he was still aiming a gun at him.

"Keep any and all smart-ass comments to yourself," Heather Wallace said as she patted him down, sliding her hands along his jeans-clad legs.

"Hell," Alex muttered. "Talk about killing the mood."

Heather's hands moved sure and quick, with an expert's thoroughness. She retrieved the iPod, his smokes, car keys, cell phone, USB drive, and lighter from his hoodie pockets. He heard clinking and soft thuds as she tossed everything onto the sofa.

"Okay. Turn around," she said.

Alex swiveled around. Shifting her weight onto one hip, Heather studied him, her lovely face all business. Even dressed down in faded boot-cut jeans and a tight cobalt-blue turtleneck, she was sexy. The turtleneck showcased her creamy complexion, vivid blue eyes, and the deep red hair tumbling past her shoulders like a jeweler's velvet cloth.

Behind her on the sofa, the other two members of Prejean's band watched Alex intently, their dark faces somber. To his right was Jack and his gun, to his left the recliner with its throw-shrouded vampire.

"Take off your hoodie," Heather said.

"Why? You already patted me down," Alex said, his fingers hesitating above the zipper. "I'm kinda chilly."

"You can have it back, don't worry."

Not having much of a choice, Alex sighed and nodded. He unzipped the hoodie, pulled it off, and handed it to her.

Brows knitted, Heather stared at his chest, at the INFERNO logo emblazoned on the black T-shirt he wore. She straightened and lifted her gaze to his. Her face was cold, but anger scorched the color of her eyes almost black.

"You were at the show last night."

Sexy *and* pissed. "I know you think that I'm playing you—"

A dark smile touched Heather's lips. "Are you trying to pretend that you aren't? You followed us here from Vespers," she said. "Am I wrong?"

"No," Alex allowed. On his right, Jack stepped closer. Alex held up a hand, palm out. "I told you the truth. They're coming for you."

"So when were you planning on warning me?" Heather asked. "Before or after they dragged me away?"

"Who's dragging who away?"

Alex glanced to the right. Heather's sister stood in the hallway's mouth, blue-purple-black hair tousled, and wearing only a purple tank top and black bikini-cut panties. She gave him the once-over, curiosity in her blue eyes.

"Morning, Annie," Heather said. "Get a robe on."

"I don't have one."

"Use mine."

"Fine."

But Annie didn't move. Instead, she leaned against the wall, hands behind her back, hips out, and watched.

"Eyes front and center, Lyons."

Alex looked at Heather. Fire still burned in her eyes. She tossed his hoodie back to him. "Now's the time. Spill. Tell me everything."

Alex shrugged the hoodie on, then trailed a hand

through his curls. He felt Jack shift beside him. "They got word that Dante Prejean—"

"Baptiste," Heather murmured. "His name's Baptiste. And who's 'they'?"

"The SB."

Heather lifted an eyebrow and folded her arms under her breasts. Alex could just imagine what she was thinking: *No such thing.* Or, *This guy's full of shit.*

"The Shadow Branch exists and some of its projects intersect with the Bureau's."

"Bad Seed," Heather said, skepticism fading from her face.

Alex nodded. "Exactly. Your dad contacted a member of the SB and told this person that Dante Baptiste saved your life *without* using his blood. So the SB decided to bring you in for tests to determine what he did to you. And how."

Heather glanced toward the hall. "Annie," she said softly. "Go get my robe."

Face stricken, Heather's sister padded down the dark hall. When Alex returned his attention to Heather, she was rubbing the bridge of her nose.

"What do they have planned for Dante?" she said, dropping her hand. "Are they gonna try to pick him up too?"

"I need to talk to Dante," Alex said. "What I have to say is for him alone."

The dark smile returned to Heather's lips. "Why am I not surprised?"

"I'm on your side, Heather. Yours and Dante's."

"Somehow I doubt that. And you're mistaken if you think we're going to let you talk to Dante alone."

We're? Alex's gaze skipped around the room, from face to face—white, cream-in-coffee, black—each was watchful and serious and hard. A worm of doubt wriggled into Alex's mind. Had he made an error in judgment by allowing Heather to find him?

"Sit on the sofa," Heather said, stepping aside. "Get comfy. You're gonna be waiting for a while." She glanced at Jack. "Keep an eye on him."

"Damn straight," the drummer said.

Heather walked from the room and into the kitchen. Alex heard her rummaging through drawers. Jack motioned at the sofa with the gun. "Sit, you."

Alex sat at the unoccupied end and did as Heather had suggested, making himself as comfortable as possible. She returned a few minutes later with a roll of duct tape and, kneeling, carefully bound his wrists together.

She regarded him for a long, silent moment before standing. "Do you know how long we have?"

Alex met her gaze and knew he'd lose her completely if he didn't give her something. "I killed the pickup team," he confessed, keeping his voice low. "I bought you some time, but I don't know how much. Maybe a day, maybe two."

Heather sucked in a breath. "Why would you do that?"

"I like you and I hated the thought of what would happen to you if they succeeded." He glanced toward the empty hall. "And because you have a sister who needs you like mine needs me."

"What else do you know about me?"

"Everything."

"Just everything on *record*," Heather said, then stood and walked away, her .38 tucked into the back of her jeans once again.

True, but Alex had a feeling it would be more than enough.

32

REVELATIONS

Seattle, WA
March 24

A LOW, DEEP INHALATION drew Heather's attention from the box she was packing at the dining room table. Von pushed the throw off and, yawning, stretched. She noted with amusement that even stripped down for Sleeping—black jeans, socks, and white wifebeater—he still wore his double shoulder holsters.

Bet anything he was a scout when he was mortal, checking the road ahead for his clan, searching for welcome or danger.

Von sniffed the air and was on his feet and at the sofa before Heather realized he'd even moved from the recliner. Attention on the napping Lyons, Von said, "Who's Sleeping Beauty?"

"SAC Alex Lyons," she answered. "I caught him spying on the house."

"Once again, paranoia pays off. So what's the plan?"

"Good question," Heather said, tucking the box's flaps closed. "He knows about Bad Seed and who's behind it. I'm not sure who he's working for. He claims no one sent him, but I don't find that very reassuring, y'know?"

"I hear ya, doll." A pause, then, "Bad Seed, huh?"

The quiet menace in Von's voice snapped Heather's head up. He leaned over Lyons, his hands knuckled into hard fists, his jaw tight. "He one of the assholes who messed with Dante?"

"I don't think so," Heather said. Wiping her dusty hands against her jeans, she stepped around the table and walked into the front room. She stopped beside Von. "But he *does* have information."

The nomad's gaze was fixed on Lyons's throat. "Info, huh? Stuff we need, no fucking doubt."

"No doubt," Heather agreed. "He says he needs to speak to Dante alone."

Von snorted. "That ain't happening." He straightened, then rolled back his shoulders. Exhaled. His hands relaxed.

"Spy Man also said some team was coming for Heather," Jack tossed into the conversation. "But he intercepted them. Said he killed them, he did."

Heather glanced over her shoulder. The drummer sauntered from the kitchen, pulling the Browning from the back of his jeans as he crossed the room. He handed the gun back to Von.

The nomad holstered the Browning. He looked at Heather, cocked an eyebrow. "That's twice, darlin'. I ain't gonna put up with it a third time."

Whistling innocently, Jack whirled and returned to

the kitchen where Eli and Antoine worked at the counter making sandwiches for the evening flight home.

"Second time, what?" Heather asked.

"Second time you neglected to mention you were in trouble too."

Heather stared at him. All playfulness had vanished from Von's green eyes. "I . . . it wasn't intentional . . . I was worried about Dante, and I . . ." Her words trailed off. It had never occurred to her to tell Von about the trouble *she* was facing. Never occurred to her that they had more than Dante in common. But, judging by the nomad's ain't-brooking-no-nonsense expression, they did. She felt a smile tip up the corners of her mouth.

"Sorry about that," she said, meaning it. "It won't happen again."

Von nodded, then shifted his gaze back to the man on the sofa. "So he claims he put the smackdown on the bad guys, huh? Whattaya think, doll? He telling the truth?"

"Yes." Heather remembered the steadiness of Lyons's gaze. "*That* I believe."

Von glanced around the room. "Looks like you're packing."

"I am. But just stuff I can't replace. Everything else—furniture, dishes, TV—I'm leaving behind." Lyons's story, true or not, had convinced her of what had been simmering in the back of her mind ever since her meeting with Rodriguez, Rutgers, and her father.

Time is running out. Disappear.

And thanks to her father, the hourglass had just run dry.

The image of James William Wallace standing beneath the buzzing fluorescent lights of the parking garage flipped into her memory. *I want us to be a family again.*

Heather's jaw tightened. *We were* never *a family.* Her father had lied to her, but she expected that from him. The realization that he'd used the same lie to sweet-talk information from Annie tied Heather's stomach into knots. She'd never forgive him for using Annie.

Heather had tried to talk to her sister about what she'd overheard Lyons say, but Annie, finally wearing Heather's robe, had refused to even meet her eyes and retreated to her room.

"We can talk about where you're planning on going later," Von said.

Heather looked at him. He nodded at Lyons. The crescent moon tattoo beneath the nomad's eye glittered like moonlit frost in the room's curtained gloom. "What are you, exactly?" she asked.

"The hell kinda question's that, woman?"

"In nightkind society, I mean. *Llygad.*"

Von smoothed his mustache with thumb and forefinger, his face thoughtful. "Okay." He returned to the recliner, sat, and tugged on his boots. Reaching back, he pulled the elastic tie from his ponytail and shook his hair free. It swung just past his shoulders, a deep and glossy brown.

Just as Heather had decided that was his entire answer—*Okay*, he said, "We're the keepers of nightkind history, the impartial Eyes of truth."

Heather mulled that over. She thought back to when he'd stood motionless beside Dante during his meeting with Ronin in Club Hell. "So, like witnesses?"

"Close enough." Von slid the hair-tie around his wrist for safekeeping. "In another age, or so I was told, we were called *filidh*, warrior-bards. We protected and educated, shaped history and truth into lyrical stories, but hell, even that's an incomplete naming."

"So are *llygad*s only nightkind or can they be mortal? Fallen?"

"*Llygaid*, doll. The plural is *llygaid*. And only nightkind need apply." Von's gaze shifted to the sofa. "Someone's awake now and pretending to be sleeping."

Lyons slivered open one eye, then the other at Von's comment. He scooted upright and rubbed his face. "Was there a shift in my breathing pattern that gave me away? Something different in my scent?" A smile curved his lips, warm and friendly and open.

Probably works like magic for him, Heather mused. *Bet that smile gets perps and fellow agents alike to drop their guards.*

"Ain't telling." Cold and sharp, Von's voice was an icicle. He rose to his feet.

"I did a little research while you were snoozing," Heather said. "I found your home address in Damascus and learned the property title belongs to Gloria Lyons." Lyons's smile dimmed. "Your mother."

Lyons nodded, his intense sea-green eyes locked on her face.

"But I couldn't find a thing about your father," Heather continued, shifting her weight onto one hip. "Which is curious. But the thing that really fascinated me is your twin sister's name—Athena *Wells*. Care to explain?"

"It's complicated," Lyons said.

"What's complicated?" Dante said from behind Heather, his voice low and husky.

ALEX'S MOUTH DRIED. The nomad's hand clamped onto his shoulder.

Dante Baptiste stood in the archway leading into the hall, dog-collared, shirtless, and barefoot, his white fingers buckling his belt, his eyes gleaming in the twilight-darkened room. He shook his sleek black hair back from his pale face.

An orange cat wound between his legs. Dante dropped to one knee and stroked his hand along the purring cat's back.

Alex's heart hammered against his ribs as he struggled to resist the True Blood's beauty-lust-nightwebbed spell.

As Heather swiveled to face Dante, he looked up at her and smiled—a tilted, intimate smile—and released Alex.

Given the look that Dante and Heather had just exchanged, Alex had no doubt they were lovers. He tried to focus on that, tried to figure how to use it against Dante. Hurt him with it. Hurt him deep. Alex drew in a long, deliberate breath, then another, as he willed his racing pulse to downshift a few gears.

Trigger him. Break him. Control him. Use him.

"*Another* duct-taped Inferno fan?" Dante asked, nodding at Alex.

Heather blinked. "Another . . . ?" The orange cat bunted its head against her leg, then wandered toward the kitchen.

"A story for another night," Dante murmured. "So who are you?"

Alex met Dante's dark eyes. He curved his lips into a smile. "Alexander Lyons," he said. "But feel free to call me Alex."

"He's the agent who went with me to my mother's murder site," Heather said.

Dante stood and joined her in two graceful strides. His gaze turned inward for a second, then he refocused on Alex. "Von says Heather caught you spying outside. Says you know something about Bad Seed."

Lovely thing, telepathy. Think I'll keep mine secret for the time being. "True enough," Alex said, resting his bound hands against his knees. "I have info for you, but I'd like to speak to you alone."

"Nope. Anything you gotta say, you can say in front of Heather and Von."

"Okay, then. Like I said, it's complicated," Alex said. "It involves my father."

A wary expression crossed Dante's face. "Who's your dad?"

Comprehension sparked in Heather's eyes, quickly followed by alarm. She grabbed Dante's arm and stepped in front of him as if she could shield him from words. As if she could protect him from the truth—a truth he needed.

"Dr. Robert Wells," Alex said.

Dante's face blanked, then pain flickered in his eyes. "Give me that name again. Say it slow."

"Robert—"

"No!" Heather interrupted. "Shut up, Lyons." She turned to face Dante, her hand still on his arm, her voice urgent. "Look at me, Baptiste."

It'd bothered Alex that she'd switched from calling

him *Alex* to *Lyons*. Hell, he thought he'd even prefer *sir* to the cold and distant way she now used his last name.

And yet the way she said *Baptiste* was warm and intimate, a special naming.

Dante shifted his gaze to her. "Just like before, huh? The name I can't hold."

Can't hold? A stark, cold realization burned holes through Alex's assumptions like dry ice. His father had added a personal safeguard into Dante's programming to prevent the True Blood from being used *against* him.

Heather nodded. "The very same." She squeezed Dante's arm, then her fingers slid away from him. She swiveled around and faced Alex again, her face cold. "Don't say that name again."

Alex nodded. "I didn't know," he said.

"What's this all about?" Dante asked him.

"I have something you need."

"Like I ain't heard *that* before," Dante snorted. "So what's this thing I need?"

Alex looked at the iPod resting on the cushion at the other end of the sofa. Not the right time to trigger the young True Blood, too many people around to see, too many chances for interference. He'd prefer a more intimate gathering to test his father's work, just him, Dante and Heather.

Glancing up at the nomad, Alex said, "Could you hand him the flash drive from my stuff there?"

The nomad—*Von?*—looked at Dante, and Dante nodded. Von picked up the small, plastic-encased flash drive and tossed it to him.

Dante caught it and turned it over in his hand. "What's on it?"

"Your past," Alex said. "Your mother. Your birth. All of your documented experiences with Bad Seed including your encounters with my father and Dr. Moore. Everything is on there."

Heather drew in a sharp breath.

Dante stared at the drive. His body tensed, his muscles coiling beneath his white skin as if expecting a blow or getting ready to deliver one—maybe both. Emotions chased across his face too quickly for Alex to name.

But one thing he *could* name, one fascinating thing: pain stark upon that damned and beautiful face. Dante was hurting. As much as that realization buoyed him, Alex wondered *why* he was hurting—Dante shouldn't *feel* or *remember* anything.

"Baptiste." Heather's voice was clear and strong. "Dante, I'm here."

Dante drew in a shuddering breath, pulled his gaze away from the drive and looked up. Heather's hand closed over his, her fingers interlacing through his, both sets of fingers folding the flash drive against his palm.

"*J'su ici,*" he said.

"Do you want to see what's on there?"

"*Oui.* I do, yeah. But not now."

"I've seen what's on there and you shouldn't watch it alone," Heather said. "I'll be with you, if you want."

Dante pressed the flash drive into her hand. "I want. You hold it for me then, *chérie.* When the time comes we'll watch it together."

"Together." Heather stretched up and kissed his lips.

For a moment, Alex felt a twinge of regret. Wished he could keep Heather out of what was to come. Wished she'd been strong enough to resist Dante in the first place.

"So what's the price on that invisible tag, Lyons?" Heather slid the flash drive into her front pocket.

"No price," Alex replied. "I just hope that once you've looked at that, Dante, you'll make my father answer for it."

"Yeah? Why do you care?"

"My sister is ill because of the work he did on us before we were even born. But I've seen what you can do," Alex said, leaning forward on the sofa. The nomad's fingers squeezed. A bolt of hot pain shot down Alex's arm to his pinkie. He went still and the pressure eased. "I know you can help her."

"So much for 'no price,' " Heather muttered.

Dante looked into Alex's eyes, looked deep, and Alex truth-wrapped his mind with thoughts of Athena and her never-ending whispers, her inward-turned Aegean gaze.

I'm losing her and she's all I have.

"What makes you think I can help your sister?"

"I saw recorded footage of what you did to Moore at the center. I also know you saved Heather's life." Alex nodded at Heather. "They're hunting her now because of that. And they'll take her apart to figure out how you did it."

Dante sucked in a sharp breath. He looked at Heather. "That true?"

"That's what he says, yes," Heather said, leveling a wintry glare at Lyons. "And he claims he killed the team assigned to pick me up." Shifting her gaze to Dante, she added, "We'll talk about this later, okay?"

Dante held her gaze for a long, silent moment. Then he nodded. Leaning in, he brushed her hair away from her ear and whispered to her. Concern flashed across her face. She placed her lips near Dante's ear and whispered a reply. She pulled the USB drive from her pocket and tucked it back into Dante's hand.

Not for the first time, Alex wished he possessed a vampire's keen hearing. "I bought Heather some time," he said. "A couple more days to get underground."

"I appreciate that," Dante said, returning his attention to Alex. "And I'm sorry about your sister, for true. But—you and me?—we're done." He tossed back the drive. "If you wanna help your sister, get her as far from your dad as you can."

Alex caught the drive reflexively. "That was a gift."

"No, it wasn't. Ain't gonna be game-played or blackmailed or guilt-tripped."

"I'll give you my father on a fucking silver platter. All you have to do is heal my sister."

A dark smile tilted Dante's lips. "I'll be coming for your old man, you can fucking put that in the bank. But in my own time and on my own terms."

The nomad's hand slid from Alex's shoulder. "Time to go," he said, slicing a fingernail through the duct tape binding his wrists.

Reluctantly, Alex stood and dropped the USB drive back onto the sofa as he gathered up his belongings, stuffing them into his hoodie's pockets. He glanced at Heather. "Can I have my gun back?"

"Sure." Heather went to the dining room table and picked up the S&W. She removed the magazine, then unchambered the round already loaded. Walking back to the sofa, she extended the empty gun to Alex.

"You know the way out," she said.

With a wry smile, Alex took the gun from her, then tucked it into the back of his jeans and pulled his hoodie over it. *Time to take a chance and plant a few seeds.*

He stopped beside Dante. "Genevieve begged to hold you after you were born. She was denied the chance. Every minute you let my father breathe, you deny her justice."

Dante *moved*. His hand latched around Alex's biceps and, in an instant, Alex was flying as the vampire hauled him across the room and outside—*sounds blur past, a sharp gasp, Heather; the crunch of drywall, the doorknob punching into the wall*—and flung him against a Jeep parked at the curb.

Alex hit hard, and bruising pain radiated down from his right shoulder to his ribs. He struggled to catch a breath. Fury lit Dante's beautiful face, blazed red in his eyes.

"What part of *in my own time* don't you fucking understand?"

The True Blood stared at Alex's throat and, for one cold-sweat-heart-pounding moment, Alex was positive that not only had he grossly miscalculated Dante's reaction, but that Dante was going to tear into him, rip him open, and *feast*.

But instead, Dante's hands knotted into fists, and he yanked his gaze back up to Alex's face. "Stay away from me. Stay the fuck away from Heather." His white skin seemed to drink in what little moonlight there was, channeling it into his veins.

"From what I've seen," Alex said, straightening against the car and rubbing his aching shoulder, "it's *you* who should stay away from Heather. How long do you think she'll last with you at her side? They're hunting her *because* of you."

"Fuck you. Ain't your worry." But uncertainty flickered across Dante's face, and his gaze turned inward like he was listening to someone. "Shhh," he whispered, soothing that someone. He touched his fingers to his temple.

A chill rippled through Alex. Just how stable was Dante's mind? How secure his father's programming? From where Alex was standing, Dante was slipping in a big way.

Exhilaration and adrenaline rushed through Alex, chasing away the chill, and feeding him strength. The True Blood looked ripe for conquering.

All Alex needed was the right moment.

Over Dante's shoulder, Alex saw Heather standing on the front step, her expression troubled. The nomad rested a hand on her shoulder, but watched Dante.

"I can help you remember my dad. Get you past his safeguards and programming. I can put him in your hands."

"Fuck you. Ain't playing. *Va jouer dans ta cour a toi.*" Dante backed up several paces, then, turning, he loped back to the house.

Heather and the vampire nomad went inside with Dante, and then the door shut with a solid thunk. Light spilled into the yard from the front room windows as someone turned on lamps.

Alex sprinted down the block to his truck and climbed inside. He keyed on the ignition. The engine started with a deep, powerful roar, and he let it idle. He had to admit Dante had thrown him for a loop when he'd given back the USB drive; he hadn't anticipated that the vampire's stubborn anger would outweigh his curiosity, his hunger for the truth.

Alex drummed his fingers against the steering wheel. The interaction between Dante and Heather was intriguing. It seemed like her presence helped anchor Dante in the here and now. But judging by her expression just now, his violence disturbed her.

Alex switched on the wipers. As the blades whisked across the windshield, wiping away the last remaining drops from an earlier shower, he spotted movement at one of the darkened bedroom windows.

Something dropped from the window into the bushes below. Then a figure climbed out and jumped to the ground. The slender shadow glanced around, then plucked a bag from the bushes and slung it over its shoulder. The shadow jogged down the street, then hooked a left.

Turning off the wipers, Alex clicked on the headlights, shifted the truck into gear, and drove down the street following the shadow's path. He was pretty certain the shadow had been female, given the curves and the hip-swinging gait.

And just like that, there it was, the right moment.

Amen, brother, amen.

* * *

GYM BAG STRAP LOOPED around her shoulder, Annie strolled backward along the sidewalk, thumb out. Car headlights and winking neon signs from trendy bistros, shops, and gas stations dazzled her eyes, adding to the pain throbbing above her right eye. A budding migraine. Just fucking great.

She felt around in her hoodie pocket in case she'd missed an oxy tab last night, but no such luck. Not even a smoke. She felt her muscles coil tighter. She needed something to push back the pain and clear her head. Needed something to sweep away all the dark shit bouncing around in her mind.

Your dad contacted a member of the SB . . . the SB decided to bring you in for tests to determine what he did to you. And how.

Heather must have realized that Annie had blabbed her secret to Dad. Heather probably hated her now. *At last, right? The last chain has fallen away.* No reason to stick around. All she'd ever been was a thin shadow angling away from Heather.

But not to Silver. He'd been fun in and out of bed and, unlike mortal guys, could keep it up forever. Even though he was twenty-six, he'd been turned at fifteen, so rolling around with him had made her feel a little pervy, but in a delicious way. Silver had also made her feel lighter than air, an upward-bound leaf falling into the sky.

Silver wraps his fingers around her hand. He slips his arm around her waist, and then he moves. *Annie's breath catches in her throat as they streak through the crowd on the sidewalk and everything rushes past in thin finger-trails of color and light, of sound.*

Annie's flying.

She feels like Silver is her training wheels as she wings through the sky, low to the ground, her hand in his, his arm around her waist—hell, her feet might be only inches above the sidewalk, if that. But she flies, glides, in his arms.

And she never wants to stop.

But when she'd told Silver she wanted to be night-kind and asked him to turn her, he'd refused. Had said he was trying hard to get back on Dante's good side after fucking up big time, and that turning her probably wasn't the best idea in the world.

Silver's pensive face and tight muscles had told Annie plenty, as had his wistful voice—he *loved* Dante, pined for him. She'd known that she had no hope of changing his mind. At least, not in the time remaining before the band left for the airport.

Annie'd decided if she couldn't fly or be trans-formed, then she wanted to disappear. And get blind *did-we-just-fuck* drunk. All she needed was a beer or twelve.

And man, Heather was going to be *so* pissed when she discovered Annie had swiped a few souvenirs from Dante's duffel bag on her way out.

Annie laughed, the sound as brittle as she felt. If she tripped and took a header to the pavement, would she shatter? Like good old Humpty-Dumpty? She drew in a deep breath of air and immediately regretted it as the spicy smells of curry and sausage made her migraine-queasy stomach clench.

Tires hissed over the wet pavement as cars passed her, headlights unfurling banners of blue-white light along the glistening street. A pair of headlights bright as twin suns going nova blinded Annie. She lifted a hand to shield her eyes. The vehicle—a big, rumbling pickup—

pulled over to the curb. She walked up to the passenger-side door just as it swung open.

The cute curly-haired blond Heather had been questioning at the house was leaning across the seat, a warm smile on his lips. "Need a ride, Annie?" he asked.

Because a tiny voice inside of her was yelling no, Annie climbed into the pickup and, pulse thundering, shut the door.

33

NIGHT DESCENDS

Seattle, WA
March 24

*N**ah-nah-nah! I'm out having fun! Leave a fuck-*
ing message! Or not!

Heather didn't bother leaving a message. She ended the call, then spiked the cell phone onto the rumpled bed in frustration. "Shit!" She couldn't help but think that Annie had taken off because of what she'd heard Lyons say.

She doesn't know I blame Dad, not her.

But that wasn't even the worst of it. Annie'd ransacked Dante's duffel bag on her way out the window, had stolen his iPod, a couple of shirts, a bottle of absinthe, and his song journal.

"She can fucking keep the other stuff. The only thing I care about is that journal," Dante had said softly, then had shrugged—no big deal. But Heather had heard the distress in his voice; the journal was special.

She had a feeling that, somehow, Annie had gut-

known which item's loss would hurt Dante the most. Maybe because she was a musician too. Heather wasn't exactly sure why Annie wanted to hurt Dante, maybe just to see if she could, maybe because she liked him. And maybe it wasn't even Dante she wanted to hurt, but Heather.

Maybe it'd been all of those things.

Heather could puzzle out a killer's identity, decipher his motives, and sometimes predict his next move, but she couldn't figure out her own baby sister no matter how hard she tried.

Heather plopped down on the bed and rubbed her face. She felt drained, tired. Annie could be anywhere, with anyone, doing anything. And time was running out fast. For herself, for Dante, for Annie, even. Heather refused to leave her sister behind to be used by their father or the powers that be.

The SB exists. A chill rippled along her spine.

And Dr. Robert Wells . . .

Though Dante hadn't said anything, she knew Lyons's words—*Every minute you let my father breathe, you're denying her justice*—had cut deep. Dante wanted Wells and she didn't blame him. But it'd be impossible. How could he confront the man when he couldn't even keep Wells's name in his mind?

Dante walked into the bedroom, his hair wet from the shower, a blue bath towel tied around his waist. "Still nothing?" he asked.

Heather sighed and shook her head. "She might be headed to Portland. She's got an apartment there and our dad's in Portland too. She might want to confront him."

"Yeah, she might." Dante took off the towel and draped it over the doorknob. "I would. I bet you would, too."

"Still might." Heather's pulse raced as she watched Dante dress, muscles rippling beneath his pale skin. She wished she could keep him naked for a while longer, wished they had the time to play.

Dante pulled on black leather pants and a twilight-purple PVC shirt crisscrossed with black latex-and-metal straps. He sat on the bed beside her. She caught a faint whiff of her honeysuckle shampoo laced beneath his autumn scent.

"We'll find her," he promised. He wrapped an arm around her shoulders.

Heather closed her eyes and leaned into him. "You need to fly home with the guys," she said. "It's not safe for you here."

"Don't tell me what I need to do, *chérie*. I ain't leaving you alone."

"Lyons could've been lying through his teeth."

"Lyin' Lyons. Probably, yeah. But not about everything. I think he told the truth about you. I ain't leaving you alone."

"Pigheaded."

"And you ain't?" Dante brushed the backs of his fingers against her cheek. "Where you planning on going?"

Heather opened her eyes. "I don't know, to be honest. Just out of Seattle. My brother's in New York, but I hate the thought of bringing trouble or worse to his doorstep."

"How 'bout you, Annie, and Eerie come to New Orleans? Stay with me until it's safe," Dante said. "I'm the reason you're in this fucking mess. Let me help, Heather."

"*None* of this is your fault." She held his dark gaze, studied his beautiful face. She could tell he thought otherwise. "I got into this by doing my job. And I don't regret that. We're in this mess together."

"Then let's fight them together, *catin*."

Together, guarding each other's backs. That felt right, just like it had backstage at Vespers while she'd protected him as he'd Slept. An intuitive rhythm pulsed between them, electric and elemental and night-blooded. She touched the spot where the bullet had entered her chest. He had no idea how special he was.

"I'll have to check with Eerie. If he's against the idea . . ." She shrugged.

A smile tugged at one corner of Dante's mouth. A devilish smile. And sexy, damn him. "I promised him my seat on the plane."

"You can do that?"

"Make promises?"

"No, the other thing."

"Yup. First class and Eerie-*minou* can lounge in his carrier on my paid-for seat."

"Good idea," Heather said. "Less stress for Eerie."

"*Oui.*"

"We can take the guys to the airport, then come back, load up the boxes I packed, and head for Portland," Heather said, mulling over their options. "We'll find Annie, drive to New Orleans, stay in motels during the day." She stroked a finger along Dante's jaw, touched his lips. Lips like a cupid's bow. He kissed her fingertip. "This could work."

"*Je pense bien,* especially since you said it aloud," Dante said. "Von told me that whatcha say from the heart has power. That a spoken thing or a wished-hard thing takes a shape in the heart and becomes real."

"I like that," Heather said softly. She lowered her hand to her lap. "I like it a lot and I'd like to think it was true."

"Me too."

"I'll say this aloud, then. I picked up the flash drive Lyons left behind," she said. "When you're ready, we'll watch it together. Maybe seeing your past will help you keep the memories." Even though she wished he *didn't* have to see all the nasty, fucked-up shit that Wells and Moore had put him through.

"*Bon, chérie.* I want to know."

"About what happened?"

"What I've done. What I've become. What I am."

Heather sucked in a breath. "Dante, no—"

"Things are unraveling inside. I feel it and I'm fighting it, but . . ."

"But nothing. I trust you."

"Don't."

That single husky-voiced word shocked the air from her lungs like a bucket of ice water over the head. She suddenly saw him on the stage floor at Vespers, Von's arms wrapped around him. Heard him ask: *I didn't hurt no one, did I?*

"I've seen you unmake a woman, true, but you also saved my life and you restored Eerie's leg," Heather said. She grasped his hand and threaded her fingers through his. "You'd sacrifice yourself without a second thought for those you love. Your heart won me, Dante Baptiste, not your looks. You need healing, and maybe you'll never heal completely, but you won't have to do it alone."

"T'es sûr de sa?" His dark eyes searched hers.

"Yeah, I'm sure. For now. So shut up, Baptiste." Heather stroked his hair, tucked a shower-damp tendril behind his silver-hoop-rimmed ear. "Time to go."

Dante kissed her lips, a heated, lingering kiss that sent hot flutters through her belly as she savored his amaretto taste. When the kiss ended, he lifted their joined hands, kissed her knuckles, then released her. Bending, he pulled on his socks and strapped on his boots. Stood, and offered her a hand up. A hand she was happy to accept.

A new future was taking shape in her heart.

PANIC FLASHED THROUGH SHERIDAN as he watched a cab pull up to the curb in front of Wallace's house. Three men, none of them Prejean, exited the house, loaded their bags in the cab's trunk, then piled into the vehicle.

Sweat beaded Sheridan's forehead, stuck his shirt to his back. Was he about to miss his moment? If Prejean left and returned to New Orleans, then he'd have to fly to New Orleans as well, and hunt the vampire on his own turf. That possibility left him cold. And still no sign of Cortini. He thought it likely she was waiting to catch Wallace alone.

Maybe she was watching right now.

Sheridan's heart triple-timed and, for a moment, he couldn't catch his breath. Too many pick-me-ups, too many hours crammed in the SUV, breathing his own ever-ripening odor, and chewing stick after endless stick of spearmint gum.

He watched the mini-mon, the screen quivering with every hard beat of his heart. Wallace and a dreadlocked male carrying a pet container walked out of the house. She unlocked the trunk to her Trans Am. Prejean and what looked like a punked-up teenager carried suitcases to the opened trunk.

Prejean *was* leaving.

"Fuck," Sheridan breathed.

Then the teenager called, "What about your bag?"

Prejean shook his head. "Leave it. We're coming back to load up Heather's stuff. I'll grab it then."

The teen nodded, then climbed into the backseat of the car.

We're coming back . . .

Sheridan exhaled. Blotted sweat from his face with his shirt sleeve. He hoped to hell Prejean was referring to just himself and Wallace. Sheridan felt confident he could find a way to justify Wallace as collateral damage to Rutgers. He just needed to be damn sure that he caught Prejean off guard and put him down with the first shot. If he didn't, he wouldn't live long enough to fire a second.

ALEX TUGGED A BLACK-AND-WHITE composition notebook from Annie's gym bag and paged through it. He studied the lyrics slanting southpaw style across the white sheets, beautiful and raw phrases; he had to admit Dante was a poet, a dark poet. He thumbed past pages full of musical composition—measures and chords, along with margin doodles and notes to himself: *Start drums here; loop the bass; falsetto chorus . . .*

Closing the notebook, Alex tossed it back into the gym bag and continued rummaging through lavender-scented clothes for the other item Annie had bragged about stealing. His fingers glided over the bottle's smooth shape and wrapped around it. Pulled it free.

Athena's words whispered though Alex's memory: *Green waters of remembrance. He'll need the green waters.*

Excitement spun through him as he examined the sealed, green-tinted bottle. Although Alex didn't know what role the absinthe would play in Dante's upcoming immersion into his past, Athena's visions were always right.

Alex tucked the absinthe back into the nest of perfumed undies, then zipped the bag shut. He scooted the bag onto the floorboards between Annie's booted feet.

She'd been talkative when she'd hopped into the truck, bouncing from subject to subject like a Slinky flipping from stair to stair, usually switching midsentence. And for one awful moment, he'd expected her to start whispering in an effort to keep up with her racing thoughts.

Then the moment had passed, and Alex's pulse had slowed. Not Athena, but Annie. A pang of regret had pricked him. Annie's mind was nearly as ravaged as his sister's.

Annie had kept thumping the end of one fist against her forehead and Alex had finally realized she was in pain, had realized she'd probably welcome the syringe.

It hadn't taken him long to find an ill-lit alley to pull the truck into.

As the needle pierces her throat, he says: It's nothing personal. All I want is Dante.

Annie laughs: Get in line, motherfucker.

Alex pushes the plunger.

He twisted flex-cuffs around Annie's wrists and ankles. Brushing a purple strand of hair away from her lips, he stretched a wide piece of duct tape across her mouth. Alex clicked a picture of her using her own phone. Sliding the phone into his hoodie pocket, he got out of the Dodge Ram and unsnapped the black tonneau cover over the bed and folded it back.

With Annie slung across his shoulders in a fireman's carry, Alex returned to the truck bed and eased her down into it as best he could. Her head bounced against the runneled metal, fanning multicolored hair across her face, but she didn't stir. She wouldn't for hours.

Alex snapped the tonneau cover back in place. He leaned against the truck, lit up a Winston, and smoked in silence for a few moments. He hoped he was right about Dante's feelings for Heather. Even so, it was still possible the True Blood might tell him to fuck off again.

Alex pulled his cell from his pocket and called Athena. After six rings, her voice mail switched on, a message he'd recorded for her years ago: *You've reached the voice mail of Dr. Athena Wells. Please leave a message.*

Anxiety coiling through his guts, Alex rang his father's cell, then the land line. Six rings, voice mail. Maybe she was so absorbed studying the center footage on the laptop she didn't hear the phone. Or was ignoring it.

He wished he and Athena shared the long-range telepathy that vampires used so effortlessly, but they'd learned through trial and error that they couldn't touch each other's minds or anyone else's unless they were within a certain proximity.

Taking one last drag from his cigarette, the butt-end smoke harsh against his throat, he flicked it into a puddle. Alex thumbed the END button on his cell, then slid the phone into his pocket. He climbed back into the Dodge Ram and started up the engine. The powerful rumble reverberated against the alley's stone walls.

Even if Athena was ignoring the phone, the Tightrope Walker should've picked up. She'd want to know about his progress since she seemed to be so invested in seeing his father in Dante Baptiste's hands.

But maybe she *couldn't* answer the phone.

Maybe Athena had decided to conduct another experiment.

TRANS AM IDLING IN a passenger unloading zone in front of the main terminal at Sea-Tac, Heather said her good-byes, giving Jack, Eli, and Antoine quick hugs before offering her hand to Silver. With a slight smile, Silver shook her hand.

"I hope you find Annie," he said. His strange silver eyes glittered like sun-sparked water beneath the lights. "She's cool, but she's chewed herself up ragged inside, y'know? She needs an easy touch."

Heather nodded, surprised by his insight. "She does. Thanks."

Silver shrugged, then stepped back a few paces to join the guys as Dante, the hood of his black hoodie pulled up to shadow his face, said his good-byes with kisses and murmured words.

"He asked me to shepherd everyone home, make sure they get there safe," Von said, stepping up beside Heather, his gaze on Dante. "But I goddamned hate leaving him. Between the migraines and the seizures . . ." He shook his head.

"Has he ever said anything about what Jordan did to him in that van?"

"Nope. Not a word."

"That's something else he shouldn't have to carry alone," she said softly.

"Yeah, good luck trying to convince *him* of that." The nomad bent and dug through the well-weathered olive-green knapsack at his booted feet. He pulled something out, then straightened. "Here, doll." He held the black, zippered bag in his hands. "You're gonna need this."

Heather took the vinyl bag, feeling cold. "Thanks. I hope I won't have to use it."

Von shook his head. "Sorry, darlin', but you will."

Heather pulled one of her business cards from her purse and handed it to Von. "My cell phone number's on there," she said. "Check in with me anytime. Once you're back home, give me a call. I'll keep you posted on our progress each night and where we're staying."

The nomad nodded. "Good enough." He slipped the card into an inner pocket of his leather jacket.

Heather caught a whiff of frost-rimed autumn leaves and then Dante was beside her. He hooked his arm around her waist. "Safe flight, *mon ami*. I appreciate you seeing everyone home. *Merci beaucoup* for everything."

"No, thank *you*. You helped me attain my lifelong

goal of roadie-hood," Von drawled dryly, then something tender warmed his green eyes. He pushed Dante's hood back and cupped his pale face with his road-weathered hands. "Let them see, little brother." Then he bent and kissed him.

Let them see.

Heather realized Von wasn't talking about the voyeuristic appeal of watching two men kiss, he was telling Dante not to hide his beauty inside a hood, and he was also speaking about who and what Dante was—musician, friend, True Blood, and Fallen.

Unique. Brimming with magic and beauty and heart; dark, untamed, and deadly.

Let them see you.

I agree, but not yet, Heather thought. *Not until his life is completely his own.*

The kiss ended and the nomad released Dante with a pat to his cheek. "Take care, little brother," he said. He cat-nudged Heather with his shoulder and she bumped him back. "And see if you can keep your gorgeous kick-ass woman outta trouble."

Dante snorted. Pointed to himself. "Gasoline." Pointed at Heather. "Match." He winked at her as Von laughed. "As soon as we find Annie, we'll head home."

Von held Dante's gaze for a few moments, and Heather knew they were speaking mind-to-mind. Something sad and yearning suddenly shadowed Dante's unguarded face, and he looked away, jaw tight.

Von watched him for a moment, then sighed. "Like a goddamned mule." Looking at Heather, he said, "Wishing ya easy roads, doll. See ya in a week or two."

"Take care of Eerie," she said.

Von snorted. "That cat's got Eli wrapped around his paw, woman."

Heather grinned. "That's my kitty boy."

Motioning for the guys to move their asses, Von strode toward the terminal entrance, pausing to exchange greetings with a couple of nomads on gear-laden bikes.

Dante untucked his shades from the front of his shirt and slid them on. He looked at Heather. "Let's go find Annie."

"FUCKING HELL," DANTE MUTTERED. He hated restraints. Unbuckling his seat belt, he shifted in the seat, his leather pants squeaking against vinyl, and rested his back against the passenger door. He rested one booted foot on the seat. *Better.*

Heather glanced at him. "That's the face I want to remember," she said, returning her gaze to the road. "The one *before* the accident."

"So don't crash," Dante teased. "And anyway, the airbag will suffocate me first."

"Smart ass."

"Yup."

The smooth, high-pitched thrum of the Trans Am's engine filled the silence. But the silence wasn't tense or awkward, Dante reflected, his gaze on Heather's face. They were comfortable together even without words, content with their own thoughts.

And that was dangerous.

It would make it even harder to walk away from her when the time came, when he was sure she was safe from the Bureau and anyone else hunting her.

The words Von had arrowed into his mind at the airport darted through his memory: *Don't deny your heart, little brother.*

Gotta. She'll die if I don't.

No, Dante, no . . .

A song suddenly disrupted the silence, a tinny version of Rob Zombie's "Living Dead Girl." "That's Annie's ringtone," Heather breathed. "Phone's in my purse." She steered the Trans Am to the shoulder of the road. "Talk to her until I get stopped."

Dante swiveled around in his seat, grabbed Heather's purse from the backseat, and fished out the Zombie-rocking cell. He flipped it open. "Annie?"

The Trans Am slowed to a stop. Heather pulled up the emergency brake.

"No, but you're not who I was expecting either." Alex Lyons's voice was level and warm. "You're who I wanted to speak to, though."

"Fi' de garce," Dante spat. "Where's Annie?"

Heather stared at Dante, fear flickering across her face. "Who is it?"

"Lyin' Lyons," Dante told her. "Where the fuck's Annie?"

"She's with me and she's safe, for the moment."

"Give me the phone," Heather said, holding out her hand. All fear was gone from her face, but her hand trembled. Dante gave her the phone.

"What have you done with my sister, Lyons?"

Heather's expression tightened as she listened to whatever the motherfucker was saying. Dante trailed a hand through his hair. Annie was in trouble. Bad trouble. Because of him.

He should've killed Lyons when he'd had the chance. Should've torn into his throat and fed.

Heather lowered the cell from her ear. The phone beeped and she looked at what appeared on the tiny monitor. Her breath caught in her throat. Wordlessly, she extended the phone to Dante so he could see too.

The screen held a photo of Annie, eyes closed, duct tape across her mouth. Anger burned through Dante's veins.

"He wants to talk to you," Heather said, her voice strained.

Dante took the phone from her fingers. He knew what she was thinking because he was thinking it too. "How do we know she's alive?" he said into the cell.

"You'll just have to take my word for it," Lyons said. "She is, but if you want to keep her that way, you need to meet me."

"Where?"

"Heather's house. If you aren't there in ten minutes, Annie *will* be dead." Lyons ended the call.

Dante flipped the cell closed and dropped it back into Heather's purse. "Your house in ten minutes," he told her.

Heather nodded, jaw tight. She dropped the emergency brake, slammed the Trans Am into gear and burned rubber out onto the road. Dante listened to the rapid, furious rhythm of her heart. Adrenaline heated her scent, edging its lilacs-in-the-rain sweetness with the sharp tang of steel.

"Hang on, *p'tite*," Dante said under his breath, wishing hard and from the heart. Memory whirled through him, edging his vision with white light.

Jay, straitjacketed and dying on the slaughterhouse's cold floor, blood from his slashed throat pooling around him, staining his blond hair red . . .

He'd told Jay to hang on, too. Dante's hands clenched into fists. He refused to add Annie's name to the litany of the lost, the long list of all those he'd failed.

"He'll want me," Dante said. "And he can have me. As soon as he gives you Annie, you get the hell outta Seattle and head for New Orleans."

"I'm not letting you sacrifice yourself," Heather said, voice tight. "We need to think of something else."

"He wants me to heal his sister. He ain't gonna hurt me."

"I'm *not* letting Lyons leave with you."

Dante shrugged. "I'll just kill him first chance I get."

"No, you won't."

"Yeah? Why won't I?"

"Because you're going to prepare two syringes with just enough morphine to knock a mortal into slumberland for a few hours. That's why. Whoever gets to him first can give him the shot. Will you be able to get into his mind? Find where Annie is?"

"Yeah, I can do that." White light danced at the edges of Dante's vision and thorn-sharp pain prickled at his temples, scraped behind his left eye. He willed the pain below. He could only hope it'd stay there. And if it didn't? He shivered, a chill breathing against the back of his neck.

I'll have to use it before it uses me.

"Promise me that both syringes will have a nonfatal dose."

Dante looked at Heather for a long moment, reading the tension in her body, the trust in her eyes. She knew he'd never lie. He reached into the backseat, grabbed the black bag, and unzipped it. He plucked out a syringe and uncapped it.

"Ain't promising."

In the depths, wasps droned.

He'd do whatever it took to keep Heather and Annie safe. No matter the cost.

34

LIMITLESS DEPTHS

Seattle, WA
March 24

SHERIDAN WATCHED ON THE mini-mon as the Trans Am pulled into Wallace's driveway. The headlights went out. The passenger door opened and Dante Prejean stepped out of the car. Streetlight shimmered along his leather pants and latex shirt, gleamed blue in his hair.

Prejean strode down the driveway and Sheridan couldn't help but admire his smooth and predatory grace. He also noticed that the vampire's body language whispered of coiled muscles, of agitation. Of hunger.

Prejean glanced up the street in both directions, skimmed a hand through his hair, then turned and paced up the driveway.

Interesting. Waiting for someone, but not happy about it.

Let's see who.

* * *

DANTE WALKED AROUND THE car to Heather, gravel crunching beneath his boots. It had started sprinkling again, more of a mist than actual rain, and droplets of water glistened on her black trenchcoat, jeweled her hair.

"If this goes south, and Lyons leaves with you," she said, her voice husky, pained, "I *will* find you. I won't give up. Do you hear me, Baptiste?"

Dante cupped Heather's rain-cool face. "I hear you, *chérie*. And ditto." He lowered his face to hers. "For luck." He kissed her and she kissed him back hard, her lips parting beneath his, her hands on his hips.

Inside, the droning wasps washed away beneath a wave of white silence and the pain in Dante's head eased.

The deep rumbling of a powerful engine drew Dante's head up. He released Heather. "Truck coming."

"Which direction?" She reached inside her trench for her gun. "Lyons drives a Dodge Ram."

"East."

Headlight glare stabbed blue-white light into Dante's eyes. Pain pierced his head, ratcheted his headache into high gear. Squinting, he lifted a hand to shield his eyes.

The rumble stopped. The headlights winked out. Brilliant pinpoints flecked Dante's vision. He plucked his shades from his shirt front and slid them on.

Heather studied the red truck parked against the curb, yellow parking lights glowing. "Is Annie with him?"

Dante saw only one occupant in the truck's shadowed interior—Lyons. Filtering out the steady rhythm of Heather's heart, he listened. The truck contained one heartbeat, a mortal's fast, smooth patter. Dante's hands curled into fists.

"No. She's not with him." Dante refused to voice the other possibility—she *was* with him, but her heart no longer beat.

"Shit," Heather whispered.

The passenger window slid down with a low hum. A thin coil of cigarette smoke curled out, disappearing in the drizzle. "Put the gun down, Heather," Lyons called.

"Where's Annie?" Dante asked as Heather bent and placed her gun on the gravel at the driveway's edge.

"Somewhere." Amusement buoyed Lyons's voice, amusement Dante wanted to prick full of holes.

Heather straightened. "How do we know Annie's all right?" she asked.

"You'll just have to take my word for it. That's the only option available."

No, it ain't.

Closing his eyes, Dante pushed the pain throbbing in his head below, and focused his thoughts. He reached for Lyons's mind. And bounced against a steel-smooth shield. Dante's eyes flew open. Squiggles of light edged his vision. "Fuck," he whispered.

"You okay?" Heather's hand grasped his arm.

"I was wondering when you'd try that," Lyons said.

"He's a telepath," Dante said. Blood hot trickled from his nose. He wiped at it with the back of his hand. "I can't get past his shields. Not without a fight."

"Shit." Heather released his arm. "How do we get Annie back?" she called. "What do you want?"

"I want Dante to listen to a little something on my iPod," Lyons said.

"I thought you wanted him to heal your sister," Heather said.

"I do," Lyons agreed. "But I also want to see how well he follows instructions."

"Fuck you," Dante said. "Throw me the damned iPod already."

"I'll send it to you," Lyons replied.

As Dante mulled over that comment—*Send? As in e-mail? As in fucking FedEx?*—he felt a surge of power, electric and strong, and a small shape floated out of the truck's passenger window. An iPod sailed up the driveway on a rippling wave of energy.

Dante stared as the iPod stopped in front of him at chest level, hovering in the air on tiny pulsations of energy. He looked at Lyons. Shadows and light crosshatched the mortal's face. Not only a telepath, but telekinetic. That gift was rare even among nightkind from what Dante knew. Natural or more of his dad's tampering?

Dante closed his fingers around the iPod and snatched it from the air. The moment he did, Heather's gun floated up from the foot of the drive like a windcaught leaf. It fluttered over to the truck and in through the open window.

"He's not going to listen to that until we have Annie back!" Heather yelled.

"I really don't want to hurt your sister, so don't force me," Lyons said. "Dante has ten seconds to comply, then I'm driving away."

Truth and mingled lies wove the fabric of Lyons's

words. Dante knew he'd hurt Annie with little hesitation.

"Don't listen to the iPod. I think he's trying to trigger you." Heather looked at Dante, her eyes nearly black with emotion. "There's got to be another—"

"Move away from me, *chérie*," Dante whispered. "Get outta reach."

Jaw tight, eyes glistening, Heather backed away from him.

Dante worked the earbuds into his ears, then, heart hammering against his ribs, he touched the play arrow. A smooth voice burrowed into his ears.

"S, time to awaken, my Sleeping Beauty. You have work to do."

A *familiar* voice. One Dante still couldn't name. Pain ripped through his mind, rising up from below and shredding his thoughts, his sense of self. Voices, whispering, screaming, and everything in between, cycloned up from the shattered depths. Droning wasps winged up in a dark and furious cloud, needling venom into his heart.

Pain shoved him below.

And Dante tumbled into limitless depths.

The unnamed voice continued to speak.

35

LOCKED INSIDE HIS HEAD

Seattle, WA
March 24

DANTE DROPPED TO HIS knees on the gravel and doubled over, his hand fisting around the iPod. His rain-damp hair swung forward, hiding his face.

Pulse thundering in her ears, Heather stepped toward him. He hissed, the low sound a warning as primal as a rattlesnake's. She froze.

"Stay away from him," Lyons called from the truck.

The hiss faded. Dante swayed on his knees. Heather wanted to yank the headphones from his ears, but had a feeling it was too late. And, for all she knew, interrupting the process might do him more harm than good.

A car door thunked, then Heather heard footsteps approaching from the street. Her hands knotted into fists when Lyons stopped beside her in a cloud of cigarette smoke and Drakkar Noir.

"So what's the plan?" she asked, her voice flat.

"When he stands up again, throw him your car keys."

"What?" Heather looked at Lyons. He met her gaze, his own curious.

"I think I know where my father's sending him," Lyons said. "Give Dante the keys and stay out of his way. We'll follow."

"He's doing this for Annie, so tell me where she is."

"After," Alex said, nodding at Dante. "Ah," he breathed.

Dante pulled the earbuds free and dropped the iPod in the gravel. He pushed his hair back from his face with both hands, then rose to his feet. Rain dewed his hair, glistened in beads on his leather pants and on the shoulders of his hoodie, on the lenses of his sunglasses.

He swiveled around, a movement so quick she'd nearly missed it. He watched her from behind his shades, his pale face still and, suddenly, unknown to her. Blood trickled from his nose. Fear hollowed Heather out.

She was looking at S, not Dante.

"Give him the keys," Lyons murmured, touching her arm.

Heather pulled the keys from her purse and tossed them. Dante snatched the jingling keys in midair. Without a word, he walked to the Trans Am, slid inside, and started up the engine. He backed the car out of the driveway, gravel crunching beneath the tires, then drove away, exhaust pluming in the chilly, moist air.

Heather watched, eyes burning. Her promises twisted around her heart.

I will find you. I won't give up.

"Aren't we following?" she asked, looking at Lyons.

A smile curved his lips, a wide, dark smile. "Amen, sister, that we are," he said. "But first, I want you to put your hands on the hood of the truck and assume the position. Need to search you."

Fury blazed through Heather's veins. "Payback time, huh?"

Lyons laughed. "Absolutely. Give me your purse and take off your coat."

Knowing she had promises to keep to Annie and Dante both and no time to waste, Heather gave Lyons her purse. He slung the strap over his shoulder and waited as she unbelted her trench and shrugged out of it. She threw it at him, then marched over to the Dodge Ram, placed her hands on the rain-slick hood and spread her feet apart.

"Keep any and all smart-ass comments to yourself," Lyons said as he patted her down, his hands sliding under her arms and down her sides, across her breasts.

When his hands dropped down to her legs, Heather tensed, expecting him to take full advantage of the situation, but his pat-down remained quick and professional.

"Turn around."

Heather did as Lyons instructed. He held up the morphine-dosed syringe. "Not even an overdose," he commented. "Feeling merciful, *Wallace*?"

"Not anymore."

Lyons handed back her trenchcoat and waited as Heather slipped into it and belted it. He kept her purse. He nodded at his truck, blond curls tumbling into eyes. "Inside."

After Heather had strapped her seatbelt shut, Lyons fastened flex-cuffs around her wrists. "This isn't necessary," she said, heart pounding. "You've got my sister—"

Lyons shrugged, and keyed on the engine. "Sometimes family relations aren't what they should be."

Thinking of her father, Heather silently agreed. She fixed her gaze on the street beyond the windshield. She pictured Dante in her mind, visualized a cord stretching between them—the temporary link formed when Dante'd sipped blood from her throat the night before.

You're not alone, Heather sent, hoping that wherever Dante was trapped inside his mind, he could hear her. *Come back to me, Baptiste.*

SAC Alberto Rodriguez poured another cup of French roasted coffee, stirring in a thick dollop of cream. He took a sip, savoring the rich flavor. He carried the cup back into the living room and set it on the coffee table.

He glanced at the fight occurring on the TV, a middleweight bout between the reigning champ, Miguel Garcia, and up-and-comer, Mickey Dowd. Always favoring the underdog, Rodriguez's money was on Dowd.

It was Friday night, which meant he had the house to himself. Sylvia was visiting her folks in Bellevue and the girls were spending the night with friends. Friday night was always Daddy's alone night.

Rodriguez sat on the sofa. He picked up the hardcopy he'd printed of Heather Wallace's Seattle physician's report to compare with the one from the hospital in D.C. Propping his feet on the coffee table, he picked up a yellow highlighter pen, and started marking pertinent facts.

Damage should have been fatal. Between the time Special Agent Wallace was wounded and when she arrived in Emergency, she should have bled out.

*During surgery to remove the bullet, it was noticed that the
aorta had clearly discernible new tissue . . .*

The wild cheers of the crowd and the announcer's
excited voice drew Rodriguez's attention up from the
report. Garcia was down on the mat, struggling to get
onto his hands and knees before the referee counted
him out. Dowd bounced on the balls of his feet in his
corner, a sheen of sweat on his youthful face.

Rodriguez watched as Garcia grabbed at the ropes,
trying, but failing, to haul himself onto his feet. The
bell rang. Dowd punched his fists into the air, head
back.

But beneath the cheering, bell ringing, and shouts,
Rodriguez thought he heard something he shouldn't
have—a quick snap from the rear of the house.

He sat up, listening. Had he heard the *shush* of a
window rising?

Setting the report aside, Rodriguez rose to his feet
and walked swiftly to his darkened office. His Smith &
Wesson M&P .45 was in the gun safe beside his desk.
He knelt and worked the combination lock. Opening
the safe, he grabbed his gun. He flipped off the safety.
Chambered a round.

Just as Rodriguez stood, his skin prickled. Someone
was behind him. He spun around, lifting the S&W.
"Don't mo . . ." His words shriveled in his throat.

Dante Prejean stood in the doorway. Bad Seed in
the flesh. And Rodriguez had no doubt who had sent
him.

The vampire *moved.*

Rodriguez pulled the trigger.

* * *

LYONS PULLED UP BEHIND the empty Trans Am and switched off the Ram's engine. "Our little True Blood must be doing his thing," he said.

"Where is he?" Heather asked. "Who did your father send him after?"

"Two houses up," Lyons said. "SAC Rodriguez's place."

"Christ!" Heather stared at the neat green house. "Maybe there's still time to stop this. You said you hated your father for what he's done to you and your sister. Why are you letting him use Dante? How can you expect Dante to help you after this?"

Fingers grasped Heather's chin and forced her head around. Lyons's gaze churned, a storm-tossed sea. "Dante will help because he'll have no other choice," he said, voice coiled tight. "Since *he* gave *me* no other choice."

Heather jerked free of his fingers. "Bullshit. Everything you've done has been a choice."

A smile flickered across Lyons's lips. "Did I mention you won't have any choices in this little scenario either?"

"Am I supposed to be surprised?"

"Guess not." Lyons reached under his seat, feeling around for something. He pulled out a small black gun and put it on the seat between them. "You have a job to do."

Trank gun, Heather realized, cold icing her heart. A cold that intensified with each word from Lyons's lips.

"You need to go into Rodriguez's house and dose Dante," Lyons said, reaching across her. He flipped open the glove box and rummaged through the contents. Finding whatever he was searching for, he closed the glove box and straightened.

He flipped open the blade of a small pocketknife and sliced through the flex-cuffs. "Once he's unconscious, I'll retrieve him."

Heather rubbed her wrists. "And after that?"

"After that, I'll tell you where Annie is and you can go get her. I'll keep Dante."

Heather thought it more likely he'd kill her and Annie. Why the hell would he leave them alive?

Unless . . . he planned to use them to keep twisting Dante's arm.

"Just so you know, there's only one dose in that gun. If you want to keep breathing, don't miss."

Heather picked up the trank gun, wrapped her fingers around its grip. The urge to use it on Lyons plucked at her control. Whatever the drug was, it'd been designed for nightkind, not mortals. She didn't know if it'd kill Lyons instantly or if he'd suffer a nasty, painful death.

And Dante?

Heather drew in a deep breath and closed her eyes. *Hold on, Baptiste.*

She opened her eyes and met Lyons's gaze. His smile vanished. She opened the passenger door and jumped down to the street, renewed rain cooling her face. A gunshot cracked the silence.

Heather ran.

A FIST SLAMMED INTO S's chest, knocking the air from his lungs. He tackled the man who'd just shot him, bulldogging the fucker to the floor. He yanked the gun from the mortal's hand and flung it away. Inside, voices capered and screamed and whispered.

Wantitneeditdoitkillit.

Givehimwhathedeserves. Giveitalltohim.

S wrenched aside the arm shielding the man's throat and tore into the warm flesh with his fangs. S swallowed mouthful after heady mouthful of adrenaline-spiked blood. Sharp pain radiated from the bullet wound in his chest, the exit wound in his back. His lung burned with each breath he drew. ·

Wantitneeditkillit.

Burnburnburnburnburnitalldown.

He burrowed his face deeper into the mortal's throat, seeking every last tart-berry drop of blood.

Dante-angel?

S went still. Listened.

Dante-angel? Where are we?

Princess . . .

Pain ice-picked S's mind. Stole his breath. He lifted his face from the mortal's ruined throat. Dizziness whirled through him, spun his thoughts like a carousel. He looked at the man sprawled beneath him. His eyes were huge in his pale, blood-flecked face. He gurgled. Then went silent.

Where's Papa Prejean taking us, Dante-angel?

A bad place I've been before. Get behind me and stay there.

I'm scared.

Pain twisted, jabbed, gouged. Dante squeezed his eyes shut. His muscles trembled. He heard a door open, then click shut.

A voice called, "Daddy? I forgot my iPod!"

Dante opened his eyes. He uncoiled from the body cooling beneath him and *moved*.

HEATHER CLIMBED IN THROUGH the open window, blinds rattling as she ducked under them. She straightened. A white washer and dryer stood side-by-side in the tidy laundry room. Dark spots of blood marred the sage-green tiled floor, leading out of the room.

She followed Dante's trail through the kitchen and down a hall decorated with framed family photos, the thick, coppery reek of blood filling her nostrils.

She glanced in each doorway she passed, trank gun held at her side. In the last room on the right side of the hall, she saw a man's body—*Rodriguez*—motionless on the floor. Blood glistened on his ravaged throat and chest. Her heart sank.

I'm too late.

From the front room, pitched voices discussed boxing strategies—TV talking heads. But underneath that, Heather heard soft sobbing, followed by a voice she recognized, Cajun-thick and low, ragged with pain.

"Shhh, don't cry. *J'su ici, mon princesse, j'su ici.*"

Dante wasn't alone.

Heather dashed to the living room, then halted, heart in her throat.

A girl of about nine or ten in jeans and a Tinker Bell tee stood rigid against a cinnamon-colored sofa littered with papers. Dante was crouched in front of her, stroking her long dark hair with one pale, blood-smeared hand. "Shhhh," he soothed. "*J'su ici.*"

Her face wet with tears, the girl cast a sidelong look at Heather. "Help me," she whispered.

Heather lifted the trank gun, pulse pounding hard and furious. She aimed.

Dante *moved*. In a blurring streak of leather and pale flesh, he grabbed the girl and shoved her behind him as he whirled to face Heather. He hissed. Bared his fangs.

The girl squeaked, then fell silent, eyes wide.

"Get down, Chloe. I won't let 'em have you." Dante's shades were gone and Heather saw rage blazing in his dilated, red-streaked eyes, a fevered fire that underscored the resolve on his blood-smeared face. "You ain't taking her."

"Baptiste, listen to me," Heather said softly. "That's not Chloe. She's long gone. Alex Lyons triggered you with a message from his father, Dr. Robert *Wells*."

Dante sucked in a breath. Touched trembling fingers to his temple. More blood trickled from his nose. Heather took a step closer. Lifted the trank gun and aimed.

"Just you and me, princess," he said. "Forever and ever."

He lifted his burning gaze to Heather's and the desolation she glimpsed in the dark depths of his eyes broke her heart. His muscles flexed. "Run," he whispered.

She knew in that moment, she would hate Alexander Lyons forever.

She squeezed the trigger.

36

THE UNDERWORLD

Damascus, OR
March 24

D ANTE *MOVED*.

Heather jumped back, shielding her throat with her arms, hoping to hell she'd hit her mark. Dante stumbled to a stop about two feet from her, staggered. He plucked the dart from his throat. A familiar smile tilted his lips and, for an instant as he looked at her, he was himself again.

Relief flickered in his dark eyes.

The dart tumbled from his fingers. Then he followed it, sprawling belly down on the oatmeal-shaded carpet, his black hair spilling across Heather's Skechers.

Heather lowered her arms. She tossed the trank gun aside, then dropped to her knees beside Dante. She grabbed his shoulders and rolled him over. She touched his face. He was burning up, his skin hot beneath her shaking fingers.

"Good shootin', Tex," Lyons said from behind her–

in the hall. "I kinda thought he'd tear you apart. Gotta admit, I'm glad he didn't."

Heather glanced at him from over her shoulder. "You're so full of shit, I'm surprised you haven't suffocated yet."

"Ouch," Lyons murmured, voice amused. He sauntered into the room and crouched beside her. "Looks like he took a bullet."

Heather followed his gaze to the hole in Dante's PVC shirt above the left pec. *Almost a heart shot.* Not fatal, but Rodriguez would still be alive if he hadn't missed. But where would that have left Dante?

"Move away, Wallace. I'll truss him up."

"Where's my dad?"

Heather lifted her gaze to the girl still standing wide-eyed and trembling beside the sofa where Dante had shoved her for safekeeping. "Is my dad here?"

Heather's throat tightened. "I don't know, honey," she said softly, rising to her feet. "What's your name?"

"Brisia," she said. "Shouldn't we call 911? My dad always told me—"

"You've been very brave, Brisia," Heather said, crossing to the sofa. She knelt beside the dark-haired girl. "Your dad would be proud of you. You just need to be brave for a little while longer, okay sweetie?"

Brisia nodded, expression uncertain, her eyes glassy with shock. Heather stroked her arm, knowing her attempt to soothe the girl was hollow, at best.

Brisia's father was dead, his body in another room, just yards away. She'd learn the truth soon enough and it wouldn't matter to her that Dante'd had no choice, that he'd been programmed to kill on a madman's whim.

All Brisia would know was that he'd murdered her father.

The mingled smells of coffee, blood, and burning leaves wove a pungent latticework throughout the room, a scent of pending grief. A scent Heather knew Brisia would always remember.

Lyons flipped Dante back onto his belly and cuffed his hands behind him. Then, still face-down, Dante's unconscious body lifted into the air, his hair swinging forward to curtain his face.

Heather felt Brisia tense beneath her hand. She looked at the girl just as she hid her face behind her hands as if she was a three-year-old watching a monster movie.

But she was a ten-year-old and the monsters were real.

"Back in a sec to tie up loose ends." Lyons accompanied Dante's floating body down the dark hall and out of sight.

Heather squeezed Brisia's arm, then rose to her feet. The girl dropped her hands from her face. Heather hurried her to the front door. "I want you to run to a neighbor's house and have them call 911, okay?"

Brisia nodded. She grasped the doorknob, then glanced at Heather. "Do you need help too?" she asked.

"Don't worry about me," Heather said. "Just go."

Brisia yanked the door open and dashed out into the night and across the street, her long hair streaming behind her.

Breathing a little easier, Heather closed the door. She left the house by the back door and trotted over to Lyons's truck. He finished snapping the black cover over the truck bed, then looked up.

Heather's hands curled into fists. Lyons had stashed Dante in the back of the truck like a piece of equipment. "We need to move," she said. "Cops'll be on their way."

Lyons shook his head, his expression amused. "So you let the kid go. I figured you would." He shrugged. "It's Dante she'll remember. I'll bet his face will be burned into her memory."

Heather had a feeling he was right. "Dante's done everything you asked; so have I. Where the hell's Annie?"

"Listen, Wallace," Lyons said, all humor gone from his face, his eyes cold and still, "and listen very close. Screw up my instructions and your sister pays."

SHERIDAN FOLLOWED A LONG stream of traffic onto I-5 south, merging the SUV at high speed into the interstate flow of red taillights. Lyons's address in Damascus glowed in green letters across the GPS screen mounted on the dash.

Rutgers's voice curled into his ear from the Bluetooth hooked around it. "I just got the word from the Seattle PD, Rodriguez is dead. Murdered."

"Prejean," Sheridan murmured.

"I believe so. The Seattle PD said it looked like a wild animal had torn into Rodriguez. I certainly couldn't tell them that a vampire was more likely."

"No."

"I assured them that I'd be sending a team in. There's also a witness, a daughter. She mentioned two men, one woman."

"Prejean, Lyons, and Wallace."

"Given your intel about what occurred between Prejean, Lyons, and Wallace at her house this evening, I did a little digging. Hell, I roto-rootered the files and uncovered a classified gem."

"Ma'am?"

"Lyons is the son of Robert Wells."

Sheridan whistled. "Do you think Wells sent him to intercept Prejean?"

"I do. And to use Prejean."

"Mission accomplished," Sheridan murmured. "And Wallace?"

"Still Prejean's. Nothing's changed there. And since Lyons loaded the vampire into his truck bed and drove away with him, I think it's safe to assume Lyons or his father or both plan to keep using him."

"Instructions?"

"It chaps my ass that the SB was right, even if for the wrong reasons."

"Ma'am?"

"Wells and Wallace." Rutgers sighed, the sound low and weary. "I rescind my order on Cortini. But if she gets in the way, don't hesitate to remove her."

"Yes, ma'am. And Lyons?"

"He takes Cortini's place in your list."

"Roger that," Sheridan said.

"And Brian? Be careful. Do you have your rifle?"

"Yes."

"Use it." The connection ended.

Buzzing on yet more pick-me-ups, exhaustion sanding his eyes, Sheridan arrowed the SUV into the fast lane.

* * *

HEATHER STEERED THE TRANS AM around a lumbering semi, gliding into the fast lane, the truck's red and yellow lights streaking into one long carnival streamer of color as she passed. Through the windshield, the road merged with the night, endless and black.

Her heart drummed a relentless, angry cadence.

Rain beaded the windshield and Heather flipped on the wipers. She realized her hands were aching and she eased her white-knuckled grip on the steering wheel.

Almost there, she told herself. *Almost there.*

Lyons's instructions after they'd left Rodriguez's house had been clear: Take the Trans Am and wait in a nearby Safeway parking lot for a half hour, while Lyons fetched Annie. After the half hour was up, Heather was to drive to Damascus, to the address she'd looked up earlier on the computer.

If she didn't pull into Lyons's driveway within ten minutes of his arrival, Annie would never wake up again. Heather had only Lyons's word that Annie was still alive.

If she wasn't, if Dante had sacrificed his sanity and freedom for nothing . . .

She *had* to be.

Heather goosed the gas and edged the speedometer past 80 mph.

ALEX WALKED INTO THE cottage's front room. "Athena?" he called. Unzipping his hoodie, he pulled it off and tossed it onto the sofa. *<Athena?>*

White noise—telepathic busy signal—buzzed into his head. She was either out-of-range or on her meds. He believed the out-of-range option more likely and, given that her laptop wasn't on the coffee table, she and it were most likely in the main house.

Watching Father.

Wonder if he's begged yet? Promised Athena love and miracles?

Wonder what he'll promise me?

Alex pulled his currently useless S&W from the back of his jeans, freed Heather's Colt from his hoodie pocket, and headed for his room.

His nose wrinkled. The cottage smelled dank and stale, but as he stepped into the darkened hall, he detected a faint, fetid odor layered underneath the mustiness.

He flipped on the hall light and frowned at the clumps scattered across the carpet. Looked like dried mud or dirt clods. Alex followed the trail to his sister's bedroom. He pushed open the door.

A *thing* lay in Athena's bed, a dirty thing dressed in a nightgown, a thing with scrawny arms, clawed fingers, and no head. The thing's torso ended in a raw-edged neck stump. It took Alex several heart-pounding moments to realize that the thing was his mother. Or what was left of her.

Alex leaned against the threshold, his muscles weak with relief.

She promised not to kill Mother, but did anyway. No wonder she's not answering.

Alex rubbed his face with his hands. A tendril of unease curled through his thoughts. The fact that Athena had finally murdered their mother didn't bother him, not really. But what surprised him was the body's condition and location—Athena's bedroom, not her lab.

And where was Mother's head?

Dropping his hands from his face, Alex pushed away from the threshold and the thing in Athena's bed, and crossed the hall to his room. He dialed open the gun safe on the bureau, and pulled out a fresh magazine for his S&W. Stashing the Colt inside the safe, he locked it up again. Alex slapped the magazine in place, then retucked the S&W into the back of his jeans.

Time to unload the sleepers and check in on Father.

Alex dropped Annie's gym bag with its lingerie-wrapped bottle of absinthe on the carpet beside the main house's front door. Dante was stretched out on the sofa, his blood-smeared hands cuffed behind him. The vampire was still unconscious, but at least he no longer bled from his nose or from the bullet wound in his chest.

Alex strode across the room and into the hall. He glanced into the guest room. Annie slept curled on her left side atop the quilted comforter, her wrists and ankles flex-cuffed. He'd stripped the duct tape from her mouth. She'd be awake soon, and here in the boonies, she could make all the noise she wanted.

Alex walked down the hall to his mother's dark room, following the sound of his sister's whispers. He paused in the doorway, his finger hovering below the light switch. He closed his eyes, basking in his twin's warm and electric presence—a cat in sunlight—and ignored the mingled stink of clotted blood and decay curdling the air.

"Threeintoonethreeintoonethreeintoone . . ."

"Athena?" he asked softly, opening his eyes. The whispers stopped.

"Alexander returns triumphant," she said, her voice vibrant and proud. "Behold the Lord of the Under-world."

Alex flicked on the switch, bathing the room in light.

THE INDIAN MOTORCYCLE RUMBLED through the night, the sound vibrating up Von's spine as he leaned against the gear strapped to Marley Wilde's bike, his right hand perched on her hip. The wind whipped through his hair and needled his face with cold rain, rain he finger-wiped from the goggles protecting his eyes. Marley's blonde dreads writhed around her skull like Medusa snakes.

Her partner, Glen One-Eighty, gunned his cobalt-blue Kawasaki Versys beside them, jerking ahead a few meters. The black, bird-shaped V tattooed on his right cheek named his clan—Raven. As he dropped back, Von extended both middle fingers—*fuck you twice*. He caught the gleam of teeth as the nomad grinned.

Fuck you twice. Dante's phrase. And Dante and Heather were the reason Von was on the road flying toward Portland and Damascus at 75 mph on the back of a Raven's Indian instead of sitting beside Silver on a plane winging to New Orleans.

One moment, Von's chatting with the pair of Ravens at a Dutch Bros. coffee kiosk inside the terminal; the next moment, pain ragged as a chainsaw blade chews through his relaxed

In the Blood   373

shields and into his mind. Literally knocks him on his ass.

Dante.

Von funnels energy into his shields, tightens and strengthens them. The pain vanishes, but his head still aches, the throb a phantom, a memory ghost.

He jumps to his feet and runs, blurring past the weekend tourist crowds, to the bank of pay phones. Fumbling Heather's card from his jacket pocket, Von plugs a debit spike into the pay slot and punches in her number.

Von grows colder with each unanswered ring. He leaves a message on her voice mail, then decides to ask a favor.

The Ravens had been happy—*Honored, nightwalker bro*—to take Von to Heather's house. No Trans Am. Von had vaulted the fence and walked around to the back of the house and looked in through the dining room window. The boxes Heather had packed were still there. So was Dante's duffel bag.

And Von had *known*. Calm and cold and intuitive.

Not a second team trying to snatch Heather. Not a car accident. Not even the goddamned Fallen.

Alex Lyons had refused to take no for an answer.

All you have to do is heal my sister.

Lyons knew how to trigger Dante. Knew how best to hurt him.

Remembering what Heather had said about Lyons's home in Damascus, Von had sent to Trey in New Orleans and asked him to search the Internet for the address. Ninety seconds later, Von had asked the Ravens for a ride south.

Hand on Marley's hip, raindrops stinging his face like pissed-off honeybees, Von wished they could eat up the road faster.

Shoulda never left Dante's side. Shoulda never let him walk away.

ALEX STARED AT THE Lord of the Underworld, the blood chilling in his veins.

She stood between the occupied beds, a smile on her lips, her mud-streaked face luminous as though a fire burned just beneath her skin and behind her eyes. Her hair was twisted with mud into dark coils sweeping against her shoulders. A long, white, gore-streaked tunic belted at the waist graced her slender form.

In one grimy hand, she held a spear from their father's collection, and in the other what looked like an apple or pomegranate or—no, too big, Alex thought, too misshapen and moist. She held a heart.

"Welcome home, my Xander," Athena/Hades said.

Alex's goddess of wisdom was drifting away from him with each breath she drew, a kite with a broken string.

A string Dante could not only mend, but reel back in and tether. Alex would make sure of it.

"I brought Dante home," Alex said, joining his sister between the beds.

"I know." She tilted her head, then shuddered. "He's dreaming."

"Thank God you're back," his father said from the right-hand bed, his voice thin with relief. "She's betrayed us. She helped the assassin into the house. She murdered your mother—" Rage throttled his words into silence.

"Consider it a mercy," Alex said. "Mother's been

dying for years." He looked around the room, cataloguing all of his sister's additions to the décor.

A garland of bluish-gray intestines looped across the top of the closed curtains and hung down each side of the window.

A man's head, a small bullet hole marring the forehead, was perched on the nightstand beside Mother's bed. And in Mother's bed, a dark-haired woman in black slept, her wrists and ankles wrapped in leather restraints.

"The Tightrope Walker?" Alex asked.

"Yes, once," Athena/Hades said. "Now she's a meal for our Dante."

Still holding his sister's hand, Alex turned to face his father. Robert Wells stared at him with red-rimmed and furious eyes, helpless and full of hate. A well-deserved karmic kick in the gonads, Alex mused.

"I triggered Dante," Alex said, holding his father's gaze. "He did as you instructed. Rodriguez is dead. And I don't think it was a pleasant death. Dante's an effective tool, but not a very subtle one."

Father drew in a deep breath, then nodded. "If you hope to have any success using him, you need me, Alexander."

"I noticed your little safeguard. He can't even hold your name in his mind."

A smug smile curved his father's lips. "Keep this word in mind: Safe*guards*."

"Keep this word in mind: Hood." His father's smile faltered. "Here's another: Duct tape. If Dante can't see your face or hear your voice, I've got a feeling he'll have no problem killing you."

"Unmaking you," Athena/Hades added.

Their father paled. "You still need me. I have the map."

"No," Athena/Hades said. "Dante needs to *remember*. When he does, he'll take you apart." Swiveling, she walked from the room.

"I can coax S into healing Athena," Father said. Sweat gleamed on his forehead.

"Y'know, I always thought Mother was right about one thing," Alex said, walking to the doorway. Pausing at the threshold, he continued, "I think Alexander the Great *did* have his good ol' dad, King Philip, murdered. Goodnight, Father."

Alex flipped off the light and closed the door.

HEATHER PULLED IN BEHIND Alex's Dodge Ram. She slid the Trans Am's gearshift into neutral, switched off the headlights, then the engine. The night, deep and endless, swept in and swallowed up all the places the doused headlights had abandoned.

She climbed out of the Trans Am and pocketed the keys. Not wanting to give Lyons another excuse to search her, she left her trenchcoat in the backseat. The air was thick with the smell of pine and moist earth, of the woods surrounding the houses. A nearby stream gurgled over rocks.

Pale light spilled from the windows and across the dark curves of shrubs and bushes. She glanced from one house to another, wondering which one she was supposed to go to; Alex had neglected to mention two houses.

Just as Heather started across the yard toward the

main house, the front door opened and a light-haloed form stepped outside onto the porch, a gun in one hand.

"Cutting it close," Lyons said.

"It's not an easy place to find," Heather said. She stopped at the foot of the steps leading to the porch. "Let me give the car keys to Annie. Let her go. Why do you need all three of us?"

Lyons raked a hand through his curls, his face thoughtful. "You might have a point. C'mon in, let's see if we can reach an agreement."

Heather placed a foot on the bottom step. "You've lied to me before. I need a show of good faith," she said. "You let Annie take the car and leave, I'm yours."

"I've got Dante, so you're mine anyway." Lyons turned around and sauntered back inside the house. "Annie's negotiable."

Body tight as a fist, Heather climbed the steps. She walked into the house. Her heart skipped a beat when she saw Dante on the sofa, still unconscious.

"He's fine," Lyons said, a knowing smile on his lips.

Telepath. She was going to have to be very careful. "Where's Annie?" Her gaze skipped around the room— leather recliners, wide-screen TV, bookcases, coffee table—marking window locations, possible exits, hall, kitchen archway.

"My sister's fetching her." Lyons nodded at the recliner closest to the sofa. "Take a seat, Wallace. Get comfy. You're gonna be here a while. Oh, and hands out, wrists together."

After her wrists had been secured again with flex-cuffs, Heather perched on the edge of the recliner, the leather squeaking beneath her. Alex went to the sofa, bent, and waved a capsule of some kind under Dante's nose. Dante stirred, then his head jerked away from the capsule. Heather caught a whiff of something acrid.

"Rise and shine," Lyons murmured. He slipped the capsule into his jeans pocket. Hooking a hand around Dante's bicep, he hauled him upright.

Dante shook his hair back from his face. Blinking, he looked around the room and Heather could just imagine what he was thinking: *Where the hell am I now?* He looked at Lyons and something very dark and dangerous flashed across his pale face.

"Did I pay for Annie?" Dante asked, his Cajun accent thick, his words slightly slurred. "She safe?"

"No," Heather threw in before Lyons could answer him. "He lied to us. He's still holding Annie."

Dante's gaze shifted to Heather and the dangerous light faded from his face. "You okay, *chérie?*" His eyes were glassy and dilated, just a thin ring of deepest brown slashed with red circled each pupil.

"I'm good," she said. "I'm just trying to convince Lyons to give Annie the car keys so she can go."

Dante's gaze returned to Lyons. "Did I do what I was fucking supposed to do?"

Lyons nodded. "You did."

A muscle in Dante's jaw flexed. "Yeah? Then why you still holding Heather and Annie? You want me to heal your sister? I'll do it."

Lyons chuckled. "Just like that?"

Dante nodded. "I can be as easy as you want me to be. Just let them go." His nostrils flared as though he'd caught a whiff of something bad, then he turned and looked toward the hall. "Fuck," he whispered.

The stench of death wafted into the air, greasy and thick, and carried on a murmured tide of words Heather couldn't make out. A tall, slender woman in a white Grecian-style gown streaked with dark smears and smudges walked into the room. She held a spear in one grimy hand, her other hand locked around a wide-eyed Annie's arm.

"My sister," Lyons said. A strange mix of love and despair swept across his face. "The Lord of the Underworld."

A chill rippled down Heather's spine. If this was Lyons's sister, then she was worse off than Heather had imagined, much worse.

"What do you see, my Hades?" Lyons asked, his voice hushed.

The murmured tide of whispers stopped. Athena Wells looked at Dante.

"I can't see beyond his beautiful face," she said, her voice low and full of wonder. "I've tried and tried and tried. Either he blocks the way or he *is* the way."

"The way?" Lyons questioned. He moved around the sofa and pulled Annie from his sister's grasp, walked her to Heather's recliner.

Heather saw the fear in Annie's eyes. "It'll be okay," she promised. "We'll get you out of here."

"I fucked up," Annie whispered. She looked away, blinking, jaw tight.

"Give me the car keys," Lyons said, holding out his hand.

Rising to her feet, Heather worked her fingers into

her jeans pocket, snagged her keys and pulled them from her pocket. She flashed a look at Annie, one her sister caught, then fumbled the keys. They jingled to the carpet.

Annie scooped them up like a first baseman diving for a low ball.

"Whoops," Heather said.

Lyons looked at her, an almost smile on his lips. "Smooth, Wallace." Opening up his pocketknife, he cut through the flex-cuffs binding Annie's wrists. "Okay, all right, Annie can go. I'll even walk her out to the car."

The glint in Lyons's eyes hinted of nastiness to come: a bullet fired into Annie's skull underneath the evergreens, her body dumped into the trunk of Heather's car, or maybe out in the woods.

Cold lanced through Heather. "No, wait—"

With a quick shove of his hand to her chest, Lyons pushed Heather back into the recliner. She landed hard, her head bouncing against the back of the chair.

A blur of fluid motion rocketed across Heather's field of vision, a blur of leather and white skin launched from the sofa. Lyons slammed to the floor, Dante on top of him. The gun Lyons had just pulled somersaulted from his hand, across the carpet, and disappeared under the TV stand.

Heather jumped to her feet. "Annie! Run!"

Annie whirled and bolted out the front door.

"Both of you!" Dante yelled, straddling Lyons. "Fucking *run!*" Hands still cuffed behind him, he dipped his face toward Lyons's throat. A flash of fangs and then he slashed into either the arm Lyons had flung up or into his throat.

Outside on the porch, Annie stopped in front of the

window and mouthed *run*. But Heather shook her head and motioned for Annie to keep going. She wouldn't, she *couldn't*, abandon Dante. They were in this fight together.

Annie's eyes widened in horror and she clapped a hand over her mouth.

Skin prickling, Heather spun around.

The Lord of the Underworld drove her spear into Dante's back, just beneath his left shoulder blade. Dante sucked in a sharp, pained breath. She yanked the spear free, the tip flinging dark droplets of blood through the air. She swiveled around to face Heather, a breath-stealing smile on her lips. Heather froze.

Outside the Trans Am revved to life. Gravel scattered under tires.

"Welcome to Hell," Athena Wells said.

37

BROKEN

Damascus, OR
March 24/25

ANNIE SLAMMED THE TRANS AM into fifth gear as she peeled down the dark road and away from the winding driveway marked PRIVATE, peeled away from the image of the Lord of the Underworld driving her spear into Dante. Peeled away from the image of her cuffed sister still trapped inside that house of horrors.

Annie! Run!

But she couldn't peel away from the truth.

Because of her stupidity, Heather and Dante might die.

Slamming on the brake and clutch, Annie brought the Trans Am to a stuttering, rubber-burning, smoking stop. Her heart launched into a moshing frenzy and she felt faint, sick. She sucked in a breath and it stuck in her throat, a ragged sob.

I almost lost Heather once. She's still alive and here because of Dante.

Don't walk away! Man up! Fucking do something!

Annie searched the car for a cell phone, rifled Heather's abandoned trenchcoat, the glove box, but turned up nothing. She pounded her fists against the steering wheel. "Fuck! Fuck! *Fuck!*" she screamed.

Who was she going to call, anyway? The cops? She had no idea where she was and she'd never trusted cops. Call Dad? Bitter anger percolated within her.

She looked out the windshield. The night stretched down the road and merged with the dark, tree-bristling humps of the hills and, in the distance, scattered lights glowed like tiny candles.

Candles. Candlelight glinting in Silver's eyes. His voice whispered through her memory: *Temporary links are formed when we take blood from someone, that's why you can hear my thoughts right now. Blood-forged, my* père de sang *says. You could say good-bye to me in the air, Annie, and I could say good-bye back.*

Fuck your good-bye and fuck you.

Closing her eyes and swallowing her pride, Annie called to Silver.

DANTE COUGHED UP BLOOD. Pain burned through his back, his chest. His entire body ached. He felt himself lifted, then lowered, but didn't feel hands.

I'm back in the Perv's van. Hurtling through the night. Musta dreamed I escaped.

Something warm and wet stroked his stinging eyelids. He tasted blood, his own, mingled with alcohol and the wormwood-bitter, anise-sweet flavor of absinthe. Green light skipped like a stone along the surface of his thoughts.

Constant murmuring whispers, like the rush of wind through the trees, or maybe the sweep of strong wings through the night, flowed all around him.

Holytrinitydantewillmakeusoneholytrinitydantewill-makeusoneholytrinity . . .

He felt the hot trickle of blood from his nose. A hand smacked his cheek. Fingers snapped in front of his face. "Dante? C'mon, boy, wake up. Focus."

"Leave him alone, goddammit!" Heather's voice?

"Heather," Dante croaked. His throat felt raw, sand-paper scrubbed.

"Here, Baptiste, I'm here."

Dante opened his eyes, but instead of the Perv's grinning face, he looked up into a handsome, beard-stubbled face, a familiar face, then it clicked and memory slid into place—Lyin' Lyons. A taped-on gauze pad bandaged the bites in Lyons's forearm, but Dante still smelled the blood, and the aroma slammed straight into his aching head.

The whispers stopped. A woman's voice said, "You've had another seizure. Did you keep any of the memories?"

Those words trailed cold fingers down Dante's spine. He glanced in the direction of the voice, at his feet. He realized he was stretched out on the sofa, his head pillowed in Lyons's lap, his legs across the Lord of the Underworld's thighs. Realized she held a laptop computer.

Lyons's twin, the mud-haired, tunic-wearing chick with the spear, smiled at him, a strangely shy and girlish smile. "Did you keep any?" she asked again.

Another seizure? Panic coiled through Dante. How

much time had passed? He looked past Lyons's sister to Heather sitting rigidly in the recliner. She met his gaze, her face pale and strained, her bound hands clenched into fists in her lap. "Annie got away," she said. "Thanks to you."

"*Bon*. Let Heather go—"

Heather shook her head. "I'm staying with you."

Fingers stroked Dante's hair, stroked and tugged, a hurtful caress—Lyons. "You haven't answered Athena," he chided.

"Go fuck yourself."

"Hades," his sister corrected. "Did you keep any memories this time?"

"You can fuck yourself too."

Lyons yanked Dante's hair. "Answer the question. Or I start in on Heather."

Jaw tight, Dante said, "Nothing. I remember nothing." But deep within, wasps stirred, droned, and a chill shuddered through him. Sweat trickled down his temples. *Sure about that?*

Lyons sighed. "Okay, let's go again. I hate to keep doing this to you."

"Liar," Dante said. The fed's voice said he liked doing this to him, liked it a lot. And hoped to keep doing it. "How many times already?"

"Five," the Lord of the Underworld said.

Fear curled into Dante. *Five?* "How many seizures?"

Lyons laughed. "Five, gorgeous, five. I keep thinking you're gonna tear yourself apart, but you don't. Not yet, anyway." He paused. "Ready, Athe—Hades?"

The whispers breezed awake: "Holytrinitydantewillmakeusoneholytrinitydante . . ."

Alex lifted a green bottle, *his* stolen bottle of absinthe. "Open wide, time for more medicine."

"The green waters of remembrance," Athena/Hades murmured. "Drink deep, so when you're killing our father, you'll know why. Then our rebirth can begin."

Dante clamped his lips shut and turned his face away. He wanted his past, wanted to see, wanted to know, but on his own terms and with Heather. Jordan had tortured him with the past and now Lyons and his gone-gone-gone sister were doing the same.

No more. Fuck each one of them.

"Your choice," Lyons muttered. He grasped Dante's jaw with hard fingers, forced his head around.

A prickling column of energy pried at Dante's lips, forcing his mouth open, and wedging into one corner. His heart trip-hammered against his ribs, triggering hot, liquid pain in his chest. Sweat trickled down his face, stung his eyes.

Athena/Hades watched, a gore-smeared hand resting on Dante's leather-clad shins, her pale brows drawn down. "You're hurting him, again," she said. "You shouldn't. He's a part of us."

"He isn't yet. And I don't have time to be gentle."

A thought brushed against his blazing mind, and Dante became aware of two things: His shields were down, drug-dropped, and Lyons was scared.

<You've got to heal her. She's almost gone. But she's convinced you need to be whole first and foremost. So fucking remember or fucking lie.>

Lyons positioned the absinthe bottle between

Dante's lips and poured. The pale green liquor filled his mouth faster than he could swallow. He choked, and coughed, breathless.

"That's the last of it," Lyons said.

The wedge of energy vanished and Dante, coughing, jaw aching, closed his mouth. He saw Athena/Hades lifting a laptop. Images flickered across the monitor. *Familiar* images. Pain chiseled at his thoughts. He squeezed his eyes shut. They couldn't keep torturing him if he didn't look.

But Lyons sighed and said, "Again with the closed eyes? You really *don't* remember, do you? Or maybe you're just fucking stubborn."

"Both and both and both," Athena/Hades chanted.

Absinthe-green light pinwheeled and flickered behind Dante's eyes as the heavy dose of wormwood burned though his veins like gasoline and pooled in his mind, just waiting for a match.

"You're not alone, Baptiste." Heather's voice, as cool and steady as river water. "I'm with you. I'm with you. I'm here and I'm with you."

And Dante held onto that promise with all his strength, refused to let go even as tiny metal hooks pierced his eyelids and hoisted them up—again. Even as the laptop with its flickering images—*Is that me?*—descended over his face—again. Even as pain shuddered through him, cracking his psyche like an egg against the hidden past—again.

Images quaked up from the jagged depths below, each one a struck match tossed into his wormwood-soaked mind.

Papa Prejean uses the special straps to bind Dante's hands, then shoves him onto his knees in front of the bathtub full of steaming hot water.

You wanna take her punishment, p'tit? D'accord, if you so hellfire eager, take it.

Papa grabs Dante's hair and plunges his head and upper body into the scalding water, holds him down and holds him under until he finally sucks in a lungful of water and drowns . . .

Dante drains the last of the men, the men that came to do bad things to Chloe, and wipes a hand across his mouth. He swivels on his knees and reaches for his princess, but she's lying on the floor in a pool of her own blood, her empty blue eyes wide with shock . . .

Whoomf!

On their burning wings, wasps carried voices aloft.

Dante-angel? I'm cold. Can I sleep with you?

Time to get yo' ass down in the basement, p'tit.

What's he screamin'?

A very clear demand: Kill me.

You're not alone. I'm here and I'm with you.

Dante held onto that promise.

Even when he couldn't hold onto anything else.

Even after he could no longer scream.

He held onto her promise.

ANNIE CROUCHED DOWN BESIDE the main house's back door, away from the light streaming through the small window in its center, and tucked herself into the shadow-draped bushes beside the door with a minimum of twig snapping and leaf rustling. She hunkered down, her knees against her chest, her back against the house.

Her fingers slid along the handle of the pocketknife she'd swiped from Alex's red truck. Dante's anguished screams had masked any noise she might've made while ransacking the vehicle. Her eyes stung.

Silver had let her know that Von was on his way. But *when* had been something they'd been unable to communicate, for whatever reason.

Stay right where you are. Von will find you.

But Annie had whipped the Trans Am around and had torn up the highway going back the way she'd come. She'd parked at the mouth of the long, steep driveway, then had hiked up to the house.

Annie unlaced her Docs, tugged them off her feet, and stashed them in the bushes. Pulse racing, and wishing for a drink of beer, water, *anything*, she rose to her feet. Before she could think herself out of it, she opened the back door and slipped into the brightly lit kitchen.

HEATHER WIPED THE TEARS from her face with the back of one bound hand. Dante was sprawled half on the sofa, his booted feet on the floor. His eyes were open, but his gaze was turned inward, unseeing, his body knotted with pain.

Her breath caught in her throat. He looked *broken*. A toy shaken apart by an angry child, then tossed aside.

She'd lost count of how many times Lyons and his sister had tried to awaken Dante's memories. Had lost count of the number of seizures Dante'd endured.

Dante falls silent when the seizure ripples the length of his body. His muscles lock, his back arches, and his limbs twist. His head whips back and forth, a blur. Blood flings into the air from his nose, his mouth, his pierced eyelids. The twins push Dante onto the floor and allow the seizure to have its way with him.

Athena kneels on the blood-flecked carpet beside Dante's convulsing body and whispers to him: Rememberand-rememberandrememberandremember . . .

The seizure ends and Dante curls up on the floor, dazed and trembling, sweat-damp black hair clinging to his forehead, his cheek.

Lyons floats Dante up into the air and back onto the sofa. He bends over Dante with a washrag and wipes the blood from his face. And the process starts all over again.

And each seizure is worse than the one before.

Athena paced at the opposite end of the room, her spear thumping against the carpet with each step. Her reflection in the windows behind her echoed her movement. "I can't see past Dante. Nothing stretches beyond him." She looked at her brother. "He's either the end of us or the beginning."

"I don't think we're going to be able to make him whole again," Lyons said. He trailed both hands through his curls. "Not without Father's help. Maybe he told the truth about the labyrinth."

"He'd tell us anything to get free." Athena stopped pacing and faced her twin. A bitter smile touched her lips. "But he'd only lead us to the minotaur within the labyrinth's heart."

Heather went still. Wells was *here*? And a prisoner of his own warped children? She felt a dark smile twist across her lips. Maybe there was such a thing as karma, after all. She hoped he remained a prisoner. She didn't want to think about what he could do to Dante if freed. Or worse, what he would make Dante do.

Didn't want to think about what *she* might do to Wells, given the chance.

"Blood might give Dante the strength to reclaim his past," Athena/Hades said.

Lyons nodded. "I'll fetch his meal." He walked from the room.

With a low sigh, the Athena-wind gusted into the air. "Holytrinitydante . . ." She resumed pacing, her spear once again thumping against the floor. Her eyes closed. "Holytrinitydantewillmakeusoneholytrinity . . ."

Hoping Athena was as lost in thought as she appeared, Heather rose from the recliner. Pulse racing, she knelt beside the sofa and touched Dante's face. "Can you get up?" she murmured.

He closed his eyes, the lashes black against his skin. Three words whispered from his lips and knotted around Heather's heart.

"Little fucking psycho."

LITTLE FUCKING PSYCHO.

Chains looped around his ankles, he hangs upside down above the bodies of the men he killed. Above the body of the girl he tried to protect, but slaughtered instead.

Chloe. Chloe. Chloe.

A heart pulsed, hummingbird fast and delicate, and Dante smelled sage and lilac and smoky sorrow. Hunger scraped his heart hollow.

You're not alone. I'm with you. I'm here and I'm with you.

Cool white light encircled him, a sacrament of silence. Heather's promise.

"On your feet, Baptiste," a voice whispered. "C'mon."

Dante opened his eyes and looked into Heather's blue eyes. Fear glimmered in their twilight depths. "*Chérie*," he breathed.

The fear faded and she nodded, a smile brushing her lips. "We gotta move now."

Dante slid the rest of the way off the sofa. The room spun around him. His head felt full of broken glass. Heather slid her flex-cuffed hands through his arm and tried to haul him to his feet. Black spots flecked his vision. Pain prickled through him, twisting like a thorned vine through his insides. He stumbled upright with Heather's help. She steered him toward the door while he concentrated on moving his feet.

The quiet shush of wind through the treetops stopped.

A chill crawled up Dante's spine. Heather pushed him forward, urging him on.

"Little god," a woman's voice said, a familiar voice. Lyons's whacked-out sister. "If you want to rescue Heather from death again, I'll be pleased to oblige you."

Dante pulled free of Heather's grasp, and turned around. Athena/Hades stood a yard behind them, her spear lifted and aimed at Heather. Curiosity lit her eyes. Dante stepped in front of Heather. Pressed his back against hers. "Keep walking for the door," he said.

"Gotcha." But as Heather took another step forward, Dante felt some splintered thing shift inside his head and an electric shock surged through his skull. His muscles locked. A blinding burst of light exploded through his vision, scintillating white light.

Memory sheared up.

Très joli, dis one, like an angel. Play with him all you want, but don't put nuthin' in his mouth. Boy bites.

Like an angel, ah, kiddo, that doesn't even begin to cover it.

The man strokes Dante's hair, curls a black lock around his finger. Fucker's name is Eddie. He's visited Dante in the basement a bunch of times. This time he brought a present—a handful of comics. Dante wishes he'd finish and leave so he can look at the comics and practice his reading. And, later, share them with Chloe.

This time Eddie's tender and full of careful kisses. Some of the things he does feel good, make Dante close his eyes and suck in a breath. Yeah, feels good, but he still hates Eddie and everyone else who tromps down those fucking basement steps.

Do you think you could love me?

Nope.

If I had Papa remove your handcuffs, could you love me then?

Nope. I'd kill you then.

When Eddie leaves, the fucker takes the comics with him.

And Papa, pissed as hell, comes downstairs.

The world spun away. Time spun away.

And Dante felt himself falling and falling and falling.

38

UNTIL THE VERY END
OF ME, UNTIL THE VERY
END OF YOU

Damascus, OR
March 25

T HE SEIZURE ENDED.
    Dante laid motionless on the floor, eyes closed, his breathing ragged. Sweat trickled down his temples, blood from his mouth and nose. Heather knelt beside him. She blinked hard until her vision cleared. Her hands trembled as she pushed his hair back from his face.

"You're killing him," she said, her throat almost too tight for words. She shifted her gaze to Athena/Hades. "He's *not* going to remember. For all you know, your father programmed a self-destruct safeguard into Dante's mind."

"Self-destruct," Athena/Hades mused. She tilted her head. "You might be right. I wanted him to know *why* he was killing father, but maybe that doesn't matter."

"I thought Dante was supposed to heal you."

"Heal me?" Athena/Hades smiled. "No."

"But your brother said—"

"I said what?" Lyons asked. He walked into the room, a body slung over his shoulder. Sneakers, taped ankles, black jeans, and a black sweater, hands flex-cuffed behind the back, slim but rounded hips—female.

"That you wanted Dante to heal your sister," Heather said.

"I don't need to be healed," Athena/Hades said. "I'm who I was intended to be."

A dark, desperate emotion flitted across Lyons's face. "Of course, but Dante can make it so you'll never need meds again. You'll be able to sleep."

"We won't need sleep once we're joined—Conqueror, Counselor, and Creator."

"Do you know *how* we'll be joined?"

The whisper-wind sprang to life. "Holytrinity-dantewillmakeusoneholytrinity . . ."

Shooting Heather a furious look, Lyons dumped the woman he was carrying onto the sofa. She landed on her side, her dark hair fanning across her face. Duct tape sealed her lips. She was conscious and her calm gaze skipped from Heather to Dante. Recognition sparked in her hazel eyes.

She knows who we are or who Dante is, at least.

She also seemed to be very cool and collected for a woman bound and gagged and about to be offered to nightkind. Heather wondered who she was and how she'd ended up on Lyons's sofa.

"Your father wanted to know if Dante had compromised your humanity," Lyons said, his gaze locking with

Heather's. "Betcha he'd give you up to the SB without hesitation if he believed Dante had."

Heather held his gaze. "Is that the best you can do?"

A muscle in Lyons's jaw flexed. "Just warming up." Reaching into his jeans pocket, he pulled out a pocket-knife. He flipped open the blade. "Ever seen your boy-friend feed?"

A chill touched Heather's heart. She remembered Rodriguez's body sprawled on the floor of his office. Remembered how Dante had torn into Étienne at the slaughterhouse in New Orleans. Remembered the pungent tang of spilled blood.

Lyons bent over the woman on the sofa and nicked her throat with the knife. A thin line of blood trickled from the cut, disappearing into the collar of her sweater. Then Lyons swiveled around and passed the knife's bloodied blade underneath Dante's nose.

"Wake up and feast," Lyons said.

Dante's nostrils flared. His eyes opened. *"J'ai faim,"* he whispered.

HOLDING HER BREATH IN the stinking room, Annie hurriedly unbuckled the last strap around the man's ankle. He eased up into a sitting position, then swung his legs off the bed. One slippered foot brushed against the IV stand, an IV stand topped with a woman's gray-haired head, her face with its gaping mouth aimed like a spotlight—a *flesh* spotlight—at his bed. Something Annie was trying hard to avoid looking at again.

And failing.

When she'd seen Alex come out of this room with a woman draped over his shoulder, she'd wondered just how many people the Psycho Twins had stashed in their House of Horrors. Wondered if anyone she found and freed would help her rescue Heather and Dante.

"Who are you?" the man whispered. He seemed to be close to her father's age, maybe a bit older, with graying blond hair.

"Annie," she whispered. "Who are you?"

"Bob."

Annie glanced at the door. It was awfully quiet out there. She crept across the carpeted floor to the doorway and listened. A low voice, then another. No sound of footsteps headed down the hall. She released her breath, relief curling through her.

Glancing back at Bob, she noticed the glass sitting on the nightstand beside his bed/prison. Her throat felt cactus-spiked. "Is that water?"

Bob followed her gaze to the glass. "Yes."

Carefully skirting the IV stand and its flesh spotlight, Annie laid the pocketknife down on the nightstand and grabbed up the glass. She drank the room-temperature water down in two throat-stretching gulps and wished for more. When she set the glass back down on the nightstand, she noticed the pocketknife was gone.

Musta fallen, she thought, scanning the beige carpet.

The bedsprings squeaked as Bob stood up.

"Did you see where my knife went?" she whispered.

Bob's arm slipped around her shoulders as if for support and he leaned against her, stinking of BO and piss like an old wino. "It's right here," he murmured and pressed something sharp and steel-cold against her throat.

DANTE BAPTISTE ROLLED ONTO his knees, his gaze on Caterina's bleeding throat. Hunger and delirium burned in his dark, dilated eyes. His beautiful face was etched with pain. Weariness smudged the skin beneath his eyes blue. He knee-walked to the sofa, then pressed himself against it.

Heather Wallace was kneeling on the floor behind him, her attention *not* on Dante, but focused on something either on the floor or maybe under the sofa. Caterina wondered what she'd discovered, hoped it was a possible weapon. She'd seen bitter hatred simmering in Wallace's eyes when she'd locked gazes with Lyons.

A hatred Caterina understood and shared.

Dante's screams still echoed in her mind. Dante might have escaped Bad Seed but his torture had never ended.

Dante leaned over Caterina. He lowered his face to her throat, his lips parting and revealing the points of his fangs. Wishing she had the use of her hands, Caterina tried to shake her hair back, then arched her neck to make it easier for him to feed since he also didn't have the use of his hands.

She felt the heated touch of his lips and her heart raced. She forced herself to remain still as his fangs pierced her skin. Renata had taught her the skills necessary to keep her alive among vampires.

Never struggle, my little love. That will awaken the hunter, especially among the young ones. If you struggle, they will tear

*and rend, seize their prey. Keep still. Keep centered. And shout
your thoughts—you* will *be heard. And that will save your life.*

Dante's body, hard and coiled and fevered, pressed
against hers as he drank her down in deep ravenous
swallows. Caterina caught a whiff of his autumn scent,
fallen leaves and rich, dark soil, earthy and warm. Her
eyes closed.

She felt like curling up and sleeping. Dreaming
deep. Dreaming long.

A thought darted into her mind: *Dead, how can you
protect this True Blood prince, this Fallen child? If you nourish
him with every drop of your blood, who will guard him?*

Caterina forced her eyes open. Her heart no longer
raced. Its rhythm had slowed. Biting the inside of her
cheek, she used pain to push back the tide of sleepiness
washing over her. Cold sweat beaded her forehead. She
focused her thoughts at Dante.

I'd be honored to be your fille de sang, *if you would be
my* père de sang.

Dante paused in his swallowing, held himself still.
Listening.

Caterina funneled all of her concentration, her remaining energy into what might become her last words:
*I always thought that when I was ready, I'd take the blood
sacrament from my mother, but I'd be honored to be your* fille
de sang, *Dante Baptiste, if you would have me.*

His head lifted. His gaze now seemed clear, lucid—
his delirium gone. He licked her blood from his lips,
gorgeous lips, Caterina thought drowsily. Gold light
glimmered in the depths of his eyes.

"Your mother's nightkind?"

Caterina nodded. Wonder flashed across Dante's

face. "*Merci* for the gift of your blood," he said, voice low, the cadence of his words Cajun-musical. "But I ain't taking any more. I'll leave the night of choosing between you and your mom."

Despite the hunger lingering in his eyes, Dante pulled away from her. Caterina regretted losing the fevered heat of his body. Her skin goosebumped and she shivered, cold inside and out.

"Your name," he said. "You know mine."

Caterina, daughter of Renata Alessa Cortini, she thought, finally sliding into the long deep dream promised when his lips had first touched her throat.

WITH THE TASTE OF Caterina's blood on his tongue, Dante swung around on his knees to face Heather. She sat back on her heels, her gaze on his face.

"Did you . . . ?" She glanced past him to the sofa. "Is she . . . ?"

"No."

Relief flickered across Heather's face.

But if Caterina hadn't arrowed her thoughts to him the way she had, he would've drained her without thought, and that troubled him. It was one thing to hunt those who hurt others, or to accept offered blood, but it was another thing altogether to feed upon a trussed-up and helpless mortal.

Von's words returned to him: *You're too young and in too much pain.*

Maybe so, mon ami. *Still ain't no excuse.*

"Don't you want to finish your meal?" Athena/ Hades asked.

Dante shook his head, and the broken glass in his head shifted and scraped. Light danced through his mind in green electric sparks. His breath caught in his throat.

Heather reached for him, a tendril of red hair sliding across her face, and Dante's vision whited-out . . .

Chloe bounces out of the bedroom wearing the purple Winnie the Pooh shirt he nabbed for her from Walgreens. Grinning, blue eyes bright, she throws her arms around him and hugs him. She smells like strawberries and soap.

It fits, Dante-angel! It's perfect!

He laughs.

Dante blinked. The ceiling with its dark wood beams whirled into focus. He tasted blood, his own. His muscles trembled from strain. Pain bit into his joints.

"Do you need more blood?" Heather leaned over him, her eyes glistening, her lashes wet. "I'll feed you, if you need more."

Crying? For him? His throat tightened. He wished he could touch her. *"Merci beaucoup, chérie,* but no. Help me up."

"I'll do that." Lyin' Lyons locked a hand around Dante's bicep and yanked him upright. The room spun, dipped, and Dante struggled to get his feet under him. Once he had his balance, he jerked free of Lyons's grip.

"You've fed," Lyons said. "You should be strong enough to do what you promised."

"Ça y est. Fuck yourself. I promised nothing."

With a soft sigh, the whisper-wind awakened. "Holytrinitydantewillmakeusone . . ."

"You said you'd heal my sister."

"Yeah, if you let Heather and Annie go, but 'cha didn't."

Lyons glanced at his sister as she circled the sofa, her spear tapping out the rhythm of her whispers against the carpet. He blinked hard several times. "All right. What's it going to take?"

"Ain't doing nothing till these fucking cuffs come off. Heather's too."

Lyons looked at Dante. His pale brows angled down. "How can I trust you?"

"You can't," Dante said, holding his gaze. "Gonna hafta take your chances."

Shaking his head, Lyons walked over to Heather, pulling his gun from the back of his jeans at the same time. "Up," he told her, motioning with the gun. She unfolded gracefully from the floor, her chin lifted.

"You think threatening Heather's gonna put me in a helpful mood?"

"No," Lyons said. He pushed aside a lock of her hair with the muzzle of his gun. "I'm hoping the fact that I'll kill her will keep you from doing something stupid."

"Go to hell, Lyons," Heather said.

Lyons shoved the muzzle's mouth against her temple. Wrapped his finger around the trigger. "We're already there."

Dante's pulse double-timed. Fire raged through his veins, his mind. "You hurt her and I'll put you in the ground."

The whisper-wind fell silent. The Lord of the Underworld stopped pacing. "My realm. No one goes underground except through me."

A fetid graveyard reek followed Athena/Hades as

she walked around the sofa and joined her brother. Mud flaked from her skin, her coiled hair. "Maybe it's time to give father to him."

Dante's heart thumped hard against his chest. "He's here?" The room suddenly whirled, and his vision grayed. He sat down on the sofa and lowered his head. He drew in deep, slow breaths. From beside him, he heard the steady beat of Caterina's heart.

"You okay?" Lyons asked.

"Blow me."

"I need you—"

"*Tais toi,*" Dante said, raising his head. The room remained in one place, a good sign. "Don't wanna hear it. You can still go fuck yourself—twice and hard."

"It's time for the transformation," Athena/Hades said, her voice light and girlish again. "To rule the Underworld, I must first enter it as one of the dead."

"No, no, no, Athena . . ."

"Hades," she corrected gently. She cupped a mud-streaked hand against her brother's face. "Once our Dante has resurrected me, we shall rule the Underworld together. Isn't that what it says in *Godhead and Divinity for Dummies*?" she teased.

Lyons laughed, the sound a near sob. "All I want is you, my little oracle. Healthy and happy, the circuit closed."

The Lord of the Underworld smiled. "But I *am* healthy and happy, Xander." She lowered her hand from his face. She walked into the center of the living room, spear in hand. "And soon the circuit *will* be closed forever and always."

She fixed her luminous, self-torched gaze on Dante.

"Once you resurrect me, little god, and I return from the Underworld to rule it, I'll bring your mother back with me. You can create a body to hold her. Give it any form or shape you wish."

Dante stared at her. *Create a body*. Those words strummed across his thoughts like fingers across guitar strings, resonated deep.

Athena propped the butt of her spear on the carpet in front of her, then leaned forward until the point rested between her breasts.

"NO!" Lyons yelled, bolting for his sister. But just as he reached her, her gaze lifted past him. A smile trembled upon her lips.

"See, Daddy? See?"

Athena/Hades threw herself onto the spear.

39

A SHAPE IN THE HEART

Damascus, OR
March 25

*S*ee, Daddy? See?

Dante jumped to his feet and spun around. The room whirled and he tipped back into Heather. "Gotcha," she said, then she sucked in a sharp breath. "Shit!"

A man stood at the hall's dark mouth, Annie hugged against his side. He held a knife to her throat. And nestled inside the crook of Annie's arm was a woman's severed head.

"I'm here to rescue you," Annie muttered, a disgusted expression on her face. "Luke Skywalker I ain't. Fuck."

Dante looked at the man's face. Or tried to, anyway. His face was a blur, a blank, and the sight of it slid away from Dante's mind. Pain pierced his eyes as though he'd looked into a bright, dazzling light, throbbed at his temples. He couldn't remember what he'd been doing or thinking.

"Your coup has failed, Alexander," the man said, contempt icing his tone. "You couldn't even control your lunatic sister. How could you hope to wield S? I expected more from you, much more. Now I'll have to begin again with a resurrected bride and fresh off-spring."

Faceless Man's voice was a finger tripping a switch. Something jagged and off-center inside Dante ratcheted into gear. His heart drummed a fierce and rapid rhythm.

Hoping to stop whatever was happening to him, hoping to keep the wrong things from clicking into place, Dante squeezed his eyes shut and dove into the droning, wasp-riddled depths within.

"Get out of here, Baptiste!" Heather pushed and shoved at him, desperation threaded through her scent.

"Ain't leaving you," he whispered.

And plunged deeper.

Holytrinitydantewillmakeusoneholytrinitydantewill-makeusoneholytrinity . . .

She trusted you. Guess she got what she deserved.

Time to take yo' medicine, p'tit.

What's he screamin'?

Kill me.

But he couldn't fall deep enough or fast enough.

"Open your eyes, S, my beautiful angel *sans merci.* Open your eyes and look at me. *Rip Van Winkle.*"

The voice looped around Dante like a noose and yanked him up again.

And, unable to stop himself, Dante opened his eyes and looked.

* * *

MARLEY'S INDIAN AND GLEN'S Kawasaki rumbled away, the engines swallowing the silence as they gunned the bikes up the dark, rain-glistening road. Von frowned at the empty Trans Am. Annie hadn't waited. He shook his head.

Foolish, darlin'. More than a little.

Maybe heart and steel runs in the Wallace family—at least in the kick-ass women.

Von opened the driver's-side door and grabbed the black vinyl bag from the backseat. Unzipping it, he pulled out a handful of hypes and several vials of dope and shoved them in his pockets. He tossed the bag back into the car and shut the door.

His gaze shifted up the night-shrouded driveway. All manner of bad shit hammered at his shields. From what he could tell, Dante's shields were down and his demons were awake and in full voice.

He hoped the morphine would be enough.

Von took note of the SUV with a bicycle rack on top parked alongside the road a little ways up. A currently unoccupied SUV, one he remembered parked on Heather's street.

Looks like I ain't the only one sneaking around tonight.

Unholstering both Brownings, Von *moved*.

FAIRY-TALE TRIGGER WORDS.

Cold fingers closed around Heather's heart when Dante's eyes sprang open at Wells's command. Red streaked his dark irises. Pain dilated the pupils. His attention was riveted on Wells, but a deep and primal rage blazed in his eyes.

She touched Dante's arm and he shuddered. His muscles quivered, taut. "Don't listen to him, Baptiste, listen to *me*."

"He's not allowed to listen to anyone else, Agent Wallace," Wells said, looking the worse for wear, hair uncombed, face beard-shadowed, his clothes rumpled. "He won't hear you."

Heather met Wells's confident gaze. "That's what Johanna Moore thought too."

Wells's confidence dimmed a notch. He nodded. "Point taken." He pressed the knife a little deeper into Annie's throat. She held still, clearly trying not to swallow. A line of blood appeared beneath the blade. "Kindly step away from S, Agent Wallace," Wells said.

"His name's Dante Baptiste. Not S."

"If you say so. Now move. Sit on the floor."

Sliding her fingers from Dante's arm, Heather paced aside a couple of steps, then knelt beside the sofa. She studied her sister. She looked pale and disheveled, but more than okay for a woman with a knife at her throat and a severed head in her arms, her gaze steady.

She'd never expected Annie to return, to attempt to help her. And even though it moved her that her sister *had* returned, Heather desperately wished she hadn't.

"Let Annie go," she said, voice level. "You don't need her."

"I don't, true, but S will need her blood sooner or later." Wells looked past Heather to the living room.

She glanced over her shoulder. Lyons had pulled the spear from his twin's body and tossed its bloodied length to the floor. He cradled Athena/Hades in his lap, rocking back and forth. "Nonononono," he whispered over and over, his voice raw and broken.

As raw and broken as Dante's voice had sounded while the twins had tortured him. Any sympathy Heather might've felt shriveled in the heat of her anger. A muscle flexed in her jaw and she looked away.

She wasn't sure she liked what she was feeling, but she'd have to deal with that later. Right now, she couldn't, *wouldn't* let Wells use Dante.

With Wells's attention focused on his grieving son, Heather slipped her hands underneath the sofa. She groped along the carpet for the thing she'd glimpsed beneath the sofa when Dante had been feeding.

A syringe.

Heather's fingers bumped against a smooth, cylindrical shape. Curling her hand around it, she pulled it free.

"Thank you for bringing Wallace home, Alexander," Wells said. "I'll enjoy studying her to see what changes S made when he healed her."

I'll just bet you would, Heather thought. *You and the SB both.*

A covert glance at the syringe cupped in her palm revealed that it was completely filled. That alone told her that it hadn't been intended for humans—too much, even for a fatal dose.

But for nightkind?

It won't do nothing but ease him into sleep, doll.

Desperation tightened around her throat. She hoped that was true for any drug.

Rising to her feet, Heather stepped beside Dante, slipping the syringe between her fingers. Wells couldn't command him if he was unconscious. Wouldn't be able to force him to do anything. She jabbed the needle into Dante's throat.

"No!" Wells shouted.

Just as Heather's thumb touched the plunger, a static-electricity jolt zapped her hand. The syringe twitched free of her grasp, jerked from Dante's throat, and zipped across the room.

Heather spun around.

Lyons met her gaze, his own a pale green sea of bitter hate and grief. "Can't let you do that," he said, easing his twin's limp body onto the carpet. "I still need the bloodsucking bastard to heal Athena."

Then he rose to his feet in one smooth, athletic motion, lifted his gun, and fired.

Heather twisted around, heart pounding, and saw a widening circle of blood in the center of Wells's shirt.

THE BULLET HIT THE side of Von's shades, shattering them. El Diablo styled shrapnel thistled his face. "*Moth-er*fucker!"

Von whirled, dropping into a crouch as he spun, and opened up with both barrels. Muzzle flash from the Brownings lit up the shadowed yard and dazzled his vision as he emptied both clips. He dove behind a stack of cordwood smelling of sawdust, mold, and oak. Wood splinters flew into the air when the next bullet slammed into the stack.

On his back, his gaze on a night sky gone pale with rain clouds, Von ejected the clips, pulled two more from his jacket pockets, and slapped them home—one, two.

He wiped his stinging face with the back of one

hand. His hand came back blood-smeared. "*Mother-fucker*," he repeated. Blinking the retinal flash ghosts from his eyes, Von rolled up to his knees.

He caught the glow of muzzle fire across the yard and up an evergreen- and oak-sheltered hill. A split second later a bullet *thwipp*ed into the wood stack.

Von grinned. *Gotcha, Mr. SUV Sniper Man.* Squeezing off a couple of rounds to keep the asshole busy, he jumped to his feet and *ran*.

WELLS STARED, STUNNED BY his son's display of telekinesis. A natural talent, not one he'd implanted or manipulated, one Alexander had kept secret. Then the bullet hit Wells in the chest, staggering him back a step like a hard-knuckled punch. He looked down at the hole in his shirt and the blood soaking into its fabric. The pocketknife slipped from his fingers.

Annie jerked away from him. He heard a dull thud and looked down to see Gloria's head rolling on the floor.

"No!" Wells dropped to his knees and seized the head by the wispy gray hair. He gathered it into his arms. Gunfire cracked through the night outside, a series of shots, then silence. His thundering heart leapt into his throat. Had the SB sent more assassins?

"Shit!" Wallace said. "Annie, get on the floor! Stay there!"

S was wincing, his sensitive ears no doubt hurting from the explosive sound of the round Alexander had fired.

Alexander lowered the gun and strode to the door. Flipped the dead bolt.

"S, protect me. Kill Alexander!" Pain ripped through Wells's chest.

"Listen to me, Baptiste," Wallace said. "You're not the killer he's tried to shape you into since birth. You're the man your mother wished you to be, wished aloud and from the heart."

A muscle jumped in S's jaw. His eyes squeezed shut, his lashes trembling as though he fought to keep them closed. His taut muscles quivered.

"Protect me, S!"

"Shut him out, Dante. You deserve a life of your own, shaped however you want. Shaped from the heart. We're in this together, all the way."

Sweat beaded S's forehead. *"T'es sûr de sa?"* he whispered, voice strained.

"Yeah, Baptiste, I'm sure," Wallace answered softly.

Wells stared at S. "Hush," he commanded, his voice a breathless wheeze. "Open your eyes, S, and look at me. *Rip Van Winkle.*"

"Snow White," S replied. Blood trickled from his nose, spattered on the sofa, the carpet. A dark smile tilted his lips. The tension uncoiled from his body. "Sleeping fucking Beauty."

Fear iced Wells's blood. He struggled for breath. S was somehow circumventing his programming. Maybe it'd been short-circuited when the twins had tried to force his past down his throat. Or maybe it was Wallace. Maybe it was both. Or neither.

Should've made him kill Wallace, like Chloe.

Wells scooted back against the wall. The coppery taste of blood filled his mouth.

More shots popped outside.

S opened his eyes.

Wells caught peripheral flashes of movement around him—Wallace's sister crawling to the sofa, Wallace reaching for S—but he couldn't tear his gaze from S's beautiful, blood-streaked face, from his golden gleaming eyes.

Gold, just like when he'd been born. Just like when he'd unmade Johanna.

Blue flames flickered out from behind S, from his cuffed hands.

S's smile deepened at whatever he glimpsed in the depths of Wells's eyes.

"This'll make it easier to kill him," Alexander said. "But *after* you bring my sister back from the Underworld."

Wells watched, cold and slicked in sweat, as a small key floated across the room and disappeared behind S. He heard a sharp click, then a thud as S shook off the unlocked cuffs. S worked his shoulders, swinging his hands forward.

Hands haloed in blue flames.

He's the one, Dante-angel.

I know, princess.

Dante's song swelled in the dark of his soul, intoxicating and free, a primal aria. Energy crackled along his fingers.

Vaulting the sofa, Dante landed in a crouch beside the man whose face he couldn't keep in his mind, Lyin' Lyons's dad. The pungent smell of fear oozed from every pore of the Faceless Man's body.

"My beautiful boy, my S," the man said, his voice bubbling, "it's time to bid you goodnight for—"

"*No!*" Heather yelled. "Shut up!"

White light strobed at the edges of Dante's vision. Pain blurred his thoughts. He slapped a hand over the man's mouth. His song raged in wild ascending chords, strumming fast and sharp as he sealed the man's mouth with blue fire. Blue flames blazed across the man's face, wiping away all features, making it easy for Dante to look at him. The pain throbbing in his head throttled down a notch.

The Faceless Man screamed and screamed and screamed, the muffled sound locked inside his throat.

But inside Dante, the voices whispered.

Wantitneeditkillitburnit . . .

Is he getting what he deserves, Dante-angel?

Nah, princess, not even close.

"Little fucking psycho," Dante said, his song resonating from his heart and into the night, aflame and unfettered.

DANTE'S *anhrefncathl,* dark and burning and razor-edged, pulsed into Lucien, drawing him up from restless sleep. His muscles flexed and, instinctively, he tried to unfurl his wings, tried to launch himself into the sky.

Pain pierced his wings, his shoulders, and Lucien awakened. Embers glowed orange-yellow-red underneath him, and Gehenna bled away above.

As did he.

A cold knot of dread settled into Lucien's chest. His

child's powerful chaos song stabbed into Gehenna's fading night sky, madness glimmering in each exquisite and haunting note.

Wybrcathl trilled through the skies above, crystalline and pure, and *chalkydri* chittered below, their excited voices echoing throughout Sheol's tunnels.

Anhrefncathl! Creawdwr! *The song of a Maker!*

And so, we must face the things we fear.

Dante was no longer hidden. All of Gehenna now knew a *creawdwr* existed, and the Elohim would stop at nothing to find him. Soon they would wing to the mortal world seeking the source of the chaos song—a damaged and beautiful boy, his furious son.

Once again, Lucien's absence was about to condemn Dante to a hellish existence. Once again he was breaking his promises.

You'll never be alone again.

I will keep our son safe.

Lucien twisted in his chains. The barbs corkscrewed deeper into his shoulders and blood trickled hot down his back. Pain blackened his vision. A rush of wings and servile chittering from the *chalkydri* announced the descent of one of the Elohim.

Swept up by wing gust, sulphurous, stinking air blew over Lucien, but layered underneath was a hint of cedar and warm amber, of myrrh. As his vision cleared, he saw Lilith hovering in front of him, her lush body gowned in deepest blue.

"Your son has announced himself," she said, her ember-shadowed face tight with an emotion Lucien couldn't quite name. "We're out of time."

"He didn't intend to," Lucien said. "He's in pain."

If the past had finally risen like a tsunami from the depths and broken over Dante, he hoped that Von was close, hoped he had a syringe ready. "You must find him before Gabriel or the Morningstar do. Tell Dante I sent you."

"What if he doesn't believe me?"

"Tell him he once gave me a gift, one that I cherished, an X-rune pendant."

"For friendship." Lilith's expression softened. "What happened to it?"

"It was taken from me," Lucien said, voice low.

Lilith glanced up as shadows winged overhead. "Now, Lucien, hurry."

Lucien closed his eyes, dropped his ever-weakening shields, and revealed the coiled ethereal bond linking him to Dante—father to son, creator to created, *aingeal* to *creawdwr.*

<Follow it to my son.>

Closing her eyes, Lilith dipped into Lucien's consciousness, a mind she'd once known intimately. He felt her presence, intelligent and warm and strong. He felt her trace the bond, tap into its rhythm. Felt it resonate within her mind. Together, they forged a temporary link to each other.

<As soon as you find Dante, let me know so I can sever the bond.>

Lilith stared at him, gold flecks gleaming in her violet eyes. *<Severing the bond might kill you both.>*

<True, but it's a risk I have to take. I refuse to let others discover the bond and use it to find my son.>

A sudden *burr* of wings opened Lucien's eyes. One of the *chalkydri,* scaled hide gleaming in the ember light, buzzed away. It fluted/chittered in a mock-*wybrcathl*: "The Nightbringer has a bond with the *creawdwr*!"

The *chalkydri*'s fluting ended in a startled squeak. The strong flap of Elohim wings echoed from the nearest tunnel. Lucien's heart turned to stone when white wings cut through the darkness at the tunnel's mouth. He threw his shields back into place.

The Morningstar emerged into the pit proper, the *chalkydri* hanging limp from his taloned hand. He dropped the scaled body into the embers. Its delicate wings sizzled on the coals, and the sickening smell of roasting flesh wafted into the air.

A smile blazed upon the Morningstar's radiant face. "Still planting seeds of trust, my love?"

Lilith spun away, her black wings stroking through the gloom for the pale sky above. Lucien focused on keeping his bond bright enough for her to follow. He wished her fletched-arrow speed.

"I find it amusing that the slayer of one *creawdwr* fathers the next," the Morningstar said. "Dante, an intriguing name, but inappropriate, don't you think? Once he's seated upon the Chaos Seat, he'll finally be far and safe from the hell politely referred to as the mortal world."

White wings slashing through the reeking air, the Morningstar whirled up to Sheol's mouth. "And he'll be mine."

Lucien stared after him, cold to his core.

And Dante's *anhrefncathl* still raged through Gehenna's sky.

* * *

HEATHER STARED, HEART POUNDING against her ribs, as Dante lifted his glowing hands from Wells's face. Or what *used* to be a face. Only smooth skin remained. And behind his absent lips, Wells's trapped screams faded. Her stomach clenched and, swallowing hard, she looked away.

He couldn't hold Wells's face in his mind any more than he could his name.

Looks like he fixed that problem.

A self-destruct safeguard *had* been programmed into Dante. And Wells had been about to trigger it until . . . well, until Dante'd made sure he could never speak again.

Drawing in a deep breath, Heather returned her gaze to Dante, carefully avoiding looking at Wells. Dante absently wiped at his bleeding nose with the back of his hand, then knotted his hands into fists—fists engulfed in blue fire. Pain glimmered in his golden eyes. He stood with quick and easy grace, and looked at her.

The sight of him tore at her. Exhaustion was pooled in blue shadows beneath his eyes. And blood slicked the front of his purple PVC shirt, dripped dark onto the carpet.

"Heather," he breathed, the pain fading from his eyes. Then he stiffened, his body so tight, Heather was afraid another seizure was about to knock him to the floor. But he lifted into the air, instead, his expression startled.

"Shit!" Heather watched as Lyons floated Dante across the room. "Are you nuts? He doesn't have control of his power!"

"Don't have anything to lose." Lyons lowered Dante to the floor beside Athena's white-gowned body.

Heather thought of his father's face and thought, *Yes, you do*. But kept that thought to herself. Anything Dante did to Lyons, Lyons had coming. In spades.

Had coming, yes, but Dante yearned for redemption, to be free of the past. Yearned to know who and what he was. How would he ever be free if she just stepped aside and let him kill? She'd be even more guilty than him, because she truly knew better. Dante didn't . . . not yet.

"Hey," Annie whispered.

Heather looked down. Her sister was kneeling on the floor, the pocketknife previously pressed against her throat now in her fingers. She smiled. After a quick glance at Lyons, she sliced away the flex-cuffs binding Heather's wrists.

Annie started to rise to her feet, but not wanting her to see Wells, Heather shook her head. "Keep low," she whispered.

Annie searched her eyes for a moment, then she bit her lower lip, and nodded. She crawled to the sofa, multicolored hair hanging in her face, and started cutting through the sleeping woman's cuffs.

Rubbing her wrists, Heather glanced around the room for a weapon, found none. "Give me the knife," she told Annie.

She wouldn't let Lyons damn Dante. Or let Dante damn himself.

GABRIEL DESCENDED INTO THE pit, his face lit and triumphant, his golden wings gleaming in the last of the moonlight. *Wybrcathl* trilled and warbled in the skies above.

"I *knew* you were hiding a Maker," Gabriel said. "My scouts have already left."

Lilith's sending arrowed through Lucien's mind: <*I've located your son.*>

His eyes not leaving Gabriel's smug face, Lucien sent, <*Hide him, keep him safe.*>

<*I'll do my best.*>

And that, Lucien thought, would have to be good enough.

Gabriel's tawny brows slanted down, he fluttered closer. "Samael? Who are you sending to?" He probed Lucien's shields, flexed against them. "Who?"

Lucien flicked open the link between him and Dante, unsealed their bond. His child's mind burned, pain-ravaged, a concerto of fire—his shields breached or down. Grief whispered through Lucien.

Closing his eyes, Lucien sent one last thought to Dante, then severed their bond.

TELEKINETIC ENERGY BOUND DANTE in tingling ropes. He tensed his muscles, but even with his strength renewed by Caterina's blood, he couldn't twist free.

"She believed you could bring her back from the dead," Lyons said, his voice thick with pain, face shadowed. "She was . . . *is* . . . an oracle and her vision's always right."

"Not about this."

"If you won't bring Athena back, then you can join her in the Underworld." Alex swung up his S&W. Aimed the muzzle at Dante's forehead. "Your choice."

"Pull the trigger—"

<Je t'aime, mon fils. Toujours.>

The sudden thought glimmered in Dante's mind, stroked across his fevered consciousness like a cool and soothing hand.

<*Lucien?*>

The bond between them sprang apart as though sliced with a fire-heated blade, either end coiling away into the ether. And a part of himself unraveled as well. Pain blasted through Dante; an explosion of fire squalled through his mind, his heart, his soul, and whipped his song into a savage bonfire aria.

His song burned, an inferno, chaotic and hungry.

And Dante burned with it.

FUCKER HAD A HELLUVA eye and was a helluva shot, too. *Spotted me even when I was* moving. Von dropped belly-down to the ground. Pine needles crunched beneath him, fragrant enough to make him sneeze.

A bullet *whing*ed into the soil a yard to Von's right. God*damn*. Fucker had sharp ears too. Could be nightkind, could be enhanced, or just good at his job. Rain started again, drops pattering against leaves and tree trunks.

Wishing for a downpour, Von rolled to his feet, and *moved*. He heard a small *thip* behind him as a bullet notched a tree trunk. A moment later, he crested the rise. Racing past the man in a suit jacket lying down in the dirt, his eye to the scope on his tripod-steadied rifle, Von angled to a stop behind him. Lifted the Brownings.

"Hey motherfucker. You owe me a pair of shades."

The skies opened up and rain fell hard and fast

and heavy. The man froze, his mortal heart drumming louder than Von's wished-for downpour.

So this comes true, but not my wish for a winning lottery ticket?

"Toss the rifle."

Hand trembling, the shooter flung the rifle down the hill. It crashed through the underbrush for several seconds before thudding to a stop.

Just as Von opened his mouth to ask the guy who he was working for and who he was gunning for, pain hammered against his shield—raw, primal, and soul-deep—staggering him.

"Little brother," he whispered, glancing back down the slope. Blue light spiked from the windows of the main house.

Fear laced cold around his heart. Von fired a round into the mortal's thigh to keep him from moving too much or too far. The man screamed between clenched teeth.

Von *ran*.

STILL LOCKED WITHIN LYONS'S telekinetic grip, Dante convulsed upright, head whipping, back arching, his limbs and body twisting in a violent and heart-wrenching blur of motion.

Lyons tilted his head, adjusted his aim.

Slipping up beside him, Heather punched the pocketknife blade into his side, between the ribs. Lyons gasped, but squeezed the trigger anyway, the gunfire cracking through the room like thinning winter ice. The smell of cordite curled into the air.

But his concentration had been broken. Dante hit the floor with a hard thump, his rigid body still spasming, contorting.

Heather yanked the knife free and jumped back out of reach as Lyons whirled around, gun held in both hands. "Annie, *go!*" she yelled.

"Maybe he'll go to the Underworld for *you*," Lyons said. He fired again and Heather threw herself to the floor, rolling to her knees, then diving behind the recliner.

Dante's seizure ended. He curled up on the carpet, shivering, his breathing rough. Spokes of blue flame wheeled around his hands, spinning out wider with every revolution.

Transforming everything they touched.

The floor rippled, shifted into a forest floor of pine-needled dirt, thick underbrush, and tiny blue wildflowers.

Heather's adrenaline-hyped pulse jumped into overdrive. Despite the gunfire she'd heard outside, she yelled, "Annie! Get out! Go out the back door!" She leaned past the recliner and risked a glance at the sofa.

Annie, blue light reflected in her wide eyes, screamed, *"What! The! Fuck!"*

"Just *go!*"

The dark-haired woman was sitting up, no longer asleep. Annie grabbed her hand and yanked her to her feet. The woman flashed a look at Heather, her eyes full of wonder and blue light. "I'll make sure she's safe," she said, a faint European accent to her voice.

Heather shifted back around and her heart slammed into her throat. Lyons stood in front of her, his gun dead-aimed at her head. Dante had risen to his knees, his golden-eyed gaze stunned. Blood spilled from his nose and from his ear, trickling along the line of his jaw.

"Fetch my sister from the Underworld," Lyons ordered, "or I'm sending Heather down below to keep her company."

Heather locked her fingers around the knife handle and slammed the blade through one of Lyons's Rippers, into his foot and through to the floor . . . *earth* . . . beneath. A strained scream escaped from between Lyons's clenched teeth.

Leaping up, Heather shoved him as hard as she could. Lyons stumbled, arms pinwheeling for balance, tripping over thick, blue-thorned vines snaking across the floor.

Dante caught him with both glowing hands and pulled him down. Blue light whipped around Lyons, through him, shafting out from his opened mouth and shocked sea-green eyes. The gun tumbled from his hand to the dirt. It curved into a black-carapaced turtle that crawled under the recliner.

Heather backed away from the rays of light lashing around Dante and Lyons. Lyons twisted like a rope of licorice in Dante's grasp, his arms twining around his body, his face shifting. Lyons screamed, the sound edged with blind animal rage and pain.

Energy crackled like lightning into the air, lifting the hair on Heather's arms and head. Pressure thrummed through the house, pushed against the walls. Her ears popped, and she winced, working her jaw. The mingled smells of ozone and burning leaves and graveyard soil curled into her nostrils.

The house quaked. Trembled. Cracks zigzagged up the walls to the ceiling. Plaster dusted the air. The front window exploded in a spray of glass shrapnel-shards that morphed into a constellation of blinking, blue crystal fireflies flitting past the porch and into the night.

Dante's song pulsed within Heather, dark and wild and heartbroken, its rhythm vibrating against her heart, *within* her heart. She stared at him, unable to look away, not wanting to look away.

Dante closed his eyes and shuddered. Pain flickered across his pale face. Two blue bolts of fire spiked out from his hands; one lanced through Athena's body, the other arrowing across the room to impale her faceless father.

Athena's dead flesh undulated. As though boneless, her body slithered through the blue-vined underbrush to twist like hot taffy into her brother's spiraling, stretching form. Lyons's golden curls rippled into hay-colored fur. Athena's gown morphed into white feathers. Fur and feathers and hot taffy flesh braided together. The twins were now a single entity.

Lassoed in blue flame, Wells was dragged over the top of the red-berried hedge that had once been the sofa. One slipper caught on a branch and remained behind, dangling like a sun-browned leaf. He clutched the severed head to his blood-soaked chest like a child's bedtime plushie.

Wells entwined with his children, twirling around and into them, his flesh stretching as though elastic. The decapitated head slid up from his arms and over his featureless face like a mask. Only now the head was that of a young woman with vibrant blonde hair, taut skin, and a gaping mouth.

They rose into the air, bathed in cool, blue fire, a three-faced pillar of flesh. Arms and legs streamlined into feathered tails. Eyes blinked open in the triune creature's braided torso and back. Rotating mouths opened in a chorus of song: "Threeintoone . . ."

One of the thick wood ceiling beams cracked, jutting through the roof. Huge chunks of plaster crashed to the floor just feet in front of Heather.

The house continued to quake and shudder. With a rifle-sharp crack, another ceiling beam split and part of the ceiling collapsed across the sofa-hedge.

Heather jumped to her feet, the floor rocking and rippling underneath her.

Dante's eyes opened, and recognition sparked in his gaze. *"Catin,"* he said, his voice an anguished whisper. The blue tongues of fire licking out from around him vanished like wind-snuffed candles. He fell to his knees, head bowed, his black hair a lamplight-streaked curtain.

"Threeintooneholytrinitythreeintooneholyholy-holy . . ." The triune beast sang its multiple-voiced hymn as it slithered and humped its way toward the dark hall.

The front door yawned open, then froze in its warping frame. A breeze smelling of pine and rain and cordite gusted into the room. Von came to a stop, struggling to keep his balance as the house shook itself apart, his gaze on Dante's singing triune beast.

"Holy fuck," the nomad whispered, holstering his Brownings.

"Yeah," Heather agreed, her voice shaky.

She crawled to Dante. Kneeling beside him, she pushed his hair back from his face, her fingers skimming across his cheek, his temple; his skin was fevered and heat radiated from him, baked into her. Blood was pooled in his hoop-rimmed ear. That scared her, a lot.

"Dante? Baptiste?"

He lifted his head. His eyes were no longer golden, the irises now rims of deepest brown ringing dilated pupils. She looped an arm around his waist and tugged. "On your feet, Baptiste. We gotta move."

More windows exploded into shrapnel clouds of glass. Groaning masonry crumbled. Beams splintered. Debris hurtled to the floor.

"I've got him, doll," Von said. "Get the fuck out."

Heather rose to her feet. "Together," she said.

Bending, the nomad grabbed Dante's arm and slung him over his leather-jacketed shoulder. Straightening, he looked at Heather. "Move your ass, woman."

Noticing Annie's gym bag by the front door, Heather scooped it up on her way out through the warped doorway, Von hot on her heels.

AS VON FOLLOWED HEATHER off the porch and into the yard, his arm locked across the backs of Dante's thighs, he heard a familiar sound through the pouring rain—the rush of wings. Relief spun warm tendrils through him.

So Lucien was all right; after all. After what he'd felt from Dante, and Lucien's continued absence, he'd feared the worst. Because, closed bond or not, Von had known that Lucien would've flown to his son's aid even if he had to wing across oceans and time and hell itself.

<*Where the fuck you been?*> Von sent, slowing to a halt and turning.

His thought bounced back, unheard. His relief vanished. Wiping rain from his eyes with the back of one arm, he looked at the black-winged figure standing beneath the evergreens.

Not Lucien. *She* fluttered her wings, flinging droplets of rain into the downpour. Her long black hair snaked up into the air and her eyes gleamed like golden stars. The chilly air steamed against her skin.

"We don't have much time," she said, her musical voice urgent. She stepped from beneath the trees. "The others are on their way. Give me Lucien's son so I can hide him."

Lucien's words sounded deep and clear through Von's memory: *Guard him from the Fallen,* llygad. *Guard him from them, most of all.*

As Von reached his left hand inside his jacket for his gun, the house exploded. And a giant, heated hand hammered him into the ground.

40

THE GREAT BELOW

Damascus, OR
March 25

DANTE HIT THE GROUND hard shoulder first, rolling and bouncing across the wet grass until he slammed into a tree and came to a stop. Bright specks flecked his vision and pain shimmered like heat in his mind.

Lucien . . .

Je t'aime, mon fils, toujours.

Voices crooned and whispered and demanded, buzzing up from the shattered depths within on the backs of fire-scorched wasps.

You look so much like her.

You wanna take her punishment, p'tit?

How come Papa Prejean handcuffs you at bedtime?

Your heart won me, Dante Baptiste.

Heather's face flashed behind his eyes as the bright specks faded. Dante tried to catch his breath, but his ribs ached and he couldn't seem to get air down into his lungs.

Focus on Heather.

He rolled over and onto his knees, pressed his arm against his damaged ribs. Rain cooled his face. He swiveled around. The house was nothing more than a smoking pile of rubble, masonry, and wood. He stumbled to his feet. *Heather . . .*

Music trilled into the air, burning and bright, and his song soared up from his core in spontaneous answer. *Lucien!* He reached for their bond, but found nothing, just a searing emptiness where the bond had *been*. Pain jabbed Dante's mind and sucked away his hard-won breath.

The ground rushed up to meet him.

COLD RAIN PLASTERED HEATHER'S hair to her skull and her clothes to her body. Wet grass prickled against her nose. She rose to her knees, ears ringing and head aching. The blast had sledgehammered her to the ground, knocking the air from her lungs.

"Heather! Fuck!" a voice yelled. Just as Heather gained her feet, Annie skidded to a stop beside her and grabbed her arm. "Are you okay?"

"I think so," Heather replied. "You?"

"Yeah, but when the house blew up, I thought you . . . I was scared . . ."

"Shit," Heather breathed, spinning around. Von and Dante had been right behind her. Through the rain, she spotted a figure rising to its knees several yards from the twisted and rubbled remains of the main house. Grabbing her sister's wet hand, Heather loped across the yard to Von.

"You okay?" she asked. She scanned the yard, looking for Dante. Her pulse pounded through her veins. She didn't see him.

Von blinked, then his eyes focused. He jumped to his feet in one smooth, light-blurring movement. Did a whirling 360. "Where the hell is Dante? Did she take him?"

"Who?" Heather asked, cold seeping in through her wet skin.

"One of the Fallen, a chick," Von said. "She ordered me to give Dante to her. Said others were on their way. God*dammit*! Lucien asked me to guard Dante from the Fallen."

Heather pushed her wet hair away from her face. "But Dante's part Fallen too, why would he need—"

"Dante Baptiste is a Maker." The dark-haired woman's voice joined the conversation. She stepped beside Annie. "And a True Blood prince."

Von fixed a hard gaze on her. "And who the hell are you?"

"Caterina Cortini, *llygad*," she answered, her voice laced with respect. "I was sent by the SB to kill Wells." She looked at Heather, her gaze steady. "And you."

Von's hand blurred to his jacket, a creak of leather. Heather blinked. A Browning muzzle was shoved against Cortini's temple. "Care to explain that comment before I pull this trigger?"

Cortini's gaze remained steady, but Heather had caught a flash of surprise in her eyes at Von's action. "The order changed," Cortini said to her. "The SB sent another team to bring you in. But even before then, I'd decided to protect both you and Dante Baptiste."

The muzzle didn't waver, not one iota.

"Why would you do that?" Heather asked.

"Because I learned who and what Dante is and guessed at what you mean to him."

"And why do you care?" Heather replied, voice tight.

"My mother is vampire." Cortini's chin lifted a shade. "I was raised in a vampire household and I've listened to fables about True Blood all my life."

"A child of the heart," Von said. "Who's your mom?"

"Renata Alessa Cortini."

Von whistled. "Holy hell. One of the *Cercle de Druide*." He lowered the gun to his side. He looked at Heather. "I say, let's trust her for the moment. She fucks up, she's dead."

Cortini inclined her head toward Von. "Thank you, *llygad*."

"Good enough for me," Heather said. "Let's find Dante."

WINGS RUSTLED. DANTE SMELLED wing musk and smoky incense. Heat radiated against him. The ache in his heart eased.

Lucien's here and safe.

But the scent was wrong and the scent was female.

Dante opened his eyes and looked into a woman's rain-beaded face—golden eyes, midnight hair, a slender sapphire-blue torc around her throat. The black tips of her wings arched above her head, sheltering him from the rain. She traced a finger along his jaw, trailing down to his collar.

"You had a seizure, Dante. But you mustn't rest for long, we need to leave."

"You know my name. You a friend of Lucien's?"

"Yes, he sent me," she said. "And you may call me Lilith." She flicked a glance at the sky. "We need to leave."

"No, ain't leaving. Why'd Lucien send you and not come himself?" Dante pushed himself up off the ground. Pain lanced through his ribs. Scraped through his mind. The night pinwheeled around him and he would've taken another header if Lilith hadn't steadied him with a hand to his shoulder.

"Merci," he murmured, stepping free of her support. "Is Lucien okay?"

The light in Lilith's eyes softened. "Your father's dead, little one."

"Liar. I don't fucking believe you!" He reached for his bond with Lucien again and touched emptiness. Pain burned like acid through his mind. He reeled, touched trembling fingers to his temple.

"He died to protect you from his enemies," Lilith said. "And that sacrifice has injured you, more than you know. Let me help you."

Dante couldn't catch his breath. His heart felt cold and still, the blood cooling in his veins. He shivered convulsively, his hands knuckling into fists. "No," he choked out. *"T'a menti.* He ain't dead, he *ain't.*"

Je t'aime, mon fils, toujours.

I shoved him away and now he's gone forever.

Will he be with me now, Dante-angel?

Red hair, freckles, blue eyes, and giggles. Chloe. This time her name didn't slide from his mind, a pebble skittering across ice. This time, her name, her face, *stayed.*

Chloe.

Dante's breath caught in his throat. Grief knifed his heart. His muscles coiled, trembled. Blood trickled from his nose. "My princess," he breathed.

"We need to go," Lilith urged. "I promised your father I'd keep you safe."

Lucien's voice whispered through Dante's memory: *I tried to keep you safe in silence.*

You promised me I'd never be alone again. And I *abandoned you.*

Dante's eyes stung. He met Lilith's golden gaze. "Why should I trust you?"

"Lucien told me that you once gave him a gift he cherished, an X-rune pendant."

Memory splashed acid through Dante's mind.

"Hey, mon ami, I saw this in a boutique. And I thought of you."

A sterling silver and tungsten chain slides from Dante's hand into Lucien's palm.

"The rune for friendship," Lucien murmurs. A pleased light warms his eyes. He teases: "What possessed you to think of me?"

Dante shrugs, a smile tilting his lips. "Dunno. Just happens from time to time."

"Where's his body?" Dante said, voice low and raw. "Wanna see it."

Lilith blinked. "Gone to ash. Nothing remains."

A muscle flexed in Dante's jaw. Lucien's words flashed through his burning thoughts: *I hid you from others. Powerful others who would use you without mercy.*

The Fallen will *find you. And bind you.*

Lilith pointed a taloned finger at the sky. "*They* are why you should trust me. *They* murdered your father so they could claim you."

Dante looked up into waves of intense blue and purple and green light shimmering across the sky. Song suddenly resonated through the night air, warbling from many throats, each individual rhythm and melodic strand weaving into a flawless whole; an ethereal concerto ringing to Dante's core.

Ain't binding me. Not ever. Not unless they know how to bind a fucking corpse.

Dante's song rose in response, a dark and furious aria.

The rain stopped.

Sheridan knotted his tie around his thigh, hoping to slow the bleeding. The pain hadn't set in really, not yet, but he knew it would soon. He wondered if he could make it down the slope, down the driveway and to the road before the vampire . . .

Something flared in the sky.

Sheridan looked up.

And his mind quietly and irrevocably unwound.

"There," Von said, pointing across the yard and up the wooded slope.

Heather peered into the darkness. Dante wasn't alone; a winged figure stood beside him—the Fallen female. The night rustled, a massive rushing sound, like a powerful wind gusting ahead of a storm or a tidal surge or hundreds of wings.

"Holy fuck," Von whispered, his gaze on the sky.

Heather looked up and gasped. An aurora borealis

of ghostly light danced and shifted across the night. Huge black Vs circled beneath the clouds; dozens of the Fallen swooped back and forth in a figure-eight loop like thermal-gliding hawks, their stroking, black and gold wings glistening with rain and vibrant light.

One broke away from the others, a male with a flowing mane of red hair, the moist air steaming against his bare chest. His golden wings cut through the night with strength and precision as he soared down to skim the tops of the trees, then angled back up into the sky in a graceful pirouette of wings and body; a breathtaking aerial ballet repeated by each, one after the other. And they sang; a choir of crystal voices chiming and pealing through the night.

Like a courtship ritual, Heather thought.

The Fallen circled above Dante.

"They're calling to him," she said, pulse hammering through her veins.

"They can't have him," Von growled. "C'mon, doll."

"Stay here," she said to Annie. Heather caught a whiff of frost and leather, then felt a muscle-corded arm loop around her waist. Von held her close as they *moved*.

She heard thudding footsteps far behind and knew Annie followed. Of course. She never listened. That was her little sister. She had a feeling Cortini also followed.

Von breezed to a stop ten yards from Dante. "Keep back, doll," he murmured.

Heather drew in a sharp breath as spears of blue light spiked out from around Dante, stabbing into the night.

The air prickled with power. His pale face was tipped up to the sky and the fallen angels wheeling above him.

One descended, black wings kiting him down to the mist-shrouded ground. His wings flared once, then folded behind him, his red kilt swirling like silk around his hips. He bowed to Dante, then dropped to his knees in the wet grass, strands of his long champagne-pale hair lifting on the breeze.

"We've come to help you home, young Maker," he said, his words clear and respectful. "To guide you to Gehenna and your rightful place upon the Chaos Seat."

Dante lowered his head, his black hair beaded with iridescent pearls of rain. He leveled his burning and golden-eyed gaze on the flaxen-haired Fallen. "Gehenna?"

The fallen angel stared, lips parting. "Ah! So beautiful, little *creawdwr*!"

The winged woman standing beneath the trees behind Dante stepped forward and whispered into his ear. Dante listened, wiping absently at his bleeding nose with the back of one glowing hand.

A deep pang of sympathy pierced Heather. *Can't they see how much he's hurting?* She started forward, intending to stand at his side. A steel-fingered hand latched onto her shoulder and jerked her back.

"No," Von hissed. "Too dangerous."

"I don't care. Let me go."

The nomad shook his head. "Forget it, doll. Dante'd never forgive me if anything happened to you."

"And *I'll* never forgive *you* if anything more happens to him. Dammit! Let go!" But Von kept a tight and hard grip on her shoulder. She realized with frustration that she wasn't going anywhere until he allowed it.

Several other Fallen swooped down to the ground and landed. Black wings and gold wings fluttered, flinging away moisture, then closed. Blue and black and purple and red kilts and gowns settled against limbs. Gold and silver torcs glinted with tiny slivers of captured moonlight.

One by one, they approached Dante crooning, "Douse the fire, young one. Douse the fire and silence your song so that we may help you. Guide you. Beautiful little *creawdwr*, we will take you home."

"Did you kill him?" Dante said, fury lighting his face, seething in his husky voice. His gaze skipped from face to face. "Did you? Or you?"

The Fallen looked at one another, expressions bewildered. "Kill who, little *creawdwr*?" one questioned. His gaze shifted to the Fallen female behind Dante. "Perhaps the Lady Lilith has misinformed—"

"Lucien. My father."

Von sucked in a breath. Dismay shadowed his face. "That's what I felt. A broken bond."

"De Noir, dead?" Heather whispered.

"We don't know this Lucien, your father," the champagne-haired Fallen said, rising to his feet. "The Lord Gabriel and the Morningstar sent us—"

Dante slammed his hands against the fallen angel's shoulders, shoved him back a step. *"T'a menti,"* he snarled. "Liar, liar, goddamned fucking *liar*!"

"Uh-oh." Von's hand slid from Heather's shoulder to her bicep and he quickly backed them both up.

Blue light starred out from around Dante, shafting into the aurora-glimmering air and into the Fallen, those on the ground and those still in the sky. Heather smelled ozone. Electricity crackled through her hair and goosebumped her skin. She grabbed ahold of Von's arm.

A spear of blue light pierced the fallen angel Dante had shoved. The angel's mouth opened in shock, then fear tremored across his face as blue flames lit him up from within, turning his skin translucent. The light flickered out. A stone statue stood on the wet grass beneath the evergreens, stone wings half-opened, features terrified, kilt frozen in motion around the hips.

"Dante, shit," Heather breathed. Pain and loss etched his beautiful face. His fury had swallowed him whole.

Screams and panicked trilling rang beneath the trees and in the sky.

Blue rays spiked into the fleeing Fallen, one by one. And turned them to stone. Those winging frantically through the air plummeted to the ground, those on the ground, kneeling or bowing or standing, remained there. All were transformed into statues of exquisite detail and captured motion—tendrils of hair lifted into the air, bodies half-twisted, faces averted, hands raised—in gleaming white, blue-edged stone.

The aurora vanished. Silence wound thick through the woods like river mist.

Dante spun around and faced the Fallen female. Her golden eyes were wide, her hands at her mouth. "You ain't binding me, either," he said, voice strained.

"I have no desire to bind you, Dante," she said, lowering her hands. "I still need to hide you before others come. Your father sent me to keep you safe. To teach you what it means to be a *creawdwr*—"

"He woulda told me about you!"

"He couldn't!" she cried. "He was afraid they'd find you through him!"

Dante's black hair snaked into the air, merged with the night. "Liar," he whispered. "Lucien warned me . . ."

She fell to her knees in the grass. "Please, little Maker, my daughter needs me," she said, desperation stark on her face. "I couldn't keep her safe, but with your—"

"He fucking warned me."

A rope of blue fire snaked around the black-haired woman. Her wings curved forward and she closed her eyes, her hands clenched in her lap. Caught within glimmering blue coils, she morphed from flesh to stone, her long hair a white curtain framing her bowed head.

Light continued to whip around Dante and his pale, grief-stricken face burned with both rage and ecstasy. His song poured into Heather, brimming with wild, searing chords and pounding rhythm; each beautiful note vibrated into her heart.

She stumbled against Von, clutching at him for balance. He slipped an arm around her as Dante's haunting and powerful song rang from her heart to his and back, rippling within her in ever-widening circles.

And Dante's triune beast sang a layered refrain: *Holyholyholy* . . .

Eyes closed, face rapt, Dante funneled a fountain of blue fire into one spot—the remains of the main house. Geysers of dirt spumed into the sky. The ground rolled and quaked, spasmed. Split open.

"Aw, hell, little brother." Von tightened his arm around Heather's shoulder and moved them closer to Dante and away from the showers of dirt and rock.

Trees disappeared, sucked down into the convulsing earth. Wood cracked and snapped, and the smell of deep, dark soil and green leaves swirled through the air, cutting through the sharp odor of ozone.

A whirlpool of dirt, splintered trees, and house rubble spun and roared, spiraling deep into the land's core.

The quaking slowed, then stopped. The mouth of a huge cave yawned where the main house had once stood. Heather caught a glimpse of the triune beast's feathered tail as it slithered, singing, into the cave.

Holyholyholy . . .

"The Underworld," Annie said, voice low, scared.

Mouth dry, Heather stared as lashes of blue light wrapped around the winged stone statues and lifted them into the air. One by one, the statues were placed around the mouth of the cave, the fallen angels caught in winged flight stretched across the tops of pairs of standing or kneeling statues.

A Fallen Stonehenge.

Guarding the deep mouth of the Underworld.

Dante's song ended.

The blue light winked out and Dante staggered as though drunk or exhausted. He fell to his knees. The night was suddenly black again, and Heather blinked away blue retinal ghosts from her eyes until they finally adjusted to the darkness.

Dawn wasn't far away. She needed to get Dante somewhere safe, and soon. Later, she would think about all she'd seen, experienced. Think about what it all meant. Think about how much it scared her.

Heather pulled away from Von's embrace and started forward, but he stopped her with a touch to her arm.

"Morphine, doll." He reached into his pocket and drew out a syringe and a vial. "I'll do it. He's hurting. Bad."

"I know he is," Heather said, "but thanks. Let me do it. I need to get used to it. He's my man, after all."

"Your man, huh?" the nomad said, handing her the vial and syringe. "Does Dante know that?"

Anytime you want, I'm yours.

I ain't leaving you alone.

T'es sûr de sa?

"He'd better," Heather whispered, throat tight. "He'd better." Flicking the cap off from the needle's end, she stuck it into the vial and filled it with morphine.

"No, Heather, stay away from him," Annie said, her eyes huge, her face drained of all color, nightkind-pale.

Heather turned and caressed her sister's cheek with cold fingers. "It'll be okay," she said, wishing hard from the heart. She crossed the yard, Von at her side.

Dante's head was bowed, his arms at his sides, his hands clenched into fists.

"Baptiste?" Heather asked, stopping just a foot from him. "Can you hear me?"

He lifted his head and his red-streaked dark eyes fixed her. "Heather," he said, his voice husky-raw, a near whisper. "*Oui. . . .*"

She knelt in the wet grass, drew in a deep breath, then grasped his chin. "You're a mess," she said, voice firm. "Your nose is bleeding. Put your head back."

Dante *moved*. He jerked free of Heather's hand, seized her upper arms and yanked her in close. Her pulse thundered in her ears.

"Keep still," Cortini said.

"Let go, little brother."

Heather caught a peripheral flash of movement as Von stepped forward.

Dante hissed, a low, intense sound that stood the hair on the back of Heather's neck. Then he shuddered. "Get the fuck away from me," he whispered, shoving Heather with both hands.

Von caught her before she hit the grass, but she pushed free of his hold and returned to Dante. "I'm staying right beside you, Baptiste. This is *our* fight. Back-to-back and side-by-side. Remember?"

"You'll never be safe with me." Dante's eyes squeezed shut. Fresh blood trickled from his nose.

"Who says I want to be safe?"

Dante stiffened, his eyes rolling up, and Heather lunged for him as the seizure locked up his muscles. She slid the needle into his taut-muscled neck and thumbed the plunger. His head whipped back.

She wrapped her arms around his fevered, trembling body, holding him as the morphine aborted the convulsion. With a sigh, Dante folded against her. She sat down on the wet grass with him in her arms, her heart pounding hard and fast.

"I was falling," Dante slurred. "But Lucien . . ." The words caught in his throat. He looked at Heather through his thick lashes. He reached up and touched a finger to her lips. "Her name was Chloe. She was my princess. And I killed her." His eyes closed. A tear slipped out from beneath his lashes, sliding to his ear.

Her name was Chloe.

A hot burr of pain pricked Heather's heart. She stared at him, eyes burning. He'd remembered a part of his past, and not with the help of someone who cared for him and in his own time, but with drugs and torture-induced seizures. Was Chloe all he remembered?

Heather stroked his wet hair away from his face. Lowering her head, her lips just touching his, she murmured, "I love you, Dante Baptiste."

But her words went unheard; Dante slept a false Sleep, lost to morphine.

"Dawn's coming, doll. We need to move."

"I have a motel room in Portland," Cortini said.

Heather nodded. "We can hole up for the day."

"And when it's night again?" Annie asked.

Heather looked down at Dante's peaceful, blood-streaked face. Tried to believe in its illusion. "Then we start a new life and we create a future."

EPILOGUE

THE NEVER-ENDING ROAD

Outside Portland, OR
March 25

THE TRANS AM'S ENGINE thrummed with power as Von slammed it into sixth gear. They burned up the road, burned up the night, a flaming arrow. Cortini sat in the passenger seat, her attention fixed on the dying night ahead.

Heather sat in the back seat, Annie beside her, Dante stretched across them both, doped and unconscious. His rain-damp hoodie was torn, ruined with spear gashes and bullet holes. His physical injuries would heal. What scared her was the damage done to his mind. His heart. She was afraid he'd been hurt beyond what she could help him heal.

Her name was Chloe. She was my princess. And I killed her.

Heather stroked his wet, black hair. She curled one lock behind his ear. Saw the dried blood. He'd given himself without hesitation for her and Annie. Had never asked the cost. Had risked his sanity, his life, his freedom.

I won't lose you, she promised him.

She was exhausted, all out of energy, drained of adrenaline. She was so tired her body vibrated like a downed power line. But her mind plotted and planned and refused to shut up.

She'd arrange to have a moving service pick up the boxes in her house, including the Portland PD and Bureau files on her mother's murder and on the Claw-Hammer Killer. One day, she hoped to be a voice for her mother. For Annie.

For Dante.

Especially for him. So he could be free, his life his own.

His future shaped within his own heart—not by Bad Seed, or the Shadow Branch or the Fallen. Her future had already taken shape and she raced toward it, eyes open.

A red neon sign flashed to the left: MOTEL VACANCY, and a neon beaver with a twig in its nibbling mouth winked. Von aimed the bulleting Trans Am for the motel.

Relief curled through Heather, and for a moment, her mind shut up. Sleep, for all of them. And when twilight shimmered across the horizon once more, they'd tear up the highway once again.

She looked at Dante and traced the edge of his beautiful face. Smelled autumn leaves and blood. Von's words glimmered like gold in her mind: *He* is *the neverending Road.*

She would follow the road home to New Orleans. Her and Annie and Eerie.

"I'm right here beside you, Baptiste," Heather whispered.

Ahead, the road unwound.

GLOSSARY

To make things as simple as possible, I've listed not only words, but phrases used in the story. Please keep in mind that Cajun is different from Parisian French and the French generally spoken in Europe. Different grammatically and even, sometimes, in pronunciation and spelling.

For the Irish and Welsh words—including the ones I've created—pronunciation is provided.

One final thing: **Prejean** is pronounced PRAY-zhawn.

Aingeal (AIN-gyahl), angel. Fallen/Elohim word.

Ami, (m) friend, (f) **amie. Mon ami**, my friend.

Ami intime, close friend, beloved friend.

Anhrefncathl (ann-HREVN-cathl), chaos song; the song of a Maker. Fallen/Elohim word.

Bien, well, very.

Bon, good, nice, fine, kind.

Bonne chance ce soir, good luck tonight.

Bonne nuit, good night.

Buono, (Italian) good.

Ça fait pas rien, you're welcome, it's nothing.

Calon-cyfaill (KAW-lawn-CUHV-aisle), bondmate, heartmate.

Cara mia, (Italian) my beloved.

Catin, (f) doll, dear, sweetheart.

Ça y est, that's it.

Cercle de Druide, Circle of Druids, a conclave of vampire Elders.

C'est bon, that's good.

Chalkydri (chal-KOO-dree), winged serpentine demons of Sheol, subservient to the Elohim.

Cher, dear, beloved. **Mon cher**, (m) my dear or my beloved.

Cher ami, mon, (m) my dearest friend, my best friend; intimate, implying a special relationship.

Chéri, (m) dearest, darling, honey, (f) **chérie.**

Comme çi, comme ça, so-so.

Coup d'état, rebellion, revolution, uprising.

Creawdwr (KRAY-OW-dooer), creator; maker/unmaker; an extremely rare branch of the Elohim believed to be extinct. Last known creawdwr was Yahweh.

Cydymaith (kuh-DUH-mith), companion.

D'accord, okay.

De mal en pire, from bad to worse.

Elohim, (s and pl) the Fallen; the beings mythologized as fallen angels.

Et toi, and you.

Fallen, see Elohim.

Fi' de garce, son of a bitch.

Filidh, Irish poet caste whose members were believed to be a combination of poet, magician, lawgiver, judge, and counselor to the ruling chiefs and king.

Fille de sang, (f) blood-daughter; "turned" female offspring of a vampire.

Fils, son.

Fola Fior, True Blood, pure.

Gêné toi pas, don't be bashful.

Gris-gris, (m) spell, charm.

J'ai faim, I'm hungry.

Je comprend, I understand.

Je m'en fichu, I could care less.

Je pense bien, I think so.

Je regrette, I'm sorry.

Je sais pas, I don't know.

Je t'aime, mon fils. Toujours, I love you, my son. Always.

Je te manque, I miss you.

J'su ici, I'm here.

J'su ici, mon princesse, j'su ici, I'm here, my princess, I'm here.

J'su pas fou de ça, I'm not crazy about that.

La passée, the night hunt.

Llygad (THLOO-gad), (s) eye; a watcher; keeper of immortal history; story-shaper. **Llygaid** (THLOO-guide), pl.

Loa, (Haitian) spirit; associated with voodoo.

Ma mère, my mother.

Merci, thank you. **Merci beaucoup**, thanks a lot. **Merci bien**, thanks very much.

Merde, shit.

Minou, (m) endearing name for a cat.

M'selle, (f) abbreviated spoken form of **mademoiselle**, Miss, young lady.

M'sieu, (m) abbreviated spoken form of **monsieur**, Mr., sir, gentleman.

Naturellement, naturally, of course.

Nephilim, the offspring resulting from Fallen and mortal unions.

Nightbringer, a name/title given to Lucien De Noir.

Nightkind, (s and pl) vampire; term for vampires.

Nomad, name for the pagan, gypsy-style clans who ride across the land.

Oui, yes.

Père de sang, (m) blood-father; male vampire who has turned another and become their "parent."

Peut-être que oui, peut-être que non, maybe yes, maybe no.

Pourquoi, why.

P'tit, mon, (m) my little one; **p'tite, ma** (f). (Generally affectionate.)

Sì, (Italian) yes.

S'il te plaît, please (informal).

Tais toi, shut up.

T'a menti, you lied, you lie.

T'es sûr de sa, are you sure about that? **T'es sûr**, you sure?

Toi t'a pas de la place pour parler, you have no room to talk.

Tracassé toi pas, don't worry.

Très, very.

Très belle, (f) very beautiful.

Très bien, very good, very well.

Très joli, (m) very pretty.

True Blood, born vampire, rare and powerful.

Va jouer dans ta cour a toi, go play in your own yard.

Vévé, an intricate symbol of a loa, used in rituals.

Wybrcathl (OOEEBR-cathl), sky-song. Fallen/Elohim word.

The song Dante sings to Annie: *Laissez-faire, laissez-faire, ma jolie, bons temps rouler, allons danser, toute la nuit* . . . Let it be, let it be, my pretty one, good times roll, let's dance all night . . . *Si toi t'es presse et occupe, mon ami, courir ici, courir la-bas* . . . If you're rushed and busy, my friend, running here, running there . . .

From "Laissez Faire" by Bruce Daigrepont (Bayou PonPon, ASCAP) from *Stir up the Roux* on Rounder Records. Used with permission.

The song Caterina sings to Athena: *Fi la nana, e mi bel fiol / Fi la nana, e mi bel fiol / Fa si la nana / Fa si la nana / Dormi ben, e mi bel fiol / Dormi ben, e mi bel fiol* . . .

Hush-a-bye, my lovely child / Hush-a-bye, my lovely child / Hush, hush and go to sleep / Hush, hush and go to sleep / Sleep well, my lovely child / Sleep well, my lovely child . . .

—Traditional Italian lullaby in an old dialect

Read on for a sneak peak of Beneath the Skin, *the third novel of The Maker's Song, coming in January 2010 from Pocket Books!*

PROLOGUE

LIKE MOLTEN GLASS

Seattle, WA
March 24/25

"**A**RE THESE THE PEOPLE who broke into your house, sweetie?"

Brisia Rodriguez didn't look up from her cup of hot cocoa. She studied the white swirls of whipped cream melting into the chocolate instead of the pictures Mr. Díon slid across the polished wood table.

Interview station, her dad would've called the small, pale green–painted room with its table and two chairs. But this wasn't a police station or the FBI field office. She knew because she and her fifth-grade class had visited both with her dad on a career day field trip.

"Is my dad okay?" she asked.

"He's in the hospital," Mr. Díon said. "But your mom and sisters are with him right now. As soon as we're done here, sweetie, I'll drive you over there, okay?"

Brisia curled her fingers tighter around the warm mug. "Will he be . . . all right?" She prayed she wouldn't have to ask the other thing, the *horrible* thing she never, ever wanted to say aloud. She was scared that if she did, it'd come true like a reverse wish.

Nononono. Don't even think *it!*

She drew in a shuddering breath laced with the thick scent

of creamy, hot milk and dark chocolate. Her stomach knotted.

"Brisia," Mr. Díon's low, soothing voice felt like a hand to her chin, gently tugging her gaze up from the depths of her hot cocoa. "You're the only one who can help us find the people who hurt your dad."

She looked at Mr. Díon. His purple eyes reminded her of sun-lit violets. "I told the police everything," she said. "They wrote it all down."

"Yes, but the police don't know who they're looking for. But I believe *we* do," Mr. Díon said, his voice as soft and warm as his eyes. "All you have to do is look at the pictures, okay?"

"Okay," Brisia said. She lowered her gaze to the trio of photographs lined up neatly on the table between her and Mr. Díon. The first one showed a man with curly blond hair, a smile curving his lips. Laugh crinkles V-ed out from beside each green eye. He reminded her of that actor, Matthew McConaughey.

Standing in the hall inside her house, Matthew McConaughey Guy smiles, all warm and friendly, almost like he's supposed to be there, even with the gun in his hand. But when his gaze flicks over to Brisia, his eyes are purest frost.

"He was there," Brisia said. "He had a gun too."

"Alexander Lyons. Good job, Brisia. What about the next photo?"

Brisia shifted her attention to the middle picture and recognized the pretty, red-haired woman. Only a hint of a smile touched the woman's lips, but her blue-eyed gaze was open and direct. Brisia remembered the hushed urgency in the woman's voice as she'd hurried Brisia to the front door after Matthew McConaughey Guy had sauntered from the room.

I want you to run to a neighbor's house and have them call 911, okay?

Do you need help too?

Don't worry about me. Just go.

"Heather Wallace," Mr. Díon said. "Why did you think she needed help too?"

Brisia glanced at Mr. Díon. Had she spoken aloud? "Well . . . I could tell she didn't like this guy," she said, touching a fingertip against the first photo. "And she asked me to call 911. I don't think she would've done that if she was one of the bad guys."

Mr. Díon nodded. "Good observation. I'll bet your dad's proud of you," he said, his violet eyes full of light. "Are you planning to be an FBI agent like your dad?"

"Yeah," Brisia said, even though up until that moment, all she'd ever wanted to be was a veterinarian. Helping and healing dogs and cats and guinea pigs. She wasn't sure if that was a new truth revealing itself to her or if she was just saying it as a bargain-promise to God. "Are you an FBI agent too? Do you work with my dad?"

"I'm FBI, yes. But I haven't had the pleasure of working with your dad."

Brisia wanted to believe Mr. Díon. She really did. Dad had told her the FBI was a part of their family—a family that stretched all across the country and around the world. You trusted family, went to them when trouble knocked on your door.

But he'd said he was *Mr.* Díon, not *Special Agent* Díon.

She lifted her mug and swallowed her doubt with a sip of cocoa and whipped cream, sweet and warm. She carefully set the mug back on the table, trying to slide it back inside the little chocolate-colored ring it'd made on the polished wood surface.

You trusted family.

"I've never been here before," Brisia said, looking around the room. It still smelled faintly of paint. "Is this a new office? I don't see a two-way mirror in here. There's not even a camera up in the corner."

Mr. Díon laughed, his voice as soothing as the cocoa in her mug. "You'll make a good agent, sweetie. This is a special room we use to interview FBI agents and their families when . . . tragedy . . . strikes, so we don't need to monitor anyone. It's a safe place from the bad guys." Leaning forward, he rested his clasped hands on the table. "One more photo, then you're done."

"Okay." Brisia looked at the last photo and she inhaled in sharp surprise at the man captured in the picture. He looked way young, for one thing, younger than she remembered. Black hair, dark chocolate–colored eyes, white skin, a tilted smile on his lips, a black collar strapped around his throat; he looked happy and sure of himself. And that was what surprised her. Without all the blood on his skin, he was cute, like pin-the-poster-to-your-wall-and-sigh-over-it cute.

He didn't look like a monster.

But she knew he was.

He—POOF—appears in front of her in a gust of air smelling of autumn leaves and Halloween apples. Blood smears his white face. She backs up until she bumps into the sofa. She freezes, her heart drumming, frantic and wild. He kneels down on one knee in front of her, leather pants creaking. A smile tugs at his bloodstained lips. Happiness rises like the sun in his dark eyes. He reaches a trembling, blood-smeared hand for her hair and slides a lock between his fingers.

She catches a whiff of something pungent and coppery. She sees blood on his pale fingers, glistening on his shirt, trickling from his nose. So much blood. But he's not acting like he's hurt. Maybe it isn't all his blood.

A thought loops cold through her mind, numbing her heart and stealing her voice.

Where's Daddy?

"Did he hurt you?"

Brisia shook her head. She tried to blink away the tears blurring her vision, but she couldn't blink fast enough. Tears spilled over her lashes and slid hot down her cheeks. No longer ten, but a bawling baby. And a baby couldn't help Dad.

"He was there," she said, her throat so tight, the words hurt. "He came outta my dad's office."

"Are you sure he didn't hurt you? Absolutely sure?"

"He didn't hurt me." She remembered the blood glistening on his shirt, smeared on his face, his hands. *He didn't hurt me, but he hurt Daddy.* She wiped at her eyes with the heels of her hands and another memory flashed into her mind.

The red-haired woman walks out of the hallway's darkness and stops beside the office door, a small black gun clenched in her hands. She looks at Brisia and her eyes widen.

"Help me," Brisia whispers.

The woman, face tight, lifts the gun, and aims it at the blood-smeared man kneeling in front of Brisia, stroking her hair and speaking to her in a language she doesn't know.

But it isn't anger she sees on the woman's face or even horror. It's sorrow.

Sniffing, Brisia wiped at her nose with the back of her hand.

"I don't see any Kleenex." Mr. Díon brushed a hand over his short caramel-brown hair as he glanced around the room.

"A lot of times it's kept under the interview table or in a drawer," Brisia said. Shoving her chair back over the low beige carpet, she peeked under the table. No box of Kleenex. Just Mr. Díon's polished black shoes and gray trousered legs.

"I think we're about done, Brisia."

"So I get to go see my dad now?" she asked, sitting up and scooting her chair back to the table. She lifted her mug and took a swallow of the cooling cocoa.

Mr. Díon stood up and walked around the table. He crouched down beside her chair. Brisia's fingers clenched around the mug, and for a moment, she thought she smelled copper and Halloween apples, saw blood against white skin. Her stomach rolled, queasy. She set the mug back down on the table.

"Before I take you to the hospital to see your dad," Mr. Díon said, his voice low and smooth, "I want you to close your eyes and go back to the moment you walked into the house this evening."

Brisia looked into his eyes. His violet gaze was flecked with gold and burning bright—rimmed with fire like molten glass. She'd learned in art class last year that molten glass could be shaped into anything.

Offering Mr. Díon a smile, Brisia said, "Okay." She closed her eyes.

You trusted family.

"I'm going to touch your temples, but keep your eyes closed, sweetie."

Brisia nodded. Fingers brushed aside the hair at either side of Brisia's head, then settled against her skin. Their heat made her feel drowsy, all floaty, like a balloon.

"Go to the beginning," Mr. Díon whispered.

A wave of dizziness swirled through her and when she tried to open her eyes, she couldn't. Fear rippled in, black and cold. "Mr. Díon? I don't feel good."

"Shhh. It'll pass. Just focus on what happened tonight."

The dizziness vanished, but an icy ball of dread lodged in her tummy. She gripped the sides of her chair to make sure she didn't fall out of it.

A thought breezed through her mind. *Everything's okay. You're safe and you'll be seeing Daddy soon.* She relaxed and let the thought curl through her like hot cocoa steam as she shifted her thoughts backward a few hours.

She opens the front door and walks into the empty living room. "Daddy?" she calls. "I forgot my iPod!"

And even as the memory and its sounds and images flowed through her mind, she felt each one being unthreaded and undone like when her mom unhooked her knitting if she didn't like how the piece had turned out.

Until it was just yarn, waiting to be knitted into something new. Or molten glass waiting to be shaped.

Then even those thoughts unraveled.

1

A NECESSARY EVIL

E MMETT THIBODAUX STOOD AT the threshold of the victim's home office, light from the hall casting his shadow across the body on the floor, weaving illusions.

SAC Alberto Rodriguez was stretched out on the carpet like a man seeking relief for an aching back. But the thick, coppery reek of blood and the squelching of police radios from the living room told a different story.

Emmett flipped on the light.

Rodriguez stared up at the glass-domed ceiling light with half-lidded, milky eyes. His throat looked shredded, savaged. Blood had soaked into the front of his cream-colored sweater, staining it a dark maroon, matching the blood halo soaked into the carpet around his head.

"Christ, did his daughter see him like this?" Emmett asked.

"No," his partner murmured from just behind him. He heard the whisper of suede against his windbreaker as Merri Goodnight leaned forward to look into the murder room. Caught a faint whiff of cloves. "Not according to what Abano told me. The kid only saw the perps. She didn't know about her dad."

"Abano? He the fed in charge of the scene?"

"You mean the fed that *was* in charge of the scene?" Merri replied dryly. "That'd be him."

"No doubt he's one unhappy camper at the moment."

"Given that the vic's one of their own, that's putting it mildly."

"Yeah, well, wonder how he'd feel to learn that some of his own might be involved in the killing?" Emmett murmured. "The feds'll be even unhappier when they realize we're shutting this crime scene down altogether."

Controlling and sanitizing the situation. A clean wipe. Scraping clinkers into the furnace to watch them burn, as his granddad used to say. No matter how you put it, the result was the same. Events were being altered at best and erased at worst.

A necessary evil in his line of work.

From the front room, Emmett caught a low murmur of voices from the TV that no one had turned off, hoping to catch the result of the Garcia-Dowd middleweight championship bout and the latest sports scores while processing the scene. No more police radio squelches or low, irked mutters.

The Bureau's people had vacated along with the Seattle PD's people. Hell, maybe they all had gone to a local tavern and had brewed up a booze-fueled bitchfest about the Shadow Bureau's glory-stealing theft of their case.

But nothing was ever what it seemed to be. Especially here.

Emmett stepped into the room, carefully avoiding the spatters of blood marring the cream-colored carpet near the threshold. He caught a faint whiff of piss just under the blood reek.

"ETA for our cleanup crew is ten minutes," Merri said. "Gillespie's supposed to drop by with instructions from HQ."

"Wonder what's taking so long? Usually Gillespie's first on scene."

"HQ probably put the chief on hold while they were busy trying to figure out who to smear the sticky, gooey blame on. Once they have that figured out . . ."

"Heads are gonna roll," Emmett agreed. He allowed his gaze to rove around the room, ticking off each item in the room as normal or not, a mental what's-wrong-with-this-picture game that he played at each assignment. Hell, not just at assignments or crime scenes anymore. He found himself doing it everywhere he went—at Safeways, the mall, in a movie theater.

Gun on the carpet against the north wall, a Smith & Wesson—not normal.

Desk with neatly parked chair—normal. Black, four-drawer file cabinet—normal.

Opened gun safe containing a single box of ammo—probably not normal.

And the late Alberto Rodriguez sprawled on the carpet in a drying pool of his own blood—well, hell, not even close to normal.

But normal had nothing to do with what had happened in this house.

"Abano and his people have no clue about vampires," Merri said, as though reading Emmett's mind. But he knew she hadn't; that was an issue they'd hashed out years ago. "They think Rodriguez was killed by multiple slash and stab wounds to the throat. And I sure as hell wasn't going to enlighten them."

Emmett chuckled. "They wouldn't've believed you anyway."

"Not at first," Merri said, a smile quirking at the corners of her mouth. "You didn't either, as I recall."

"Still don't," Emmett drawled.

Merri folded her arms across her chest, slung her weight onto one hip, and arched an eyebrow. "Uh-huh. Don't make me prove it to you, Thibodaux. Again."

Emmett shook his head, smiling. "Once was enough, thanks." He pinched up his trousers at the thighs, then crouched down beside Rodriguez's body. His ruined throat had been pierced and torn by sharp teeth.

"Not the neatest work I've ever seen," Merri said, her voice pitched low, and now right beside him. After five years working together, her speed and stealth no longer startled him. Most times, he even forgot what she was.

"Looks to me like one outta control vamp." Emmett glanced up at his partner.

Merri tilted her head, her dark brown eyes studying all that remained of Special Agent in Charge Alberto Rodriguez—husband, father, Bureau man. "Young, maybe. Or hungry as hell." She shifted and glanced back at the doorway and Emmett followed her gaze.

High-velocity blood spatter speckled the doorway's wood frame and the peach-colored wall beside it. "Looks like Rodriguez got one good shot off, though," she said.

"He did," Emmett agreed.

Merri nodded at the gun on the carpet. "For all it was worth."

"So what stopped the vamp from killing Rodriguez's daughter?" Emmett said. "Why didn't he snatch up that kid and drain her dry?"

"Good question." Merri crouched down beside Emmett and he smelled spice and cloves from the cigarettes she smoked. "And I think I have the answer."

"Yeah? Let's hear it, then, Goodnight," Emmett said, voice a low drawl, a little bit of Louisiana creeping in underneath his words. "You gonna tell me this vamp's got a soft spot for kids?"

Merri shook her head, and her straightened black hair, gathered and glossed into a high and neat ponytail, swung like a pendulum across her shoulder blades. "Nope. Someone else shot him again."

"Yeah? Who?"

A smug smile curved Merri's rosy full lips. She lifted her hand and displayed a small, slender dart pinched between two fingers. "One of the other perps dropped the vamp with a trank gun. I relieved Abano's techs of the one they'd bagged while processing the scene. But they missed finding the dart in the carpet."

Emmett grinned. "I knew there was a reason I kept you around."

"Because I'm a better field agent than you'll ever be?"

"That'd be it."

"Truth, brothah," Merri said, then chuckled, the sound warm and throaty. She slid the dart into an inside pocket of her black suede jacket. "Makes me wonder what else they missed."

"Truth, sistah. I'm guessing tons, but it doesn't matter. It's never going to court." Emmett rose to his feet, his knees creaking with the movement. An annoying new voice in the body-choir his joints, tendons, and bones had orchestrated ever since he'd turned forty. A body-choir that sang loud and strong when it rained. Given that he lived in Seattle, the singing was almost year-round and lusty as hell.

Looks like all those years of karate sparring are catching up with me.

"Do we know for certain that feds are involved in this?" Merri asked.

"HQ just said it was possible and to keep everything hush-hush until the perps were positively identified," Emmett said, offering a hand up to his partner.

Merri snorted. "When *isn't* something hush-hush?" She grasped his hand, her dark brown skin bleaching out his hard-won tan, and he pulled all five-foot-nothing of her up onto her booted feet. "It isn't called the Shadow Branch for nothing."

"Sing it, sistah. Wanna bet that even the director's dumps are classified?"

Merri shook her head. "Man, that's nasty. What's the matter with—" She straightened, her hand sliding free of his, her alert posture reminding Emmett of a hunting dog on point. She swiveled smoothly to face the doorway. "Our people are here."

Emmett heard the front door open, then click shut. A cold draft of air swept into the room and goosebumped his skin. Heard the squeak of wheels underneath the background noise of the TV, felt the thud of footsteps coming up the hall.

"Three," Merri murmured. "And Gillespie's reeking of Jovan Musk as usual. Maybe that's why his wife left him."

"*Christ*, Merri."

"Just saying."

A white-uniformed medic with a neat 'fro and hipster black-framed rectangular glasses paused at the doorway. He nodded at Rodriguez's body. "He ready to go?"

"More than ready, actually," Merri said.

The medic stepped aside as Merri and Emmett walked from the room. They passed the gurney parked in the hall waiting to receive Rodriguez's remains and the blonde female medic standing at its head. She nodded as they passed, a nod Emmett returned.

Section Chief Sam Gillespie stood in front of the cinnamon-colored sofa, his hair buzz-cut to black stubble, the outline revealing a hairline in high retreat. At six one, he stood two inches shorter than Emmett, his skin just a shade lighter than Merri's. Beads of rain glistened on his wire-framed glasses and on the shoulders and collar of his deep blue Gor-Tex jacket. He held the handle of a black satchel in his right hand.

Gillespie's lips stretched into the taut line that he considered a smile. "Thibodaux," he greeted. "Goodnight."

"Chief," Emmett returned, stopping beside the sofa. His gaze fell upon a mug resting on the coffee table. The red letters etched upon its white surface read: GROUCH, a mug Rodriguez was most likely sipping from just a few hours ago, unaware that death was climbing in through the laundry room window.

"Chief," Merri muttered as she strode past him to the front door. She flung it open, drawing in deep breaths of the chilly, moist air in noisy, drama-queen style. Rain pattered against the front steps and the taped-off crime-scene paving stones leading to the front door.

Gillespie *was* a little heavy-handed with the cologne, but at the moment, Emmett was grateful to smell something besides blood and piss and death.

"How's Rodriguez's daughter doing?" Emmett asked.

"Okay, I imagine," Gillespie said. "Her memory's been scrubbed by now."

"Christ," Merri muttered from the doorway. "She's just a kid."

"One who's still alive," Gillespie said, "*because* of the memory scrub. In the bad old days, she would've been turned into another victim of this official and tragic 'burglary gone wrong.'"

Emmett nodded, and shoved his hands into the pockets of his trousers. True enough. Lost time, missing memories, and a few misfiring synapses were a helluva lot better than the cold and permanent alternative.

But nothing said he had to like either option.

"Seems the Bureau has a few rotten apples in the proverbial barrel." Gillespie dropped the satchel onto the carpet. "The daughter positively IDed the suspects as SAC Lyons, SA Wallace, and Dante Prejean,—a vamp member of some top-secret project."

Emmett whistled. "Wallace? Wasn't she just named as a hero by the Bureau a couple of weeks ago for taking down that serial killer?"

"The Cross Country Killer—Elroy Jordan," Merri supplied from the doorway.

Gillespie nodded. "She was. But she ran into Prejean during the course of that investigation. It's now believed he corrupted her."

Merri snorted. "If he did, then he was only working what was already inside her."

Gillespie lanced a cold, icicle-sharp gaze her way. "Wallace just kicked her career into the gutter, Goodnight, and after she'd been offered the Seattle SAC position. Her service record was sparkling with intelligence, ability, and drive—full of promise. I think *corrupted by bloodsucker* is as good an explanation as any."

Emmett agreed, but he kept that opinion unvoiced. A rush of cold air smelling of cloves and rain swirled to a stop beside him.

"No offense," Gillespie said.

Merri held his gaze for a moment before asking in a crisp voice, "So what's the lowdown, Chief?"

"We're confiscating all evidence gathered by the SPD and the FBI," Gillespie said, his gaze traveling around the living room, as if envisioning how the scene would be officially reimagined and restaged. "We're making sure that statements already given to the SPD and the feds by the Rodriguez girl and her neighbors vanish."

"Any of the neighbors facing a wipe?" Merri said.

Gillespie shrugged. "Could be. That's for someone else to decide."

"What kinda TSP was Prejean a part of?" Emmett asked.

"HQ's playing this one real close to the vest," Gillespie replied. "All I was told was that it was a joint project—us and the feds—devoted to the study of sociopaths."

The image of Rodriguez's ravaged throat and empty eyes popped into Emmett's mind. *The study of sociopaths.* A chill touched his spine.

"In other words, their monster slipped its leash and they want us to fetch it. Do I have that right, Chief?" Merri said.

Gillespie nodded. "Pretty much."

Emmett nudged the satchel with the brown toe of his Dingo boot. "What's that?"

A wry smile tugged up one corner of Gillespie's mouth. "It's your monster-catching kit. Cuffs, drugs, chains."

"We know how to handle vampires," Emmett said. "Monster or not."

"Not this vampire. He's enhanced."

"Enhanced?" Merri asked. "You fucking kidding me?" She dropped a hand to her hip, her dark brown gaze direct and challenging. "Why the hell would a vamp be enhanced?"

"I wasn't enlightened on that account," Gillespie said. He removed his glasses, held them up to the overhead light, and peered at the rain-spotted lenses. "But I *was* told that adrenaline implants to boost his speed, dexterity, and strength had been installed."

"Oh. Of course," Merri said. "All the stuff vamps have in such short supply."

Emmett stared at Gillespie, a knot of dread pulling tight in his guts. Had the chief just *lied* to them? He tapped a *listen close* finger against the back of Merri's hand.

"Our assignment, Chief?" Emmett said.

Gillespie slid his glasses back on. "Intercept and detain our perps. Prejean is priority one, Wallace priority two, Lyons three." He slipped a hand inside his Gor-Tex jacket and withdrew a plastic-encased flash drive that he handed to Emmett. "All pertinent data, including files, photos, destination, and instructions. Study it on your way to Damascus."

The medics, the blonde in the lead, wheeled the gurney and its dark, plastic body-bagged contents through the living room and out the open front door, wheels thumping down the steps. Hipster pulled the door shut behind him.

Even through the fog of Jovan Musk, Emmett caught the nostril-pinching stench of blood and death.

"Our perps are in Damascus, Oregon?" Emmett asked, curling his fingers around the flash drive, tucking it tight against his palm.

Gillespie nodded. "We have reason to believe that Lyons might've taken Prejean home. Satellite scans of the area and of Lyons's home in particular revealed Wallace's Trans Am and Lyons's Dodge Ram parked in the driveway."

"A safe bet that Prejean's with them," Merri commented.

"HQ's thought too," Gillespie said as he walked around the sofa to the hallway. He stopped in front of the murder room. "And they've got a good five or six hours' head start, so move your asses. We've got a plane waiting for you at Sea-Tac. Rendezvous with Holmes and Miklowitz at the airport and bring them up to speed. You got stay-awake pills, Goodnight?"

Merri nodded. "I do."

"Good." Gillespie's jacket rustled as he folded his arms over his chest. He stared into the office.

Slipping the flash drive into his trousers pocket, Emmett

bent and wrapped his fingers around the satchel's handle. "Chief," he said, straightening. "Is there anything else we should know about the project or Prejean's *enhancements*?"

Gillespie swiveled around to face them, the lenses of his glasses reflecting light, his arms still folded over his chest. "I wish I knew," he said quietly. "Be careful out there. Don't take any chances—especially with Prejean. Hell, not even with Wallace and Lyons. I know HQ wants them alive, but it's not worth your lives. Not to me."

"Might be better to take our time and wait for Prejean to Sleep," Merri said.

"Maybe so," Emmett said. "But then he could hole up someplace we wouldn't find him. So I think moving our asses is our best option."

"Then let's hit the friendly skies and catch us some bad mofos."

"Truth, sistah."

"Be careful," Gillespie said again, voice low. His gaze once again fixed on the office's blood-spattered interior. "And *that's* a direct order."

"Roger that, Chief." Emmett exchanged a glance with Merri as he strode for the front door and the fresh air beyond. Doubt and a frown pinched the skin between her eyes. A dark realization glimmered in her eyes, the same realization rolling around in Emmett's skull.

They'd just been lied to. Gillespie had passed along the lie he'd been given.

And worse? The chief *knew* it.

Emmett's pulse drummed hard and fast through his veins. He and Merri were being ordered into the forested hills of Damascus on a goddamned bureaucratic ass-covering operation without knowing the truth of what they were up against.

A monster waited for them in the forest's dark heart, a monster who savaged a man in his own home, but left his daughter untouched.

A monster named Dante Prejean.